Worldwide Praise for the Erotica of

C000121130

"If you're an avid reader of all-male erot[ica]
John Patrick's series of torrid antholo[gies]
will provide hours of cost-e[...]
— *Lance Sterling, [*

"John Patrick is a modern master of the genre! ...This writing is what being brave is all about. It brings up the kinds of things that are usually kept so private that you think you're the only one who experiences them."
— *Gay Times, London*

"'Barely Legal' is a great potpourri...and the cover boy is gorgeous!"
— *Ian Young, Torso magazine*

"A huge collection of highly erotic, short and steamy one-handed tales. Perfect bedtime reading, though you probably won't get much sleep! Prepare to be shocked! Highly recommended!"
— *Vulcan magazine*

"Tantalizing tales of porn stars, hustlers, and other lost boys...John Patrick set the pace with 'Angel'!"
- *The Weekly News, Miami*

"...We guarantee you that this book will last you for many, many evenings to come as you relive your youth, or fulfill your fantasies with some of the horniest, hottest and most desirable young guys in fiction."
— *Blueboy*

"'Dreamboys' is so hot I had to put extra baby oil on my fingers, just to turn the pages! ...Those blue eyes on the cover are gonna reach out and touch you..."
— *Bookazine's Hot Flashes*

"I just got 'Intimate Strangers' and by the end of the week I had read it all. Great stories! Love it!"
— *L.C., Oregon*

"'Superstars' is a fast read...if you'd like a nice round of fireworks before the Fourth, read this aloud at your next church picnic..."
— *Welcomat, Philadelphia*

"Yes, it's another of those bumper collections of steamy tales from STARbooks. The rate at which John Patrick turns out these compilations you'd be forgiven for thinking it's not exactly quality prose. Wrong. These

INTIMATE
Strangers
A Collection of Erotic Tales
Edited By
JOHN PATRICK

STARbooks Press
Herndon, VA

Books by John Patrick

Published in the United States
STARbooks Press
PO Box 711612
Herndon VA 20171
Printed in the United States

Many thanks to graphic artist John Nail for the cover design. Mr. Nail may be reached at: tojonail@juno.com.

Book and text design by Milton Stern. Mr. Stern can be reached at miltonstern@miltonstern.com.

First Edition Published in the U.S. in May, 1998
Library of Congress Card Catalogue No. 97-065251
Second Edition Published in the U.S. in May, 2007

CONTENTS

EDITOR'S NOTE

Most of the stories appearing in this book take place prior to the years of The Plague; the editor and each of the authors represented herein advocate the practice of safe sex at all times. And, because these stories trespass the boundaries of fiction and non-fiction, to respect the privacy of those involved, we've changed all of the names and other identifying details.

INTRODUCTION: A PART OF BEING ALIVE
John Patrick

Intimacy with strangers can often be the most exhilarating experiences one can have. And one's first such encounter can be truly unforgettable. In his classic coming-of-age novel, Milkman's On His Way, David Rees describes his first intimate encounter with a stranger. He was taking the sun at the beach when a man who had been with two other guys remained after they left. "There was a lot of joking and laughter; the dark-haired one didn't want to go for some reason, and the others found this very funny. They walked off in the direction of Sandy Mouth. The man who was left turned over and looked at me.

"I decided to go for a swim. As I went past him, he smiled and said 'Hi.'

"I stopped. I felt, suddenly, very tense: that knotted-up sensation in the stomach again. 'Hi,' I answered.

"'I think I'll join you,' he said. He had a chain round his neck, on it a flashy silver pendant. He was very hairy. From his throat down to where it disappeared inside his shorts.

"We ran into the sea. It was warm, and almost as flat as a swimming pool, only a hint of rise and fall. 'You swim well,' he said, then dived and grabbed at my legs, pulling me under. I surfaced, shook the water from my eyes, and grinned. 'What's your name?' he asked.

"'Ewan.'

"'I'm Paul. The others are Jay and Derek. Del for short. We're on holiday, renting a cottage in Coombe Valley.'

"'I live here,' I said. 'In Bude, that is.'

"He made a face. 'Don't like Bude.'

"'It's a dump.'

"'Come on. Let's sunbathe.' We walked up the beach. 'Bring your things over here,' he said. I did so, wondering why I was obeying the commands of a total stranger so easily.

"We talked for a long time. He had just completed his probationary year as a teacher, at Deptford in south-east London. He was twenty-three. A surf enthusiast, but, he said ruefully, he'd obviously chosen the wrong week. I told him about sharing first prize in the competition. 'We're just amateurs,' he said, 'me and Del and Jay. If we get a fortnight each year in the sea, we're lucky.'

"The conversation drifted on, technical stuff: types of wave, different equipment, the personalities in the England team. How nice it would be to practice in Hawaii. But certain things in the talk seemed odd: half-finished statements he left hanging in the air, as if he wanted me to pick them up and work them out for myself, or maybe throw him back something of a similar nature.

"'Del and Jay are together,' he said. Then gazing at me, a wide smile on his face, 'I'm just looking. Looking around, that is'. But I didn't know what the answers were that he expected, so I said nothing. He had green eyes: open, trusting. Green as wet grass. There were some long silences. After one of them, he asked 'Do you have a girl-friend?'

"'No.'

"'Between girls, is it?'

"'No. Not really.'

"Another silence. 'Maybe it's a boy you're interested in.' I shut my eyes. 'Or maybe you aren't sure yet.' He rolled over, his hand brushing my leg. He didn't take it away. The effect was the same as Leslie touching me.

"'Perhaps I should go,' he said, laughing. 'I don't want to be accused of corrupting the young.'

"I opened my eyes and sat up. 'Don't go! Please don't go!'

"He said, very quietly, 'You're beautiful.' And he kissed me. The first time in my life I had been kissed by someone of my own sex. 'Is it safe here?' he asked.

"'Safe for what?'

"'Oh, you are young and inexperienced!'

"'Yes, I am.' I looked round. There was no one in sight. And he was touching my skin, caressing me, sucking my cock, arousing me so much that I felt there could be no stopping now even if coach-loads of people suddenly appeared on top of the cliffs. It wasn't a bit like it had been with Leslie. This was making love: so much feeling passing between us, so much gentleness. We came at exactly the same moment, in each other's hands.

"'I think, somehow, you needed that,' he said.

"'I did! Christ, oh, I did! You just don't know! My first time. My first proper time, that is. I feel . . . oh, I can't explain! Terrified.'

"'Terrified?'

"'I don't want to be gay! Suppose people find out? And how can you ever be happy?'

"'Aren't you happy at this moment?'

"'Yes. Yes!' I stood up, ran down the beach, then jumped in the air and shouted at the top of my voice 'I am happy!!'"

Speaking of happiness, flight attendant Patrick Drahos, known as the "Jet Lag Fag," finds strangers to be intimate with all across America.

When in New York City, Drahos suggests a visit to The Big Cup cafe, where "on a sunny afternoon you'll find yummy college students, local residents, muscle boys and anyone else who needs a really big mocha; the men will supply that extra shot of cream.

"Once you've gotten your caffeine boost and your bootie busted, you might want to go work off some of that energy at the Chelsea Gym.

Absolutely the place to bump, grind, and moan, groan, and otherwise pump. You can even lift weights, too, if you ever make it out of the showers.

"...Should you find yourself far from home and long for a piece of California with its sun, beaches and, of course, surfer boys, then head to The Splash. The recently remodeled establishment features surf boards set up as cocktail tables, hunky strippers...and a clientele that tends to be very preppy and suburban, so you'll have no problems finding the boy of your wet dreams. SURF'S UP! And so were my legs. After I did my own version of Don Ho-ing around, I understood what they meant by the terms Big Kahuna and Hang Ten. ...I staggered to King on 6th Avenue. I was greeted in the royal style by a muscular, naked, beautiful knave on a small stage gyrating, stripping, and sporting a raging hard scepter of sorts. ...This dark little den of depravity offers one other attraction: for a minimal fee you can venture upstairs and experience one of New York's biggest, cruisiest, darkly lit backrooms, where anything can, and usually does, go on."

In Love Sucks, Ken Shakin describes how much fun he had in New York City: "As I mindlessly strut down the boulevard my attention is drawn to the men and boys I find desirable. I'm not the only one playing that game. You can tell that everyone is checking out everyone on the street, for whatever reason. The TV is on. You watch. It's channel surfing as they drift by. I check out every last man, woman, and beast. When something cute and butch goes by I stare into his eyes and look down at his crotch. It's a fun game. Along the way I realize that right there next to me, walking parallel in the same direction, is something very cute and butch. I wonder that I hadn't noticed him before. He's tall, dark and handsome and he seems to be brooding about something, walking with hands in pockets, kicking a can. My heart goes out to him. Let me make it better. I follow him. Though we are independently going the same way. But as soon as I notice him and begin to follow he seems to be aware of the fact and stops kicking the can. He becomes self-conscious. He looks over. I look away. Force of habit. I look back. He looks away. We walk side by side for many blocks. Our stride is in sync. Does he have the same thing in mind? I look over again. He turns slightly and raises his eyebrows at me, but there isn't enough body language to entitle me to speak to him unless I just blurt out something. What would I say? We follow each other in silence, our shadows extending behind us at an angle. Parallel. Not once crossing. Could he be thinking what I'm thinking? Our movements are as one. Our stride. We notice the same things. The argument on the corner. The ambulance whirling by. The graffiti on the wall. Unintelligible scribble. But we both study it. Because it attracts our attention. Only the artist knows what he's really trying to say, if even he does. But that doesn't stop us from looking. I have in the past met men simply walking down the street. The right eye contact and a few minutes later you're off doing it in some alley.

"...One turned into a lover for a while, though we never got along. I think sometimes of calling him out of the blue. What would I say now? I think about all the old lovers who came and went and maybe never really were lovers or boyfriends or whatever we called ourselves. In the end we returned to being strangers."

At one point, Shakin decides to leave New York, but not without one last tour: "...So I go to the park for one last tour. I get it on with a rather hunky little guy with a big cock. We play with each other's cock like babies with pacifiers. Silly as it is, I can't get enough. I know I've said it before. Proof that enough is never enough. And when we shoot our stuff I feel a bond with this stranger. Our intimacy speaks for itself. Two souls coming together in a city of lost souls. So maybe we're gonna die, but right now we're living. We shoot our seed on a tree holding on to each other's manhood, feeling the warm pulse of the other in our grasp, holding on for dear life. He smiles at me, a cute, brotherly smile and I know I'm alive."

Lately, even New York magazine has gotten in on the act, making the point that sex is still alive in Manhattan despite the present mayor's attempts to stamp it out. Reported Lily Burana, "Tucked neatly away in a heavily trafficked tourist area is a snug little bar where the pretty boys roam. For a modest $5 cover charge, a person can enter the disco thrum and enjoy what is perhaps best described as the homoerotic iteration of a taxi-dance hall. Buff gym dandies in jockstraps and tight briefs, dollars waving out of their waistbands, go-go dance atop the bar and mingle with the customers – offering touch dances, massage, or simple conversation in exchange for tips. At 1 A.M., the place bursts with archetypal specimens from the urban gay Diaspora – grizzled workies in down vests and Caterpillar caps who look like they're just out of the cabs of their Peterbilts and barely out of the closet; clusters of drag queens; and the omnipresent fashionably pierced PIBs (persons in black) of all races.

"The social dance here is more convivial and celebratory than frantic and predatory. The barely clad men and their patrons tease each other, chat, and sway entwined to George Michael. One dancer sits on the bar with a man's head on his knees and assiduously rubs his neck. Surely, in their heads the dancers mull over student-loan payments, the weekly roster of auditions and go-sees, who waits for them at home, and how much they can get out of their customers, but such preoccupation doesn't show. They assume a totally polished facade that combines the requisite hormonal push with an efficient tenderness.

"Although the clientele and the attendant muscle corps are almost exclusively gay men, women aren't made to feel unwelcome. A number of the dancers are quite enthused by womanly presence, actually. Once one gets the chance to press his well-maintained physique against a girl, he hovers close and whispers in confessional tones, 'I'm straight.' Which could very well be true. Passing isn't just for gays in heterosexual society – it's also quite common for straights working a gay trade.

"It's quite a clever arrangement – do an end run around potential pimping and prostitution charges (make no mistake, however; there are plenty of fingers walking into criminal territory) and at the same time offer a more genteel alternative to the more, shall we say explosive, live gay male theater. Outside, the never-ending stream of out-of-towners troops on, none the wiser that mere steps away, worshippers gather at a Temple of the Body, where, appropriate to our age, the sacrament is sanitary and the access is on demand."

For some, access to this Temple can cost. In one of the stories in his collection, The Risk of His Music, Peter Weltner describes one of these encounters: "His arms outstretched, resting back against the bar, facing Bourbon Street, Brice Landry sat on his stool like a king on his throne, poised to receive the worshipful, ready to dismiss with a flick of his head or hand anyone who might attempt to approach his person without having waited for the subtle sign that granted permission. He was a star who knew he had been born uniquely blessed, as if God had intended him to be always distant from the rest of humanity and radiantly self-luminous."

Once, in New Orleans on spring break, Brice "beheld for the first time the solution to those desires which thus far he had so rarely fulfilled. Having encouraged the brothers to return to the safety of the campus on their own, he stayed an extra week, moving from bar to bar as he followed the path of increasingly higher praise, satisfied to know that it was his nature to deserve it, whatever the source. Watching him undress, one man said it was like seeing a Donatello strip off his armor only to reveal the body of a Michelangelo beneath. Brice understood what he meant and liked the sound of it. It was in fact, he quickly discovered, such words that he seemed to enjoy most, the hymns to his body all others sang. Even when he did not let a man touch him, he nonetheless made him feel almost rewarded simply to be allowed to stand at a distance and adore."

Arthur, a deeply closeted school teacher attending a convention in the city, becomes obsessed with Brice, seeing him every day sitting on his usual stool at the Bourbon Pub, "sitting turned toward the door, an impatient look on his too-handsome face. As Arthur steadied his nerves and slowly strode across the street to where the boy sat, having at last convinced himself that there was no further virtue to be learned in continued struggle, a swirl of water tugged at his feet as if to stop him. When he attempted actually to speak, his tongue stumbled against his teeth and saliva flew out instead of words. The boy, grimacing, ducked and turned away.

"Arthur poked his shoulder with two fingers. "Excuse me."

"'Go away,' Brice ordered.

"'Oh, no. I'm afraid I can't. That's exactly what I mustn't do. It's too late.'

"Brice glided his body back around. 'What?'

"'I hate to be a nuisance and I can't believe I'm saying this, but I think I need to know how much.'

"'You're joking, right? How much?'

"' Please . '

"Brice rested his elbows on the bar and examined Arthur up and down like a buyer his prospective slave. 'Three hundred bucks.'

"'So much? Must it be so much?'

"Brice shrugged. 'Take it or leave it. And I don't touch you and you don't touch me, understand?'

"'I'm not a wealthy man. Three hundred,' Arthur repeated, stunned.

"Brice massaged the back of his neck, demonstratively flexing his bicep. 'I don't haggle, friend.'

"'No, of course not, of course not. All right then. But you'll go with me now, please, before I lose my nerve.'

"Brice hopped off the stool... "

Brice follows Arthur to his room, where Arthur is still regretting what he had started: "'I find this deeply humiliating. Don't you?'

"With a flick of his head, Brice tossed back his sleek wet hair. 'No. Why should I?' He immediately started to unbuckle his belt.

"...Brice snapped the band of his briefs. 'You going to just sit there or what?'

"'I don't know. I'm not sure. What do men like me usually do in these circumstances?'

"Brice teasingly inched down his underwear. 'Most guys like to jerk off.'

"Arthur looked astonished. 'Oh, no. No, I can't.'

"'Suit yourself. It's your bread.' Brice poked a fist into the pouch of his briefs to shove them down further, stepped out of them, kicking them toward his shorts, then positioned himself at the foot of the bed, directly in the line of Arthur's worried eyes. 'You know, this all really would feel a whole lot better if you could work up a little excitement or enthusiasm, Arthur. I like to get them real excited. Do you understand?'

"'I'm ugly,' Arthur suddenly cried out, blocking his sight with his fists which pounded against his eyes. 'I've always been ugly.

"'I've seen worse.'

"Please go away. Please, boy.'"

Of course, Brice does not leave. Arthur consents to get nude himself, and then Brice says, "'You're supposed to be excited. What do you think this is all about? You're supposed to have a hard-on. It's part of being alive.'

"'I've never liked being alive,' Arthur confessed.

"'Don't talk crazy. Stare at me. Go ahead. Admire me. Tell me how good my body is making you feel.'"

Finally, Arthur is ready: "'Please, Brice. Please touch me.'

"'I don't do that, Arthur.'

"'Leave part of yourself in me. Let me possess some small part of your beauty.'

"'No. I don't do that. Never.'

"'Please.'

"'No,' Brice barked.

"'But I love you,' Arthur wailed.

"'Oh, Christ!' Brice swore. 'But you damn well really better be a virgin,' he shouted, violently wedging himself between Arthur's knobby knees."

Later, remembering the encounter, Brice says, "All the tricks were like that, wanting me so bad they'd almost die for it, pleading and begging and trying to bargain their way into being loved."

Jack Fritscher, the San Francisco-based author of Some Dance to Remember, a novel about the 1970's circus of rough-trade set, one day found himself, inexplicably, in Hollywood. When in Rome, the saying goes, so he went to a world-famous hustler bar. "I had to remember that the johns, many of whom were more attractive to me than were some of the hustlers, aren't looking for mutual gay sex. They're looking for a 'straight' guy who will ball them the way sex used to be before sex was a lifestyle. The mutual satisfaction is a combo of money, power, and sex. So there I stood, leaned, sat, paced, smiled, watched, cruised with fifty bucks hot in my jeans, begging to pay for it, so I could cross the line and know what the fuck it felt like to buy my way into a specific section of street-smart, low-life, talk-show trash that without cash no gay man has any access to. Rough-trade tricks are usually born in trailer parks in the American South, raised in foster homes, tattooed in juvenile facilities, saddled with one or two young sons by 15-year-old bitches, and are, educated in prison, where the one important lesson they learn is that gay men are an easy mark.

"I felt as confident as a kid in a candy store. Actually, a john need never fear rejection, because all he has to do is flash more money at the young and the dangerous. The lower classes are eternally attractive to the middle and upper classes. (Ask Pasolini, the martyred Patron Saint of Rough Trade!) Even heterosexually, every class knows what it's for.

"No matter what sex trip you want – SM, rough trade, suck/fuck, water sports, dirty feet, you name it – anything goes in a hustler bar where the level of play is the kind of primal sex once found in rest stops, YMCAs, bus stations, and carnival midways with mechanics, sailors, hitchhikers, and gypsy men with dirty fingernails who'd do anything for a buck. The natural-born rough-trade hustlers, in their wonderful anonymity, danger and wild taste, should not be confused with the slick urban-gay hustlers who advertise through the 'Models Classifieds' in gay papers where the 'muscle sex' or 'dominance sex' is highly stylized Kabuki ritual. Gay hustlers are high concept. Rough trade is just plain basic fundamental what-it-is.

"It's Friday evening becoming Friday night on a full moon weekend in LA, and the two camps of hustlers and johns sport with each other like friendly Montagues and Capulets. If, in America, money can rent you what you want, then a hustler bar is almost as close as a man can get to sex-with-satisfaction practically guaranteed. Hustlers, in fact, invariably 'can guarantee you, man, we'll have a good time.'

"Twenty-five bucks, average, gets a john a hustler for the first time: no frills, just some laid-back trade getting his dick sucked until the john comes. A return bout costs less. Prices vary depending on the time of night, the night of the week, the proportion of johns to hustlers, and the specifics of the sex trip that the john wants out of the hustler. Frequently, there's cab fare or a tip of about ten bucks tacked on when the 'boy' has done his best at turning out a good performance. The essence of hustling, after all, is show biz. And a taxi to a hustler is a status symbol equal to a limo.

"A tattooed, well-built, blond, goateed hustler with a buzz cut eyes my table and heads to the jukebox. He plays 'I Don't Want to Walk Without You.' I stand up and move in near to him, a quarter in my sweaty hand, and scan the selections for a musical reply. My choice: 'Hit Me with Your Best Shot.' We listen to the music, eyeing each other. Who is the matador? Who is the bull? He's more wary that I am.

"'You wanna beer?'

"'Yeah,' he says, 'Bud.'

"At the bar service station, a john leans over to me. 'That one,' he says pointing at the blond goatee leaning his butt against the jukebox, 'will do it for twenty bucks. He's raunchy. Likes to get blown and have his ass eaten. He's quiet. Believe me, I know. He's a bit player in B-movies. Action-adventure flicks. I've licked all those tattoos on his arms. I sucked on him for maybe an hour and jerked myself off.'

"'Oh,' I say.

"...When sex combines with money, I think of the stereotype that johns ought to be old and ugly and degenerate, like this guy revealing these things to me. Well, I'm not yet old or ugly. But the degeneracy of paying for sex squats awkwardly on my head this night in this hustler bar. I laugh to myself that my bourgeois conscience is much ado about nothing. Actually, I find I really have an almost politically correct 'attitude' about going through with this pay-for-play trip even with this guy nobody would believe would have sex with a man unless he actually was paid! I remember the words my buddy, Old Reliable, who lives to love hustlers, said to me earlier in the evening: 'Hustlers are actors. You're the producer. You got the money. You're also the director. Hustlers are minimalist artists. They'll do as little performance art as they can. Unless you direct them. Hiring a hustler is like ordering a la carte. You get exactly what you want. This is Hollywood. It's a circus. But at least it's the Big Top. All the movie stars and TV people hire hustlers. Judy Garland loved rough trade boys. Rock Hudson loved pay-for-play tricks. Stars pay for performances because they themselves are paid for performances. Hollywood is where America brings its dreams. You can hire your fantasy. The world's great performances aren't on screen. Great performances take place in the sack.'

"I hand Blue-Eyes-with-Buzz-Cut his Budweiser. I want to proposition him. I want to do it. But I can't. He's so shy or sly, he's not helping. Why do I have to pick the quiet type? I came out tonight prepared with cold cash to be nasty, to go slumming, to fucking buy sex! How un-American to suddenly become a reluctant consumer. I feel the power is in my pocket: the cash. I think: Show him the money! God! Blue-Eyes-with-Buzz-Cut is hot as a street in Venice Beach! The kind of sweaty macho based on the kind of clean you can maintain when you're living out of a knapsack and brushing your teeth at an IHOP. He's my speed. In a post-Judas minute, I'd take him straight to the barroom toilet, flop him back against a urinal, and, do him – if only coins weren't changing hands. Then good old lust, like cavalry riding over the ridge in the last reel, develops its own logic. I stare into his incredible eyes. Hustling, I rationalize, is the world's oldest profession. Moral-religious trips can't reject thousands of years of sex-theater history. I laugh at my puritanical head but take very seriously my hardening dick, which has no conscience. He takes a swig of beer and peers at me hard. Inexplicably, I blurt out: 'I want to exploit you.'

"'Cool,' he says.

"Nervous as a virgin-bidder at a white-slave auction, I say: 'Ya wanna mess around for fifty bucks?' Fifty? Why did I say fifty? My subconscious is worried whether or not he'll like me. I forget rough trade doesn't give a fuck about me. His blue eyes pierce into my face.

"'You ain't a cop, are you?'

"'Flattered,' I say, 'No.'

"His face lights up. He actually says, 'Show me the money.' Hustlers are able to work out deals with a john in a heartbeat. 'Let's go,' he says, and we stroll out together, with the bar full of johns and hustlers watching our cool-ass exit.

"...That night, Blue-Eyes-with-Buzz-cut was what he has long been: a terrific piece of ass. That night, I became, at least for once, what I had long had an attitude about: a john. Mmm, I mean, a patron of the arts."

One sure way to become intimate with a stranger, rough trade or whatever, is to hitchhike. But, while it can be fun at times, it is not without its dangers. After a few harrowing incidents while hitching, something seemed to have changed for David Sedaris, as he explains in the book Naked: "It felt as though I'd been marked somehow. I had always counted upon people to trust me, but now I no longer trusted them. A driver would introduce himself as Tony and I'd wonder why he'd chosen that name. They were liars, every last one of them. My suspicion was a beacon, attracting the very people I'd hoped to avoid. Drivers began picking me up with the idea I had more to offer than my gratitude. Drugs were the easy part; I carried them as a courtesy and offered them whenever asked. What threw me were the sexual advances. How much did they expect to accomplish at fifty miles per hour, and why choose me, a perfect stranger? When I thought of sex, I pictured someone standing before me crying, 'I love you so much that . . . I don't even know who I am anymore.' My imaginary boyfriend was of no particular age or race; all that mattered was that he was crazy about me. Our first encounter would take place under bizarre circumstances: at the christening of a warship, or maybe a hurricane might bring us together in a crowded storm shelter. I thought about our courtship and the subsequent anniversaries, when our adopted children would gather at our feet saying, 'Tell us again about your first date.' I suppose we could have met in a car or van but not while I was hitchhiking; it would have to be more complicated than that. Maybe the driver of my vehicle would suffer a heart attack, and he would be one of the medics. The important thing was that I wouldn't be looking for it; that's what would make it so romantic.

"'You fool around much when you hitchhike?' The most overt were the men with the wedding rings and the child safety seats, whose secret double lives demanded quick, anonymous partnerships. I had an unpleasant experience with a married couple outside Atlanta. Two o'clock in the morning and they were driving their Cadillac nude from the waist down. They invited me to spend the night in their home, the husband casually masturbating as his wife styled her hair. 'We'll fix you something to eat,' she offered. 'I'm a damned good cook, you can ask anyone.'

"A few days later in Fayetteville I was driven down a dark dirt road by a man who offered to crush my skull like a peanut. Cowering in the bushes had become something of a hobby, and I knew it was time to ask myself some serious questions. I walked the eight miles back to town, boarded a bus, and never hitchhiked again.

"...Nowadays I'll find myself in a car driven by some friend and we'll pass someone standing by the side of the road. His hair is rowdy from the rush of passing traffic, and his lips move in what is either a curse or a prayer. I want to tell the driver to pull over and stop, but instead, pretending a sudden problem with the radio reception, I lower my head until the ghost has receded from the rearview mirror."

"On my trips around the country," a man told Boyd McDonald in Raunch, "I would often spend my free time in malls cruising. At one time Denver had a terrific mall called Southglen that I would frequent. The toilets were upstairs and had four stalls, all with glory holes. I would spend hours in there playing. It was especially hot around 3:30 to 4:30 in the afternoons. The local high school was a block away and every kid with a hard-on must have known about those toilets. If I had known about toilets when I was that age I would have been there too. The young fuckers had dicks like blue steel and they shot warm, sweet loads into my mouth.

"In Oklahoma City, I was at a mall every day for a week. There were three stalls and since it was a new mall I decided I would get things going. I went in early one morning with tools and opened up a hole just made for sucking hot rods through. "In Houston, the Galleria was the place to be. I would spend all my free days there cruising between the first floor west toilet and the one upstairs on the east side. A lot of office workers came through this mall at lunch time and since there was a large parking garage on one side of the mall with several enclosed stairwells, there were plenty of places to escape to once contact was made.

"Both toilets were hot and equally busy. The west side had peep holes but low partitions so you could stand and work your prick and look over and see into the next stall.

"The upstairs toilet had thick walls that were also low between the heads. It also had a polished aluminum ceiling that made cruising so easy. Just had to lean back, look up, and there, usually, was the other guy checking you out also.

"This east toilet was probably a bit busier in the afternoons. Once I picked up a hot-looking man, tall, dark, in western drag. He had a seven-inch, uncut, thick tool and wanted it worked on. We headed for the stairwells in the parking garage. We went in and climbed up two levels and looked out to see how busy that level was. Hardly any cars so we got to it. I fell to my knees and he pulled out his prick and waved it at my face, then slapped me with it. Suddenly we heard some shuffling and started to cover up. Down the stairs came two guys who just grinned at us. They'd obviously just finished having sex and were on their way back down. They passed by, and I passed my hand to this guy's prick. I pulled it to my mouth and began to slowly pull it deep into my throat, where I could swallow around it, making myself gag on its length and width. Hardly anything makes my cock harder than to choke on a fat, juicy, stiff dick.

"He let me work him in this way until he was close and then he pushed my head against the wall and fucked my face deeply with sure, penetrating strokes.

"I came in my fist. He emptied his load into my throat. Never even got a taste of it, just the sensation of his cum pumping into my gullet."

Marcus O'Donnell, in "Blood's Promises" (from the anthology Hard, from Black Wattle Press), introduces us to a lad who desperately wanted to know a stranger intimately. At least he knew the man's name: Tagget. "He didn't like the name, but the lilt of the remembered accent – Irish, Scottish, Welsh even – washed over the harshness of the name's consonants. The name was buried deep inside the accent. It was that sound constituted my memory of him although we had exchanged only a few words. I followed him mercilessly. It all seemed to no avail. He kept walking, set on his own private trajectory. It seemed as if it would never intersect with mine.

"He wore a serious yet slightly vulnerable expression that lurked not on, but somehow inside, the lips; lurking precisely at that indistinguishable point where the lips become the mouth. A point that is neither surface nor interior.

"I went straight towards him after he had finally settled: slouched against the wall. I looked directly into his eyes, stood so that my body was touching his, began to stroke his chest with the back of my fingers then to explore his torso for nipples to squeeze. His head looked away from me, seemingly ignoring this unambiguous advance, but his eyes crept back in their sockets towards me. He made no move in return but neither did he push me away.

"To my surprise he agreed to come to a room. Inside, he warmed towards me. Kissing, pressing, stroking, pushing, looking into my eyes. I held the back of his head with my open palm and dug my tongue deep inside his

- 11 -

mouth, which softened and filled with saliva. He kissed me back, his tongue forcing its way past mine. Then he pulled back his mouth, pushed me against the wall, his crotch pinning me down, his fingers nimbly finding and working my now-erect nipples.

"I ripped at his denim shirt to find underneath, a leather harness crisscrossing his slightly sunken chest. The image registered as both revelation and confusion. Pale, formed but not worked or pumped, skin smooth and soft to touch, glowing in the low light. Now the boy was a memory that flickered in and out of focus. I couldn't remember much past those initial moments. My clothes had come off. I lay back on the vinyl- covered bench of the cubicle and the boy, his leather pants around his ankles, his crisscrossing harness against his chest, had eased his fingers deep inside my arse. We sniffed amyl and both flew, our thoughts and bodies ricocheting against the enclosure of the small darkened room. Neither of us came but somehow it all moved to a mutually acceptable climax and end. It was then, as we dressed, that I first heard his voice telling me his name. Then he was gone, leaving only the breath of sound for me to sniff."

In his memoir The World, the Flesh and Myself, Michael Davidson recounts many years of meeting strangers and making them his friends throughout the world. In Berlin, he met Werner. "I had, of course, surveyed the city's swimming-baths; and most afternoons was going to those in the Barwaldstrasse, somewhere in the wilderness beyond Hallesches Tor. And there one day, naked beneath the showers, I found the most startlingly beautiful person I'd ever seen: a living, and lively, Beardsley decoration for 'Salome' – he might have been the original Beardsley prototype, except that he was an improvement on the artist's invention. He had all the Beardsley sin, but none of the corruption; all the grace and uniqueness, but without the epicene languor. His was the face Beardsley would have drawn, had he not been dying of consumption. Ivory-white skin, parchment-pale, with a fervent scarlet mouth and huge sable eyes, full of black fire; a mass of romping black hair, thick and lively as a bear's, and the figure of a Gemito fisher boy. To Beardsley he added something of the Della Robbia choristers in Florence and a great deal of the famous 'Tripod' satyrs in the Naples Museum. It didn't surprise me to find that this face had been chosen from all over Germany to go on the cover of the magazine published by the Socialist Labor Youth – whose blue blouse and red scarf he wore.

"But, I quickly found, it wasn't only his face that was intoxicating; it was a glittering personality and the incomparable friendship that he gave – in his magic company differences of age, culture, language, vanished: he made me his equal and partner. 'Was ist mein ist Dein, 'he pronounced early on; and that remained his rule for the next few years – what was his was mine: he would share, when I was broke, his last cigarettes; and gave to the last drop his love and loyalty. I had found at last the 'divine friend much desired'; if one of us was faithless it was I – never he.

"Before I knew what was happening, that first day, I'd been swept on to the back of his bicycle and was whirling down the Friedrichstrasse – to a schwules Lokal, one of those 'queer' bars whose discreetly blacked-out facades and somberly curtained doorways proclaimed out loud their nature, where we drank cognac. He was not quite fifteen."

Scott O'Hara, in Autopornography, started at fifteen as well. He had his first real sex when he seduced a twenty-eight-year-old: "Maybe the proper word is 'raped'. I certainly didn't give him a chance to say no. I knew he was gay, and I knew I wanted it; therefore surely it followed that he should want me...? I cringe, today, at my youthful certainty, just as I marvel at his tact and gentility. He also marveled at the size of my dick, leading me to assume that this was standard gay speak during sex (which is, I've found, the case): 'God, you've got a big dick!' 'Fuck me with that big dick!' etc.

"The second man who I had sex with, some two weeks later, may have made similar comments; I don't remember. I remember the fourth man (not long after), who I met at the county library. He took me back to his apartment and asked me to piss on him, in his bathtub.

"Today, I'd be delighted to oblige; at age fifteen, I was terminally pee-shy, and completely unable to comply. I was mortified, and surprisingly turned off. He talked a lot about how big my dick was, but I discounted everything he said because he spent the rest of my visit trying to fuck me, which I didn't want him to do. He literally had me pinned down on his bed at one point, while I was struggling to get loose.

"I'm not especially proud of the fact that I resorted to reminding him that I was a minor, and I could get him in a lot of trouble . . . he did let me up then, and I promptly put on my clothes and fled. It's experiences like this that make me so skeptical of so many stories of 'boy rape' – most men are perfectly well aware that the boy has all the power in any sexual encounter, and most boys are equally cocksure, so the 'intimidation' argument doesn't cut much ice with me."

To see just how "cocksure" boys get that way, it is interesting to review the book Male Colors, in which Gary P. Leupp opens the window on the complex and varied patterns of sexual relations between males in early modern Japan. He says that Seikenji, which lay near the Okitsu stop on the Tokaido highway, was famous for two attractions – medicinal plaster and boy-prostitutes. Engelbert Kaempfer, passing through the town with the Dutch mission in the 1690s, described the relationship between these two: "On the chief street of this town were built nine or ten neat houses, or booths, before each of which sat one, two, or three young boys, of ten or twelve years of age, well dressed, with their faces painted, and feminine gestures, kept by their lewd and cruel masters for the secret pleasure and entertainment of rich travelers, the Japanese being very much addicted to this vice. However, to save the outward appearances, and lest the virtuous should be scandalized, or the ignorant and poor presume to engage with them, they sit there, as it were, to sell the aforesaid plaster to travelers."

"Such wayside prostitution (like unlicensed female prostitution) was not officially approved," Leupp says. "The hawking of medicinal plaster provided the boys with a convenient front. But many shogunate officials were probably inclined to overlook the infraction. Kaempfer expresses surprise that the commissioner escorting the mission in its travels – normally a model of dignified impassivity – could scarcely contain his excitement at the sight of these boys and detained the whole procession half an hour as he enjoyed one's company."

In his masterpiece, Koshoku ichidai otoko (The life of an amorous man, 1682), Ihara Saikaku wrote of a brothel featuring tobiko ("flying boys," or itinerant boy-prostitutes) in the village of Niodo, near the ancient capital of Nara. Here the hero, Yonosuke, meets a youth who has been selling his body since childhood. After enjoying his services, Yonosuke asks him to recount the tale of his perambulations. The young man's story provides a list of male prostitution hot spots and reveals something of the instability of the lives of such boys. The boy began in Kyoto, working as a female-role actor on the stage while doubling as a prostitute, and later lived in Miyajima (Aki province) with a theater patron. After an interval serving as a daimyo's boy in Bitchu province, he found himself homeless, soliciting priestly customers at Konpira Shrine in Sanuki. He then plied his trade in the Anryu pleasure quarter in Sumiyoshi, between Osaka and Sakai; in the Kashiwara licensed quarters in Kochi, Tosa province; and finally in Niodo in Yamato province. At age twenty-four, he looks forward to the imminent expiration of his current contract.

"...In some Edo wards," Leupp says, "men seeking male prostitutes patronized a standard 'teahouse,' or chaya, and asked the management to call in a boy-prostitute rather than one of the resident female prostitutes.

"One episode in the kabuki play Narukami Fudo Kitayama zakura, the hero, Danjiro, lingers in an antechamber awaiting an audience with a lord. Retainers of the household come to attend to him. First Hidetaro, a delicate boy of twelve or thirteen, enters to offer him tobacco. A delighted Danjiro compliments him on his beauty and asks about the progress of his martial training. The boy replies that he has been studying archery but has not yet learned to ride a horse.

"Danjiro thereupon offers to instruct Hidetaro in horseback riding. When the boy enthusiastically accepts the offer, the stalwart squeezes the boy between his thighs, explaining, 'Press tightly against the flanks of your mount, thus.' Embracing the boy, he rocks him back and forth suggestively, but when he attempts a kiss, Hidetaro panics and runs off. Danjiro laughs, bows to the audience, and facetiously pronounces his own conduct 'shameful'.

"Clearly, this samurai hero is equally amenable to having sex with boys or with women. So too, apparently, were many commoners, particularly the young libertines glamorized in much of Tokugawa popular literature.

"...The young rakes in Saikaku's works are generally bisexual. Four wealthy youths in one of his stories did nothing but have sex from dawn to dusk. ...Saikaku's most memorable character, the Casanova-like merchant Yonosuke (short for Ukiyonosuke), patronizes both male and female brothels. He reaches age fifty-four having dallied with 3,742 women and 725 young men, numbers that probably represent the sexual fantasies of many men of the time.

"Although Yonosuke's sexual history is of heroic proportions, he is merely a contemporary man-about-town writ large. It is altogether possible that one trip to the nanshoku teahouse per five to the courtesan brothel may have been the standard routine of many a wealthy urban rake.

"...An early seventeenth-century work called Shiratama no soshi (The white ball book) suggests that a male was considered most suitable as a homosexual sex partner from age seven to twenty-five, during which time he would develop from a child to a youth to a man. These categories roughly correspond to the more poetically defined stages given in the Wakashu no haru (Springtime of youths): from age eleven to fourteen, the boy was a 'blossoming flower'; from fifteen to eighteen, a 'flourishing flower'; and from nineteen to twenty-two, a 'falling flower'. Sixteen (fifteen by Western reckoning, as the Japanese regarded babies as one year old at birth), was thus the boy's 'springtime'. Saikaku also declares that sixteen 'is the age when youths are most attractive to other males.'

"The Sino-Japanese term saibi, which means homosexual anal sex and is written with the characters 'to plant' and 'tail', recalls the notion, common in some other societies, that anal sex with a boy confers manly qualities upon him and indeed is essential for his growth. An obscure passage in the Kojiki, meanwhile, thought by some to represent advice about heterosexual intercourse conferred upon the initiate during genpuku, may in fact refer to homosexual anal sex. In any case, if such ritualized pederasty once occurred in Japan, the practice had long been forgotten by the Tokugawa period.

"Men seem to have been rather universally drawn to beautiful youths. But how did boys respond to the adult male's advances? Certainly one finds literary examples of youths sexually harassed by men they despise; in Ishikawa Masamochi's Hida no takumi monogatari (Tale of a Hida craftsman, 1808) the hero, Yamabito, continually attracts such unwanted attentions. Yamamoto's Hagakure recommends that a youth cut down an obnoxious suitor. However, it is the poor qualities of the suitor, rather than the reception of homosexual interest, that meet with disgust.

"But literature also commonly portrays nanshoku as an emotionally rewarding experience for the boys pursued. For example, they may be deeply touched by love letters from male admirers. They frequently take the initiative in offering themselves to men who attract them. Some lack an older lover but pine for one. In one Saikaku tale, the thirteen-year-old page of a daimyo, who shares the latter's bed but does not love him, declares that 'if one day someone should tell me he loves me, I shall risk my life for him.' In ancient Sparta, boys lacking male lovers apparently suffered embarrassment. In Japan, such relationships met with more ambivalence, but Saikaku notes that 'a youth with no male lover is like a maiden without a betrothed', i.e., the object of pity.

"In ancient Greece, Kenneth Dover suggests that the adult lover in a homosexual relationship (erastes), who could easily buy a male prostitute or slave boy, was obliged to court his beloved youth (eromenos), impressing him with his qualities before winning his sexual favors. The boy, who could also find sexual outlets in prostitutes and slaves but who knew nothing of heterosexual courtship, may have been flattered by such attentions and have found satisfaction in 'being welcomed for his own sake by a sexual partner of equal status.'"

Well, guys, we welcome you, and trust you will find great satisfaction in the varied tales of intimacy with strangers in this spirited new collection.

INTIMATE STRANGERS
John Patrick

"The guys there were so beautiful – they've lost that wounded look that fags all had 10 years ago."

– Allen Ginsberg in 1969, after visiting the bar Stonewall

He slid his hard cock inside me. Deep, deeper. I had never had anything so big, or so hard, inside me. I held my breath as he kept coming into me; we were breathing and then not breathing in unison, and he brought his hand up to my mouth to cover it, suppress any sound, and then I began sucking his fingers, one at a time, then two at a time, then three. His fingers tasted of cum, of my own cum, since he had just jerked me off as he fucked me.

"Suck," he said, and pushed into me, harder still, as if by trying he could disappear up inside me.

When he came, his face became contorted as if it hurt him to come. He pulled out and rolled off me. We lay quietly for a while, and then he began to lick at my cock, making me come again, with his tongue, his lips, and his fingertips. I cried when I came, and doubled up, curling into myself.

He began kissing me, from my toes up along my legs and the insides of my thighs, over my belly, up my neck and onto my face and in my hair. He said this was his way of kissing me hello and good-bye at the same time. That's the way it is with strangers. Intimate strangers.

It had begun only hours before, when I stepped aboard a train at New York's Penn Station for a brief and normally uneventful journey to Philadelphia to visit my maiden aunt. It was something I did three or four times year.

I spotted an aisle seat on the right, beside a man who stared out the window, an open book across his lap.

This odd posture of contemplation made me ask for permission to sit beside him, and he gestured a welcome. He was an attractive man with dark hair and friendly eyes. He wore a black suit and looked vaguely Italian. The man may have been 40.

I pulled out my own book, and he politely asked what I was reading. It was "Breakfast at Tiffany's." I explained that I had just seen the movie and wanted to know what the "real" story was. He chuckled at this, and told me that he knew Mr. Capote and, despite what I may have heard, the heroine really was based on a girl the author knew. Before long, we were wrapped in fervent conversation about Mr. Capote and other authors he knew. He said he was a literary agent, and while he didn't represent Mr. Capote, he represented several authors whose names I would know if he said them. He had a warm and expressive face and I grew rather fond of him as we rolled on to the City of Brotherly Love, cocooned by our mutual interests from the crowded and noisy car.

Our newfound intimacy was interrupted by a man who stumbled from the first seat down the aisle toward the middle of the car, where we were sitting. The man had the look of a person most New Yorkers work hard to avoid. He was old, ragged but not dirty, and with only a tooth or so left in his head. I avoided eye contact and turned back to my neighbor, but sensed his approach.

He muttered something I chose not to understand. "Sorry, I don't smoke," I said, and waved him off. I figured he was bumming a cigarette.

He returned a look somewhere between pity and disgust. "No," he said, quite clearly now. "I'd like to borrow a pen."

I was embarrassed. He needed a pen and had identified me as a student, and all students have pens. I told him I was on a holiday and didn't have one, but I could see he didn't believe me.

"Here." My neighbor had pulled a pen from inside his suit jacket. "Take this. In fact, you can have it."

The old man looked at the pen and then at my neighbor with surprise. I too was surprised because I knew a silver Cross pen when I saw one. And so the man scribbled something on a tiny piece of paper and quickly offered to return it.

"Please, go ahead and keep it. In case you need it again."

The old man looked hard into my neighbor's eyes, then nodded and waved in appreciation.

"I thought he wanted a cigarette," I explained.

He shrugged. "My good deed for the day." He touched my elbow. "And what can I do for you today?"

I blinked. I wanted to tell him, but I was still not sure, despite all the insider talk about Mr. Capote.

"Your book," I said, "What are you reading?"

He showed me the book he had nearly finished. It was Allen Ginsberg's Howl. "It's a few years old now, but I've never read it. I wanted to see what the courts thought was obscene."

The man held the book up and I examined it. "Do you know him, too?" I asked.

"Oh, yes. We have similar tastes in – " He paused, then squeezed my knee. "Friends."

I blushed and looked away. I never knew how to react once strangers revealed themselves to me.

As we pulled into the station, he handed me the book. "Here," he said. "Please take it. As my gift."

"I can't," I said. "You're not finished with it."

"Oh, I can get another. Just like I can get another pen."

I accepted. "What's your name?" I asked him.

"Harrison. Frank Harrison."

I introduced myself to him and we held hands for a long moment.

John Patrick

"Do you have to rush off to your aunt's?" Frank asked in the cab. No, of course I didn't. I could always make some excuse.

Earlier, on the subway to Penn Station, I had placed myself fully between a young Hispanic and the old woman next to me. I glanced down at the bulge in his pants. I gave him time to figure it out, to refuse me. I kept looking at his face, the bulge, his sneakered feet.

A year ago, on a good night, when I was new to it, this was enough most of the time. I would cruise, be cruised in return, and leave satisfied.

But now I had waited, to follow the object of my desire. He led me to his building. We didn't speak until we were inside his little apartment. It was dark, even with a lamp left on.

My hand moved to his waist, came to rest on the leather belt, took hold of the thick buckle. I played with it lightly.

My hand moved slowly, willing him to stop me if he wished. Under the denim, his cock was swelling against my palm. I stroked along his bulge, around it, pretending it wasn't really anything all that exciting, but he knew better.

Still, it was all up to him. I traced his shape as it grew. He drew a deep breath in anticipation. He couldn't wait to have me sucking. There could be no doubt which of us wanted this encounter between strangers, which of us has asked for it. I unzipped him and his enormous sex was filling my hand. I curled my fingers around him, stroking.

"Don't come, yet. Not yet. Please," I begged. He looked down at it, how I was stroking it. I kept stroking, admiring the mass of foreskin, the heft of it, the sheer beauty of it. I kissed it, nibbled on the head.

On a scale from one to ten, I would say it had been an eight plus orgasm.

I would have liked to have hung around to see him recover, but I had a train to catch to Philadelphia.

Now Frank, he was a ten if ever there was one. And what made it all so memorable was that after he gave me the tongue bath he held me for several minutes, sucking my naked shoulder blades, squeezing my asscheeks.

Dressed, I stood at the door with my Capote book and my gift of Ginsberg under my arm. Frank gave me his card, asked me to call him, whenever I was free. Then he kissed me one last time, saying hello and good-bye.

- Excerpted from John Patrick's forthcoming erotic novella, "Brother Love," which will be published next year.

THE EXCHANGE
John Patrick

Okay, yes, I admit it. I paid for sex: paid for a stud. Two hundred, at my hotel.

I'd been in L.A. for the preview of the new TV season and that always means two weeks of meeting after meeting, most of them boring, and then dragging myself back to the room at night. I decided, this year, I'd skip the finale party and have a little party of my own.

Then I saw the ad, under "Masseurs." A massage was what I needed. I'd seen many of these ads before, of course, but this one really captured my attention. "The Ultimate Treat: Nude massage by very handsome, caring bi-stud." What harm in calling the number, just to see, just to have a feel for how these things work? Not that I would ever consider, not that I would have an interest in sex for hire, but a massage....

I expected little really. But before I knew what had hit me, I was caught in the middle of a sex-for-hire transaction. I got a message that I had to leave my number; Chet would call me back.

We got the time and place decided, but then he got friendly, probably to check me out. I was forthcoming, but not too much. Then came, "What you into?"

My mind was racing. The drop in my belly was reminiscent of a roller coaster ride. The slamming of my heart drowned out my feeble words. Requirements seemed to be spilling from me. What was I doing? Why couldn't I slow this exchange down? "Anything and everything," I shot back, attempting to sound in control, although I certainly wasn't. Oh shit, I was out of control! My cock was throbbing. I stroked it. I should have hung up. But I didn't. I held fast that receiver like a kid does a balloon on a windy day and muttered my demands. "Everything," I insisted. After all, for two-hundred hard-earned dollars for a massage, for chrissakes... "Yes. In an hour. Yes. I have cash."

We hung up. How surprisingly easy this was! I stared at the black-edged ad. In an hour? Had I actually consented? The transaction whirled around me like a hurricane. Two hundred dollars. Oh my God.

I sat in my room like a reluctant patient in a dentist's chair. I had gone to the front desk and cashed some checks so I had four one-hundred dollar bills crammed in the pocket of my bathrobe. Not that I would actually go through with this scheme. Not that I would end up in bed with a man for hire...but a massage....

My heart thumped recklessly. I fished out the condoms I always carried in my toiletry kit. Life being what it was, circumstances twisting as they do, it was always best to be prepared on the off chance that – On the off chance that what? The sudden urge to hurry out of the hotel, climb into my rental car and screech out of the parking lot overwhelmed me. What was I thinking?

There was a knock on the door. I opened it. "Hi, how you doin'?" The voice gushed through me like liquid heat. There he stood. All six-one, six-two of him. In a gray jogging outfit, massage table in hand.

"Hello there." My voice cracked.

He nodded, his dark hair flopping over his forehead, and I let him into the room. He was set up in a moment. A harsh hollowness ballooned in my chest. I stood immobilized. Now what the hell did I do? My gaze slid from his flurry of activity to linger on those hands. Huge, browned by the sun.

"Okay. You wanna get down on your stomach and we'll get started."

I obeyed, tossing off my robe and making myself comfortable. I felt abruptly transported out of my hesitations and into the steamy sensation of his touch.

"You're very attractive," I told him. "I thought you were going to do this in the nude."

"Of course. Just getting you comfortable."

He was standing at the end of the table, his crotch in my face. Slowly, deliberately, he pulled off his sweatshirt. His torso was incredibly muscular. I had an immediate hunger to see more. He took my head in his hands and pulled me forward. I was breathing hard and my mouth felt sucked dry. He pushed me into his crotch. I could feel the flesh under the fabric. He wore no jockstrap. I started to nip, to kiss. He loosened the sweats and they fell away.

My god, it was thicker than I could have dreamed, larger than I could have hoped. I felt suddenly dizzy. A creamy aching throbbed between my legs. His sweats dropped to the floor and he stepped from them. The fragrance of sex hung heavy in the air. Entrancing musk blended with an intoxicating spice into a primal, raw scent. All I could think of was his semi-hard cock. All I could consider was the hugeness of it. Like a desperate baby, I opened my mouth wide for the what I considered to be the "ultimate treat."

He was all slippery heat. Submerged in dark desire, I found his cock with my mouth and sucked, sucked, sucked. I was all over him, and he reached down and cleaved my asscheeks open. I was ravenous, but I pulled back. His ballsac dangled like a dark pink ornament. I licked it once, lapped it. Wanting more, needing more, I grabbed the cock again. It was now fully hard and sex juice shimmered on the head. I licked if off, went back to sucking.

Meanwhile, he'd been busy making me warm and oily, massaging my aching muscles. Then he started to probe. In and out, he pumped his finger into me. Again and again, over and over. Engulfed in pinks and reds, surrounded in the hot perfume of lust, I spun in a vortex of pleasure. It was dark. It was light. I was swimming in slippery gels, floating on a sun-baked lake, swirling in a tropical storm. The slapping sounds as he pounded his cock into my mouth lifted me high in the air. Again and again, more and more. But suddenly, he pulled back, saying he had work to do.

He stood on the side of the table and massaged my muscles, occasionally pushing my hand away from his cock. He was soon concentrating all his efforts on my buttocks, kneading and squeezing and spreading them. His oily fingertips gently teased until my asshole was begging for it. He accommodated by sliding two fingers inside the snug chasm and waiting, letting me get used to it.

Then he went back to massaging. He spoke for the first time in several minutes, telling me, "Oh, man, I just love the spring and roll of a good ass. Too bad the skin's always so rough there from sitting." At that he applied more oil to the area and I thought of how great it would be to have him fuck it. He rubbed my inner thighs, his fingers brushing my cock, as if inadvertently. After teasing me awhile, he turned me on my back and parted my legs with professional exactitude.

My cock throbbed, long, hard, glistening with pre-cum. He stared at it. "I think you need a little extra massaging today, but that's fifty dollars extra. My time, you know."

"Certainly," I said. "Go right ahead."

"God," he said, squeezing my balls, "I'll bet you pump a hell of a load."

I followed his gaze down to my crotch. "Yeah, I...I guess so," I stammered.

Before I knew it, he was licking the sweat off my nuts. As he moved his tongue, my dick jerked, leaving a trail of pre-cum on his forehead.

Every time his tongue lapped across my balls, I felt it all over my body. He rolled them around on his tongue, then he sucked them, stretching my cords out tight. My dick began slapping up against my belly.

When my balls popped out of his mouth and he started licking my shaft, I clasped my hands around his thick neck. His pink tongue flicked around my knob, licking away the honey that was oozing out, and then he winked at me and capped my cock.

I'd never felt anything like this masseur's practiced mouth on my meat. He kept his lips in this tight little circle as his head bobbed up and down. Then he swallowed me up to the short hairs, and I began to shudder. He kept it there a long time, shaking his head and swallowing, giving my dick a terrific massage. Then he came up, nipped the tip of my prick a couple of times, took a deep breath, and went down on me again. I gripped his biceps, squeezed hard, closed my eyes, and just let it happen. Within a couple of minutes I was ready. My toes were all curled up, and I was twitching all over. He just kept on sucking till it happened. I thrust my hips up off the bench and let him have it. My expensive masseur really got off on it. He sucked and swallowed, smacking his lips and making these happy little grunting noises. Spent, I flopped back against table, closed my eyes.

"Shall I finish your massage now?" he asked.

I opened my eyes. He was standing beside the table, his fingers toying with my anus. His rigid cock was right in my face. "God, I don't know. It's huge."

"It will feel very good." He slid a condom on it, then said, "Turn over, please."

I turned to lie on my stomach again. He entered me easily, so relaxed was I now.

Snug inside me, he lifted me up so he could stroke my cock while he fucked me. In this position, I could look in the mirror across the room and see him over me. The muscles in his arms were knotted, and there were veins standing out under his tanned skin like a road map. Sweat trickled down his chest, and his belly popped out in thick ridges every time he hunched his hips forward. He kept slamming into me faster and harder till my head was banging against the table and I was grunting as loud as he was. By the time he shouted, "I'm ready," I was close again. I shuddered as my jism soaked the towel under me.

This was service, I had to admit. I wanted it to last, but within seconds, he exploded.

Okay, yes, I admit it. I paid for sex. Not that I would ever consider, not that I would have an interest . . . but I can't tell you how sad I was when, the following year, back in L.A. for the same round of meetings, I called Chet's number and a disconnect notice was all I got.

FLASH

Rick Jackson

Venice, California, doesn't have border guards to keep out the old or ugly or otherwise annoying, but it might as well have. Even the letter carriers are cute and young and trendy – at least mine is. A real dream boy if ever there was one. He's only been around, delivering the mail on his in-line skates, for a little more than six months, but the very first time I ran into him, he made one hell of an impression.

I guess I should say he ran into me. I was just coming down the stairs when young studly streaked up to our mailboxes and slammed into me like a greased Ganymede on wheels. By the time I pried my ass off the sidewalk, Flash had more or less collected his far-flung mail and gotten back to his wheels. While I was taking stock of the kid – and that took a while – I noticed he had scraped the living shit out of his right kneecap. His uniform shorts weren't torn, but they obviously held too big a package for their own good. Besides, it was pretty clear that if I let Flash continue on his duly-appointed rounds the way he was, his sock and skate would be a gory mess in no time. It was my civic duty to invite the kid inside and tend to his wounds!

I started off doing just that, but by the time we had peroxide bubbling away on his scraped knee, my mind was drifting higher – up to that long, thick bulge snaking down his left thigh or the twin mounds of massive man-nut swelling from between his legs. I was the living picture of compassion as I rubbed some Vaseline-based pain killer across his scrape and longed to slide my hands higher, up across his strong, tanned thigh and hard around what I really wanted him to deliver. For a long moment, I watched his lean young body deal with its minor set-back and waited for a sign.

Even in Venice, where everyone is pretty, Flash was something else. He must have been about 24, but looked closer to 14. Part of the credit for that deception went to his high cheekbones and massive brow and jaw. Part went to his sun-bleached blond hair and huge brown eyes. Part was due to his solid-packed muscles and soft, youthful skin. Mostly, though, it was that damned shy goofy smile of his that did me in. He was open and innocent and trusting as a fool. The guy may have been put together like a Greek god, but he grinned like a cross between Jimmy Stewart and Gomer Pyle. Maybe if he'd been wearing underwear, I'd have stood a chance. As it was, the massive outline that postal dick made as it stretched his grey shorts tight was too savory for anything human to resist.

Flash didn't say dick as I slid my hand slowly up his thigh and latched onto what he had hanging. His brown eyes cocked sideways and looked at me for a moment, reminding me rather of a spaniel the first time he catches his master having sex. If his top head started off trying to figure me out, his bottom one was with the program from the get-go. I had no sooner locked on target than I felt his thick shank pulse and throb with welcome in my hand. It had a surprising heat and the supple youthful softness of skin one seldom finds on men past their teens. Most of all, though, that dick had an agenda. It bucked and heaved in my hand and did everything but pay me to jack it.

I was so cranked up that I wasn't thinking straight. I should have plucked off his shorts and gotten seriously busy. Instead, I gave his civil service unit the special handling it needed. I even eased my left hand up his other leg so I could play with his nuts while I worked. His sky-kissed blond head lay back against the chair by then, his eyes shut and mouth agape in pleasure; but I felt for all the world like one of those nuclear-research guys, my hands operating some remote experiment my eyes couldn't see. Besides, the hot Venice day had turned his dick and nuts all hot and sweaty. I've been around men enough to know there's nothing this goose likes so much as a fine slow-poached gander.

When I reached up to solve Flash's trou problem, he seemed almost relieved. I was careful not to scrape the shorts across his bum knee, but I was also quick to get back down to business. His shorts were still flying across the room when my mouth wrapped around his big, sweaty `nads. They were delicious as only a man's nuts baked crotch-deep for hours in the California sun can be. The melded flavors of man-musk and sweat blended to perfection across the outside of his heavy male-bag while the inside throbbed with virile power and the promise of buckets of jism ready to be delivered.

I was kneeling between his wide-spread legs as he lounged in my chair so I could lap and suck at those wrinkled sperm-pods in comfort. His hard thighs were rich with flavor and promise whenever I felt the need to give his stones a rest – but that wasn't often. Flash seemed to like kicking back with his feet up while I snuffled up and down his crotch, licking his nuts the way I wish I could lick my own. When the flavor started to fade, though, and I started chewing harder on his balls, the kid started having second thoughts. His hands still pressed my head against his crotch, mind, but the little chipmunk squeaks of pleasure he had been making suddenly matured to yelps of anxious concern for his future.

When I looked up to check out his expression, I saw that he had taken advantage of having my face buried in his crotch to lose his shirt. Except for his skates and socks, Flash was naked as a monk's wet-dream and twice as arousing. His broad chest was tanned and hairless, descending in easy ripples from impossibly wide shoulders down across rose-tipped tits and a flat belly to a waist small enough to hang off a Sri Lankan mystic.

I had been licking his balls so long that my leg had cramped up. Since I needed to stretch anyway, I left him to his own devices long enough to haul a bucket of rubbers and lube from the bedroom. I suppose we could have moved in there for Act II, but the way his legs were spread wide was too perfect a picture to improve. I think he started to give me shit when he saw me rubbering up, but my hand slid down to pry wide his ass-crack. Once he felt my fingers sliding along the sweaty depths of his hairless crack, gliding across his shithole and teasing it with a man's possibilities, he lay back and let Nature happen.

I took my time, of course – not because I was afraid my dick would hurt him. I knew damned well my thick nine inches of angry occupant was going to rip his ass wide. I just love foreplay for its own sake. Except for the obvious, there's no pleasure greater than taking an up-tight asshole and teasing it happy using nothing but a couple of fingers, a bucket of lube, and the length of a sunny afternoon to work the magic.

Flash seemed to agree with me. His ass rolled upwards to give me more room and his jaw soon went slack and even more goofy. As I rubbed his asshole the right way and then made it habit, I couldn't help noticing that his squeaks had turned to long, low moans of pleasure. I've never rubbed a gator's belly, but I've seen film of it being done – and that's the same sublime expression of absolute contentment that Flash had on his face during the ten or so minutes I was massaging my way into his affections.

When I got all wild and slipped my first finger up his ass, he let out a little gasp, but bore down around me like a trained boy-toy. His body shivered with pleasure as my fuckfinger slipped across his prostate and scratched an itch that had been so deeply buried, the kid hadn't even realized it had been nagging away at him for years. He instinctively rolled his ass to grind my finger harder across his butt nut, proving himself to be just exactly my kind of civil servant.

His slick guts trilled along my fingers like an Easter carillon, coasting here and there as my finger stretched at his asshole. When, after a time, I added a second and then a third finger to splay his ass wide, his eyes went temporarily buggy and then settled back into neutral as his young male body sucked sweet succor from life. I might still be kneeling between his knees, playing with his ass and worshiping his classic beauty and tight perfection, if he hadn't finally let out a thunderous mournful sigh that seemed at once to bubble up from the very depths of the earth and rattle down from marble Olympus.

His muscled body gave another little shiver and then, eyes bright with wicked relish, he spoke his first words in almost an hour: "That feels so . . . . Your hand feels perfect up there, but I'd like to try more if you don't mind."

I didn't mind. I was having a good time, but the very best times come from helping out a stranger in need. I spread more lube down my dick than you could scrape off a shoat at the Mississippi State Fair, but that was more to grease the skids of my own pleasure than to help Flash out of the problem he was about to back in to. Out of consideration for his knee – and because I'm just nasty enough to like to see my bitches when I dick them deep – I didn't flip his ass over. Instead, I lifted his legs until his skates clinked together behind my neck and then I pressed my advantage.

Even through the rubber, I could feel the slut's asshole trying to gobble my bone for lunch, but it was like a gnat trying to suck down a mountain. Flash moaned and twirled his eyes as I slid my fat dickhead across his anus, but he was about to find out what a pain in the ass a really good time could be.

I reached low to brush his lips with an encouraging kiss and then parked my eyes about a foot from his so I could see every flicker and nuance. Then my ass reared back to gather steam and drove my deadly dick back down past the tight defenses of his glutes and through the tortured, shredding tissues of his asshole. The kid's eyes nearly erupted like a Saturday morning cartoon caricature's – wide with wonder and terror and perhaps the first tentative wisps of wisdom. Then those blond lashes clamped shut, his nails raked across my back in a vain effort to claw away the agony, and his hard male body learned what being on the receiving end of a really special delivery felt like.

I held him in my arms for a long, slow moment of unaccustomed tenderness. Then, gently at first, I eased my thick dick up and out of his ass. His guts caved in behind me, desperate for relief, yet clinging tight around my tool because he was even more desperate for satisfaction. Flash needed to be had. He needed to feel a man's thick dick digging deep up his ass. Without knowing why, he yearned to be taken, to be roughly possessed like some Barbara Cartland heroine, to be dominated and owned by a man more powerful than he. As much as his body needed to be ravished, his soul needed it even more.

My dick picked up speed and sliced snicker-snack deeper and faster and harder through the tender pink ruins of his shithole with every passing second. His eyes had long since opened, scintillating bright with the greedy glow of one who has seen the transcendent and made it his own. His moans and growls grew apace, and his hands outdistanced even them, tearing their way along my flanks, across my ass, and back up to claw at my shoulders. Against the feral background of his woodland noises, the quickening clogged-drain sound of dick meeting hole, and the sloppy, sweaty smack of hips slamming into up-reared butt kept me from growing bored.

The magical rhythms and heavenly smells of man and sex and summer lured me away from mere carnal pleasure and wafted us both to a weightless realm where thought gave way to feeling and feeling hoisted the soul's sails to glide across a sweet, sting-less, honeyed sea towards nirvana. Time and the very cosmos itself both wobbled and spun to a stop as Flash and I lost ourselves and found each other. In a perfect world, we would still be floating there, bound by bone and tail forever.

Years too soon, my body turned on me and jolted time forward once again. I came back to myself to find I had dropped one of Flash's legs but instinctively held his bad knee close to my shoulder. He had twisted about slightly in the chair and was taking the full brunt of my attack up the ass, but sideways. The glassy look on his eyes and the strands of frothy jism dripping down across his chest and bare belly proved he had made a male delivery of his own while I'd been busy customer-servicing his ass.

We both did plenty of yelling over the next minute or so, but once I found myself dry-humping his ass, I saw no reason not to drop onto his sweat- and jism-stained chest for a quick time out. Flash didn't let me rest on his chest or my laurels for long. He was soon whining about getting back to his route – but needing another serious dicking first. I talked him into sharing a cool shower with me to wash off the day's sweat before I led him to my bed, but I might as well have saved the water. Flash wasn't much interested in cleaning up, and by the time he limped into his skates and rolled out the door, the sweat that drenched us both was only one of Nature's little souvenirs of our good time.

You can believe Flash was back for more the very next day – more interested in being serviced than in servicing his route. Lately, though, I've found a way to keep the mail moving on time. I've moved his ass into my apartment and use it so long and hard all night long that the bastard is almost glad to slide off to work. I know I'm glad to see him go. Of course I'm happy to see the nation's mails being delivered, but mostly, I just need the rest.

AULD LANG SYNE
Thomas C. Humphrey

"Leave 'em off, Willard." Jimmy reached for my glasses as I scrubbed them on my shirttail to wipe off the fog that kept building up as the cabin got warmer. He leaned over and peered close in my face. "You're a good-lookin' dude without 'em."

I giggled as if he had said the funniest thing in the world. I was high for the first time in my life, and it was wonderful! Everything was wonderful! I plopped back down on the carpet and watched the lambent blue flames dance over the artificial logs, fascinated by the intense color.

Jimmy stretched beside me and leaned on an elbow. I could feel his eyes exploring me without turning to look at him. He was as high as I was, but not for the first time – or the five-hundredth, probably.

"It's weird, you know, man. You and me here together on New Year's Eve – the school nerd and the school fuck-up, high as kites, waiting for a new year full of the same old shit." His voice was dreamy, without a touch of bitterness or cynicism, and it floated into my consciousness from a great distance.

"They say whatever you do New Year's Day you'll do all year," I said. "Maybe I'll just stay high. Can you stay stoned three hundred and sixty-five days in a row?"

"You sure as hell can give it your best shot, dude. But there's other things that'd be more fun sometime." He lifted up my hand and dropped it in his crotch. "Like this, maybe."

I jerked my hand back as if he had thrust it into the fireplace. My whole body felt on fire, and beads of sweat popped out on my forehead. My heart threatened to tear through my chest.

"What's the matter, Willard? Ain't you ever helped a buddy out before? I bet you want what I got, don't you?" He matter-of-factly put my hand back between his legs and pressed it into the tight, hot mound that steadily grew under my touch.

I did want it. I had even thought what it would be like as we drove around swigging our beers and toking on the joint he dug out of a cigarette pack. Now that I had it in my hand, though, it scared me. Then Jimmy reached between my legs, and high excitement and driving need won out over my fear.

I had boldly walked up to Jimmy in the pool hall a couple of hours earlier. "Want to shoot a game?" I asked.

For just a second, a peculiar expression swept across Jimmy's face, then he nodded. "If you're paying," he said.

I did know how to hold a cue stick, and I knew the difference between eight ball and rotation, but this was the second or third time I'd ever been in the pool hall. I grew up in a rigid Baptist family, where it seemed that everything fun was sinful.

This New Year's Eve, though, I was restless. For once in my life, I wanted to do something exciting, maybe even sinful. Especially something sinful. I had been home from college almost two weeks, had made the rounds visiting relatives, had seen the few high school classmates I remotely could call friends, had discovered everybody but me had dates and parties to attend. I had the choice of staying at home and going to bed early or driving around in the family car, hoping against hope for something out of the ordinary.

My little hometown was closed tighter than a bank vault, except for a diner and the pool hall. I drove around in the steadily increasing rain mixed with sleet and listened to some big band group entertain until the ball would drop and everybody would hug and kiss and go ape over the world being a year older. And, as usual, I would be alone and self-pitying and miserable.

The light battling through the frosted plate glass window announcing "Wayne Street Billiards" beckoned to me. As I stepped inside, I experienced the usual tingling excitement of being in forbidden territory. The room was shabby and not very clean. The unpainted wooden floors were worn from a constant tread of feet. Paint was peeling from the dingy green walls. Only the velvet of the tables gleamed with cleanliness under the strong lights above them. The room was virtually dark except for the pools of light cast around a couple of tables.

The place was practically deserted. The bartender leaned on an elbow and thumbed through a well-worn girlie magazine. A couple of old men shot nine ball at a front table, their occasional deep laughter resounding, and a heavy fog of cigarette smoke hovered over the table, curling away lightly as one of the men bent to shoot. Toward the back, three redneck types, slightly older than me, cussed and loudly taunted each other in a very heated game. And Jimmy Reese sat in his tight jeans on a bench against a side wall, legs splayed, bored.

Jimmy and I had gone to high school together until he dropped out at the beginning of eleventh grade. Our little school was split into definite cliques, and everybody was forced into one or another of them. There were the jocks, the preppies, the nerds, and the fuck-ups. Jimmy was a fuck-up, a drug-using tough guy with no interest in school. He wore faded tight jeans with rips and white threadbare spots in all the right places and usually a black Metallica or Guns 'n' Roses tee shirt. He either ignored or smart-mouthed teachers in class. He defied a smoking ban by sitting on the side steps before school and during lunch puffing away – sometimes on weed instead of tobacco. Most of his jeans had FTW – fuck the world – inked into the thighs along with bloody daggers and skulls and crossbones.

Jimmy actually was rather slightly built, but he had a well-proportioned, lithe body, raven-black hair that just covered his ears, and a pouty, bad-boy demeanor that rivaled film star Johnny Depp's. Girls from all the cliques hung on him, fascinated by his teenage angst and almost palpable sexual aura. For years, I watched and dreamed about him from a distance without ever speaking a dozen words to him.

Now, there I was – Willard Baker, class valedictorian, Most Likely to Succeed, National Merit Finalist – Willard Baker, the best little boy in town – Willard Baker, nerd – lying on the carpet in a strange lake cabin Jimmy had broken into, completely stoned, kneading Jimmy's hard-on through his jeans, wondering where we went from there.

"Let's get rid of some clothes," Jimmy said, a new huskiness in his voice. He bounded up and started shucking coat and shoes and shirt. Seeing that I hadn't moved, he tugged me to my feet. "Come on, let's get naked," he insisted. Just the way he said it sent a shiver of excitement through me.

Although I had a pretty good body that I wasn't ashamed of, I was an only child and had been indoctrinated with the idea that modesty is a supreme virtue. Throughout high school, I had finagled to schedule gym classes for last period so I could shower at home instead of with a gang of other boys. The only naked bodies I had seen were pictures of Greek and Roman sculptures and those I created in my fantasies.

Jimmy had been a frequent and favorite subject of these fantasies, and I had mentally posed him in every conceivable position. I could hardly wait for him to stand before me naked in the flesh, but getting undressed myself was an entirely different matter. I just stood immobile, hypnotized by the sight of him unpeeling his tight jeans from his hips, his calves, his ankles, his feet.

He kicked his pants aside and moved to me, his white briefs gleaming in the dim blue light. "Looks like you need some help there, buddy," he said.

He ran his hand up and down my crotch, and my hard-on swelled so tight I decided it would split through my pants, saving me the effort of taking them off. Jimmy slid my heavy jacket off and snaked my sweatshirt over my head. When he moved to my waistband, I stopped him. After all, I wasn't going to be completely passive in all this. I unfastened my jeans and shoved them down.

Reaching for my stiffer again, Jimmy guided my hand to his briefs. I squeezed and kneaded, conscious of the intense heat radiating through the thin cotton. It was a fantasy come true – Jimmy standing nearly naked close to me, playing with my dick as I felt him up and tried to determine how much was tucked into the tight pouch beneath my hand.

"Get your clothes off," he said, stepping back to strip his briefs down.

After I pried off my sneakers and bent to take my jeans off, I straightened up to feast on the sight before me. Jimmy was in a hipshot stance, most of his weight on one leg, and he pressed his hard-on straight out with a thumb on its base. I had a quick vision of Donatello's "David." That vision dissolved, though, as I noticed that Jimmy had a much more pronounced masculinity than the androgynous statue. His chest was well-muscled, with large dark nipples, and a slight black fuzz nestled in the cleft between his pectorals. His ridged abdomen led downward to a fishbone trail of black hair that expanded into a tangled mass above his cock. His narrow hips melded into tight, nearly hairless thighs.

After surveying him from head to toe, my eyes hurried back to his stiff cock. In my fantasies, I had kept recreating and improving upon it until I turned it into a phallic icon as imposing as the enormous genitalia depicted on primitive fertility gods. As I put it under the microscope of vision heightened by desire, I realized that my fantasies had been far from accurate. Jimmy's endowment was all too humanly average – no larger than my own, if as large. The reality of it did not dampen my enthusiasm for it, though. My breathing was so short and my heart was pumping so fast I felt dizzy-headed.

Jimmy posed and preened while I ogled him for a minute or so and then stepped in close. "Let's see your equipment," he said. In one clean move, he stripped my briefs to my thighs, freeing my hard cock, which reared straight up. Jimmy grabbed it and slowly moved his hand up and down the shaft. Without prodding, I reached for him.

"Come on, go down on me," he whispered after we had stroked each other a few times.

"Huh?" I asked dumbly. I was so naive I didn't know what he was talking about.

"Go down on me. Give me some head, dude," he insisted.

"Uh-uh," I said, catching on.

"What's the matter? You want it; I know you do."

"I – I..." was all I could manage. I felt like a complete dork.

"Are you virgin?" he asked with a note of disbelief.

"Yeah. I – I've never done anything," I confessed. The blood rushed to my face until I was sure I was lighting up the whole room.

"Well, how about that!" he said around a good-natured chuckle. "I've found myself a cherry! But you just relax. Ole Jimmy'll teach you everything you need to know. Man, will I ever teach you!"

He guided me down onto the carpet and tugged my briefs the rest of the way off. Before I knew what was happening, he pried my cock away from my body and took it into his mouth. His warm lips and flicking tongue were almost too much to bear. I shoved my ass hard against the carpet and shrank away. Almost at the same time, though, I wanted that warm wetness to absorb me completely. Going for the best of both extremes, I set up a frantic hunching and drove my cock back and forth, back and forth into his mouth.

"Whoa! Slow down and enjoy it. Let me do the work," he advised.

I managed to lie still, except for the trembling in my taut thighs and the frantic, involuntary wandering of my fingers through his hair. What he was doing was the best thing that had ever happened to me. I wanted it to last forever, but I knew that it was rapidly coming to its end.

Just before I reached that point, Jimmy took his mouth off my cock. "That's how you do it," he said. He scrambled onto my chest, his knees under my armpits, his dick in my face. "Now, suck mine," he said, jabbing at my lips.

I saw a clear drop of pre-cum ooze from the head of his cock just before I closed my eyes and opened my mouth. Jimmy raised up over me, his weight on his hands above my head, and started a slow movement in my mouth. Remembering what he had done to my dick, I started using my lips and tongue. I had dreamed about this very cock being in my mouth countless times, but the reality was much better than the dream.

Jimmy sat back on his haunches, most of his weight on my chest, and raised my head off the carpet. Without him thrusting into my throat, I could explore and savor his cock at my own pace. I ran my tongue all over the head and played with different depths of penetration and different degrees of pressure on the silky-hard shaft. In no time, I had him moaning and groaning, and he grabbed me by the hair and moved my head back and forth on his rod. Just before I knew he was going to shoot, he pulled his cock away from me.

"Man, you were shitting me about being virgin. You suck cock like a pro!" he said.

"Uh-uh, this is my first time," I insisted. I strained upward to reach his dick, which was tantalizingly just out of reach.

"You really want it, don't you?" he said. He slapped my cheeks a few times with his dick and rubbed it all around my lips, teasingly pulling it away every time I tried to get it back in my mouth. Then he didn't pull away, and as I took him in, he leaned forward and lifted my head and fed me his cock until it brushed my tonsils.

"Now, go ahead and suck me off," he said, rocking his dick back and forth in my mouth.

I barely had started working on him when his dick swelled against my lips. "Yeah! Suck that cock! Suck it dry!" he growled out. He made some primitive animal sounds deep in his throat and the unfamiliar blast of his come hit the back of my mouth. The sudden force and heat and taste of it caught me by surprise and I tried to twist away, but Jimmy pulled forward on my head and held me on his dick until the fat tube on its underside quit throbbing against my lower lip. The first blast of his come had gone clear down my throat, so when he pulled out of my mouth, I gulped the rest of it down and then pulled him back close and just held his cock in my mouth until it began to soften.

He tumbled off my chest and sprawled on his back. "Man, that was good – real good," he said. "When I rest up, we'll have to go for seconds!"

I had hoped that he would settle in to give me the same as he got, but without touching me, he sat up and reached for his jacket. He fumbled around until he pulled out another joint, which he lit up and passed to me after he had a couple of hits.

I propped on an elbow and watched him as we shared the joint. My dick was so hard and my balls were so tight they hurt. I hoped he'd give me the relief I craved when we got another buzz on.

"Whose cabin is this?" I asked.

"Belongs to John Hemphill down at the bank. He's outta town."

"How'd you know how to get in and turn on the gas?"

"I been here before – with John."

"You mean. . . ."

"Yeah, don't let his wife and kids fool you. He's been swinging on my dick since I was fourteen – and treating me pretty good in exchange."

"But I always thought – I mean – The way girls used to hang on you at school, I figured you were screwing whenever you felt like it. I never thought you -"

"What? Would go for gay sex? I ain't gay or nothing, understand, but when I'm horny I'll go for anything."

"You were sure about me, weren't you?"

"I had my suspicions all along. But tonight you popped up when I was just horny enough to try you."

"I'm glad I caught you in the mood," I said. The weed was working like a truth serum, and I felt like confessing. "I used to think about doing it with you all the time. You wouldn't believe how many times I've jacked off with a picture of you in mind."

"Was having it as good as you thought?"

"Better. But I didn't suspect you'd suck my cock, too." I desperately wanted him to do it some more.

"I've done lots of things, 'specially if money was riding on it. And shy as you are, I figured you needed some warming up. Hell, didn't take much warming. But I usually don't go for getting somebody off like that. I mostly just go for what I can get. If I'm horny enough, I'll fuck anything, even a snake – if he'll open his mouth."

Jimmy had been slowly fingering his dick, which was fully erect again. I watched and my dick got harder and harder. He cupped his hand around the nape of my neck and tugged me toward him. "Speaking of opening mouths, I'm all hot again. Get back on my dick."

I realized by then that Jimmy was totally selfish. There was no doubt that he planned to use me until he'd had enough, without even thinking about my feelings and needs. But one of my needs lay in the fulfillment of the fantasy I had created around him. I also was using him, in a way that I was beginning to see, but that I was sure he would never think of. When he tugged my head downward, I eagerly took his cock back in.

With him sprawled on his back, legs spread, and me crouched over him, I had more freedom to explore him than I'd had the first time. As I tongued his dick, I cradled his balls and rolled them around in my fingers. With my other hand, I caressed his tight abdomen and moved on up to pinch at his nipples.

When I sensed that he was getting close, I took my mouth off his dick and lapped at his balls, taking first one, then the other into my mouth. All the while, I lightly played my hand over the sensitive flesh of his inner thighs. He lay trembling and quaking, and slight groans escaped him. He ran his fingers through my hair and then sat up to knead both my ass cheeks. One finger probed around until it slipped inside me.

"Wait a minute," he said, pulling away and standing up. He fumbled through the dark house while I lay on my back and stroked my cock. Soon he made his way back. In the dim light of the fire, I saw that he had some kind of tube in his hand.

"I figured John would have something," he said. He kneeled between my legs and shoved them wider apart. He squeezed some kind of gel onto his fingers and dabbed at my ass.

"What're you doing?" I asked, a little afraid for the first time.

"I'm gonna break your ass in," he said. First one, then two fingers slid up in me. The intrusion stung and I flinched away.

"Uh-uh, Jimmy. There's no way, man," I said. "I can't handle that."

"Sure you can," he said. His fingers probed around inside me. "You got a hot cherry ass, and I'm gonna bust it." He hoisted my legs across his shoulders and leaned forward, raising my ass off the carpet.

"Uh-uh, you'll hurt!" I protested. Scared as I was, though, the idea of him dominating me and taking what he wanted excited me.

"I ain't that big. You'll get used to it." He guided his cockhead to my puckered hole and insistently pushed forward.

"God Almighty! Quit!" I yelled out, twisting away from the sharp pain that ran all through me. His dick popped out.

He got a grip on both my thighs and pushed against me, his unguided dick searching and poking around for entry. "Just be still and don't fight it. I'm gonna fuck you, one way or another!" His voice was hard and determined, the tough guy quality I'd always fantasized about.

I tried to relax as his probing dick found its target. When he shoved forward and buried his cock up my ass, though, it took my breath away, and I groaned and struggled against the intense pain.

"Okay, man, you got it all," he said. "Now relax and give me a good fuck."

He started moving inside me. I bit my tongue to keep from crying out and reached under to feel his cock sliding in and out of my ass. He would pull almost all the way out and then shove back in until his pubic hair crushed against my hand. I moved my hand out of the way and, with both hands, squeezed his ass cheeks, liking the feel of his flexing muscles every time he shoved forward.

"Swing your legs off and lock 'em around my back," he said. As I moved my legs, he pushed his knees out and lay down on top of me, part of his weight on his elbows. I wrapped my arms around his back and pulled him tighter against me.

Instead of the hard shoving he had been doing, he started gently fucking me, rotating his hips and wiggling his dick around inside my ass. Most of the pain vanished. He nuzzled his chin into my neck, and I mapped his back with my fingers and lifted my ass to meet his thrusts. Neither one of us was in a hurry.

When his movements became faster and harder, when I knew he was about to come up my ass, I boldly twisted his head around and kissed him. He started to draw back, but I held him tight. All at once, he opened his mouth and jabbed his tongue in mine, and we battled each other as he pounded into my ass for all he was worth. He made a couple of short, quick lunges and buried his cock as deep as possible and went rigid. As I felt his hot come spurt into me, my own dick thrashed and kicked between us and I spilled my heavy load all over us.

"Whew!" he exhaled when he broke our kiss. "I never knew popping a cherry could be so good! I shoulda come after you a long time ago." He started to pull out of me.

I stopped him with a hand on his ass. "Don't get up yet," I said. I grabbed him by the hair and kissed him again. He did not resist.

After we cleaned ourselves up in the dark, frigid bathroom, I reached for my underwear, figuring he would be ready to leave.

"Do you have to go, Will?" he asked. He stepped in close and squeezed my dick.

"No, I just figured. . ." It hit me then that he had called me Will, not Willard. For the first time in my life, I didn't feel so much like a nerd. I was Will, and Jimmy Reese, of all people, wanted me to stay with him awhile longer. I was more than ready to stay all night, even knowing the hell I'd catch when I finally got home.

"Let's fire up another joint. We both got nothing better to do." He fingered his dick, which again was showing some signs of life. "Later, I want that ass again."

"Maybe when we're good and high, I'll fuck your ass," I ventured with more confidence than I was feeling.

"Maybe," he said, a teasing glint in his eyes. "I'm liable to do anything when I'm stoned." He put his arm around my back and pulled me close. His other hand went for my crotch. "Happy New Year, nerd!"

"Happy New Year, fuck-up," I said before I pulled his head down and kissed him.

LITTLE MERCIES
John Patrick

"Life is full of little mercies like that, not big mercies but comfortable little mercies. And so we are able to keep on going...."
– *Tennessee Williams in "Summer and Smoke"*

It was Mike who said we should be merciful. It was Mike who said we should take pity on our house guest, the one we called "that gentleman from Georgia," although Joe actually was a Michigander, transplanted to Atlanta by his father years before. I had known Joe as a youth in Battle Creek, when I lived there and my dad worked for Kellogg's. We had taken separate paths, but stayed friends of a sort.

While Joe had dozens of lovers, I had Mike. Everybody said I was lucky, having Mike, since everybody wanted Mike. Mike with the perfect ass, they said. Mike, however, would have none of it. He had eyes only for me. But, as time passed, Mike was losing interest. Our sex was becoming predictable. Still, Mike wouldn't let anyone near me. This was okay since Mike, despite everything, still had that perfect ass, which, was even if he wasn't in the mood, always open to me.

I knew when I invited Joe for the weekend that Mike would show a little mercy towards the man. Joe reminded him of a sugar daddy he'd once had. "But Joe is broke," I countered.

"But he's lost his boyfriend."

"He's always losing his boyfriends."

"Yeah, and he's lonely. Show a little mercy," Mike begged.

I made up my mind to be as merciful as I could.

Mike greeted Joe as if he were his long-lost friend, not mine. What was this?, I wondered.

And Mike's goofy behavior didn't end. First at dinner and then at the bar, Mike was playing up to Joe as if he expected he would be shown some real mercy when he got home.

But that was not to be. Far from it. As anguished as Joe was over the break-up of his two-year relationship with Bill, he had no trouble drowning his sorrows in Michelob and then scoring; he went home with Keith, a boy I would not have turned down had I been single. Joe, I pointed out to Mike, didn't need our mercy.

When Joe finally dragged himself back to our place the next day, Mike was desperate for some news of his encounter. Joe dismissed the adventure with a curt, "Too short." I took this to mean that the kid was not well-endowed, but Mike decided Joe meant that the encounter was far too brief. Whatever the truth, we'd never hear it from Joe. I had known Joe fifteen years and had never seen his cock, nor ever heard him boasting of his cocksmanship. Although he didn't look it, he was a true nerd, far too intensely involved with his computers and his mother. Still, Mike insisted, he wanted to come for the weekend for some reason. I told Mike it must be to see him. "It surely is not to see me," I said. "He could have had me ages ago."

Mike's mercifulness seemed to be getting out of hand. I know he had smoked a joint or two during the day and another before dinner, but I had never seen him in such a mood. Joe's face was lined and sadder now, but he was still an attractive guy. He certainly appeared to attract Mike. What prompted it was a long discussion of Mike's affairs before he met me. I could tell Joe was delighted by the news that Mike was somewhat of a sex pig. I was growing increasingly nervous as I watched Mike cross the room to sit beside Joe on the couch in our living room. They moved closer to each other as the conversation continued. After fixing another round of drinks, when I returned to the room, Mike was kissing Joe. As they kissed, Joe reached out his hand to me, and I came to him.

I was shocked to feel Joe's fingers caressing the now quite-obvious bulge in my pants. Mike groaned and then they switched. Now Mike kissed me while he straddled one of Joe's legs to rub his crotch against Joe's knee.

I love it, I thought. Mike had carried on like this only a couple of times before. What prompted this I had no idea. Well, I decided, maybe this was Mike's idea of mercy. I could feel Mike's hands getting his pants open. Then Mike exposed his cock and Joe bent forward to suck it. I felt Mike's body, the body I knew as well as my own, beginning to hum, the tension cranking up and up. A long time had passed since I'd had two men to work on, and I had almost forgotten how exciting the prospect was.

Before long all three of us were sprawled on the shag rug before the fireplace. Mike somehow got naked without my even realizing it was happening. One moment he was dressed; the next moment, his big cock was bouncing in Joe's face. Mike pulled at my clothes to get me undressed; and then Mike helped Joe remove his shirt. I could see Joe wanted Mike's cock. Maybe he'd always wanted Mike's cock. Last night, I think he would have been happy if I had taken his trick and left him with Mike. Joe seemed to adore Mike's sweet seven-incher. He sucked it while I slowly ate and licked Mike's ass with my practiced tongue. Joe's hands were all over both of us. First Joe, who had always been so sedate, so tentative around me, took Mike deep down his throat. Mike ground his cock down and filled his mouth.

I gave up trying to understand what was happening. I knew Joe enjoyed being a top and would want to fuck Mike, eventually. At the moment, though, Joe was content just to suck. After I was finished eating out Mike's ass, he raised it high in the air, and begged me to fuck him. He started rocking as soon as I got inside him. "Oh, honey, give it to me!" he cried.

Soon I was panting. Mike was whispering something urgent in Joe's ear, his forehead lowered to the top of Joe's head.

I squeezed Mike's asscheeks as I pressed my cock into the now-steaming crevice. Joe started fingering me. I gasped as his fingers pushed into me with unexpected force. He stretched out on the sofa and I went after his cock, springing up erect from behind the zipper as I lowered it. My eyes watered when I found he smelled like the fresh, well-groomed little boy I once knew, and I wanted to suck the cum out of him. I never had a chance with him then; he was too young, too afraid.

Before long I was pumping into Mike as never before while I sucked Joe and Joe sucked Mike. Mike shot his load into Joe's mouth, and he swallowed hungrily while Mike rocked back onto my cock.

Joe let Mike's cock drop from his mouth, pulled away, and stood behind me.

His knob came into contact with my pulsating sphincter. I stepped up my assault on Mike's asshole while Joe's cock soared into my shocked butt hole.

Joe grunted and puffed. I came inside Mike and wrapped him in my arms, succumbing to the full force of Joe's savage impaling. Joe stabilized my hips with his hands and jerked faster, plowed harder, and I squeezed tighter. Joe gave a quick succession of loud pants, squirmed, and I felt the warm wetness of Joe's sperm in my ass.

Joe kept stabbing his meaty shaft into me, but eventually Mike begged to be fucked by Joe. Slowly, he withdrew, and I stepped aside, collapsed on the couch. Joe rubbed his sloppy cock into Mike's even sloppier asshole. Joe was not fully hard, and I know it hurt Mike terribly until Joe got it all the way in and started to screw him.

Then Mike sought out my mouth, kissing me as Joe fucked him. The fucking brought tears to Mike's eyes and he moaned and groaned. I held Mike down as the brutal fucking continued, and all I could think of to say was, "Have mercy on him, Joe. Have mercy on him."

AT FIRST SIGHT
John Patrick

"In 1916 Ivor Novello, Noel Coward's chief rival as king of the London musical stage and known as the 'British Adonis,' met Bobby Andrews, a 21-year-old actor. It was love at first sight...much more than friends, far more than lovers."
– Boze Hadleigh in "Sing Out!"

At first sight, I thought I knew him and I felt my blood heat, my cock stir, the breath evaporate from my lungs.

I remembered his touch, so strong, so sure. The memory of his cock shoved roughly inside me aroused a need I hadn't admitted to myself for a long time, a desire to be abused by a hot young topman.

"What is it?" asked George, my "date" for the night.

I was looking across the table at DaVinci's restaurant at the handsome face so much like the one I remembered that I couldn't stop staring at him.

"Someone you know?" George persisted.

"No," I said, taking a long swallow of the expensive red wine George had selected.

I was being truthful, in my fashion. This boy across the room was not the one I remembered. Certainly. He wouldn't be that young. The boy I remembered was my age, and that boy across the room couldn't even be legal. If he looked at me, he'd see someone nearly thirty, still attractive, but sexually invisible to a boy like him.

I looked back at the boy. He turned his head, and his clear-eyed gaze fell on me with a shock like cold water, and he smiled. "You're blushing," said George with interest. "Is he an old boyfriend?"

"No. Oh, no." Hardly old, I thought. You are old, George. "Just someone I met once – in another country. Do you want to taste my salad?"

As we ate, I remembered that I first saw the abusive stranger at the mall, drinking a milkshake by himself. He had a tumble of black curls surrounding a deeply tanned face. I admired the fit of the stranger's jeans. I got a shake myself and took a seat. I wasn't looking for trouble. I was content, I thought, to look and not touch. I liked the way his lips curled around the cigarette that he lit up after he finished his shake. I liked the way his eyes narrowed against the smoke. I liked his slender fingers as he threw his empty cup in the trash and then stood, as if waiting for me. I liked the way he moved, shifting his weight or rolling the stiffness out of his neck and shoulders as unself-consciously as an animal.

That was it – he was animalistic. A brutish-looking sort, unlike anything I had ever seen in one so young. He moved to the pavilion, but didn't sit down. He leaned against a bench, as if he was displaying himself. I gazed for a time at his intriguing, less-than-classical profile, then shifted my stare, let it fall in a caress on his shoulders, his back, down to the ass that so nicely filled his tight, faded jeans. He turned his head lazily toward me as if he'd felt, and liked, my attention. I moved my eyes back up his body to meet his eyes, and I didn't smile. He was the first to look away. Then I did smile, but only to myself.

Someone else, a gray-haired man, approached him, cigarette in hand, and he gave him a light and responded to his conversational ventures absently, his attention hooked by me. I could feel his senses straining in my direction even when his back was turned, his eyes fixed elsewhere, his ears assaulted by the blandishments of the man, who eventually gave up and took his need to someone else.

He followed me to my car. I had parked far from the buildings, in a dark corner of the lot. He said nothing. And his silence held us still. He was hungry and I had become his prey. I became uneasy about this, told him I had to be rushing home, it was getting late. This was not what the animal expected, so he pushed me into the gully beside the parking lot. He grabbed me by the belt loops and kneed me to the wet grass. It had been sprinkling earlier and it was still thundering. He fell on top of me. My pride melted into his thrusts. My cock was hard as he laced his thick, grimy fingers around my clean, skinny ones as he pushed me deeper into the wet grass. He got up on his hands and knees and whispered, "Turn over."

I did what the stranger said. I didn't care who this youth was. I just knew that he wanted me, and in his wanting I wanted him back. I rolled over, and he opened his jeans. He too was hard, or nearly so. His heavy balls hung over me like bait. I kissed them, sucked them, while he jacked himself. His moans told me I was doing what he wanted. Eventually he worked me out of my pants. The grass was warm and wet. His hands were solid and hot. He smelled like the smoky tip of a match. He had lit me: I was close to orgasm when he slicked his cock with his spit and started shoving it in. I heard nothing but the thunder overhead. We were alone. I wanted to explode as he got it in me. I pressed his ass harder against my body, to get it all in. God, it hurt, but it was wonderful at the same time. He covered my mouth with his hand. My bug eyes darted quickly from the edge of the piney brush that surrounded us to his writhing body over me. As long as we were quiet, I thought, no one would find us. He didn't seem afraid. He pulled back, to come on my belly. My body was still while he lifted up and stuffed his filthy cock into his jeans. I closed my eyes, and when I opened them again, he was gone.

It was nearly eleven o'clock by the time we had finished eating. I watched George smoking his cigarette.

"Have you always smoked?" I asked. I was now making polite conversation.

George had fallen into a funk of a sort because the busboy had made quite a nuisance of himself once he realized I was watching him. In a final flourish, he brushed against me, excused himself, but the connection was made.

After that, George was in a hurry. George was always in a hurry, it seemed, but tonight he wanted to leave in the worst way. He wanted to fuck me and then go home. He tried not to look at his watch too obviously. George tried to give the impression that he was always in control, but he was not nearly so in control as he pretended to be.

George was one of my clients who would go running back to his wife after sex, which suited me. I could never understand his need to make a "date" out of fucking me. I really would have preferred it if he had just come over, fucked me, and left. But then, I wouldn't have had the distraction of the curious busboy.

Back at my apartment, I yawned, stretched, and then looked at George. He opened his arms, as if he wanted to kiss me. I said in a flat voice, "Follow me." By now it all seemed so completely cold-blooded.

The narrow hallway to my bedroom seemed longer and darker now that I had swallowed several glasses of wine. I turned right into an open doorway. The room was dark. I felt his hand pulling me quite vigorously. He ran his hands up and down my body. In the darkness his fingertips found their way to my zipper. He pulled it, frantic now to get me out of my pants. I felt a surge of lust, a sensation so intense it was almost painful. I had never felt this with George before. Perhaps the memory of the stranger raping me had turned me on more than usual, or perhaps the idea that another boy had paid unusual attention to us during dinner had turned George on.

He pushed me on to the bed, pulled my pants off, tore off his own clothes, then straddled me. He applied the lubed condom. Tonight his going into me was ecstasy. Normally, while George's immediate, uncomplicated demands satisfied his week-long need, and paid my rent, they gave me little satisfaction. But this was different. His fucking was incredible, for him. My mind was now obliterated. He lunged into me, desperate for it. I held him fast. I could hear his gasping breath and then a long, drawn-out sigh. He hadn't finished yet, and I waited for him. I came when he did. When he finally shuddered to a halt, he rolled off me. I could see he was smiling. I watched him lying languidly on the bed. He lay with his legs splayed out in front of him. I turned on the lamp. He was flushed with a post-orgasmic flush that made his blue eyes shine brightly. I could see a patch of damp on his belly: my cum was drying there. I peeled off the rubber and stroked his cock.

"Would you like to fuck me again?"

"I can't for a while," he confessed. "That took everything out of me. You always do that, but tonight... ."

"You were good tonight."

"As good as that busboy?"

"Damn, George. That kid just looked like somebody. Somebody from a long time ago... ."

"Oh, yeah, I remember. In another country... ."

I kissed him, feeling good about him for the first time since that first night.

He pulled away. "Hey, I've got to get back. I'm sorry I can't stay, but you know how it is."

"Sure." I looked at him. My eyes were level. "I know exactly how it is."

I knew this made him felt uncomfortable, but damn him. If it weren't for him, I might well have been with the busboy.

Yet George was good tonight. I didn't want him to go. I hung on to him.

"I really have to get back. You knew I was married. I haven't tried to hide anything from you. I've really enjoyed this evening and I'd like to come back and see you next week for your birthday. You're such a darling."

Now I wiggled out of his embrace. "Don't call me darling. I'm not your darling."

I rolled over and lay flat on the bed, my ass in the air. God, I don't know why but I wanted to provoke him again.

He got to his feet. I knew he hated this bit; he much preferred it when the lights were off and he could creep into his clothes and glide away. Now he was conscious of the unforgiving light beaming on his sagging, middle-aged body. I began undulating my hips, trying to entice him to fuck me again. I burrowed into the pillows.

"I don't care what you say. You are my darling, my darling little boy."

"I'm not you're little boy. Don't keep saying I'm your little boy."

"What the fuck's gotten into you?"

He turned out the lamp. A good sign.

"You! You got into me, and I want you in me again."

"You've never talked this way before. God, I can't believe this!"

"Believe this," I snarled, rolling over, exposing my hard-on.

"Jesus!" He leaned over me, stroked me. "Did I ever tell you how much I like this cock of yours?"

"Yes. Once, a long time ago."

"It really is a gorgeous cock."

I couldn't believe this. He was actually going to suck it. He hadn't sucked it for weeks.

Slam bang, thank you...that's what it had come down to. But now, tonight, he's sucking it. He got back on the bed, on his knees, between my thighs. He started in, taking his time. He played with my asshole, still moist from his fuck. Two fingers, then three. He was splendid, sucking while finger-fucking.

"Oh, George," I moaned, over and over.

After a while he was panting, "You want me back in there, don't you?"

"Oh, yes," I pleaded.

Finally, it was over. Really over. I don't think he came again, but I did. He was pleased that he could arouse me so. He kissed me gently on the forehead, told me he'd see me on my birthday. "Thanks," I said, not really wanting to be reminded I would be turning thirty. Of course, I told him I was turning twenty-five. He probably believed me.

I waited for him to leave by the front door and then switched out the light. I lay back on my pillow and my eyes filled with tears. It hurt, a dull ache, deep inside, where his prick had been. Then I thought about the busboy, about how good he would have felt, wondered where he was now, and fell fast asleep.

\- – -

Over the phone, the busboy promised to meet me after the restaurant closed. I waited in the car, but he never came out. The next night, I honked as I saw him leave the building.

"You promised," I said, rolling the window down.

He leaned toward me. He was smiling. "I know I did, but I break all my promises." His eyes were sparkling with mischief.

"I'll keep that in mind."

He got in the car. He said he would leave his car at the restaurant. I sped off but got only a block before I had to stop for a light. He raised a hand to my face. I turned to look at him. He kissed me.

"I've been waiting to kiss you ever since I first saw you."

"Love at first sight?"

"Yeah, I guess. You've got the cutest little ass!"

The light changed. I hit the accelerator. "You wanted it that much, and yet you broke your promise?"

"Oh, I was sick last night. I knew you wouldn't want me when I was sick."

He didn't look remotely sick, or recovering from being sick, but I let it pass.

He insisted we go to his place. But it wasn't his place exactly, it was his parents' house. I didn't want to go in, preferring to take him to my little apartment.

"Where are they?" I asked, growing impatient.

"On vacation. See, they had a delay, that's why I didn't work last night."

"So you weren't sick?"

"No."

"So you tell lies too?"

He took me in his arms. "Just little ones."

"What am I doing here?" I kept asking myself.

I followed him through a large square living room. The room was furnished lavishly. The sofas were covered in a soft pink floral material. There was a big fur rug in front of the fireplace, and the lamps were mostly art deco. The floor was of polished wood, and small Persian and Indian carpets lay pleasingly on the floor. "God, what a neat house." I gazed about the room with delight.

"Yeah," Paolo said. "I'm gonna miss it."

"Oh?"

"Yeah, when I go to college in the fall."

Soon his tie was gone and a lock of his black hair fell over his face. I felt my heart thump. He was so devastatingly handsome. Even more handsome than my stranger at the mall.

He took my hand and pulled me gently to him. "I won't do anything you don't want me to do. Just let me kiss you a little. You need kissing. I can always tell when a boy has not been kissed enough."

He gently pecked at my mouth. I felt a quite extraordinary feeling invade my body. In his gentleness he was more appealing than any boy I could remember. George's kisses were often so demanding. Paolo kissed me as if we had all the time in the world. And we were in his parents' house! I found myself moving deeper into his arms. I felt his hardness, and he felt mine.

He led me to the bedroom, his bedroom, a jock's bedroom, or so it appeared. My mind was full of questions, but at that moment nothing mattered but getting his clothes off him.

He had broad shoulders, and a very long back. He climbed out of his trousers and then hung them neatly over the back of a chair by the bed. Then he slipped off his underpants. The light from the open bedroom door fell across his shoulders. I stared between his legs and Paolo saw where my eyes had settled. He gazed at me quizzically. "You don't mind if I'm uncut, do you?"

"Oh, no," I sighed. Of course not. Indeed, I had expected my young Italian stallion to be uncut; if he had not, I probably would have been disappointed. What I had not anticipated was the size of Paolo's penis: it was one of the biggest I had ever seen, at least ten inches, and thick. I wanted to suck it immediately, but he wanted more kissing. His kisses became deeper and more passionate.

He slid his hands under my buttocks and squeezed. "Oh, yes," I murmured. I felt like I might come right in my pants with the pleasure of it all. My back arched and my body fell into rhythm with his. He was on top of me, dry-humping me, while he continued kissing me. He was such a fantastic kisser!

Then I heard the sound of my own voice gasping and moaning as he removed my clothes, piece by piece, taking his time.

When he had me nude, he started stroking me. In no time, I felt the tidal wave of my orgasm taking me out of my body and into space. Somewhere so far away. When I came back to earth, he was still stroking me. "I hope you haven't finished," he said.

"Finished? We haven't even started!" I moved against his fingers, which were now lodged up my ass.

I couldn't stop thinking about that kiss. Paolo literally took my breath away. Nobody had ever kissed me like that. Most clients kisses were quick pecks or a total plundering of my mouth. I didn't know that men could kiss the way Paolo did.

I sank my fingers deep into the silky waves of Paolo's hair as his tongue slid into my mouth. Paolo caressed my back and shoulders, then moved down to the rounds of my ass.

Paolo cupped his hands around my cheeks and eased them apart. Paolo teased the sparse blond hairs, touching them with the tip of his tongue and driving me wild with excitement. Then I felt the warm tongue washing the sides of my crevice. My hole expanded, begging for something to fill the emptiness. I gasped when I felt the thickness of Paolo's tongue pushing deep inside. Involuntarily, my cheeks tightened, and Paolo's stubble rasped against the inner walls of my cleft. Paolo's tongue plunged into me, over and over again, I moaned and writhed, the pleasure almost beyond bearing. None of my clients would have dreamed of doing such a thing. It was so intensely intimate; I felt decadent, but I had never felt anything so wonderful in my life. If Paolo didn't stop, I was going to shoot again all over the sheets. "Please," I begged, "you have to stop or I'll come again." But I couldn't move one inch away from the incredible pleasure.

My words only seemed to drive Paolo to greater efforts. He reached between my legs and carefully drew my rigid cock back, driving it deep into his hand, then quickly pushing back, unwilling to lose any of the tongue driving me to such delicious sensations.

I came again, overflowing Paolo's fist with thick streams of cum. Paolo pulled me into his arms, holding me while my breathing steadied. I could feel the heavy club of Paolo's incredibly large sex throbbing between us. In a minute, he was going to have to do something about that. It had been months since I'd touched an uncut dick, and I couldn't wait to explore its mysteries.

Paolo tilted his face up and kissed me again. I lapped the stubble on Paolo's chin and kissed a wet trail down his throat. I nuzzled my face in the thick mat of chest hair and made a short excursion to his armpits. This got him going – moaning, groaning. At last my fingers wrapped around the thick cock – the skin a rich mahogany against the bronze of Paolo's thigh. The flaring head stretched the foreskin tightly, exposing the small circle of a spongy head. Paolo shivered as I circled the shiny red button with my fingertip. I tightened my hold and pushed my hand down. I watched in amazement as the skin slid smoothly behind the crown. I darted my tongue inside the glistening slit and made Paolo groan. Gently, I stretched the skin forward beneath the silky overhang and swirled it over the sensitive rim. Paolo had a hard time staying still, but he let me play as long as I wanted. I held the plump head in my mouth, sucking gently, while I weighed Paolo's furry balls in my hand. Hungrily, I drew in more of the veiny shaft. Paolo cupped the back of my head, but he let me set the pace. I wanted more, suctioning more each time my head bobbed. At last, he plunged all the way down, packing my throat, and my lips were soon pressed tightly against Paolo's wiry groin. But sucking it wasn't enough. I pleaded, "I want you inside me."

Paolo took a condom from the night stand and rolled it over his cock. He pushed my knees back and knelt over me. "You sure?" he asked, his rod nudging the portal.

I looked up into his eyes and smiled. "Oh, yes! I want every inch of you inside me."

Holding Paolo's hips, I thrust upwards to meet the descending cock. I gasped as the broad head entered, stretching me to the limit, slowly filling me until I felt Paolo's balls swing against my spine. "Oh, yeah," I sighed.

Paolo rode me slowly. My cock stood straight up, rubbing through the silky hair on Paolo's chest at every stroke and leaving a glistening trail of precum. My arms tightened, urging Paolo on. Paolo started pumping harder, his balls slamming against me with every thrust. Sweat dripped off his forehead. My tongue caught the salty trails and lapped them eagerly. Paolo groaned and kissed me, licking the salt off my lips. I started jacking my own cock. I didn't know if I could come again, but I wanted to. I rubbed my hand through Paolo's sweaty chest hair and used it as lube. My hips rose off the bed to meet every lunge, and Paolo's hips went into overdrive, pistoning wildly. It was heavenly for several minutes. Then he froze, arm and neck muscles straining as he filled the condom with his load. My own balls tightened and I shot a small volley of jizz onto Paolo's chest. Paolo collapsed, groaning, his body crushing me to the bed as the final spasms racked our bodies.

Paolo held me for a long time afterwards, kissing me passionately.

"This can't be a sin," I gasped. Nothing this wonderful could be wrong. I was holding on to Paolo as if my life depended upon him. Then I realized that I was crying. Really crying, and Paolo held me gently in his arms. "What's wrong?"

"I have to go." I raised my tear-stained face to his.

Paolo's eyes were pleading with me to stay.

"I can't stay, Paolo. I have to get back."

"Is that guy waiting for you?"

"That guy?"

"The one at the restaurant."

"Oh, no. I live alone. It's just that – "

Paolo suddenly frowned. "So he was just a john?"

"A john?"

"You are a – " He looked away, finding it hard to spit out the word.

"Professional?" I volunteered.

"Yeah, that."

I rolled away from him. What was going on here?

He rubbed my shoulder. "Look, it's what I wanted. I wanted somebody who did it for a living. That was the only way I was going to do it. I knew that's what your story was – "

"Is. That's what my story is. I'm a professional. Right now, that's what I am."

"Well, then, how much do I owe you?"

I didn't answer. All I wanted to do was leave, but I couldn't move. Finally, "First time's free."

"Oh," he said, smiling, forcing my thighs apart. He slid a fresh condom on his renewed erection. "Why's that?"

"'Cause you're so cute, that's why."

"And this, how much will this cost?" he asked, shoving his cock into me again.

"Oh, just shut up and fuck me."

And fuck me he did. Every night, after he finished work, he'd come to my apartment. During these late-night sessions, I got to know him a bit better. His father had insisted he work to help pay for college and his getting a job at the restaurant was easy because his family owned it. He had always been interested in gaysex but had never acted on his impulses. He was engaged to his high school sweetheart, a nice Italian girl who wanted to remain a virgin until she wed. "Her loss," I said.

For my birthday dinner, I insisted George take me back to DaVinci's. It was even more fun this time because, after all, the person I was gazing at across the room I really had been to bed with. None of this was lost on George, of course, and it made his fucking of me that night even more heated when we finally got back to my place.

After George had gone, I soaked in the tub for twenty minutes before Paolo arrived. He was stunned by the grand display of gifts from George: flowers, candy, a new suitcase ("For the convention," George said. Every year I went with him to the shopping center owners' convention in Las Vegas. His wife hated the place. I loved it. George owned several malls and strip centers, and DaVinci's was located in one of them. That made him Paolo's family's landlord, making my nightly trysts even more dangerous – and delightful, because Paolo had no idea who George was.)

Paolo nibbled on a chocolate and pouted, "But I have nothing for you."

"Oh, I wouldn't say that," I countered, my hand squeezing the bulge in his jeans.

But Paolo did have a surprise: He sucked my cock! Well, not really. He licked it, nibbled a bit on the head. Then he dropped my shaft from his lips and sucked in my balls, rolling them around with his tongue and sucking on the skin of my scrotum. He shifted his position so that he lay atop me and fucked my face while he traced a line on my skin on the underside of my crotch with the sharp point of his tongue. From my balls, it followed the bridge of flesh that led to my asshole and I tensed to the pinprick sensations as it circled my quivering asslips. His tongue darted into me and I groaned, my throat clogged with the enormous cock. He rolled me up onto my shoulders and I felt his face against my buttocks as his tongue lathered and stroked my hole. He spat into it, then got some lube. I could feel the blunt tip of his finger, smearing the lube around, probing. He dribbled more spit into my hole, then worked in two fingers, forcing my asshole wider with his driving knuckles.

I took his cock out of my mouth and began licking up and down the hard shaft. I wanted it in me so bad. "Fuck me," I begged.

In response, he withdrew his fingers and positioned himself between my legs. While he slid on a condom, I put my hands on my knees and pulled them back, offering myself to him. He leaned forward and kissed me, then straightened up and pressed the sheathed, swollen head of his cock against my asshole, and entered me, slowly, lovingly, so unlike George who, even this evening, had rushed it. I've always liked the entry even better than the orgasm. When you're having an orgasm, you're not as aware of yourself and your lover as you are at that exquisite moment of entry. Paolo grunted with pleasure when he was all the way in. Then he leaned forward until my own erection was rubbing against the muscled, hairy surface of his stomach. He cradled my head in his hands and put his face close to mine. "Let's come together," he whispered.

But I had come with George and I was in no hurry to come now. It was so seldom I enjoyed sex anymore and I was going to prolong this as much as possible. I had yearned for some affection, some excitement in my life again, and this was it. I was not about to rush it. I groaned in response.

"Am I hurting you?" he asked.

I met his eyes. "No," I managed to croak, and I cleared my throat. "No, I'm okay. I just...I'm fine."

Thus assured, he started in. It was a glorious fuck. Now and then, he paused in his exertions to rain kisses on my face. It seemed that his desires were increasing in proportion to the loss of my need. Only with the most ardent kisses and caresses was he able to turn my resolve to hold off my orgasm to still another victory.

As we did indeed come together, I envied his future bride as I have never envied anyone.

We stayed in that position for a while, and, as his long, thick cock slowly softened inside me, we kissed each other's face, eyes, lips. Then his cock slipped out with a smacking sound, and we fell asleep in each other's arms.

- - -

George sat across the table from me at DaVinci's, sipping his wine. He looked very sad. He looked like he'd forgotten how to smile. I asked him what was wrong.

"You're missing him, aren't you?" I asked.

"I guess. Yes."

We had come here "just for old times' sake," and George noticed the cute busboy was no longer here. George seemed to miss him almost as much as I did.

George knew more than he let on; he always did. He went on talking, eventually getting around to the subject of death. I had no idea what he was talking about, until he said: "You know, when you have been feeling so intensely for so long, and then it stops, it's like death. An orgasm is a little death in itself, and you've had quite a lot of them lately."

I looked away from his concerned gaze. He had not spoken of the end of my affair until now, but he had begun to ask questions about "that boy." He wanted to know what we did, when we did it, where. He was living vicariously, I thought, and loving it.

I looked at George in a new light, seeing Paolo thirty years from now, living a double life, with a wife and a boy kept on the side. A sad life, really, but one to which George had adjusted. Tuned into my thoughts as never before, he asked, "Will you see him again?"

"I don't know."

And George, as vague as ever, said, "Well, time will tell. It always does."

A POTENT COMBINATION
Jack Ricardo

During my teenage years, I wasn't very active sexually, but I developed a vision of what I wanted: a stud wearing black engineer boots, leather chaps, a leather vest and a leather cap perched on his head. For some reason, this vision propelled my imagination into a very sensual sphere.

On more than one lonely night, I feasted on a vision of leather while my fist worked my cock until my chest was splattered with enough cum to leave me panting in relief.

But the relief never did reach complete satisfaction. I never quite had the courage to take this fantasy that one further step into reality. It's the masculinity of black leather that turns me on and not the pain and humiliation that I've read about in various fuckbooks.

And that's what stopped me from wading into the leather pool. I wasn't about to become any leatherman's slave or even his Master; I wanted to be his partner in lust.

As the months passed, my desire to touch another guy, especially one outfitted in leather did not diminish. I longed to inhale his scent, to make love to a him, to feel his strong arms holding me tight, to hold another leatherman, to lick a leatherman's balls, to suck a leatherman's cock while caressing his boots did not diminish. If anything, this craving grew stronger. So strong, I even chanced to buy a leather vest and engineer boots. I was determined to fulfill my fantasy.

I stood before the full-length mirror. Okay, I wasn't Hollywood handsome. But I wasn't bad either. On a scale of one to ten, I might be a seven. My body wasn't overtly muscular either but it was well-defined. Little hair coated my chest but the blond hair on my head was closely cropped and shaggy, giving me what I hoped was a virile image. My pubic bush was as blond as that on my head, my cock was soft and cut and leaning to the left atop two tightly-packed balls pinched with finite hair. I fondled my cock, then stretched my jockstrap over my ass, adjusting my balls snugly inside the pouch. I drew a white T-shirt over my head, stepped into my frayed 501s, and pushed my feet into my new engineer boots. Lastly, I stretched my arms into my leather vest. The black cowhide grazing over my arms fired my nuts. I was ready, if a bit anxious. There are three leather bars in town. I've visited them all. The first two were depressing, with soused leathermen scrambling around in the dark and dangling their chains before heading for the back room. Not my scene. The third bar was The Pipe, which attracted a masculine crowd, most of whom wore Levi's. But leathermen did visit the place. I parked my car on a side street and sauntered into The Pipe, brave, but still anxious. It was a Tuesday night and not very crowded. Yet there were enough men leaning on the bar, or playing pool, or pacing the floor to encourage me. Two were geared up in leather. One leatherman looked about my age. He wore the full regalia of leather but he was also a sissy, prancing around with a wince that was an instant turnoff. I studied the second leatherman. I'd seen him at the bar before. He was tall and lean and macho to the max. A black leather Rebel cap was centered on his head. His chest was bare and centered with a thick snatch of red hair partially hidden by his leather vest. His sullied chaps fit securely on long legs bottomed with buckled engineer boots. The worn pouch of his 501s was like a strong beacon in a wicked nor'easter. The lines webbing from his eyes advertised his age and experience. He was looking at me looking at him.

Our eyes met. My mouth was dry. I gulped, backed up to the bar, and ordered a beer. With can in hand, I sipped and turned. He was standing right beside me. He said, "My name's Tod. I've seen you here before." His gaze slid over my vest with a wistful eagerness. "But never in leather."

"First time I wore it," I said. "Name's Mark." Our eyes were nailed to each other. We didn't shake hands. We both upended our cans and drank.

"So, what are you into, Mark?" Tod asked. His voice was husky yet amiable.

My anxiety was relieved. I replied, "I'm not into pain, I'm into men, masculine men, and not...."

"You into leather?"

"I guess. But not humiliation." I smiled. "Yeah, leather's a big turn-on." The hairs on Tod's chest, hairs surrounded by leather, seemed to sparkle. The unique aroma of his equipment drifted to my nose. "I'll say this: You're a turn-on," I added.

"Ha! I'm old enough to be your father," he said, and offered a sly grin that wrinkled his eyes playfully. "I don't dole out pain and I don't take it from no man."

This is so right, I thought. I told him, "I'm not looking for a father. I'm looking for a man."

"I'm that, I must admit."

"That you are."

"You ever make it with a leatherman before?"

"No."

"Then let's go."

I followed Tod to his house and parked in the driveway. At this point, I did become nervous again. What if he was lying? I asked myself. What if there was a dungeon inside that house, with chains and cuffs and paddles and whips? (And lions and tigers and bears, oh my.) I smiled to myself and stepped from my car. I can take care of myself, I knew. Not for nothing have I been taking Karate classes all these months. He opened the door. I stepped onto the porch, into the house, and dove in.

An ordinary living room inside an ordinary house. I breathed a sigh of relief. "Why don't you take off your clothes?" Tod suggested. Actually, more an order than a suggestion. "Leave your leather on. In there." He pointed to a room at the side. I walked in warily. It was barren but for two orange crates stacked with porno magazines, a box of rubbers, and a tube of KY. A soiled mattress was on the floor. One wall was fully mirrored. The bare bulb hanging from the ceiling gave off a dim erotic glow. I tugged off my boots, shrugged off my vest and my T shirt, pulled down my 501s, kept my jock on, then replaced the vest back on my back and again stepped into my boots. I stood before the mirror, one young masculine image of jockstrap and leather. Tingles zinged from my balls to my brain. Tod walked into the room. He was still wearing his leather – his cap of the Confederacy, his vest, his chaps, his boots. But there was one thing missing. His 501s. Spotlighting the center of his chaps was a massive bush of deep red hair crowned above long, low-hanging balls fronted by a cut cock half hard. My chest sizzled like bacon in a pan. I swallowed some spit. The first thing Tod said was, "A fucking jockstrap," spoken as a joyous announcement. His eyes widened and brightened, the tip of his tongue slid over his lips. He knelt in front of me and kissed the pouch of my jock. My cock immediately began to overfill that pouch.

"A fucking jock," he said again, damn near drooling, as he ran his hands over the hairs on my legs to the pipe of my boots and began licking the outline of my prick through the mesh pouch, gently yet with a passion that couldn't be faked, his tongue a thick sloppy snake that rambled over packed hard cock and full balls. But he was only tasting the meal. He wasn't ready to chow down.

He rose to his feet and held me around the waist, crushing my packed jock to his bare crotch. My cock was scrunched and smashed against his pubic hairs and had me gasping for air. His hard flesh of cock was diddling between my legs. I slid my hands under his vest and inhaled both the scent of his leather and the aroma of his sweat as my hands filled his armpits. Tod stepped back, but not out of reach. I kept my hands buried under his arms, under his vest, and scraped my face over the hairs on his chest. My tongue lapped out, sweeping over his pecs, over his ribs, up and up until I was able to scrape his leather vest with my face and lap at the hairs of his armpits. The dank aroma, the flavor of old sweat, forced my cock to battle the mesh of my pouch and spark sensations that began to consume me. I snuggled my face under his arm, holding onto his vest like it was raft in a raging sea.

"You're hungry, ain't ya, Mark?" Tod gasped, putting both hands to the side of my head to work my face over his chest and his nipples, pulling me from one armpit to the other. "One hungry cocksucker," he moaned, inching his crotch forward until I felt the head of his cock slap my stomach. It was a green light that I obeyed, and lowered myself slowly, sensually trailing my face, my mouth, my tongue, over the hairs of his chest, to the thick tangle of brush that blossomed at his crotch, until I was on my haunches at his feet. I nuzzled my nose into his cock hairs, slurping up the healthy stink of a man's sweat with my mouth. The shaft of his cock was trembling under my chin as I wrestled my neck from side to side.

My eyes happened on the image in the mirror, of me burrowing my face into the crotch of a leatherman's chaps. I damn near burst open with a certain pride of accomplishment. I shuddered with satisfaction and snapped my head from Tod's grasp. As I sat back on my boots to admire this man, the leather of my boots warmed my bare strapped ass. His cock sprang up, a stiff shaft with an enormously round cockhead, its pisshole dribbling with a string of slime. My hands gripped the sides of his chaps and I leaned over to stick my tongue out and lap up the slime from that fucking leatherman's pole poking from the field of hair and leather. The smell of his chaps, the stink of his hairs, the taste of his slime, pierced small but potent explosions in my brain that sent out thrills to inflame my skin, that made my cock throb almost painfully, yet gloriously. I opened my mouth and gobbled his cockhead inside.

I moaned in gratitude at the chance to service this fucking hard-ass leatherman, gliding my hands down the rough leather of his chaps, slurping at his cockhead clamped solidly between my lips, wrapping my tongue round the rim, sliding my fingers down to fondle the toes of his boots, then lifting my hands under his chaps to stroke the leather pipes. I lifted my eyes. I saw two images. The mirror and reality. Tod was standing with his hands on his hips staring down at me, his chest was heaving, his mouth was open, spittle flowing from the sides.

"Yeah, Mark, love that fucking cockhead, love those fucking boots."

I squeezed the tip of his boot and sucked his cockhead. A splash of oozing juice leaked from the pisshole onto my tongue. I gulped it down and slung both hands up to caress the cheeks of the bare ass probing out from behind his black chaps. I clawed at his ass. Tod groaned and shot his hips forward. His cock came with it. I breathed through my nose and took that fucking leatherman's cock down my throat like the fucking leatherman I was, then sucked up, flipping the cock from my mouth and smashing my face against the shaft, lapping my lips up and down the swollen length, lowering my face until I was able to smack my mouth onto the sweaty flesh of his balls.

"Yeah, fucker," Tod yelled, grabbing my head and pasting it to his nuts, grinding those full bags of cum over my nose, my cheeks, my mouth. "Eat those fucking knockers, cocksucker, swipe those fuckers clean with your cocksucking mouth." His words were a powerful aphrodisiac. I opened my mouth and slurped one baggy nut inside. My own nuts were aching for pleasure and relief while I sucked Tod's nuts, one by one, while I gulped and sucked both into my mouth and snuggled my nose between his legs. The entire room became an aromatic thrill that seeped into my being, filling me with the smell of sweat and leather and balls. I could see my spit covering his balls when I pulled back. They glowed. I immediately pounced down on his cockhead and sucked down his shaft, pulling my arms up to scratch at his cock hairs. Tod was pumping my face with one solid cock, I was inching my fingers to his chest to paw at his thicket of hair, to tighten my fingers over his nipples. Tod moaned, groaned, coughed, cemented my face to his cock. His cock became a steel tube that quivered. It spit. His cock blasted off. My mouth was being filled with pulsating cock, my face was buried in his cock hairs, in his chaps as I reached under his vest and again pressed my hands into the sweat of his armpits, my face crammed with cock. His cock was pulsating in my throat, spitting its load directly to my guts, his nuts trembling on my chin.

I collapsed on the mattress at Tod's feet, gasping for air. When I opened my eyes, Tod was standing over me, his legs spread. He was stroking his shining, softening cock. A contented grin covered his face. My cock in my jock was arching and painful, expectant, pleading for release. I exhaled and caressed the pouch. Tod's voice broke through the air, harsh and demanding, "Get your fucking hand away from there. This cocksucker is gonna blow that fucking dick for you, cocksucker." He stepped between my spread legs. I lay with my arms over my head as Tod knelt and bowed down to the pouch of my jock. He was ready to chow down now, and did, grinding his face into the mesh pouch of my jock, gnawing at the strong stem of my cock, mouthing my cockhead through the mesh, then tearing my pouch down and snapping my cock out, raking his mouth over it, downing my cock in one sharp gulp while he tugged my nuts still jammed in the pouch, pulled them, twisted them, wrapped them with his fingers, until I was one pulsating blob of leathermanhood, twitching and turning to watch myself in the mirror shoot my load off into this fucking leatherman's hungry mouth.

I lay like dead, my eyes closed, my breathing loud and rash. Tod lay prone between my legs, my soft, wet cock brushing his chin. His bare ass poked from his black chaps and shone like a full moon at midnight. His black leather Rebel cap was still on his head. A lovable leather cocksucker.

- – -

That initial encounter with my first leatherman wasn't my last. Well, that's not entirely true. In one sense, it was my last. Tod is the only leatherman I've made it with. It's been four months now. And always, the erotic pleasure we gain from our leathersex encounters is enormous – as enormous as the orgasms we give each other. Orgasms with leather. A potent combination. And without the pain. Pure and raw animal masculinity. I think we're becoming lovers. Leather lovers.

JOCK TALK
Leo Cardini

Every time I feel his huge balls pressing against me, sweaty and smelly from the strain of his rigorous morning workout, an indescribable thrill runs through every fiber of my cotton and elastic pouch. And if that weren't enough to satisfy my lustful cravings, there's that big dick of his, warm and flushed from his exertions, all snuggled up inside me, taking up more space than we Bike Mediums were ever made to hold.

But don't get me wrong. I'm not complaining! How could I when every time I hold my master's substantial equipment in my embrace, I'm at complete liberty to examine how neatly cut and perfectly proportioned he is, what with that thick, rubbery shaft and that enormous mushroom of a cockhead that begins to ooze a tasty overabundance of pre-cum every time he steps into the locker room after his workout and strips down for the adventures that inevitably await him down the corridor where the showers, the sauna, the steam room and the Jacuzzi are located.

Not that he would ever think of wearing me into that backroom paradise of exclusively masculine physical delights! I mean, there are men who do, you know. I can't tell you how much I envy those privileged pouches when I watch them returning to the locker room, soaking wet and proudly clinging to their masters' cocks and balls like a second skin, flaunting their ability to contain all that juicy manmeat. Though now and then you do see a waistband that, whether from too many washings, or from too large a load, sags so far below its master's navel, his pubic bush spills out in exhibitionistic display – a tantalizing sight if there ever was one.

Anyhow, here I am, once more shucked off and abandoned on the long, narrow bench that runs the length of the lockers, king-of-the-hill atop my master's other gym wear; his tank top, his stretch shorts, and his white cotton socks. All of them are as limp and sweaty as I am, and all of them are secretly envious of me for my intimate grasp of him during his workouts. Besides that, I'm always the first one on, his cock and balls lovingly scooped up inside me, and the last one off when he liberates them again to swing free in the open air for all to see as he struts into those intriguing backroom facilities, leaving me behind to witness how many men turn their heads when they pass by him, absentmindedly yanking on their dicks as they check out his fine, firm butt.

Well, this morning, I find the usual ache I feel during this cruel abandonment upstaged by my interest in the broad-chested hunk and a half who follows my master out of the gym into the locker room. Yes, I know he's deliberately trailed him in. When you serve a master like mine you get to know these things. I don't mean to brag, but after all he is a soap opera star. Tall with drop-dead, square-jawed good looks, he's got long, blond hair parted in the middle, gentle blue eyes, even white teeth all a-gleam through his rakish smile, and a dimpled chin. Add this to his wide shoulders, narrow waist, tight buns, and, of course, that provocative bulge that's my special responsibility, and it's no wonder wherever he goes all eyes turn to follow.

Well, this guy who's trailed him in is no slouch either. In fact, he reminds me of Rocky Angel. You know, that Italian-stallion heartthrob who co-starred with my master for several months? The one who played the boxer about to undergo a sex change, until he got kidnapped to Brazil, escaping only to suffer a bout of amnesia and wander off into the Amazon jungle, never to return, since he was written out of the script when he got the lead in that new hit musical "Victor's Victrola?" Yeah, that one.

Anyhow, he pulls his gym bag out of a locker several down from my master's and proceeds to strip, tossing his workout clothes into it.

Hmm. Not bad. Not bad at all! Mounds of sleek muscle, washboard abs and...oh my God!...an immense, brown-shafted brute of a dick with thick blue veins and a deeply-furrowed nutsac the size of a baseball hugging the underside of his cleanly cut cock.

Of course he's checking out my master with sly, sidelong glances. But he's more than just checking him out. I don't know why, but I get a funny feeling about him. True, one hand reaches up to his chest to tug on a nipple, like I've seen countless other men do when they gaze upon my master. And true, no sooner has he tweaked it into its own miniature erection, than he takes his free hand and reaches into his crotch to give his dick a long, slow tug, which is also expected behavior under the circumstances. But he keeps shifting his eyes to stare down at me! Down at me, up at my master, down at me, up at my master. Back and forth until my master, towel in hand, heads towards the back facilities.

That's when this guy steps over to me, reaches down and picks me up, pressing the inside of my pouch against his nose and sniffing. One dose of my master's crotch-sweat inspires him to inhale again, this time deeper, with a chest-expanding enthusiasm that sucks me up against his flared nostrils. Then he lowers me across his open mouth, pressing me against the flat of his tongue, a thin coat of saliva spreading over the damp distillation of my master's workout.

Next, he lowers me onto his muscular chest, drawing me across to his right pec. His nipple's still hard from the tweaking, and he pinches it with thumb and forefinger right through the fabric of my pouch.

I've never before been sexually assaulted by a complete stranger, I know about the terrible misfortunes that can befall a jockstrap, and I know I should be outraged and distressed...but frankly, I'm beginning to like this!

Especially when he slides me across to his other pec for another bout of tit play, and then lowers me down along the hard, hairy terrain of his chest and the bumpy badlands of his washboard abs, running me across his tight innie of a naval and plunging me deep into the rampant overgrowth of his pubic bush, fragrant with the aroma of his own workout efforts. Then, before I have time to recover from this eventful downward trek into his crotch, he moves me along the wide, rugged topside of his semi-hard, down-curving dick until he captures his cockhead in my pouch and begins masturbating himself.

Now, this is the first time I've ever touched another man's dick, and the feeling is...well...exhilarating! His over-sized cockhead is so velvety smooth, and his thickening dick shaft so responsive, growing inch by inch into what promises to be a truly magnificent erection, that I just let him have his way with me.

Shit! Just when things are beginning to get real good, we hear the approach of someone else entering the locker room and I'm hastily thrown into his gym bag, landing on top of his sweaty, workout gear, and zipped into darkness. His sweat socks, tank top and gym shorts, damp and disheveled below me, seethe with resentment at my intrusion, and his jockstrap exudes downright hostility at my trespass onto his turf.

Well, I can't tell you how relieved I am when some minutes later the zipper flies open, the light from the overhead fluorescent lamps comes flooding in, and I'm yanked out of this humid pit of hostility. I'm not prepared, however, to be hauled upwards into his crotch, my back straps stretched as he maneuvers one foot and then the other between my straps and pouch, sliding me up his muscular legs and depositing his cock and balls into me, drawing my back straps across his firm, melon-mound asscheeks with a snap, and adjusting my waistband along the circumference of his solid, compact waist. His crotch is damp, smelling faintly of soap, so I know while I've been captive in his gym bag, he's been off luxuriating in the shower room.

I've never housed the contents of another man's crotch before, so as I struggle to accommodate new needs, I feel invigorated with the novelty of discovery. For one thing, he has bigger balls than I'm used to, but since his snug nutsac imprisons his huge nuts close to his body, it's easier for me to hold them in. This gives me freedom to examine his hairy sac, which intrigues me since my master shaves his. "Once a week," he tells his friends, "whether they need it or not.". And for another thing, he positions his dick up against his abdomen – not down over his balls. It's so fat and heavy I really have to struggle to hold it in place. And even then, it lists slightly to the right, his piss slit pressed against my pouch in a prolonged kiss.

Before I've had a chance to reacclimate myself, up come his 501's, button after button enclosing me in darkness, pressing me tightly against him as we make our way out of the health club and into the streets.

Fortunately, it's an old, well-worn pair of 501's, so two of the buttons make their way out of their buttonholes, affording me a view of the way home. Turns out he lives barely a block away from my master.

Once we're inside his apartment, he impatiently strips off all his other clothes, and busies himself in tidying up his small, one-bedroom dwelling. Every chance he gets, there's his right hand kneading my pouch, encouraging his dick to swell up inside me. But, to my frustration, it never grows beyond a rubbery, supple-shafted, half-hard-on before he has to pull out his hand again to attend to some chore. And then, when his intercom buzzes, completely drawing his attention away from me, I feel a sad sense of deprivation.

"Hello," he says into the speaker.

"Lou?"

"Yeah. Hi, Danny. Happy Birthday. The door'll be unlocked. So just come on in."

"Okay. Sure."

And with that, he buzzes in Danny and dashes into his bedroom. He flings himself onto the bed, spreads his legs apart and adjusts my pouch to show himself off to full advantage. Then he lies back in the pillow with his hands behind his head.

I feel his crotch heating up as his dick begins to stir. Now let me tell you, there's nothing like the thrill of a man getting a hard-on inside you. I can't tell you how many times I've experienced the thrill of my master's growing cock filling me up, stretching every fiber of my pouch in its relentless, self-centered ascension to full erection. But this time the thrill's increased with the excitement of fresh discovery. A fatter, more deeply-veined dick grows inside me, placing greater demands on me that have ever been made before.

Just as my waistband's about to be pried away from his abdomen, I hear the front door to his apartment open.

"Lou?"

"In here," he yells out, pulling my pouch up over his pre-cummy cockhead.

In walks Danny. He's lean, smooth-skinned and clean-shaven, with long blond hair parted in the middle and spilling over his forehead. The loose, low-hanging jeans and oversized tee shirt he's wearing emphasize his youthful appearance and boyish good looks. All in all, it'd be easy to take him for my master's – or, I guess, my former master's – kid brother.

"So what'd you get me for my birthday?" he asks, leaning over to kiss Lou.

"Greedy little bugger aren't you."

"Yeah. So what'd you get me?"

"This," he says, cupping my pouch.

"That worn-out piece of meat? Hell, I've had that. Like half of everyone else in the Village."

"You fuck! The jockstrap, stupid."

"Oh?"

He leans over and sniffs me.

"What makes you think I'd want a smelly old jockstrap?"

Hey! Now, I might be smelly. But old? You can feel for yourself my elastic's as springy as the day I was pulled out of my plastic wrapper!

"Because it's not just any smelly old jockstrap."

"Yeah?"

Intrigued, he runs his palm across my pouch. Lou's semi-hard dick rebels against me with a buoyant throb it's my pleasure to restrain.

"So what makes it so special?" he asks as his fingers spread over me and he digs in the heel of his hand under Lou's balls.

"I'll give you a hint. Channel Q. Weekdays."

"Uh huh?"

"Two P.M."

"The Gays of Our Lives. Never miss it."

"I know."

"So?"

"So who's that actor you always cream over? The one who plays Broadway choreographer Tom D'Aria?"

"Lance Longfellow?"

"Yeah. That's the one. What if I told you this is his jockstrap?"

"It is?" he practically whispers.

"Yeah."

"Awesome! You're the best boyfriend a guy ever had."

Worshipfully, he slowly strokes my pouch.

"But wait a minute," he says stopping, just when I was really getting into it. "If it's his jockstrap, how'd you get it?"

"Oh...well...I asked him."

"Yeah, sure! Like you saw him on the street, walked up to him, and tapped him on the shoulder with, "Uh, excuse me, but could I have your jockstrap?"

"Well, not in so many words. And it wasn't on the street. He's been working out mornings at The Club, around the same time I do. So we're in the locker room, I ask him, and he says 'sure.' But then he says he's kinda of horny from watching me work out, so would I mind sucking him off. So...."

"You blew Lance Longfellow? You actually took his dick in your mouth and..."

"Nah. The truth of the matter is, I stole it when he wasn't looking."

"You stole it? Wow! Supposin' he ever caught me wearing it at The Club? He'd think I was the one who stole it from him."

He pauses, pondering the possibilities, and then he resumes running his palm up and down my pouch against the swollen underside of Lou's dick.

"Danny, it's not like you have to wear it there. Besides, even if you did, you work out in the afternoons, and he works out in the morning."

"But supposin' I just happened to work out some morning, and I just happened to be wearing it."

"Assuming he recognizes it's his jockstrap. I mean, how many Bike Mediums do you think there are in the world? Just in the Village alone there must be...well...hundreds. Or thousands."

"Jesus! If only they could talk, can you just imagine the stories they could tell? But anyhow, supposin' he did recognize it, and supposin' he didn't like the fact that someone else was wearing his very own jockstrap. Someone who stole it from him. God knows what he might do to me! Or force me to do to him!"

Now, what with his hand sliding up and down my pouch, with all the loving attention it's clear he'd sell his soul to lavish on Lance, Lou's dick has risen to full erection, his insistent cockhead relentlessly stretching my pouch up above my waistband, all the while his piss slit is moistening me with a generous outpour of pre-cum.

Danny grabs my waistband with both hands to lower me off Lou, but Lou intercepts, restraining him with, "So how do you say 'thank you'?"

"Uh...thank you?"

But you can tell from his smile, he knows more's expected of him.

"That's all I get for stealing Lance Longfellow's jockstrap for you? Well, maybe I won't give it to you after all. No," he says, squirming his ass into the bed, making a big show of getting nice and comfortable, "I think I'll just lie right here..."

With his right hand, he slowly reaches into me, wrapping his fingers around his dick shaft and pressing his cockhead out against me. It responds with another sticky ooze of pre-cum

"...and jack myself off, thinking about how Lance looked in the locker room, totally nude with one foot on the bench and the other on the floor as he leaned over to reach into his locker, his big piece of meat just dangling there, so close to me I could've just fallen onto my knees, opened my mouth, and...but you don't want to hear about that, do you?"

"You cockteaser," Danny says with clear delight. Taking Lou by surprise, he pulls his hand out of me, pushes both Lou's hands up over his head, and falls on top of him, forcing his tongue into Lou's mouth.

And while Lou yields to this prolonged assault, the soft, worn denim of Danny's Levi's rubs against me as he begins hunching his hips into Lou's crotch. Lou responds by hunching back, pressing his hard-on against Danny's, treating me to a delicious double-dose of hard cock as the animal inside each of them begins to take over and they struggle against each other with rapidly escalating passion that makes me fear for my well-being.

Finally Danny jumps off Lou. Standing next to the bed with wild eyes, he kicks off his sneakers and tears off his socks, tee shirt and Levi's, carelessly tossing them onto the floor. Standing there in just his briefs, he pauses to admire his boyfriend with a ferocious intensity as he that makes him look as if he's about to pounce.

I, in turn, take advantage of the moment to savor the sight of his youthful features. Ah, such a lean, tight-muscled body! And such an outrageous hard-on, barely constrained by those poor put-upon briefs of his, the broad expanse of its underside pressing outward in sidelong ascent, his enormous cockhead resting against his hip, the same way Lou's did when he first put me on.

When he pulls down his briefs and kicks them off, his truly monumental erection drops down heavily between his legs, a victim of its own weight. His pale brown shaft, networked with a thousand and one thin blue veins ends in a neat cut, below which hangs a purple-red cockhead the size of a plum. Behind, two big balls rest suspended in a low-hanging, nearly hairless ballsac. And all of this in such dramatic contrast to his slim, youthful body.

Jumping back onto the bed and straddling Lou, his balls brush lightly against my pouch as his horse dick flops forward onto Lou's belly.

Ah, all that marvelous manmeat! It nearly drives me crazy. You see, Lance always tossed me onto the floor beside the bed before things got good, so I was always on the sidelines of his sexual exploits; never up close like this.

Danny leans forward and the underside of his dick presses against my waistband as he grips Lou's nipples between his thumbs and forefingers, gently twisting them.

"Ohh!" Lou moans, hunching his crotch up against Danny.

Danny leans farther forward. He falls onto his hands, more of his dick slides down across my pouch and he bites into the nub of Lou's left nipple. He gives it a gentle tug. Lou moans and thrusts upwards again.

Aw, shit! Do you know what it's like to have two stiff, oversized dicks rubbing against you at the same time? You do? Then you can just imagine how overwhelmed with passion I feel right now.

Well, Danny tugs and tugs, first on Lou's left nipple, then on his right. And each time he does, Lou heaves his chest upwards and lets out with a low moan and a lingering cock-thrust

Danny abandons his tit-play and kisses his way down Lou's chest, following the same route I'd been forced to follow earlier when I was abducted. How distant that all seems to me now. And yet it happened not even an hour ago!

By the time he reaches Lou's navel, Lou's cockhead's once more pushing my sorely-stretched pouch up over my waistband, impatiently lunging towards Danny's mouth, begging with pre-cummy cockthrobs for the touch of Danny's lips.

But instead, Danny goes to lower me once again. Rather than rejoicing in this liberation, I feel an intense pang of loss. Fortunately Lou restrains Danny, and Danny instead repositions himself flat on his stomach in-between the vee of Lou's spread apart legs and sticks out his tongue, slithering the tip of it under my pouch where my back straps meet. Lou moans again and Danny's tongue probes the swollen, tender territory below Lou's nuts.

Then I feel the flat of Danny's tongue against the rough mesh of my pouch, licking Lou's balls right through me, drenching me in his saliva until Lou's warm nuts cling to me sticky wet. Next, he moves up to lick the throbbing underside of Lou's cockshaft. By now he's oozed out so much slippery pre-cum, his cockhead's managed to nose its way under my waistband, his piss slit all a-dribble as it takes a peek at the outside world.

Danny reaches up to take it into his mouth, but my waistband holds it flat against Lou's taut belly, so he contents himself with flicking his tongue across Lou's piss slit. Lou's dick insistently throbs against my restraining waistband as he records every stab of pleasure with a sharp, staccato "Oh!" clenching his asscheeks to hunch his hips up off the bed again.

Once more Danny goes to slide me off Lou, and once more Lou's quick to restrain him.

"Fuck me first, okay?" Lou begs, raising up his bent legs, his crack spreading open and his butt hole coming into view as I feel my back straps stretched across his asscheeks.

"Christ, that is still the most beautiful fuckhole I've ever seen in my whole life!" Danny enthuses as he stares at Lou's butt hole. Pink and puckered, with a halo of sparse hair surrounding it, Lou repeatedly clenches it until Danny succumbs to its allure and plunges his tongue deep inside, his forehead pressing against my pouch.

"Oh!" Lou groans as Danny feasts on his hole. I'm spellbound since I'd never seen anyone get rimmed before. You see, Lance was heavy into sucking cock and having his sucked. And on those few occasions when he allowed someone to rim him, I was already tossed onto the floor close to the bed with an obstructed view. Though once I was thrown into the company of a pair of Calvin Klein's discarded a few inches farther away so it could just see over the bed, relating to me in enthusiastic detail why Lance was moaning the way Lou is now. And on another occasion I was hanging out with this real pig pair of cum-stained Jockeys with a large rip in the rear who made me horny with envy when he explained he got it when one of his master's partners in a fit of passion tore him open to stick his tongue up his master's hole. The thought of actually being right there, a close-up witness, had gnawed at me ever since.

And now here I am as Danny presses his hot palms against Lou's butt cheeks, right across my back straps as he pulls them as far apart as they'd go and greedily plunges his tongue in and out of Lou's clearly over-sensitized hole like there's no tomorrow!

"Oh!" Lou moans again and again, wriggling his ass until Danny finally slides out his tongue and reaches under the bed, pulling out a plastic bottle of Vaseline lotion.

Squeezing some onto his hand, he slathers it across Lou's hole. Then he works one finger inside. Lou responds by squirming and moaning all over again. A second finger joins the first and a third joins the second and Lou's screaming and writhing out of control. His beautiful butt stretches my back straps and his swollen cock, pulsating with pleasure, drenches my pouch with pre-cum.

Once Danny's got him fully lubricated, he applies some to his own cock. A dick the size of his takes a lot of the stuff, but fortunately there's plenty left in the bottle.

Then, raising himself up onto his knees, he presses his massive, grease-up member against Lou's rear entrance. When I see this union of cockhead and butt hole, I begin to grow a bit concerned for Lou because, after all, his hole's only so big, and Danny's dick is fucking enormous. I mean, just the head alone's fat enough to stretch him well beyond the dimension of three little fingers.

But when Danny slips his fat, purplish cockhead into Lou's hole with a slight shove and Lou lets out a prolonged, deeply intoned "Ohhhh!" while slowly shaking his head from side to side, I realize I'm concerned over nothing at all.

Well, inch after inch of Danny's dick makes its way up inside Lou, whose cock grows into a fat, rock-hard, nine-incher as he slowly strokes it. Since his hand as well as his dick's still inside my pouch, which is stretched beyond anything I've ever experienced before, I begin to understand what his fortunate butt hole must feel like taking in all that cock.

Soon Danny's fucking Lou with a forceful, even-paced rhythm, each cock thrust sending a shock wave through Lou's hard body, registering against my back straps and in the constant jostling of his nuts inside my pouch. And all the time Lou's stroking his dick. My waistband gets stretched to the max as Lou's fist makes its way up and down his shaft, faster and faster until he forces his dickhead right out into the open, hovering over his navel and spewing pre-cum.

Suddenly Danny lets out a loud "Ah, shit!" and with the mightiest plunge of all drives his cock all the way up Lou's ass, draining his nuts of the first outpouring of cum and then proceeding to jackhammer the rest of his load up Lou's ass.

And at this same time, Lou – his balls are now tightly encased in his snug sac, ripe with a hot load of jism – lets loose with "Ohh! Ohh! Ohh!" as the violent discharge of spurt after spurt of cum lands all over his chest in long, ropy strands.

Their orgasms are so powerful I get blissfully lost in the effort, dizzy from their double-time buttfucking and cockstroking. Their brows are beaded with sweat, their faces are drawn into expressions of pain-pleasure, and I'm incapable of separating out their "ahs" and "ohs" as their bodies convulse pleasure.

As they come to rest and catch their breath, Lou takes his still-swollen, softening dick and stuffs it into my pouch. I willingly embrace it, appreciatively soaking up the last drops of cum that slowly seep out of his piss slit.

"Happy birthday, baby," he says, finally slipping me off. Hope you like your present."

The way Danny takes me and rubs the inside of my pouch against his cheek, I know he does.

And when he puts me on and I feel his mammoth equipment filling me up, I think he's as much a gift to me as I am to him.

- - -

You're probably not going to be surprised when I tell you that night he jacked off several times without ever taking me off, soaking me with his seed. Lance had never done this with me. The most I ever got out of him was the occasional hard-on, and a drop or two of cum lodged in his piss slit when he'd slide me back on after some sexual encounter.

The next morning, after a rejuvenating visit to those two great democratic institutions, the washer and the dryer, where brutes like me get to pal around with the likes of silk boxer shorts, he puts me on again and heads for The Club.

Now, though I'd heard he works out afternoons, I wasn't really surprised he decided to alter his routine to get there well before noon, especially since the night before Lou mentioned several times he wouldn't be there this morning.

Well, when he finally "just happens" to meet up with Lance, it's in the steam room. This is the first time I'd been in the back beyond the lockers. Let me tell you, it's like heaven. All those facilities. And all those men. Men in briefs and jockstraps, wet and clinging. Men with towels wrapped tightly around their waists, their cock heads pressing outward, swinging from side to side with every step. And men in the buff parading their stuff for all to see.

Anyhow he steps into the steam room, and there's Lance, alone, seated on the second tier.

Standing in front of him, Danny runs his hands across my pouch.

"You're Lance Longfellow, aren't you?"

"Why, yes I am," he says slowly, his eyes making their way down Danny's sleek body, coming to rest dead center on my pouch with a complete lack of recognition as to who I am, so taken is he with the way Danny fills me out.

"I knew it! Well, let me tell you, I'm one of your biggest fans!"

"Oh?" he says with peacock delight. And then he adds suggestively, "And just how big would that be?"

Danny, grips me by the waistband on either side of my pouch and slowly lowers me down over his taut lower abdomen. His blond pubic hair spills out, and then the California redwood base of his cock comes into view. He stops at that and I feel the rest of his dick stirring inside me.

"I see," Lance says, lowering himself down onto the bottom tier, right in front of Danny. "Very big indeed."

Caught in the grip of my present master I watch my former master's head come close, closer, and closer still as Danny's cock presses out against me. Sliding down onto his haunches, Lance opens his mouth, sticks out his tongue, and looks up at Danny's face with pleading eyes.

Danny continues to lower me until his dick flops out. From below Danny's thickening rod, I look up to see Lance wrap his lips around Danny's cockhead, then proceeding to take in inch after inch of his ever-hardening shaft with an ease that exceeded even my expectations of his cocksucking abilities.

Danny issues a prolonged, impassioned moan. Lance's chin begins to press against me as Danny's dick reaches full erection, his cockhead burrowing its way into Lance's throat.

Then he proceeds to give Danny, judging from his groans, the blowjob of his life.

But it's not until a few minutes later, when Lou steps into the steam room that things really begin to get hot....

PENILE SUBVERSIVES: VARIETY IS THE SPICE OF LIFE
Peter Eros

I'm fucking this dude on top of Teddy Roosevelt's head. It's that time of year. He's got a solid steel cock ring surrounding his entire genital package – not the President – the guy. He has tit-rings, spectacularly obscene, self-designed tattoos, and is the proud owner of a metal Mohawk. He has five metal inserts, with threaded holes, imbedded in his shaved pate, which allow him to screw a variety of decorative surgical steel spikes into his scalp. He's probably insane, but is sexy, amiable, bizarrely handsome and deliciously tight-assed.

When you live and work in an area this remote you don't lose an opportunity to fuck. I'm a stonemason on the fifty- million-dollar face-lift at the Mount Rushmore monument, and on the huge Crazy Horse being carved fifteen miles away. I've been here three years now, living in a trailer on the outskirts of Sturgis, sharing with one of the Park Rangers. Mike's a terrific guy and we regularly fuck and suck each other when nobody else is available. In fact, we really groove on each other but we both agree that variety is the spice of life.

This is not a national park for all tastes. It's off the beaten path, accommodations and services are just adequate, and the terrain and climatic conditions can be hard on the body. It is a place, however, for hikers, birders, botanists and those who like their landscapes wild and free. And not far away, at Lead, we've got a bunch of lonely gold miners. Fortunately for Mike and me, some of the miners and lots of the visitors like their sex wild and free as well.

One weekend in August the whole area is over-run with Harley-Davidson motorcycles, fully loaded with flesh and duffel. It's the Sturgis Rally, the annual confluence of bikers that descends on South Dakota each summer, bringing the ear-drum-blasting noise of their bikes and great gobs of cash to spend at local businesses. They eat up every hotel and motel room and every campground for two hundred miles around, and an awful lot of them are looking for some man-to-man action.

At this time of year I'm usually dressed in brief cut-offs and skimpy tank tops, amply displaying my cut muscles. Hooking sex-seeking companions is not too difficult. The area is over-run by large, burly men on larger, burlier bikes, flashing chrome and hardware. The bikes flash chrome and hardware, too. The thunder of engines is everywhere. I doubt the launch of a space shuttle could be more booming. More than a quarter-million cycles are in Sturgis.

Friday, when I'd finally crawled through downtown and got on Interstate 90 toward Rapid City, cyclists sped past me in all directions, and the escort continued all the way for the twenty-five miles into the Mount Rushmore National Memorial. The parking lots were full of lined-up Harleys, their front wheels all tilted in one direction, like a hockey crowd watching a fight in the corner of the arena.

There are few places in America that are as iconic as this granite bluff with the faces of four presidents chiseled into it. It is like the Statue of Liberty or the Golden Gate Bridge. The sixty-foot heads with twenty-foot noses make a kind of bombastic sense, which still strikes awe from most of its visitors.

Weekdays my crew is hard at work restoring climate-ravaged rock, but weekends the work area above the heads is abandoned territory, with little likelihood of unwanted intrusions, and my favorite place to bring my latest fuck-buddies. They are invariably impressed with the panorama, a topographical masterpiece that Nature has wrought: expanses of butte-broken prairie and the Badlands' sinister white spires and menacing cliffs.

Ziggy – that's what he calls himself – hails from Seattle. He sings and plays guitar, fronting a pop group called Penile Subversives. They've been gigging and fucking their way across the country on an extended bike run. We met in the Rapid City bar where they were playing a one-nighter Friday, happy to get off their crotch-rockets for a few hours.

When I came in about 1 a.m. Ziggy was between sets and skylarking with his equally skimpily clad companions, and a tittering coven of coked-up groupies. But he kept glancing his wild blue eyes approvingly in my direction. Just before returning to the stage he gave me a wink and provocatively licked his lips. He was topless and bare-ass in his black leather chaps and zip-fronted leather thong, the priapic tattoos artfully designed to emphasize his svelte and impressive musculature.

He was a refreshing change of view. When I think of bikers I generally visualize the Hollywood image of Marlon Brando in black leather, terrorizing store owners. The times have changed. The average Sturgis rallier looks more like Brando does now than he did then. And large numbers of them are obviously yuppies with money to drop on a pricey bike, slumming with the "outlaws" for a weekend once a year.

But Ziggy was something else again, and obviously available if I liked to stick around. I happily stood, enthralled through three sets, as Ziggy taunted the crowd, whirling around bare-chested, jutting and thrusting his leather-clad pelvis and shiny-chain-divided buttocks at them with sexual and musical arrogance as he breathed punk fire through the stacks: huge, scorching gusts of raunchy rock 'n' roll that made me howl with sick pleasure. Sweat was trickling down his chest and between his shoulder-blades, spinning off into the crowd. The group's warmly spot lit torsos glowed like highly polished mahogany. Ziggy sang like he'd been to hell and back and still had the taste of sulfur in his mouth. His songs were dark and deceptively beautiful. The heavy-reverb guitar licks made the human body hum like it was getting a constant low-voltage electrical charge.

The audience was swaying, clapping, shouting, all focusing their combined enthusiasm and collective will on the small platform, and the exquisitely structured electronic dance mixes. Too bad there wasn't enough room for anyone to move. It was as if a two-way intravenous drip-feed of adrenalin had been set up, with the audience feeding off the five Penile Subversives: responding to their goadings, being fueled by their music and being charged by their energy. For their part, the Subversives were being continually resuscitated by the urgings and enthusiasm of the audience.

By 4 a.m., when they finished, the place was smoke-filled, echoing with noises of music, laughter, screams and shouted conversation. It was the only place in town where you could experience the bewildering feeling of jet-lag without actually flying.

I'd sidled through the crowd so that I was leaning against the doorjamb to backstage. Ziggy grabbed my shoulder and turned me, thrusting me ahead of him through the door. The other guys passed us with a variety of salacious winks and nods as Ziggy pulled me into his embrace and thrust his tongue between my lips. His tongue twined around mine, thrusting deeply and insistently. I wrapped my arms around him and held him. We ate each other's mouth, and I could feel his ample prick stiffen in its leather pouch as it pressed against my own throbbing erection. He disengaged to gulp some air and growled, "I'm in town till Sunday midday. Got somewhere to take me so we can fuck, hot lips?"

"Sure thing. But you'd better put some clothes on. Even in August it's chilly around here at this hour, and you've been sweating like hell."

He slipped into a T-shirt on which Snow White was doing unusual things to the Seven Dwarfs, and a leather jacket with as many zips, pockets and compartments as one of those organizer bags. He deftly unscrewed his scalp attachments and pocketed them, with a knowing wink in my direction.

"I don't want to do you an injury in our first encounter."

In the cab of my 4x4 he snuggled against me, his thigh pressed to mine and one hand stroking the back of my neck as the other sneaked into my crotch. As I drove off he flicked my buttons open and set to eating my straining prick. He swallowed my dick all the way to the balls. I ran my free hand over his polished scalp, fingering the metal implants.

Every nerve in my body caught fire as his tongue played over the welcoming surface of my cock. His lips squeezed my shaft, sucking with a slow, steady rhythm. His tongue curved along the underside of my meat, the tip rasping mercilessly over the trigger of nerves just behind the crown. I squirmed both with delight and concern. My driving was at hazard. I pulled off the road as he began squeezing and manipulating my ballsac.

"I'm coming!" I gasped, my voice choked with passion. Ziggy wrapped his hand around my flexing shaft and glanced up at me as my balls snapped up tight between my legs. As my jism sprayed his throat he kept right on sucking till I was spent. As he withdrew he gave me a lop-sided grin and pressed his lips to mine, transferring some of my own juice into my gasping mouth.

I pushed him back and unzipped him. His long, fat cock, improbably tattooed with amazingly detailed decorative patterns, pulsed against his belly, stretching toward his navel. He was uncut, but his foreskin had retracted and his piss-slit was gaping, a shiny Prince Albert glinting at its tip. A steel cock-ring encircled his genitals. A clear drop of pre-cum bubbled out of his throbbing prick and caught in the spiky hairs on his gut.

I chowed down on his fleshy knob, sucking the salty bubble before consuming his rod in one deep swallow. Working my tongue up and down the fat tool, tweaking the metal ring at its tip, using my throat muscles to contract around the swelling shaft, I was intoxicated by the smell of leather and spunk. His pubic hair was black, but his ballsac was hairless. I pushed my hands up under Snow White and gave the aroused nubs of his pierced nipples a fingernail massage.

"Oh, fuck, man! That's cool," Ziggy purred, licking his lips. I felt his cock flex and vibrate. I worked up the shaft, swirling my tongue around the thickness, over and up the blood-pulsing veins. He dug his finger-nails into my shoulders as he jerked and thrashed under me, letting fly with a spout of hot, reeking jism, pumping deep into my gulping throat. I had a hard time swallowing all the delicious cream, much of it gushing out over my lips and the corners of my mouth. I kept massaging his jumping scrotum, bobbing my head up and down the slicked length of erectile muscle, extracting every drop of delicious sperm from Ziggy's contracting balls. He lay back against the window with a sigh of contentment, looking like a naughty cherub.

Driving home, he fell asleep on my shoulder. I had to shake him awake and support him with an arm around his body as we stumbled to the door in the dawn light. Mike and his sandy-haired fuck-hunk of the night were asleep in each other's arms and hardly stirred. Ziggy fell onto my bed and allowed me to undress him, then rolled over into instant slumber. I stripped and wrapped myself around his slimly muscular flesh. I didn't wake until he stirred about 2 p.m. and asked me where to piss.

Mike and his blond had gone. I lay in a lubricious daze, watching my colorful companion stumble to the john, his pendulous balls visible from behind, swaying between his sinewy thighs. I heard his stream of urine splashing forcefully in the bowl. I followed him and fondled his ass-cheek as he passed me in the doorway.

When I returned Ziggy had removed the Prince Albert and was massively rampant. He yawned, throwing his shoulders back to work out a kink in his spine. His cock flexed and bounced against his belly. I knew then that I wanted this stupendous prick to open my butt wide and deep. Without speaking I straddled his thighs and unwrapped a condom as he dipped his fingers in the tub of lube and gently pushed three fingers up into my seasoned pucker.

As I slid the latex down his prick I rocked myself forward and positioned him at my hungry entrance. His cock slid in slow and easy. I wriggled my hips and spread my butt cheeks, getting comfortable, threading his dick up my hot hole. Then I bucked back, sitting on my heels. He was embedded to the hilt. His clipped pubic hairs tickled my butt.

Ziggy smiled dreamily and began to thrust as I raised and lowered myself in time to his rhythm. I watched the decorative body move beneath me, the muscles flexing, nipples tightening, the muscles of his forearms jumping as he grasped my waist and pumped out the rhythm of passion. It was total bliss being fucked by Ziggy, hovering over him, feeling him stabbing up into my vitals again and again as I pistoned my cock in my lubed fist.

Ziggy's thrusts became more urgent, meshing with my mounting excitement. When he gasped and his hips began slapping frantically against my ass, I was ready as well. Each jolting thrust triggered a spasm that pumped my cream out of me, jetting streams the length of his torso. As Ziggy crested right along with me, I collapsed on top of him. Our bodies twitched and writhed with the intensity of our shared passion, our torsos stuck together with my musky cum.

We lay fondling and kissing and Ziggy let me examine the elaborate, continuous pattern of copulating males in every conceivable position, that decorated almost his entire body. Then I got up and made some coffee. Ziggy lay back against the propped pillows and happily answered my questions about his exotic appearance.

"I used to be a musician with the Marines, man. That's when I got my nipples pierced. It was sort of a rite of passage, and I liked it. I wanted a tattoo as well, but I didn't want the traditional eagle, globe and anchor. I've always been good at drawing, especially male anatomy. Females never interested me. I designed my first tattoo, the sixty-nining couple across my pecs, and had it done in San Diego." The focus of each sucking mouth was one of his nipples, incorporated into the design as a swollen cockhead.

"When my commanding officer saw it I was discharged from the service. I guess it was what I'd secretly wanted. I soon hooked up with the guys in the band and we're beginning to build a reputation for ourselves, musically as well as sensationally. I've kept on adding to the basic design. I don't have too many spaces left. The Prince Albert was a natural progression. It's a real turn-on."

"What about the screw-holes in your scalp?"

"I like body modification. It didn't hurt, apart from a minor headache. The guy burrowed a channel under my scalp and then shoved in the threaded plugs. It took about an hour and a half. The threads allow me to screw in a variety of spikes. They vary in length from a quarter-inch to three and a half. But I rarely use the smaller-gauge anymore. If you're going to have spikes in your head, have spikes in your head!"

"But why?"

"For personal expression. If they wanted to, anyone could have a metal Mohawk just like mine. But what would be the point of that? Where the creativity comes in would be if they arranged the spikes in some different configuration. That would be about them. Believe me, this is not something I did on a whim. A lot of personal time and effort went into this. The guy who did this for me, he's a professional body piercer, he'd been exploring the feasibility of installing a metal Mohawk for a few years when I volunteered for the project. I took antibiotics immediately after, just in case, but beyond that I didn't take any special precautions. I use common sense. I don't go round sticking my head in piles of cow shit! And it's got me on Jenny Jones and a coupla' other shows that have gotten us some good publicity. But I'm regularly baffled by security people at airports who insist on waving a metal detector over my scalp. What? I somehow planted a bomb in my own head?"

We laughed easily together as I relaxed back against the pillows with him. He kissed me as he clutched my flaccid cock, massaging it to resurrection. He traced its length with his tongue, then sucked my whole scrotum into his mouth, rolling my balls with his tongue. He came up for breath and said, "I want this up my ass, man. It's not often I find a real man to ream my pucker. There's so many flaky screamin' queens in this business."

"Pleased to oblige, babe. How do you like it?"

"Any which way, dude."

He slid a pillow under his butt, spread his legs with graceful elegance almost into a split, and I entered him with my tongue, probing deeply into his funky hole, bonding to his taste. His funky odor brought out my feral instincts. I reamed and sucked and bit his prominent and practiced rosebud, before lathering his suction cup with lube. He groaned and thrust against me with wild abandon.

Safely latexed, I impaled his orifice, pounding into him without restraint, and he rocked and rolled beneath me, grinding his ass into my groin, as I settled into a steady rhythm of deep penetrations. He flexed his sphincter in synch, never missing a beat of my inward thrusting. His anal muscle control was phenomenal. He laughed out loud between grunts and groans as he gleefully thrust back and forth meeting my challenge. His penis was rock hard and his copious drip was richly aromatic. He glistened with sweat as I fucked him, his giggles settling into deep, grunting, breathy sighs.

Supporting myself with my left arm, I began stroking his rigid, engorged prick. Gradually I strengthened my hold as my hugely engorged prostate-stimulator built to its final crescendo. Ziggy was growling his need now, shouting it out, "Oooh! Oooh! Oh, yeah, fuck!"

I was flying on automatic now, overwhelmed by the exquisite testicular stimulation of the clenching colon sucking at my juices. As my ejaculations exploded into the clasping membrane, deeply embedded in his ass, Ziggy began to blow his load. He let forth a tremendous ear-splitting cry, his teeth bared, saliva falling from his open mouth onto his chest. His muscles tensed, sweat poured, and he threw a high, arcing, voluminous, creamy stream of semen into the air. He pumped and jetted and spurted, till we were both spattered from head to toe. I fell into his embrace, both of us quaking and spasming from our intensely satisfying excavation of our deepest desires. Gradually we relaxed into a state of contented bliss.

Ziggy told me that they didn't have a performance that night and that they weren't leaving till Sunday midday. He rang the motel where he was booked and roused one of the other musicians from the arms of some hunk of rural satisfaction, telling him not to expect to see him till departure time.

After washing each other in the tight confines of the shower stall, we spent most of the day and night exploring the multiple possibilities of oral and anal stimulation, drinking a few beers and smoking a couple of joints. A massive summer thunderstorm hit about dusk, just when we were planning to go eat, so we settled for microwaved frozen pizza.

Sunday dawned warm and muggy and a heat-mist veiled the sun. The light on the white walls of the trailer was changing from pink to yellow. The first waves of another day of heat were beating on the windows. Outside the rain had ceased and watery sunshine was yellowing the church spire. Vague sounds of voices came from the streets and a low hum of traffic, the speech of an awakening town.

We were both ravenous. By the time we stumbled into Denny's the weather appeared set fair, and the sun had drawn up most of the puddles left by the rain. There was a serene blue sky flooded with golden light – all seemed well with the world.

Our hunger for food satisfied, I drove Ziggy to my open-air hideout as he deftly re-inserted his intimidating prongs. At the summit, there was a gentle cooling breeze. I spread atop Teddy Roosevelt the quilt I always carry in the truck. Ziggy stripped and pranced, exhilarated by our wicked freedom in such a hallowed place, exulting in the fantastic view, and the stunning proximity of the other massive heads, which most people only see from a considerable distance. He gazed across Jefferson's nose to the back of Washington's head, then back to the side of Lincoln face, and remarked that the play of sunlight across the granite features made them seem alive. Then he asked:

"Why Teddy Roosevelt?"

"Well, it's a flatter space here, babe. We're less likely to roll over the side in our excitement. And it's set further back than the others so we're not likely to be seen by anyone looking up here with binoculars. Besides which, it's a prettier view from here, especially your delicious bod."

"Well, let's fucking do it!"

Ziggy assumed the submissive position, facing the panorama, on elbows and knees, head down, buttocks raised and widely spread. I knelt to revere the pouting lips of joy. I thrust my tongue into the callused cincture, and Ziggy shivered with pleasure as I probed his tasty asshole. I rolled a condom on my bouncing prick and it flopped down against the warm, smooth cleavage of his buns. He reached back and spread them with his fingers and I slid into the tight passage with one shove. Ziggy exhaled sharply but otherwise didn't flinch. I gripped his waist, all my feeling concentrated in my cock.

"Oh, fu-u-uck!" I cried blissfully, gripping his smooth thighs.

"Yes! Yes!" Ziggy hissed. He wiggled his butt, massaging my prick. His ass-ring squeezed the base of my shaft so tightly, I thought I was in heaven. I couldn't hold back. In no time I shot my load in great spurts deep in his asshole, then slumped over his sweaty back.

Ziggy swiftly pushed me flat on my back, his glistening body crouched between my thighs. He lifted my legs over his shoulders and I felt my asshole exposed to the breeze. He smoothed a condom onto his prick and flashed me a brilliant smile as a shadow fell across us.

"Hullo, what's going on here?"

I recognized the voice, but Ziggy didn't and started guiltily. I grabbed his thigh to stop him jumping up. It was Mike, in uniform.

"You asshole!" I growled. "Get that fucking uniform off and join us."

He didn't need a second invitation. He threw off his clothes and straddled my head, facing Ziggy. He leaned forward and embraced the tattooed one, gobbling his mouth as Ziggy probed my gaping hole. I sighed as I felt it slide into me, spreading my ass ring. I shoved my butt up to meet his thrusts, and I felt his swinging ballsac slap against my tailbone as he pounded into me.

My nose was under Mike's scrotum and I began to lick his cleft, tasting his salty sweat, probing his pucker. I could hear him growling like an alley cat in heat. His ass ring opened and closed, squeezing my tongue tip.

"Suck my dick," Mike muttered. He moved his ass back and my face slid down his ball sac and tasted his pre-cum-smeared cock tip. I reached blindly for his pulsating shaft and sucked it into my gasping throat. While Mike fucked my mouth, and tongue-wrestled Ziggy, the frenetic musician was banging away, slamming his meat up to his balls in my manhole

"Yeah! Yeah!" Ziggy panted, growing breathless.

"Yeah! Yeah! Yeah!" echoed Mike, his voice rising to a high-pitched whimper.

Mike was the first to cum. As I was swallowing huge gobs of his cream, I tightened my ass ring against the base of Ziggy's shaft. He groaned and his cock started to jerk like a jammed piston. His hot seed filled my ass. Both guy's sweat-streaked bodies shuddered and jerked uncontrollably as they spurted their loads into me. It was the totally satisfying conclusion to a great weekend. As we disengaged and Ziggy stood silhouetted against the sky like the monument of a pagan god – I guess it was a trick of the light – Jefferson seemed to wink in complicity, but if anyone was watching, Teddy remained as stone-faced as ever.

THE PUPIL
Peter Eros

"'S'truth Jason! Caleb's been giving you the glad-eye for weeks, Mate. For a little Argonaut you're more one-eyed than Cyclops," Bruce sputtered.

My Aussie mentors, Bruce and his mate Eric, have always called me their little Argonaut, ever since I became their surfboard pupil when I was eight years old. That was more than ten years ago. My very liberal mother and father guessed they were gay, I reckon, but they also knew they were the best coaches on the coast, and both former champions of the sport. With their board-shop and workshop, and loft dwelling above it, right on the beach-front, they and their two lovable surf-dog Spaniels had become a local institution. And they were very attentive to the kids under their tutelage and no hint of scandal had ever been associated with them. Besides which, they appeared far more butch than most straight guys I know – strong, reliable, but unthreatening.

They early cottoned that I was gay, when puberty began taking its toll and I graduated from being a dry-hump orgiast. I was about eleven, as I recall, and they quietly counseled me how to handle it so as not to get myself in unnecessary scrapes with guys who weren't gay. I'm not religious, but I think of them kind of like father-confessors. They told me there was nothing to be ashamed of, that it was perfectly natural, and encouraged me to masturbate and explore solo pleasure, without qualms of conscience. They teamed me also with other kids they suspected to be gay, encouraging us to experiment with each other, sometimes even leaving us together in the loft with a selection of porno magazines to illustrate what was possible, and a ready supply of condoms with an illustrated brochure on how to use them. Sex was, after all, they said, just the ultimate sign and seal of true friendship. But they never laid a hand on any of us, apart from the occasional bone-crushing hug or affectionate caress. Not until I was eighteen, anyway. Even then, they didn't come on to me. I sort of pushed the limits one late afternoon, when their defenses were down.

Bruce is an extrovert with a zany sense of humor. He's so far over the top that he comes out the other side. He often seems just too perky and cheerful – cocky, competent and resilient. He's nearing forty but still seems like the energetic boy next door with freckles; clean-cut, with perfect uncapped teeth, wide inviting, full-lipped mouth, and sparkling blue eyes that spread the honey of sex-you-up charm. Sun-bleached blond curls crown and offset the all-over deep freckled tan on the leanly muscled six feet of buff bod.

Eric, by contrast, is a five-nine powerhouse of stacked furry muscle, honed to perfection with years of weight-training. A year younger than Bruce, Eric had straight dark hair and dark brown eyes, high cheekbones and orthodontically perfect but slightly pointed teeth, giving him a saturnine, almost sinister air, enhanced by a gruff manner that disguises his real warmth and depth of feeling. His alternate-hunk looks and a caress that seems more like a grope, are offset by his puppy-dog eyes, which suggest a conscience might lurk in the bulge of his well-filled beach bikini.

One late afternoon, a couple of weeks after my eighteenth birthday, I came in from two hours of wave riding, unthinkingly barged up the stairs to the loft and entered without knocking. Bruce and Eric were both naked on the king-size bed and getting it on. Eric lay on his back, legs raised and spread, with Bruce buried to the hilt up his ass. My cock jerked to attention as I ogled, despite my embarrassment. Bruce gave me a sideways glance and a twisted smile.

"You've caught us well and truly bare-assed this time kid. You're old enough now – you might as well hop on for the ride."

I didn't need any further encouragement. I shucked my board shorts. My fingers circled the base of my cock, now thick and erect. I peeled on a lubed condom, as Bruce greased his puckered hole. I clasped his round firm buttocks and straddled his spread-eagled body. He was still pumping Eric beneath him. I could feel the hard muscles in his taut calves and thighs as I moved my legs over his. I embraced his muscled back and clutched the pushed-up shoulders. With one thrust I buried myself deep inside him and swiftly settled into their already- established tempo. Bruce's anus pulsed around me. My sweat dripped on his back. My hands slid around his body and played with his bulging nipples. Some inner rhythm shifted speeds and urged our movements to quicken. It was as if I were fucking them both at once, which I guess I was. I grew rough and forceful in my need to dominate and possess my old masters. They responded in kind, obviously desperate to satisfy my every need. Each subtle change of position made the anticipation more overwhelming, until we all abandoned ourselves entirely and sought out the release that was maddening us. The headboard was snapping against the wall.

Bruce twisted his head back to me and we kissed. I tasted his saliva and pheromones. I was panting and half sobbing as my first gush jerked deep inside him. I came and came, whimpering with pleasure, slick with perspiration.

As we slid apart Eric surfaced, his long black hair stuck to his cheeks and temples with sweat. He rolled onto his back and I fell into his bear-like embrace. His mouth opened and engulfed my face. He was eating me. His tongue thrust through into my throat as I tried to respond in kind. One hand stripped my condom then grasped our two cocks together, massaging and stroking as the other hand fondled my low-hangers.

Bruce had moved in behind me and was nibbling and tongue-probing my virgin ass. My head was spinning wildly as I tried to deal with this bevy of new and overwhelming sensations. Eric slid down and sucked my meat into his vacuum mouth, as Bruce inserted first one, then two well-lubed fingers into my dilating asshole, sliding them in and out, feeling for my aroused prostate.

"Holy shit!" I gasped, "Oh, fuck, that's really cool, Oooooh, fuck!"

Encouraged, my tutors increased the diligence of their lesson. Eric had my cock deep in his throat, while his tongue did push-ups all over it and his lips loudly smacked and sucked. Bruce, latexed and ready, inserted the massive head of his prick in my hole and crooned in my ear,

"Just relax, little Argonaut. We'll take this real slow and steady. I'll ease in real gentle, mate. You just take it at your pace. It'll probably hurt a little, but you just persevere, petal-pie. It'll be worth it, believe me."

And it was. He was right. It did hurt like hell for a moment or two, but a few deep breaths and he slid past my sphincter, right into my colon, and seemed to be probing my guts. I'd never felt anything so good in my life. I was truly fulfilled in more ways than one. Bruce's weight pushed into me, spreading me open, until he was jack hammering my manhole and I was screaming for more.

"Don't stop! Oh fuck! Bruce, I love it. Oh God, fuck meeee!"

Eric was still slurping at my crotch, sucking harder, his mouth and throat filled with my swollen prick. I started to quicken the rocking of my hips, almost coming, riveted from both sides. I both wanted to cum and to prolong it. But I had no control. My eyes closed into darkness and something took over. We rocked together in a furious quiet rhythm. It was oblivion and we rode it for all it was worth. My anal muscles clenched and unclenched, milking the massive probe, and then I was coming, my cock and my anus spasming, like a dual orgasm, as I let myself go in Eric's mouth and Bruce's discharge erupted into the condom up my ass.

Eric disengaged with a devilish smirk and enveloped us both in a joyous hug, as he once more engulfed my mouth with his own. He'd kept some cum in his mouth so I could taste my semen and smell it, feel its slickness in my mouth and throat. I squirmed happily on the warm bed, knowing that whenever I had an aching need, I had a safe place to indulge my lust.

Our three-ways, with constant variations of roles and positions, have become a regular occurrence. And, just occasionally, when we all feel we have a safe companion or two, we have ourselves a fourgy or a five-way. But Caleb was an unknown quantity to me, undeniably attractive, but distant.

I can't say I wasn't turned on by the guy. Who wouldn't be? He's dark, Hispanic looking, but not – he says he's of Scottish descent – twenty-four and just back from the army with hot olive eyes, a square, resolute jaw, full red lips, an attractively broken nose, and tiny shell-like ears on a head covered in soft, brown wavy hair, just growing out of its Spartan military cut. He has the build of a shapely football player, which is, he tells me, how he got the nose.

Caleb was a surfer on the east coast when he was growing up. He was raised in a northern coastal town. But six years of army life didn't give him much opportunity to indulge his passion for the waves. He first came to the workshop looking for a job, and because he'd heard about Bruce and Eric's monopoly of the surf-board business in our town, and hoped to get back into the sport with a little expert advice. They really didn't need any help, but they hired him anyway and soon found they liked his company, his quickness in picking up the finer points of board-building, and his dedication to the work, which allowed them a lot more free time to indulge their pleasures. As I'd opted for college in my hometown, we were often able to surf together, or frolic above the workshop, while Caleb held the fort down below.

I don't know why I felt so shy around him. I found myself a compulsive gawker as he worked in the shop, his smooth body sweat-glassed, dressed only in tiny shorts, that emphasized his ample equipment and muscular butt, as he molded, planed and diligently finished the board he was working on, his pungent maleness rejoicing my twitching nose. But I was tongue-tied in his presence, despite the wetness from the intersection of my jeans slipping down my thigh, the glistening vision of him dancing me up to hardness. I wanted to be all wetted up, wrestling, slapping my slick body against his. So, imagine my surprise when Bruce chided me and told me that Caleb was as interested in me, if not more so, than I was in him. How could I have missed the hot looks Bruce and Eric swore Caleb had been giving me for weeks?

"We're not going to let you waste any more time, Jason, my sweet. Eric and I are going out to the clubs tonight while you and Caleb baby-sit the pooches. And our six favorite videos are on top of the TV. There's a casserole in the oven and a nicely chilled Chablis in the fridge. Caleb is closing up at six and will want to shower, by which time the food should be ready and so will his one-eyed trouser trout. It's a little beauty. I know 'cause I was in the lav one day and saw him pointing Percy at the porcelain. Bye, bye, little Argonaut, and don't do anything we wouldn't enjoy. Oh, and by the way, we won't be home till after midnight. So, Cinderella, enjoy!"

Beside myself with anxiety I paced, I looked out the window at the sea, and I fondled the dogs. I opened the oven door and peered at the casserole. I closed it and paced again. I looked at the videos, chose my favorite, put it in the machine and lined it up. I pulled off my tank top, did some chin-ups and some pushups to pump my muscles. I posed in the mirror and adjusted my cock in my shorts.

"Very inviting," Caleb husked.

He was standing in the doorway observing me. I hadn't heard him on the stairs and the dogs were so used to him by now they hadn't stirred. I blushed. He closed the door behind him, unzipped his shorts and stepped out of them, his feelings for me twitching insistently before him, encircled by a metal cock ring, glinting in his pubic forest. He stepped toward me and grasped my flushed face in his massive hands. He kissed me on the forehead, then each eyelid; he nuzzled my nose and sucked my mouth into his own. I responded like a drowned man does to mouth-to-mouth resuscitation. I was limp in his arms, gasping his breath deep into my lungs, as he picked me up bodily, laid me on the bed and stripped off my shorts.

"How do you feel, beautiful?"

"I'm nervous, I guess, but I love it. I think I love you," I gasped, and blushed again. My cock was drooling and my tits felt so pumped I thought they might split right off my body. Caleb straddled my torso, his head settled in my crotch and his muffled voice murmured, "I just want to taste you, Jason."

The voluptuous cavern of his mouth opened. His lips encircled my straining prick, sliding up and down. He opened wide and swallowed my nuts as well, sucking and tongue-probing, swirling my balls in their skin-tight case, fomenting the jism that had been awaiting his firmly gentle attention, my cock lodged deep in his throat. Then he clutched my ass cheeks and pulled them apart and back so his tongue could prime my pucker, probing deep with an ample supply of saliva.

Caleb was stroking his own cock up and down. I pushed his hand away and like a kitten to a mother's nipple, I ravaged his missile with my lips and tongue.

"Yes, lick my balls," he moaned as he let me go and slid round on the bed.

He let me push him onto his back and I mounted his swollen appendage. He rocked up to give me all of it. His firm hands reached for my waist and aided my rise and fall as my swollen pucker massaged his cock that was probing deep inside my guts. His fingers encircled my cock, vigorously rubbing and slicking it, as the sound of sliding, wet fornication overwhelmed all other sound.

I was bobbing up and down with the rhythms of his thrusting groin, my fingers tweaking and kneading his gorgeous, dark brown nipples. His penis jammed into me deeply. With each upward thrust I felt a mini-orgasm. I pounded up and down, pushing my cock forward, showing off my rising excitement. Caleb's ecstatic face, a glorious vision of arousal, urged me to seek my own. I concentrated on my anal manipulations. His hand pumped my cock hard. I felt it growing even more. I pumped his cock in and almost out, up and down, squeezing and relaxing as Caleb's throaty thrill noises brought us both closer to ecstasy.

My butt felt warm. Caleb's probe was finding its target. Total relaxation and lust concentrated in my manhole pushed my puckered hole closer. I wanted Caleb all the way in. My insides began to contract as I rode, and Caleb started to cum with each thrust of his orgasm, jabbing deeper into my bunghole. We were like wild animals rutting in guileless heat.

His climax started to duplicate itself in me. Guttural sounds began in my diaphragm, pushing through my lungs and throat. Each banshee cry of joy was followed by a contraction of my anal muscles around the gushing organ erupting at my core. My juice spurted in great gobs, spattering Caleb from chin to belly-button. My breath slowed down as my heart pounded loudly. All that we could hear were our two hearts beating as we gasped for air. We looked like we'd been oiled down. I collapsed into his embrace.

We lay like that twenty minutes or so, just fondling and kissing, enjoying the after-glow. Then I remembered the food and leapt to the stove. Happily it wasn't ruined, though it was a little overdone. We had a quick splash in the shower, soaping each other down, had a long exploratory kiss under the warm stream, then returned to eat and drink, unable to resist clutching hands across the table and bursting into inexplicable giggles and sighs of pure joy.

We needed no video to encourage further exploration. With the food warm in our bellies and the wine enhancing our euphoria, the dishes dumped in the sink, we collapsed back onto the bed, crushed in each other's arms. Caleb lay beneath me, pushed my auburn tresses back from my face and kissed me on the tip of my freckled nose. He held my face in his hands and gazed into my eyes.

"I've never seen such deep green eyes," he said. "It's like looking into the depths of the ocean. Oh God, Jason, I think I just want to love you forever," and he crushed me to him again.

Caleb went to the nightstand and opened the Crisco. He dipped out a liberal glob, eased up his legs and lubricated his anal pucker, all the while smiling at me seductively. I picked up a condom, but he shook his head. Then he applied the lube to my aroused penis and guided me in, spreading his legs, his eyes closed and a half-smile played on his parted lips. My eight -plus thick inches slid in to the hilt. Caleb let out a mighty sigh, a murmur of relief.

"Fuck me," he growled, his body heaving. "Oh, I love your hot cock in me. You're so big. Am I tight enough for you? Oh yes, fuck me Jason. Really plow my ass hard. I haven't had a real fuck in months. And I want to be yours so much. Oh, yes, babe, that's wonderful."

I began a slow rhythm, unraveling his craving, sliding my free hand over his erogenous flesh, moving it roughly over his skin to feel the blood-swollen muscles of his aroused body. Caleb cooed with each thrust, our entangled hair moist with our body's desire.

"Oh yes," I murmured. "Your hole feels like it's got baby teeth. You're gripping me so tight. It's fantastic."

"Oh," he cried out. "Fuck me hard! Slam it in!"

Our pace increased. Caleb jerked beneath me, his breathing erratic, as his hand furiously worked his cock. He cried out, the nails of his left hand digging into the soft flesh of my shoulder blade. He bucked wildly, his butt slapping against me, shoving my cock in him as far as it would go.

Without disjoining from him, I lifted Caleb's leg, as he pulled me down to him by my nipple and prodded my mouth with wet lips and a fierce tongue. His face was lost in our hair mixed with our kisses. A toss of my head sent the locks behind me and the grip on my nipple tightened.

I snatched his hands and pinned them above his head. Squirming below me, Caleb locked his legs around my waist; as my pelvis pounded the yielding ardor at the center of his responsively thrusting hips and butt. Hard, audible breaths lunged from his mouth to mine and I bit hard into his bottom lip as the sexual high fizzed at the base of my skull. The muscles of Caleb's legs crushed my body, fingernails welted my shoulder blades and Caleb arched and his mouth opened in a cry that persisted in the room moments later as the fizz reached the top of my skull and my satisfaction spilled, as he shot his load in spasming jets.

As my spent dick slipped from anchor I slurped up the thick pearls of love-juice liberally decorating Caleb's muscled torso and pooling on his solar plexus. Exhaustion kept Caleb still. My cheek cradled between his pecs, I heard the pounding of my heart in his as the gusts of our after-shocks gradually receded. I savored the delicious taste of love percolating on my tongue.

The callused hands gently stroked my face and I lay back as his fingertips meandered round my erect nipples. I could feel them stiffening even further against the palms of his hands as he gently massaged my pecs. I gasped. I took a deep breath. His hands grabbed my buttocks, pulling me towards him, and our mouths met in a frenzy of spit and tongue. This was a real man, stronger than most of the guys I'd fucked; much stronger than me. I marveled at the hard contours of his chest, the wiry black hair curled tightly against those pumped breasts, delineating his midriff and framing his newly stiff and flushed cock, the salty, musky scent of his sweat.

His tongue delicately lapped the tender tips of my nipples, slowly, and the juice began dripping from my prick onto my leg.

"You have beautiful love knobs, Jason," he murmured as his mouth gently sucked them till they stood out like pencil rubbers. I was engulfed by a dizzying flash of heat.

He grabbed my tits and gave them a fierce twist, and I cried out in pain. But I liked the roughness, the intensity of his touch. His cock knocked against my legs knowingly as he pinned my arms behind my head and bit and sucked behind my ears.

A wet finger stroked my asshole and I panted with desire.

"What would you like now, babe?" Caleb purred.

"I want you to fuck me again," I whispered hoarsely.

Caleb's big cock consumed my eyes, and the wanting in my buttocks was becoming unbearable. My hands crept down to his cock and I began to stroke and fondle it.

"Fuck me, Caleb," I husked plaintively.

"I don't believe my luck. What do you want?"

"Oh God, I want you to FUCK ME! I want to feel your red-hot cock slamming into me again. I want to squeeze out every drop of juice you have."

"Is that so?" He grinned like a schoolboy.

He straddled me, teased my anal pucker with his tongue and slid his cock smoothly in and out of my mouth. Tears rolled down my face as I choked, the corners of my mouth yearning to take all of him with each slide. My precum flowed freely as he relentlessly tongued my manhole.

Caleb turned around, brandishing the length of his beautiful hard dick, and sank his tongue into my mouth again, his hands roaming my entire body. Each touch stung my tenderized skin, firing my hot cock and anxious butt hole. I thrashed wildly in his embrace. Our kisses tasted of briny musk and his cock prodded teasingly against my wetness.

"What do you want?" he breathed huskily.

"Oh Caleb. I want your big fat cock to slam into me – please!"

My whole body was quivering, teetering on the brink of orgasm. I was intoxicated, delirious. I grabbed his cock beneath the head with two fingers and stroked it up and down quickly, and he guided it to my pucker, resting it against my wet opening. He grinned.

"My sweet Jason. Oh babe, I want to give you the fucking of a lifetime. I want to hear you scream to the gods with pleasure."

He shoved a pillow under my ass, raised and spread my legs far enough to shove his cock inside me in one swift smooth move.

He fucked me slowly at first, then hard and brutally, then slowly again whenever I moaned loudly and I guess he thought I was close.

With each slide into my crack, my legs opened a little wider and his dick slammed a little deeper. He bit my breast, hard, and I liked it.

Gut-wrenching moans started low in my abdomen, then traveled up through my chest to my mouth. All the time he was murmuring in my ear an erotic mantra, "I love fucking your tight ass."

As I moved in tandem with his thrusts I whispered, "I love it, Caleb. I love you."

He grabbed my hair and somehow pulled me round so that I was on top, riding his cock as he fondled my knobs of joy. I was close to coming.

He grabbed my waist and guided me up and down. I felt his cock buckle and jerk wildly deep inside me, and he came, bucking with frantic thrusts.

I cried out as ripping waves of extraordinary pleasure reverberated through my body with an exquisite and powerful release as it came, spattering my love in hot jets, as my anus spasmed and dilated, our bodies steeped in love juice and sweat.

Only time will tell, but I think this is the real thing, though I do have some reservations about committing to monogamy. But Bruce and Eric are already arranging the wedding ceremony.

LEARNING DISCIPLINE
Frank Brooks

"You will remain in this hotel room and you will study the Biblical passages and workbook pages I have assigned you until your mother and I return from the conference this evening. You are not to leave this room, let alone the hotel, under any circumstances. Do you understand? You will be quizzed in depth on your studies tonight, so you had best study diligently. Do I make myself clear?"

Kevin chewed his lower lip. "Yes." Now he didn't dare ask if he could be allowed to go down to the beach, which he was dying to do.

"Yes, what?"

"Yes, sir." He tried to control the defiance in his voice. Betray a hint of surliness and he'd get a whack alongside the head.

The Monster (Kevin's name for his stepfather) gave him that self-satisfied, superior look of his and turned with a smile to Kevin's mother. "He's learning, my dear, learning fast, as I told you he would. Discipline, discipline, discipline! A boy can never have enough of it. Shall we go?"

"Do as your father says," Kevin's mother admonished him as the Monster guided her out the door.

Kevin waited a full minute after the door had closed before he dared mutter, "Fuck you!" Then he flung himself face-down onto the roll-in hotel bed in the corner on which he slept and covered his head with a pillow. He wanted to die. He couldn't take anymore of the hell his life had become since the Monster had taken it over. He was no better than a prisoner.

Not that his life had been that great before the Monster's appearance, but at least it had been tolerable. His mother, though a natural nag and a snoop from the beginning of time, had at least been manageable. He'd been able to tune her out, to ignore her much of the time, and his dad – his real dad – had provided a buffer between Kevin and her, someone to distract her from focusing all her nagging attention on him. Although Dad had rarely stood up to her, jumping when Mother said, "Jump," he had at least kept out of Kevin's hair and let him have his own life. "Try to make your mother happy," was about as naggy as his father ever got with him, and his accompanying wink seemed to imply: Humor her, make her think you're listening to her, but then do your own thing.

No, life before the Monster had not been ideal, but it had at least been bearable, but then his mother had joined that religious political group and her natural tendency to mind everybody else's business except her own, and Kevin's business especially, became increasingly fanatical.

Kevin knocked the pillow off his head and jumped up. By now his mother and the Monster were miles away, probably already at the auditorium where the religious convention they'd journeyed to this country to attend was being held. He wouldn't have to set eyes on them again until this evening. He pulled open the doors onto the balcony and caught his breath at the flood of sunshine and sea air into the stuffy hotel room.

It was another world outside, one dazzlingly beautiful. It was as if he'd thrown open the door of a mausoleum. In seconds he'd stripped off all his clothes and was standing – blond, lissome, and erect – on the private balcony of the hotel room, arms resting on the stone balustrade that enclosed it. He looked down onto the golden beach and blue-green sea below at the base of the sea-cliffs and felt such longing that he had to curb an impulse to climb up onto the balustrade and dive off, ending his miserable life after a few moments of soaring freedom.

He took his erection in hand and began to jerk it with a vengeance, pumping the tight foreskin rapidly over the flange of the moist, plum-like knob. A clear, thick, slippery fluid oozed from his pisshole. It felt heavenly to stand naked in the sunshine in a strange country, working his ultra-sensitive young meat as the floral-scented breezes licked his stiff nipples and slithered between his thighs, tickling his hairless perineum and plump pink balls. He worked his smooth legs against each other and rubbed one foot on top of the other, reveling in the sensual feel of his slender young body. His free hand slid back to caress his satiny, grapefruit-sized buttocks and to tickle the moist crack and twitching, budlike anus between them. It felt so good to beat his meat again, something he hadn't dared do since being forced to accompany his prison guards on this trip.

They wanted him along so they could "keep an eye on him," they'd said, and now they'd confined him to a hotel room and forced him to study the Bible while they plotted politics and partied at their international convention of people just like themselves. "Discipline" was the Monster's favorite word, one he barked so often that Kevin could hear it repeating in his head like a buzz in the ears: "Discipline, discipline, discipline!"

"Fuck you, Monster!" Kevin humped his tight loins obscenely, buttocks dimpling, skin misted with sweat. "Fuck you!" If his mother and the Monster could see him now, they would die of heart attacks. He wished they could see him and that they'd both croak on the spot.

Maybe it would have been better if his mother had caught him with Rusty on that fateful afternoon. If she'd walked in on them and had actually seen what they'd been doing, she would have died on the spot of a heart attack and he would still be living with his real father instead of with Monster. It was a horrible, evil thought, he knew – wishing his mother dead – but he couldn't help it. It was the way he felt. He'd relived that afternoon hundreds of times in his mind. Whenever he beat his meat, which was often, he thought about it. It had been the best, most exciting afternoon of his young life – and the worst.

. . .

Rusty was a bigger, older kid from school, a quiet kid who kept to himself but who could get mean if anybody messed with him. He'd been on the wrestling team until being kicked off for breaking training rules, so he was tough enough that even the most asinine bullies didn't mess with him. The few times when Kevin had accidentally exchanged glances with Rusty, Kevin had looked quickly away. The last thing he needed was for Rusty to snarl, "What're you looking at, faggot?" He'd been called "faggot" by the bullies at school and hated it. He didn't think that Rusty even knew he existed, which is why it surprised him speechless when Rusty confronted him that afternoon after school.

"I got a six-pack," Rusty said. "And I got a hot magazine. A fuck magazine. You ever see a fuck magazine? You wanna get drunk and see some hot pictures?"

Kevin had a hard time getting any words out. The combination of Rusty's friendliness and of his proposing that they share such forbidden pleasures sent such anxious excitement through him that he almost peed in his jeans. Rusty said they needed a place to go and Kevin, his heart thumping, managed to suggest that his bedroom was available. His dad wouldn't be home from work for hours, and his mother, who attended her political-strategy meetings daily, rarely got home until even later.

In Kevin's bedroom both boys took off their shoes and socks and Rusty guzzled two cans of beer before Kevin could even swallow half a one, but even that amount of beer went straight to Kevin's brain and made him dizzy and giggly and he felt as if he were moving in slow motion. Rusty paged through a magazine called Sluts as Kevin, sitting beside him at the edge of the bed and melting because Rusty's left bare foot pressed hotly down on top of his right, gawked at the pictures of women sucking huge, hard cocks and getting fucked in positions Kevin had never dreamed of. Kevin thought he was going to come in his pants, not just because of the pictures, but he was sitting thigh to thigh, shoulder to shoulder, and foot to foot with Rusty, who he was sure had just as hard a cock as his own.

"Wow!" Kevin muttered as Rusty turned the pages. "Cool!" "Nice fuckin' tits, huh?" Rusty said, although Kevin hardly saw the women's tits because he was focusing on the huge veiny cock of the man she was sucking off.

Kevin finished his first can of beer and popped open a second one as Rusty opened his fourth.

"You ever fucked?" Rusty asked, wiggling his toes against Kevin's. He sounded as drunk as Kevin felt.

"No," he admitted, he'd never fucked. "Have you?"

"Of course! A lot of times. You ever sucked?"

"Sucked what? Tits?"

"Tits, pussy." Rusty looked at him and smiled wickedly. "Cock."

Kevin felt himself flush red as a beet and gulped more beer. "Heck no!"

"No what? What ain't you sucked?"

"Nothing," Kevin said. "I ain't sucked nothing."

"I know guys at school who suck cock," Rusty said. He opened his jeans and lowered them. His large, sweaty, teenage cock was sticking straight up in the air, its pisshole like an eye at the tip of its bulbous, maroonish head, an eye that was staring straight at Kevin. "They suck cock and they get off on it." He stroked himself. "I even let them suck my cock. I don't mind. I love getting sucked off." He kicked off his jeans, peeled off his t-shirt, and fell back stark naked on the bed, his huge cock throbbing against his muscular belly, the tip of it pecking at his navel. He picked up the magazine again. "Take off your clothes, man. Get comfortable."

Kevin gulped the rest of his beer. He was so hot that his eyes watered. He nearly fell off the bed as he struggled out of his clothes, drunk not only on the beer but on Rusty's overpowering sexual scent. He grabbed his stiff cock and started pumping it.

Rusty reached over and pressed down on Kevin's blond head: "Suck my cock, boy! I know you want it. Suck my big, ugly cock! Come on!"

Kevin was trembling. He did want it!

Rusty bent his cock up with one hand and pressed down on Kevin's head with the other. "Eat it, cocksucker!"

Suddenly Kevin's mouth was stuffed with hot, sweaty cock and he almost fainted with excitement.

Rusty groaned, arching up, rocking his loins, forcing Kevin to swallow more of his rigid eight inches. "Eat it, boy, yeah, suck my big one! Suck the cum out of it!"

Moaning, sucking, Kevin pressed against Rusty, wrapping his smooth legs around Rusty's muscular hairy thigh, humping Rusty's leg as he sucked the stud's throbbing cock. As his head bobbed, he thrilled at the feel of the cock-veins rippling against his lips. The big cock tasted so good that he wanted to bite it off and swallow it.

"Yeahhh!" Rusty sighed. "Man, suck it!" He paged through the magazine as he rocked his muscular loins. "Yeah, suck the head! Oh fuck! Pull the skin down! Lick it right there, yeah!" Kevin thought that his jaws would dislocate, but he moaned with delirious joy, sucking and tonguing and drooling and bobbing his blond head. As he devoured Rusty's delicious cock, he played with Rusty's egg-sized balls and rubbed sweat from the hairy ball-sac onto his face, getting drunker on the studly aroma than he was on the beer. He was totally and wonderfully out of his mind.

"You're good, baby, you're good," Rusty said, rocking his hips and grunting his appreciation. "Suck that big cock, baby!" His cock was swelling larger and harder by the second.

Kevin worked his own throbbing cock against Rusty's thigh, humping rapidly as he sucked and sucked and sucked.

"Oh fuck!" Rusty groaned, his muscular feet working, his toes clutching. He dropped the magazine, arched up, and drove his cock deep into Kevin's throat. "I'm coming!" His cock flexed, fucking a torrent of jism down Kevin's gullet.

Kevin choked as the thick wads of spunk splashed against his tonsils and slid down his throat like hot oysters, but he kept sucking, guzzling every hot spurt of Rusty's delicious stud-cream. As he guzzled cum, he went into a humping frenzy and saw stars, nearly passing out as his own cum exploded against Rusty's thigh. He kept humping and sucking until he'd squeezed every drop out of both of them.

They were both catching their breaths when Rusty pushed Kevin away and suddenly sat up. "What was that?"

"What?"

"That! I thought you said nobody's home." Rusty rolled off the bed and began yanking on his clothes. "How do I get out of here?"

Now Kevin heard it too: sounds of somebody else in the house.

"I'm out of here!" Rusty yanked the screen out of the window frame, dropped it, and dove through the screen-less opening like a circus acrobat through a hoop.

Kevin, in a panic, kicked the window screen under the bed just as his door swung open and his mother, in her usual no-knock fashion, invaded his bedroom and caught him standing there naked, cum still dripping from his stiff cock, empty beer cans scattered at his feet, a fuck-magazine spread open before him on the bed.

"Oh my Lord!" She clutched her throat. In her hysteria, she failed to notice the missing window screen and never guessed that Kevin had not partied alone.

. . .

Standing in the sunshine on the private balcony of a hotel in a strange country, Kevin gasped as his body twanged spastically and he pumped his pent-up boy-juices into his cupped left hand. As he spasmed ecstatically, he fell against the balustrade to keep from toppling over as the strength went out of his legs and they nearly buckled. Warm jism dripped from between his fingers and splattered on his bare feet. Licking the spunk from his hand and eating it, he pretended that he was eating Rusty's load.

Rusty, dear Rusty. He hadn't seen Rusty since that afternoon and probably never would again. His mother had gone ballistic over the "sick, perverted, unChristian behavior" of her son, consulting preachers and counselors, who had her immediately remove Kevin from his school and enroll him in the Christian Evangelical Academy where, they said, he would be "removed from the satanic influences of heathen peers and molded into a good Christian soldier."

When Kevin's dad shrugged off the incident by quipping, "Boys will be boys," Kevin's mother called him a "lax, liberal, irresponsible, unChristian father" and blamed him for Kevin's downfall from decency, and soon thereafter she divorced him. In court a sympathetic female judge found in favor of Kevin's mother, agreeing that Kevin's dad was not fit to be a father, and almost as soon as Kevin's dad was legally banished from the household, his mother remarried – to the Monster, who moved in and took over.

She had met the Monster – ordained minister, aspiring politician, licensed psychotherapist – months earlier at the Christian Evangelical Academy where her meetings were often held, and he had awed her. As Kevin's stepfather, the Monster awed her even more with his gung-ho approach to fatherhood, which involved watching Kevin's every move and "disciplining" him daily, often with beatings.

. . .

That evening in the hotel dining room, during a lull in the dinner conversation – Kevin dared not interrupt as his mother and the Monster discussed the wonderful speakers that day at the conference – Kevin finally got his chance to ask if he might please be allowed to take a walk on the beach after dinner. To his surprise, the Monster agreed, then took the wind out of Kevin's sails by saying that all three of them would go.

By the time they reached the beach, descending a steep hill via a series of zig-zagging stairs, both Kevin's mother and the Monster were in a bad mood. The climb down had exhausted them, and the climb back would surely be worse, and it was Kevin's fault for suggesting this foolishness. Still, they would walk a short distance along the sand, and no, Kevin could not take his shoes off.

A quarter mile down the beach, as they strolled in the ripe sunshine of early evening and Kevin begged for just a few more minutes before they had to turn back, the beachwear of the swimmers and sunbathers they had been passing made an abrupt change of style. It was as if they'd stepped through an invisible doorway on the beach and into another world. Suddenly the men and women, the boys and girls, were no longer dressed in skimpy swimsuits. Now they were dressed in nothing at all!

"Oh, good Lord!" said Kevin's mother, clutching at her breast near the throat.

"Incredible!" said the Monster. "This is the end!"

Just then a boy, his erection wagging like a stubby tail, came bounding out of the surf, and Kevin's mother turned pale.

"Back to the hotel!" the Monster ordered. "Immediately!"

Kevin tried to glance back for another look at the boy with the hard on, but the Monster cuffed him alongside the head and pushed forward.

"March!"

. . .

"You will remain in this hotel room and you will study the Bible passages and workbook pages I have assigned you, and you will under no circumstances leave this room, let alone this hotel. Do you understand?"

"Yes sir," Kevin said.

"And tonight I will quiz you both on today's assignment and on yesterday's. Is that understood?"

"Yes sir."

Kevin had been spared last night's Bible-study quiz as the Monster had ranted and raved and preached about sin and evil and perversion and had spent hours on the phone making calls to the hotel management, the local police, and the U.S. Embassy to complain about the nudity on the beach. Having gained no satisfaction with phone calls, he resolved to bring up the issue at the conference the next day and Kevin had fallen asleep listening to his reiterations of shock and disgust, which Kevin's mother seconded.

Ten minutes after they had left, Kevin left the hotel himself, wearing only a pair of tiny light-blue underwear briefs which he hoped would pass for a swimsuit. He hadn't been allowed to bring a swimsuit along on the trip. Once on the beach, he headed directly for the area where people went nude and immediately stripped off his briefs and carried them as he walked along as naked as everybody else.

He felt excited and scared and wonderfully free. The sea breeze licked under his balls and up his ass-cleft and within seconds he had an erection that wouldn't quit. He would have been embarrassed to death if he'd been the only boy on the beach with a hard on, but he not only passed other boys with hard-ons, who openly appraised his as he appraised theirs, but he saw an occasional hard-cocked man as well. The farther he went down the beach, leaving tracks in the wet sand at the edge of the surf, the freer he felt. He imagined himself walking on and on, walking forever, naked and free, his troubles forever left behind.

He had walked almost a mile – encountering nude men and women and boys and girls all the way – when he came to a barrier of sea rocks that jutted almost into the waves. Once around the barrier, he spotted more nude swimmers and sunbathers ahead, but he soon realized that he had entered new territory. Here there were no females, only males, men and boys, many of whom sported erections. Men smiled at him as he passed. Soon he encountered a sight that made him stop in his tracks and stare.

Two muscular men were standing in the surf, arms around each other, grinding their naked bodies against each other and kissing. He almost grabbed his cock to masturbate at the sight. When the men noticed him they called to him in what sounded like Spanish and motioned him over. Embarrassed and confused, Kevin kept walking.

He wandered in a daze, thinking about what he'd seen. What would the men have done if he'd gone to them? Why had he panicked and run away? His imagination clicked into high gear. He imagined himself sandwiched between their naked bodies. Maybe he should go back. Suddenly he became aware that somebody was walking beside him and he looked up to see a tall, blond man who could have been a basketball player. The man took one stride for every two of Kevin's, a big, floppy cock dangling and flopping in front of him like a long, fat snake. The man smiled and spoke to him in German or Polish or something, and Kevin nodded his head that he didn't understand.

"You don't possibly speak English?" said the man.

"Yes," said Kevin. "I'm American."

The man laughed. "I took you for Dutch or Scandinavian, or maybe German. Oh what luck! What's a cute American boy doing here all by himself?"

"Walking."

"Been having fun?"

Kevin shrugged. "I guess."

"By the looks of things you've been either having fun or you're ready for some fun. Nice young meat. Real nice. It looks like a rocket ready to take off. You know, you're just my type: young. My name is Hank, by the way, from St. Louis."

"I'm Kevin."

"Cute name. Would you like to go behind those rocks over there with me, Kevin, and have some fun? I'll make it worth your while."

Kevin felt panic again. "I don't know."

"I'll suck your cock and make it feel heavenly. I love young cock, and yours looks like it could use a good suck."

Just then Kevin saw a bronze-skinned boy and a man disappear behind the rocks near the cliffs.

"Come on," Hank said, taking Kevin's hand. "I'll make it worth your while."

Kevin allowed himself to be led. He was as curious and excited as he was nervous. He wanted to see what that bronze-skinned boy was up to.

The first thing Kevin saw as they stepped behind the rocks was the bronze-skinned boy lying back against a boulder, hips thrust forward as his man-friend kneeled in front of him and sucked his slender brown cock. The man growled appreciatively as he sucked, his saliva dripping from the boy's tight brown nuts, his hand jerking as he jacked off. When the boy saw Kevin, he smiled at him with dazzling white teeth, then glanced in the other direction as if to draw Kevin's attention to an even-wilder scene.

Beyond the boy getting sucked, another bronze-skinned boy crouched on all fours on the sand as a black-bearded giant with bulging muscles, kneeling behind the youth, his hands encircling the boy's slender waist, humped the boy's up-turned rump. At first, Kevin thought the man was sliding his massive cock between the boy's golden-brown thighs, but then he realized that the enormous cock was sliding in and out of the boy's body, in and out of his ass! It was an incredible sight!

"Beautiful!" Hank said, jerking off as he stared just as wide-eyed as Kevin. "Talk about an elastic hole! That monster would split me in half. Would you like a cock that big up your cute butt, Kevin?"

"I don't think so."

Hank laughed, pushing Kevin back against a boulder. "Don't worry, I'm into sucking."

Kevin relaxed against the rock as Hank dropped down in front of him and kissed his cock, which was sticking up at an acute angle at the sky. Hank licked Kevin's balls, then crouched and kissed Kevin's feet, licking across the toes. Kevin watched, fascinated. It was like the guy was worshiping him.

Hank moved back up, licking, nibbling, and kissing Kevin's shins, knees, and thighs. He growled as he nuzzled and licked Kevin's balls again, and Kevin panted, his cock flexing, youthful sap oozing from his pisshole. Hank gently sucked both of Kevin's balls into his mouth and Kevin started to jerk off.

Hank pushed Kevin's hand off his cock. "Naughty boy, don't be impatient! I'll take care of that." He kissed Kevin's hips, licked his stomach, slid up and sucked his pink, erect nipples. He lifted both of Kevin's arms so he could sniff and lick Kevin's armpits.

"God, what a smell!" Hank sighed, inhaling deeply. "Young pits drive me crazy!" He tried to kiss Kevin on the mouth but Kevin turned his head away. Hank kissed his cheek and dropped down again. Kevin gasped as the man swallowed his cock.

The bronze-skinned boy next to him grinned, watching Kevin get sucked. Now they were both getting sucked at the same time.

Kevin sighed, fucking his cock in and out of Hank's practiced mouth. The feeling was exquisite! He almost came with each wiggle and thrust of his boy-cock between the firm ring of Hank's hot lips and as Hank churned his fat, slightly rough tongue at the ultra-sensitive underside of Kevin's knob.

The boy to Kevin's right started gasping, muttering under his breath. His eyes rolled back and he cried out, "Ahhhh! Aiehhh!" Soon he was rocking his brown hips and pumping his spunk down the gulping throat of the man sucking him. Kevin rocked his own hips faster, able to sense what the other boy was feeling, on the verge of shooting off himself.

The giant fucking the other boy, as if stimulated by the sucked boy's orgasm, started to hump and grunt like a bull, plunging his cock rapidly into the slender loins of the youth whose waist his hands encircled. The fucked boy, his hand a blur on his cock, whimpered in high-pitched tones and began to squirt jism onto the sand. The giant bellowed, "Yahhhh!" and shot his load into the body of the ejaculating youth.

The sight was too much! Kevin's eyes rolled back and his toes clutched sand. A surge of ecstasy nearly blew the top of his head off and he half-screamed, his body jerking like a rag doll's as he shot his spunk down Hank's throat. He felt hot splashes against his shins and feet as Hank himself unloaded. Next to them, the man drinking the other boy's cum shot thick, juicy wads onto the boy's sinewy brown insteps and brown, pink-nailed toes. There was so much cum in the air that Kevin could smell it.

When Kevin recovered from his orgasmic trance, he saw that money was changing hands. The man who had sucked off the other boy handed him some currency that looked to Kevin like play money, but the grinning boy, his cock still half hard and shiny with saliva, flashed the bills at Kevin as if to impress him, then went running off as if to spend them. The man who'd paid him followed.

Hank closed Kevin's hand around a twenty-dollar bill, U.S. "How's that? Enough?"

"I guess," Kevin said, looking in wonder at the bill. He was actually being paid for getting sucked!

"Doll, I really wish I could stay around and enjoy you some more, but I'm flying back in a few hours and gotta run. I wish we'd met a week ago, when I first got here."

Kevin was only half listening. Distracting him was the bearded muscleman, who was standing now and had picked up the boy he'd just fucked, and was French kissing him. The boy had his arms around the man's bull-neck and his legs clamped around the man's waist as the man crushed his slender frame to his massive chest and muscled abdomen. Kevin watched, fascinated, as the man's rigid cock snaked back into the boy's hole with an easy slide.

"Lord, what a bull that man is!" Hank said. "A regular Minotaur! He's been fucking the local boys nonstop all week. Absolutely insatiable! And what a cock! Drives the boys nuts. They all want to get fucked by it. And he's filthy rich besides. You've probably seen his yacht anchored out there offshore. They call him Frederick and claim he lives in a castle near the Black Sea – or is it the Black Forest? A castle packed with boys, probably. Some men have all the luck!"

Frederick and the boy were kissing as if their mouths were permanently fused, staring into each other's eyes as Frederick, juggling the boy's asscheeks in his bearlike paws, humped upward into the boy's ass, driving all ten inches of his thick fuck-spike into the boy's tight butt. His balls looked the size of tennis balls and banged the boy's asscheeks with each upward thrust. The man shuddered, let out a cry, and began pumping another load of hot spunk up the boy's ass, some of which leaked out and dripped from his nuts. The boy gasped with each explosion into his body.

"I've really gotta go," Hank said, "or I'll miss my flight. So long, Kevin darling, I'll remember you always."

Kevin watched as Frederick gave the boy he'd fucked a wad of bills, then swatted him playfully on the ass, sending him on his way. As soon as the boy was out of sight, the man turned his attention to Kevin. His dark, fiery eyes made Kevin shiver under their scrutiny as he looked Kevin up and down. He seemed as much animal as human, and dangerous like a grizzly. When Frederick flexed his erect Satyr-cock at Kevin and smiled, Kevin blushed to his toes, then panicked and fled.

. . .

Kevin was no longer completely broke but had the twenty dollars Hank had given him, enough money at least for some food when he got hungry. And when that money ran out, he knew where he could get more.

As the day wore on, he continued scouting the long stretch of beach where only men and boys wandered nude, and he found that there were several other private areas behind sea rocks where men had sex with the local boys and with each other. Always the men, most of them tourists of various nationalities, paid for the services of the local boys they enjoyed, and the slender, grinning, bronze-skinned youths immediately ran off to spend their windfalls, only to return a few hours later to peddle their rigid young cocks and satin-skinned flesh again. Though propositioned several times himself and offered money, Kevin declined to go with his pursuers. He was still a bit timid, and he had things on his mind.

He had made a decision: he would not go back to the hotel. He would not see the Monster or his mother again and give them the pleasure of torturing him. All he had left now was a pair of underwear briefs and the twenty-dollar bill he'd wrapped up inside them. Although he was scared – nearly out of his mind scared – he felt better than he had in months. He was scared, but he was free, and he thought he could happily spend years naked on this beach, feeding men his cock in exchange for what money he needed. He couldn't think of a more pleasurable way to make a living.

"Greetings, my young friend."

Kevin jumped. He hadn't realized he had company until he felt the hand on his shoulder. He turned and found himself staring at an abdomen constructed of meshed-together segments of thick muscle. A bearded bear-of-a-man was looking down at him, the man called Frederick, the man with the yacht and the castle who fucked a dozen boys a day with his torpedo-like cock.

"You are American, yes?" the man said with a heavy accent. Kevin nodded, hardly able to face him. The man's eyes glinted as if with fire. The bearded giant both thrilled him and scared him to death. "I have been watching you for hours, beautiful boy, following you, watching you. You see, I am in love with you." His hairy paws gripped Kevin's shoulders. His enormous cock was sticking straight out, inches from Kevin's chest, its foreskin half-retracted as it throbbed with each powerful beat of the man's heart. A drop of lubricant oozed from the half-inch-long slit at the tip of the moist purple knob. "I love you and must have you. You must come with me. I will reward you beyond your wildest dreams."

Kevin, if he had any will to resist, had no strength to do so as the man guided him behind some rocks. With one hand on Kevin's blond head, Frederick used the other hand to peel back his foreskin completely and he rubbed his searing-hot glans on Kevin's cheeks, nose, and lips. The scent of uncut man-cock made Kevin dizzy and drove him slightly crazy. He moaned, licking the man's dickhead as if it were an ice cream cone. The salty, musky taste made him drunk. He stuck his tongue into the open slit of Frederick lube-oozing cock, tongue-fucking it. Then he engulfed the head, stuffing his mouth with it as if with a fist. He drilled his tongue deeper into the man's pisshole while sucking ravenously on the juicy knob.

"Oh yah, yahh, my angel!" Frederick forced his dickhead down Kevin's throat, choking him. His body shuddered and his flexing cock nearly lifted Kevin's head off as he poured a torrent of salty spunk down Kevin's gullet. Though choking, Kevin managed to swallow, drinking it all and sucking for more.

When Frederick was finished, he cupped Kevin's face in his hands and kissed him on the mouth. Kevin sucked the man's tongue. He knew he wanted Frederick as much as Frederick wanted him.

. . .

The sun had set and the sky and sea were a blaze of reds, lavenders, oranges, and blues. The yacht rocked gently, deepening the feelings of warmth and bliss Kevin felt. Across the water the lights of the tourist hotels that stood in silhouette on the hills above the beach twinkled. In one of those hotels, Kevin knew, the Monster was fuming, planning sadistic punishments for him when he returned. But he would not return. He would never return.

"More wine?" Frederick tipped the bottle's mouth over Kevin's glass. Kevin giggled. "I'm getting drunk."

Frederick, hugging Kevin from behind as they half reclined on the large, luxuriously padded chaise lounge on deck, worked his enormous hot cock against Kevin's ass and lower back. "I like drunk boys. They say Ganymede was often tipsy."

Kevin sipped his wine and squirmed in the man's arms as Frederick kissed, licked, and nibbled the back of his neck and shoulders, giving him goose bumps and hot flashes simultaneously. Kevin's cock was sticking straight up in the air between his thighs. As their master made love to Kevin, deckhands and servants, all of them handsome youths, paused to watch as they went about their duties and uttered words of approval and lust in various tongues. All the youths were as naked as Kevin and Frederick, and most of them were just as erect.

"You must not be jealous," Frederick said. "As long as you are not jealous and live harmoniously with my other boys, you will know pleasures beyond any you have dreamed. Unfortunately, some boys become jealous of my attentions to the others, make scenes, and must leave my employ prematurely. I keep fifteen to twenty boys in my inner circle. Some stay with me two, three, even four years, until they are past their prime. Others, the jealous ones, only remain a short time. Those who remain, once they pass the prime of their beauty and must leave the inner circle, are rewarded with excellent positions, becoming, for example, deckhands aboard this yacht." He licked the nape of Kevin's neck. "Delicious boy, so delectable, and a virgin no less. A prize catch."

Kevin shivered as the man licked him. It both terrified and thrilled him each time Frederick referred to his "virginity," knowing that Frederick intended to take it soon.

The man sucked on his ear, twisting his tongue into the ear canal. He shivered and squirmed. The man's attentions drove him wild. He loved the feel of Frederick's big, hairy muscles against his velvet-smooth skin. The contrast of his boyish flesh with the hairy, almost abrasive flesh of the muscular he-man made him feel more naked than naked. Frederick pushed Kevin forward onto his hands and knees on the chaise and began to lick his ass, holding apart the cheeks, slurping the length of the tingling cleft, kissing and tonguing the pink anus, wiggling his tongue into it and sliding it deep into Kevin's sensitive hole.

Kevin sighed, his cockhead pecking at his navel as his cock stood ramrod straight under his belly. Frederick could lick his ass all night if he wanted to. He'd never felt anything like it, had never realized that his asshole could feel so wonderful.

"Delicious boy," Frederick growled, eating out Kevin's throbbing young hole. He drove his tongue in deep again and Kevin almost jumped out of his skin.

One of the servants, a muscular blond youth who had stopped to watch, stood before them masturbating. His large phallus dripped as he worked the foreskin over the flange of the knob.

"You may give it to him, Karl," Frederick said. "He will appreciate it."

The young servant moved closer, put a hand on Kevin's head, and stuffed his cock into Kevin's mouth. In seconds the big cock began to quiver and ejaculate and Kevin guzzled the youth's thick, salty-sweet load. The deckhand sighed, withdrawing, and Kevin's lips smacked together as the dripping phallus left his mouth.

"You are beautiful with a cock in your mouth," Frederick said. "Not long ago Karl himself was still part of my inner circle, but, alas, you see he has grown into a handsome, muscular youth – an Adonis to be sure, but no longer a Ganymede."

Frederick smeared greasy lubricant on Kevin's anus as he spoke. He worked lube into Kevin's aching hole, then greased the entire length of his massive cock. He turned Kevin around to face him, and had Kevin, kneeling, straddle his loins. "Sit, darling."

As Kevin lowered his ass, Frederick's dickhead spread Kevin's asscheeks and seared his anus.

"Sit, darling," Frederick said again. "Just sit and relax. We are in no hurry."

Kevin knew that the huge cockhead throbbing between his asscheeks could never enter him. It was impossible. Still, it felt wonderful to have the hot phallus kiss his anus, and he rotated his butt, reveling in the sensation. He'd never dreamed his ass could be so sensitive, that it could so throb and ache. He was dying to feel Frederick's cock inside him, but he knew it could never happen because it was physically impossible. He remembered the boy Frederick had fucked on the beach and marveled at the feat. The boy, though smaller than Kevin, must have been constructed differently to allow such a stallion-cock to enter him.

Kevin felt something slip, felt something give way. Though he felt no pain, he realized that Frederick's cockhead was no longer just kissing his anus, but that it had entered him. He wiggled his loins and felt the fullness of the man's cock anchored inside him.

Frederick was sighing: "Oh, marvelous! Oh, yahhh!"

Kevin felt himself sliding – a long, long slide – and Frederick massive hairy balls tickled his asscheeks. Kevin's mouth gaped, as much with astonishment as with the sensation of being stuffed with nearly ten inches of rigid man-cock. "Fuck!"

"Yes, fuck!" Frederick eyes rolled ecstatically. His hands encircled Kevin's hips, rotating Kevin's loins as he slowly churned his phallus in Kevin's body.

Kevin clung to him, panting, his arms draped around Frederick's neck, his open mouth pressed to Frederick, tears of joy and lust running down his cheeks, tears that Frederick licked off.

"My darling!" Frederick whispered. "Yah, yah, my darling boy!" His hands slid up and down Kevin's back as Kevin squirmed against him. "Fuck me, my angel, fuck me!"

Kevin's heart jack hammered as he squirmed against the man's muscles and fucked himself on the massive cock. He'd never dreamed anything could feel like this. He felt the same sensations in his asshole as in his cock: itching, maddening, throbbing, liquid sensations that spread throughout his body. It was as if his entire being had become a huge, pulsating phallus.

He mashed his mouth to Frederick's, sucking and gnawing on the man's thick lips, inhaling his breath, sucking on his tongue, drooling into his mouth. He gazed into the man's fiery eyes as his tight virgin ass bounced, Frederick's cock sliding in and out of him. They panted and grunted in unison, with such wild abandon that their cries of pleasure could surely be heard a long way off over the water.

Frederick's eyes turned back in his skull, only the whites visible. His body shuddered. He let out a bull-like cry that was surely heard on shore. His cock flexed and his molten spunk exploded from his cock and burst into Kevin's loins as if from a volcano. The feel of the man coming inside him sent Kevin into ecstasy. His vision blurred and he cried out, his voice as high-pitched as a girl's as his entire body spasmed and his boy-jism shot against the heaving, contracting muscles of Frederick's abdomen and chest and Frederick muttered, "Yah, yah, yah!"

Dazed on pleasure, drunk on wine, Kevin giggled as Frederick lifted him as if he weighed nothing, held him up like a toy doll, and licked the jism off his stomach and chest. Frederick lowered Kevin again, back onto his upright cock, and this time the prick slipped with ease into his no-longer-virgin ass.

SLAVE AUCTION
Daniel Miller

Last June, my friend Michael and I actually traveled halfway across the country to be auctioned off as slaves. It's true: he had read about the event in a leather magazine and immediately signed us both up. His voice practically shook with excitement when he described how we'd be stripped down, exposed, and probably even fucked in front of a whole room of rugged, horny leathermen. All the while, they'd be bidding real money for the privilege of taking us home and doing all that and more to us in private!

The specifics were up to the buyer, of course, but the basic idea was that he would assume complete control of his purchase for two weeks. He could take us anywhere, and do pretty much anything with us short of injuring or marking our bodies without our consent. The club would make sure all the rules would be followed so that everyone would feel satisfied at the end. Whoever purchased us would also have to provide us with transportation home after our two weeks of voluntary servitude. It was all very civilized for those who cared to participate. The way Michael had it figured, it would be the perfect way to spend our summer vacation from college, and I couldn't help but agree!

The private club where the auction would take place was an innocuous little den, tucked into the basement of a boarded-up retail shop. We entered a shadowed passageway that smelled of man musk, and the stone walls seemed coated with perspiration. A broad-chested man, his head completely shaved and his eyes obscured by mirrored sunglasses, met us at the entrance and escorted us through a side door so draped in shadows that we would never have noticed it on our own.

We soon found ourselves in a much larger chamber already filled with guys of all ages. There must have been 20 or 30 of them. One or two of them were wrestling out of their jeans and t-shirts or tank tops, and a few were in leather thongs or jock straps. A growing number of them wore nothing at all. Their fleshy cocks, both cut and uncut, waggled around in various states of arousal as they drank in one another's unabashed nudity.

A tall man with a blond moustache suddenly came striding toward us, a short whip clenched in his gloved hand. He flicked it in front of our crotches menacingly, then gave us the same lewd smile that the first guy had. "Take off your clothes," he barked. "Then you can get in line with the others and wait for your turn on the block."

Retracting the whip, he stepped back and crossed his arms. The would-be slaves who were already naked shifted forward in a long, flesh-colored wave, craning their necks over their masters' shoulders to watch our self-conscious little striptease.

I felt my skin growing warm and sweaty all over as I slowly peeled away my shirt, socks, and finally my jeans. The only time I'd ever gotten undressed in front of so many guys before had been in a locker room. That time, though, no one was staring right at me--or at my cock as it flopped free and bounced against my blushing thigh. My shaft was already stiffening, my bulb-like glans lengthening and filling with hot blood. A thick trickle of perspiration oozed into my butt-crack as I bared my ass to the captive audience surrounding me.

Now completely naked, I lifted my chin and scanned the crowd. Most of the slaves' faces were slack with lust. A few of them were openly groping their own naked cocks and balls as their hungry gazes met mine. A sudden, overpowering excitement swept through me. The bald guy who had first brought us into the room came toward me, lifting a shiny metal strap from one of the hooks on his belt. My pulse was throbbing as he shoved two calloused fingers against my neck and fastened the collar as tightly as it would go. Then he hooked his boot around the back of my left knee and shoved me down hard. I bit back a grimace and a grunt as I hit the floor on all fours. A second later I heard a leash being snapped into place at my throat. Out of the corner of my eye, I could see the blond performing the same ritual on Michael.

The crowd of gaping slaves parted, and for the first time I saw that only a gauzy black curtain separated our chamber from a much larger room. It was toward this curtain that my master was now leading me. My hands and knees kept striking the bare floor painfully as I struggled to keep up with his long strides.

As we approached the curtain, I heard an expectant murmur of voices. This turned to outright applause and loud, ear-splitting whistles when we fluttered through the curtain. My Master tugged on my lead, forcing me to kneel upright, with my head pointed up at the high, dark ceiling. I couldn't see a single face in what sounded like a fairly large audience, but I could certainly feel the heat as their famished stares racked my pitifully enslaved body.

I heard a scuffling sound beside me, and the cheers intensified as Michael took his place beside me. We knelt side by side like raunchy bookends, our hearts pounding almost audibly and our throbbing cocks pointed straight up in the air.

While we remained on our knees, sweating hard but not daring to move, an emcee shuffled his notes at a microphone stand in the corner.

"Next we have a very special lot. This, it appears, will be their first time at auction, and some lucky top in the audience tonight will have the pleasure of breaking in both their beautiful virgin assholes at the same time!"

His words prompted another round of raucous cheers from the audience. Behind us, the blond guy and his bald colleague set to work demonstrating our best assets for the crowd.

My Master pulled on a latex glove, letting the wristband snap against his tight skin. "Squat on your feet and part yourself," he commanded, and I immediately obeyed. Knowing what was coming next, I tried to relax as he knelt and probed me roughly. His knuckles prodded painfully against the insides of my ass-cheeks as I desperately held them apart, struggling to maintain my balance. I'd tried fisting only a couple of times before, but never in this position, and never with an audience!

I trembled as the smooth, cold latex slithered up into my hot tunnel. The bald guy held nothing back, snaking his first two fingers all the way in without even pausing. Then, after tickling my inner ass-walls to get me to open farther, he shoved his pinkie and ring fingers smoothly past my clutching sphincter. I nearly went limp with enjoyment, and I had to force myself to stifle a moan.

"As you can see," the emcee drawled smoothly, "this young man has plenty of storage space should his new master care to make use of it."

I took a deep breath as the bald guy moved his whole fist deep inside my ass-canal, then started unfurling his fingers one at a time. Unable to hold back, I let out a groan that seemed to vibrate his burly hand and wrist against my guts!

We stayed in that position, my whole torso filled by that burly guy's arm and fist, my prostate pulsing with need and my mind shifting into the dizzy oblivion of ecstasy. Meanwhile, the blond guy who had taken control of Michael stepped forward and stripped away his shirt and codpiece. His meaty dick and balls swung ponderously below his sagging belt, a tiny gold hoop glistening in his pierced scrotum. Somehow it made him look even more naked, and dangerous in an almost unbearably arousing way.

"Our virgin slaves need a Master who will dominate them both physically and mentally, but with the care that a true master shows his servants," explained the emcee. The blond guy, his fat dick growing slowly erect, moved Michael into a standing position at the edge of the platform. He unclipped Michael's leash and used it to slap his bare buttocks and low-hanging balls.

In spite of myself, my own rod swelled as the red welts appeared on my friend's pale, narrow backside and thighs.

"As you are all aware, virgins aren't so easy to come by these days," the emcee joked. "These newcomers need an experienced Master who will teach them to appreciate the finer points of submission. May we now hear your offers on this pair of fine, soft young cocks?"

As the bidding began, a light shove sent Michael to his knees. His cock stirred and reddened as he went down. He remained in profile for the spectators, the hard curve of his seven-inch prick standing out in clear relief under the harsh white light. The audience seemed to take in a collective breath as the blond man started lightly tapping his short whip against the side of his thigh.

Michael posed on all fours, gazing at his Master's bared torso with a respectful, passive face. To no one's surprise, he buried his mouth between the guy's legs when he drew close enough. As Michael sucked the heavy club of flesh, his face growing red with the embarrassment he obviously craved, he spread his legs to display his swelling asshole to the audience.

I – and no doubt the bald guy who was still fisting me – watched intently as the blond man augmented his hip-thrusts with a few well-placed whip strokes along Michael's buttocks. Michael was already coming, a distinct flush spreading along his sides and across as much of his groin area as I could see. Still he bore down on the blonde's bucking cock, stifling his own orgasm with a visible effort. The bidding reached delirious proportions.

Michael spasmed suddenly, his dick distending toward the floor and gobs of stringy jizz splattering the platform beneath him. With a snarl of pleasure, the blond leaned way back, his own creamy cum bubbling visibly around Michael's straining lips. It seemed to go on forever – and then I lost track of the progress of their frenzied humping as the bald guy began to remove his fist from my fully stretched body cavity.

I felt a quiver of pleasure run through me as he reballed his fist and stimulated those same burning nerve endings as he pulled his arm out of my body. Tiny flames of the most beautiful pain I'd ever felt lapped at every fiber of my core, and I was astonished to feel a tingling glob of pre-cum spurt from my cock tip. Again the howls and gasps of the spectators reached a deafening pitch as the three of us came together, slicking the platform with triple streams of thick, gooey cum.

In that moment, my spurting cock, the sea of admiring eyes focused on my totally bare body, and the increasingly frantic beat of my excited pulse made me totally forget myself. I fell to the platform and squeezed my eyes shut as an orgasmic storm raged through me, tearing my spirit, my self-consciousness, and maybe even my throbbing cock, up by the roots!

When I opened my eyes, I found that Michael and I had both been purchased for what seemed to me a hefty sum. The audience was chanting a simple, one-syllable word that I couldn't make out at first. It took me a moment to come down to earth and understand that it was the name of our new Master, and that he was, at that very moment, standing up and making his way to the platform.

He would have been an impressive man in any setting. Now, decked out in full leathers, with his long moustache blending into the curve of his sharply defined jaw and his stern black eyes framed by thick, clay-colored beetle brows, he was positively, and excruciatingly, intimidating. I felt my balls clench all over again as he hopped up onto the stage and headed straight for Michael and me.

His imposing frame and commanding manner made me instinctively shift into utter submission. I remained flat on the floor even though my twitching cock was bent at an uncomfortable angle, my eyes focused on his chunky boots. He stopped just inches away from my head. The audience was hushed as he slowly slid one of those steel-tipped toes toward my parched mouth.

Gingerly, taking care not to move any part of my body except my jaw, I extended my tongue and licked the coarse edge of his thick sole. My tongue came away gritty and sour-tasting, but I immediately slithered it back out and repeated the boot-cleansing ritual when he slid his other foot parallel to the first.

My blood ran deliciously cold when he let out a ferocious laugh. From my position on the floor, I saw his ankles rocking as he shifted his weight and spread his legs around my head. He stopped when his big feet were about eighteen inches apart, and I heard the growl of a zipper being pulled slowly open. I heard the hiss of leather as he peeled his tight pants away from his muscular hips.

Again without moving my head, I rolled my eyes to see his fat cock, swathed in a mass of long, reddish hairs, dangling down at me. I cringed for a moment, startled to see that his glans was pierced straight through with a barbell-shaped gold ampallang which already glistened with pre-cum. As I imagined that thick, studded organ sliding into my already-ravaged asshole, my sphincter began to burn and clench up with overpowering fear and desire.

However, that particular sensation was apparently not what he had in mind for me at the moment. I had just begun to raise myself on trembling arms when my new Master bent. He shoved his pants all the way down by turning them inside out against his legs, then spun around so that his ass was poised over my face. As he reached back to part his big, hairy cheeks with his hands, he commanded that Michael crawl over to suck his cock.

"I want you two fuckers to clean me out back and front," he growled, wrenching his butt-globes farther apart with his enormous hands. The flesh of his fingers and palms looked weathered and hard, roughened no doubt by the handle of the bullwhip he wore at his side. "And believe me – I'd better not feel even one dry patch of skin anywhere between my cock and my asshole!"

As he spoke, he slowly twisted his head and looked down his shoulder at my face. His expression was rocky, and his drooping moustache curved around a lusty, sharp-toothed smile. To my surprise, though, his eyes were anything but cold or brutal, as I'd expected. Instead, I saw only was a blazing, unflinching warmth that spoke of desire and compassion as well as discipline and humiliation. In the two weeks of service we had pledged to this man, Michael and I would learn how to slake his desires by making our own fantasies real...for all three of us.

"Master," I whispered. Eagerly, I jumped up to my knees and applied my face to the musky-scented cavern between my Master's parted ass-cheeks. Salivating with need, I plied my tongue up and down his tangy crack, poking into his asshole on the upstroke and then moving down past his perineum whenever I dipped my head.

While I rimmed him hard, yet sensually, on the other side of his groin, Michael got to work tongue-bathing Master's bejeweled prick. He, too, was working himself up into a lather as he scoured glans, shaft, balls, and even that overgrown, rust-colored pubic jungle. To my intense satisfaction, we could hear Master groaning with satisfaction.

At one point, as we were both diving down to refresh the big man's best-hidden crevices, our tongues touched in that moist, murky man-grove. Both of us paused – and I almost felt like smiling ecstatically. Figuring that such a light-hearted gesture would go against the spirit of the event, though, I did my damnedest to conceal the greatest rush of pleasure I had ever felt in my life.

THE TRYST
Daniel Miller

I sat at the bar, running nervous fingers up and down my beer bottle. It was only Wednesday night, but plenty of hot guys were already milling around the smoke-filled club. A few were cruising each other on the dance floor, and one leather-clad couple were swaying close together. I watched as the taller of the two, a rough-looking, bearded guy with a snake tattoo on the left side of his neck, stuck out his pierced tongue and forced his partner's lips open with it. The smaller guy inhaled deeply, kissing him back and thrusting his torso forward. Through the smoky haze, I could just see the big dude reach down, discreetly unzip his buddy's faded jeans, and grope his exposed, meaty balls.

Shifting on my seat to relieve the pressure in my swollen balls, I glanced away from them just long enough to check my watch. How late would Devlin show up this time? I wondered. Maybe he wouldn't be here at all. He liked to keep me waiting, never doubting how feverishly I was thinking of him – or how savagely my pulse was beating in my horny cock the whole time.

I glanced back at the dance floor in time to see the guy with the tattoo heading toward the back of the club, pulling his submissive companion along by the crotch. Was that what I'd looked like on that first night with Devlin, nearly a month ago now? He hadn't been holding my nuts like that, but he might as well have been. Smirking, he'd hustled me off in the same direction, eventually shoving me through an obscure metal door behind the broken cigarette machine in the corner. I'd literally stumbled into a dingy storeroom, piled high with empty cardboard boxes and discarded bits of ruined furniture. The door immediately swung shut again, cutting off every sound except the pulsating, muddy-sounding beat from the dance floor.

I'd regained my balance just in time to pivot around and see him open his fly and wrench out his meat. The only light was what glimmered through the crack near his feet, and his mushroom-shaped cockhead glowed thick and dark through the relative gloom. He wrapped his fist around his bulging shaft, then used his wrist to flick his pendulous organ back and forth. It hardened a little each time he moved it, until it seemed to writhe like a gigantic eel in his grasp.

"I'm Devlin," he grunted. "You don't need to bother me with your name."

Helpless with the force of my lust, I dropped to my knees and wrapped my lips around his pulsating tool. His blunt head seemed to bruise my tonsils as I shoved my head forward, while his solid shank pressed my tongue down flat. I had to fight off an urge to choke as I sucked him hard, lifting my hand to rub his plum-sized balls through his jeans. I felt them tighten and the hot cum bubble up in his slit right away, and then, suddenly, he put his hand on my forehead and shoved me back roughly.

His cock slid from my mouth with a slurp, a few droplets of cum stinging the tip of my tongue as he withdrew. Instinctively, I'd started to dive forward again, but his firm hand held me in place while he came outside my gaping lips. His slit gushed like a fire hose, spraying his cream all over my cheeks and chin. In the dim light, I could see that he was clutching his shaft in his fist once again, guiding himself along the surface of my lips and then under my nose. The bittersweet scent of cum clogged my nostrils, making my head spin.

After he'd smeared the last of his load on my face, he yanked back his cock and brought it down hard once again, clubbing my jaw line with the bulbous head. Then, abruptly, he'd spun around on his boot heel and zipped himself up while he was turning to go.

"Later," he said gruffly. "Tomorrow night, maybe."

Alone in the near darkness, I yanked open my own pants and jacked myself in desperation. I had gone so hard my shaft and balls were almost numb with strain. When I had finished, I stuffed myself back inside and rushed back out into the bar. There was no sign of him, but several guys at the bar smirked at my flushed face and wild manner. I considered asking them where he'd gone, but recovered what was left of my dignity just in time and went home to jack off again. I had, of course, returned to the same bar on the following night, but Devlin didn't reappear.

My second experience with him came more than a week later. I'd been at the end of the bar, wondering if I could get up enough nerve to cruise a hot college guy on the other side of the room. I'd sensed someone moving in behind me, so I swiveled around on my barstool. I found myself looking up at Devlin, grinning at me through a two-day growth of beard on his face. To my surprise, he addressed me by my name, which I knew I'd never given him. Then he tilted his head toward the dance floor and started walking in that direction.

I slid off my stool and hurried after him. As I'd expected, he wove through a few dancing couples and headed for that metal door again. I paused, waiting for him to wrench it open, but this time he didn't bother. Instead, he turned around and fished out his dick right there in the open.

"Here?" I croaked, looking around in shock. Sucking a guy off in public wasn't something I'd ever done before. The guys on the dance floor had paused, and some of them brazenly stopped dancing and wandered over to watch. Even in that place, such an obvious display wasn't that common. I could feel my face going scarlet, the heat suffusing my groin as my nervous but excited cock sprang bolt upright. Devlin didn't speak. He just spread his feet and tilted his hips forward. His bulging meat jabbed out at me like an accusing finger.

Two minutes later, I was on my knees again, inhaling his thick meat for all I was worth. A whole crowd had gathered around us, murmuring and jostling each other with excitement while I brought his demanding tool swiftly to orgasm. Once again, though, he yanked himself away at the last minute before he came, then and aimed his spurting cock at me and covered my chin, neck, and the front of my shirt in cream.

My whole body burned with humiliation and excitement while he again went through the ritual of slapping my face with his cockhead. When I tried to crawl away, one hand ineffectually in front of the tent in my blue jeans, Devlin grabbed my shoulder and held me in place. His eyes shone with an unspoken command, and I obeyed him as if I were in a trance. In front of half the guys in the bar – or maybe it was more by that point – I jerked myself to orgasm, strewing a ribbon of pearly cum on the floor. Once again, Devlin zipped up and smirked at me as the crowd began to disperse. "Later. Next week," he growled, not specifying a day or a time.

And so it was Wednesday again – nearly seven days since he'd said it, and I was still waiting. I had been on the same barstool every night for a week, periodically scanning the crowd in hopes of a glimpse of him, finding myself disappointed if any other pair of eyes lifted to meet mine. I kept my cock hard by reliving those two previous encounters. Any inhibitions I might have felt before were gone. I was so desperate to satisfy him again that this time I would have gone down on him right there at the bar if he'd wished it.

The two leathermen on the dance floor had disappeared from view. I knew they were behind the metal door, in the same dingy storeroom where I'd first blown Devlin, the smaller guy serving his dominant lover as lustily as I'd served mine. My cock was aching so badly that I discreetly shoved a hand between my thighs and kneaded the painful denim-covered lump. I felt a few droplets of pre-cum squeeze against my cotton shorts. I exhaled deeply, partly from the relief my hand was providing, and partly from despair that I would get no further satisfaction that night. I half-closed my eyes, shifting my weight on the seat.

The first thing I felt when the figure moved in on me was the brush of hot breath on my cheek. Then a heavy hand dropped over the one I had in my lap, the fingers forcing mine deeper into my swollen mound. I snapped upright to see Devlin standing right between my splayed thighs, the collar of his leather jacket turned up until it touched his cheeks. The scruffy outgrowth on his pale face looked longer and coarser now, giving his grin an even more sinister aspect. I was afraid of the way he looked, but I was even more desperate to give myself to him utterly.

"You waited," he said unnecessarily. Then, before I could respond, he pulled his hand from my crotch, hauled me to my feet, and pressed me against the wall at the end of the bar. Bending slightly, he matter-of-factly peeled my jeans and cum-stained Jockeys down to the midpoint of my thighs. I gasped, a squawk of protest dying in my clenched throat.

I stood there by the bar, the front door only a few feet away, motionless and exposed. Along with the rest of the guys who happened to be standing nearby, Devlin stepped back and took a long, critical look at my bright red hard-on as it wavered pitifully above my hairy balls in the smoky air. The blush that spread over my body only seemed to concentrate the heat in my crotch. I thought I might pass out from the humiliation, but at the same time I wanted nothing more than for him to reach out and grab my desperate shaft.

He did no such thing, of course. Instead, he put both hands on my shoulders and spun me around, shoving my face against the gritty wall. I grunted as he parted my ass-cheeks and shoved two fingers roughly into my asshole, rummaging in there like he was measuring my canal for size. The crowd of observers were murmuring again, and one of them even laughed out loud. When Devlin jerked his fingers back out with a wet, popping sound, I didn't know whether I wanted to faint or come.

I turned back around as Devlin sniffed and licked his fingertips, then nodded his permission for me to hike up my pants. I bent over and did so, mortified tears stinging my eyelids, my cock so stiff it barely fit back inside my damp Y-fronts. When I straightened up again, Devlin's thumb strayed over the curve of my throat. He pressed on my Adam's apple for a moment, making me suck in a quick gasp. "Let's go for a walk," he said. This time, he stood aside so that I could precede him out of the bar.

It had just rained, and the air had a steely, damp smell that made me feel grungy and refreshed all at the same time. Devlin slid his hand on my ass while we were walking, and I was grateful that my Henley shirt hung low enough in the back that no one passing by could have seen him squeezing my buns and nudging my crack through my pants. As we turned down a dingy side street, he slipped his hand all the way inside and tickled my rear crease with his fingernails. I gasped when he poked against my asshole, just lightly enough to get my pisshole pulsating and wet again.

"My apartment," he grumbled, steering me toward a run-down brownstone. His finger in my asshole directed me up the stairs, and he didn't remove it until he had unlocked the door and shoved me inside his front room, flicking on an overhead light that seemed impossibly harsh after the dim secrecy of the barroom.

Fiercely, he whirled around and pulled me against his chest, wrenching my zipper open again and shoving my pants back down. My short followed a moment later, and I stood in front of him naked and sweating. He pushed me to my knees as he began to peel off his own clothes, baring his magnificent body while I salivated and trembled.

When he was naked, I realized that I had never actually seen all of him in normal light. I'd missed a lot. Devlin was a thick-torsoed, extremely hairy guy, a rough black carpet stretching from his fat nipples to his plump red cock. Another coarse forest cushioned his fat, brownish nutsac.

"Suck," he demanded, shoving his hard-on into my face. Just like before, I opened my jaws and lathered him up, tickling his slit with my tongue and drawing on his rigid shaft like a straw. He moaned, leaning into me and expelling a harsh breath. Like before, I tasted the first acidic sting of his pre-cum. And, like before, as soon as I enthusiastically speeded up, he stopped me.

"Enough," he grunted, sliding his cock from my mouth. The movement was so abrupt that I tottered on my knees for a moment. While I regained my balance, Devlin circled around to lean his shins against my ass. Reaching down again, he plugged my ass with his fingers, stretching me out mercilessly. I felt my inflamed flesh buckle and expand to accommodate his harsh plunging. The quick, hard jabs of his hand and wrist soon had my hips quaking with lechery. I was almost insane with the need to feel his powerful rod sluicing into my freshly prepared back entrance.

Finally, he dropped onto his own knees as well, aiming his rubbery cockhead between my ass-cheeks and nudging my tenderized hole with the tip. He grabbed around my chest for balance, pinching my stubby tits between his fingers, alternately stretching them out and letting them snap back into place.

After so much buildup, the first hard stroke of his cock into my hot hole felt like he'd shoved a block of ice into me. I'd been fucked up the ass before, though not often, but Devlin was big and insistent enough that it felt like his fat, hard wand was splitting me open for the very first time.

He heaved himself against me with all his strength, drilling himself so deeply into my hole that it felt like the head of his cock was pounding against the back of my ballsac from within. His scratchy bush scoured the tender flesh of my ass-globes, my inner walls flexing and tugging on his deliciously pumping shaft. All the same, it somehow just didn't feel like enough.

Grunting, I reared back on my hands on knees, forcing my ass back at him until he was skewered all the way inside me. I humped backward again, my spine tingling as I felt his low-hanging balls smack my crack. I wondered if I were only imagining the fact that his nuts felt harder now, the thin skin tighter as the bounced up and down on my cheeks.

A moment later, I knew it hadn't been my imagination when Devlin's body went tense all over. His fingers froze in the middle of squeezing my nipples, leaving them compressed more tightly than if they'd been imprisoned by steel nipple clamps. Then, with a low, gut-wrenching, almost pitiful moan, he let go and blasted my shivering rectum with a genuine splash of thick, hot jizz.

Finally feeling him empty his hot cock inside me was more pleasurable than I can even describe in words. While he was shooting, I started to wriggle and squirm underneath him, coaxing every last drop from his swollen tool. His sauce was soon overflowing my back reservoir, streaming down my spread-open crack and gushing down the backs of my thighs. That got me going, and a moment later my untouched dick was spurting just as copiously as his.

We emptied our bodies of a month's worth of pent-up lust, grunting and hissing like a pair of angry beasts as we rutted in a forgotten corner of the concrete jungle. My skin, the carpet, and Devlin's hairy body were soon drenched with the pearly strands of our mingled cum.

We finished at about the same time, his cock going soft in my groove while mine dropped and swung, like a stalled pendulum, between my legs. Devlin popped out and rolled onto his side on the floor, looking at me with shimmering black eyes. I looked back, my eyes finally settling on the pooling jizz that had gathered in his thick bush.

"Let me taste it this time," I whispered. His eyelids drooping like his cock, he nodded and opened his legs, and I stuck my head between his thighs. Ignoring his cock this time, I sucked on his drained sac and lapped at the damp hairs that sprouted around it. His cum was as strong and delicious as I'd known it would be. I was still licking wildly when he thrust his fingers into my scalp and brought my head up so that I was looking into his face. His lips were once again a hard line of desire – as was his cock, which I felt growing rigid against my leg once again.

"Later?" I asked in a playful tone, boldly stroking his damp shaft with my fingers. His grip tightened against my scalp.

"No, not later," he whispered hoarsely. "Now."

I was happy to comply.

FINALLY FUCKING FRANKIE
John Patrick

Marcel saw two boys kissing high in the balcony. He sat watching them for several minutes, until they leapt up, anxious, clinging to each other. He followed the handsome couple, thinking they might be going to the theater's infamous toilet, but they disappeared instead behind the filthy curtains.

Marcel's curiosity was aroused, but he didn't dare show himself. He easily found a gap in the curtains, and carefully opened it, just wide enough to peep through. And he was very pleased with what he saw. The curtain hid the entrance to an upper balcony, no longer used. On the stairs sat the two handsome youths. He could see them much clearer now, even though the light was dim. One was pretty, slim and blond – an angel, with blue eyes and pink lips; the other was dark, fierce-looking, perhaps Puerto Rican. They were both dressed in tight faded jeans and white T-shirts. They were talking almost in a whisper, and Marcel couldn't understand a word they were saying to each other. Then they began kissing on the mouth, slipping their hands inside each other's T-shirt to caress each other's back, stomach and chest. He watched their lips meet with a surge of emotion, as if the action were taking place in slow motion. Marcel had planned to escape the old theater, having found no one who interested him, but he simply could not leave now. He remained behind the curtains. From his position he could see that the swelling in the dark one's jeans was now stretching the cloth taut. The blond put his hand on it, then went down on his knees at the feet of the Puerto Rican, who remained sitting on the steps. The blond undid the dark one's fly. Marcel saw the boy wasn't wearing underwear. His long dick, curving back a bit near the tip, sprang up between the buttons of his jeans. The blond freed his huge balls, licked them, moved his tongue up as far as his glans, then pushed his cock inside his mouth and began sucking slowly. As the suck continued, the dark one lay back and gave out little moans.

Seeing the Puerto Rican so soon reach orgasm made Marcel bolder, and he opened the curtains wider, enough to be able to see through the gap without having to hold it open. The lovers were too wrapped up in each other to notice anything. Still standing, Marcel began stroking the bulge in his own jeans, without taking his eyes off them. The sucking of the dark one by the blond was so perfect that all three of them let out a moan of satisfaction together.

The Puerto Rican made a few final thrusts between the blonde's lips, and Marcel knew the end of this little show was near. But not before the Puerto Rican, coming off his high, noticed the movement of the curtains as Marcel shook his prick, splattering cum on the fabric, and then stuffed his equipment back into his jeans. He smiled at Marcel but the Frenchman, discovered, quickly fled.

Marcel returned to the theater nearly every day on his lunch hour, hoping to get a chance with the talented blond himself, and every day he did see the blond, but the boy was always with someone else. Instead of a show behind the curtain, however, the blond left the theater with those who picked him up.

Finally, on a snowy Saturday, Marcel went to the theater late in the afternoon. His timing was perfect this time: he found the blond sitting alone high in the balcony. Marcel wasted no time and soon they were back at Marcel's tiny but elegantly appointed apartment a dozen blocks away.

Marcel took his time with the seduction, offering Frankie a drink. They sat quietly for a few minutes, sipping one of Marcel's favorite wines, chatting pleasantly, before Frankie made the first move. He joined Marcel on the couch and opened his jeans. Frankie's fingers glided slowly down the curve of Marcel's belly, to the tuft of pubic hair, and paused there. "God," he gasped, "what a cock!"

Marcel sighed, closed his eyes, but was unable to stifle the moan of delight that rose to his lips as Frankie ran his fingers delicately up the insides of his thighs. He thought he would come immediately. He thought Frankie would suck it, but, instead, Frankie wanted to get Marcel nude. He undressed him, taking his time, kissing his skin here and there, stroking Marcel's now-hard sex occasionally. Now, Marcel thought, the boy would get down to sucking it the way he had the Puerto Rican. But, no, Frankie rose to his feet and threw off his clothes, so that he was now as naked as Marcel was. When Frankie turned, he saw Marcel's fingertips were caressing his cock. Frankie stood transfixed, staring at it, continuing to be fascinated by its size and strength.

Marcel stood. Frankie took the uncut organ in his hand and squeezed it. "This is the biggest one I've ever seen," Frankie said.

"Ha!" Marcel said, as if he didn't believe him, but of course he did, for he knew, even here in Manhattan, the Frenchman was something of a legend. He lifted Frankie in his arms and led him to his bedroom, where he spread him over the center of the double bed.

"Fuck me," the boy begged, parted his legs wide.

Marcel was stunned at first; he had been dreaming of getting one of Frankie's blowjobs for days, but this was even better. Marcel loved a blowjob, but he loved fucking even more. Showing no mercy, Marcel applied lube to Frankie's willing hole, then applied some to his cock, now achingly hard.

"You want it, eh?" Marcel chuckled. "This biggest one?"

Before Frankie could reply, Marcel lay over him, reached between his legs and guided his pulsing stiffness into him. The beautiful body Marcel had coveted for months was fully ready for his entrance – he slid deeply up into him with the easiest of pushes until his belly was flat on Frankie's. Frankie threw an arm round Marcel's neck and drew his face to his, showering him with warm kisses on his lips and cheeks, while Marcel slowly rode back and forth on top of him. Marcel was letting his new lover get used to his size.

By turning his head Marcel could see in the large mirrors the reflection of his lovemaking. He saw the naked length of his own body stretched out on top of the youth's, and the rhythmic jerking of his bottom as he stepped up his attack. Frankie's adorable face was clearly to be seen in profile, his eyes wide open.

Soon, Marcel's fast little movements produced moans of ecstasy from Frankie. Frankie's slender arms were flung about Marcel's bull neck, to hold him tightly to him. Marcel watched the younger boy's graceful legs raise themselves from the bed and clamp about his waist.

"Oh, god, you're so tight," Marcel said breathlessly, his hands under Frankie to grasp the taut cheeks of his bare little bottom.

"Fuck me," Frankie moaned, his own loins jerking up to the rhythm of Marcel's heated thrusting.

"Oh, yes," Marcel gasped, hardly able to speak as the sensation of finally fucking Frankie overwhelmed him.

He pulled him tight against him, his hips jerking out of all control. "Don't stop!" Frankie pleaded. "Please don't stop!" His breath was coming in gasps, and Marcel felt his body moving in rhythm with his. Then, for an instant, Marcel's hips stilled, their movement no longer necessary. Marcel filled Frankie to overflowing as he came in a gush – a feeling so intense that Marcel cried out in both pain and pure physical delight. Frankie held the stud still between his legs, and Marcel leaned to kiss the boy. His tongue was in his mouth, then in his ear, his teeth raking Frankie's nipples. "Oh, God!" Frankie cried.

"Oh, Frankie," Marcel sighed, little ripples of pleasure still speeding through him.

"I loved it," Frankie confessed with a little sigh.

"Oh, yes, me as well," Marcel murmured, watching Frankie's hot little cock grow stiff again in his hand.

Now Marcel rolled Frankie onto his stomach, his busy hand still grasping his stiffness while he mounted him.

"Oh, yes, put that big thing in me again," he gasped.

"Oh!" Frankie exclaimed as Marcel pushed home to the hilt. "Oh, God, this is...." But his voice trailed away, choked with emotion.

Frankie had never been fucked so vigorously as now. While he loved the length and thickness, it was Marcel's technique that was thrilling him now, to judge by the little gasps and sighs that escaped his mouth.

Marcel gazed down in adoration and wonder at the ass below him. Then he looked in the mirror and saw Frankie's face crushed to the pillow. His eyes were tightly closed, but his mouth was open wide and panting, and it was obvious that he was hovering on the edge of yet another climax. Trying not to grin, he stopped his hard thrusting into him and lay still on top of him.

"What is it? Why have you stopped?" Frankie asked.

"I want to enjoy your coming," Marcel said. Frankie's sex had not left his hand. He stroked it furiously. He could feel Frankie squirming against him as he jerked upwards in a nervous little rhythm.

"Oh, oh," he gasped. "I love it," he confessed, his velvety brown eyes tearing up.

Marcel resumed his fucking, Frankie trembling violently against him with the force of his desire.

Before Marcel had a chance to conclude his fuck, Frankie twisted beneath him with a surprising strength for his slender frame and rolled over on top of him.

"What are you doing?"

Marcel was quick to get his answer as Frankie sat on his cock. "But Frankie," was all he had time to say before he was straddling him and sliding up and down on the prick. He reached up to handle his ass, and Frankie rode him hard and fast, his mouth wide open in a grimace of concentration.

Marcel gasped, thrusting rhythmically upwards into his new lover.

As the most incredible delight throbbed through him, Frankie said, "We must do this again and again and again."

"Oh, yes, yes!" Marcel cried wildly.

The strength of his impulses, if not their vileness, carried him over the edge of bodily endurance, and his body arched up in ecstatic release. Marcel's fingers dug deeply into the lean flesh of Frankie's bottom and with short, sharp thrusts he sent his spunk surging into the boy.

He turned on his belly and leaned over him to kiss his lips and eyes. Marcel's hands took possession of Frankie's now well-fucked ass.

His breathing almost back to normal, Frankie said, "Marcel, I've wanted to be loved for so long. I didn't know it'd be like this."

"I know," Marcel said. "I could tell."

"You're the only person who's ever – ever – fucked me that hard." Frankie smiled, letting his fingers play in Marcel's coarse pubic hair, causing Marcel to tense.

"I don't think I'll be able to walk to the bathroom," Frankie said, lifting up.

"Sure you will," Marcel said, propping himself on pillows, lighting a cigarette.

When Frankie came back into the bedroom, Marcel watched him dress, his eyes dreamy, his expression smug. Their good-bye was long, involving much kissing and touching.

"Will you call me?" Frankie asked finally, standing at the door. He had written the phone number of his mother's apartment on a pad by the phone.

Marcel nodded, but somehow Frankie knew Marcel would never call him.

Marcel didn't ask people to understand why he did this. In fact, by the time they had figured out what was going on, he had moved on. "I'm not into long-term relationships," he said as an excuse. "I look for more than just anonymous sex, however." To him, it was all in the seduction – and in the getting away with it.

HURRICANE ANDY
Jesse Monteagudo

It was a balmy day in August of 1992, and all I wanted to do was to sit on the front porch of my North Miami home, with a cool beer in hand, oblivious to the world. What promised to be a nice, quiet, hot Miami weekend ended abruptly when the telephone rang in my living room. I cursed under my breath as I walked into the house to pick up the phone, only to hear my buddy from college, Hector.

"Hey," he said, "what's going on? Long time no see!"

"Well, I guess some things never change." Hector and I had a fling back in the early seventies, when we were both studying at Miami College. Our fling ended when Hector, who was basically bisexual, married Sue, a stunning young Chinese-American. Twenty years later Hector is still a hell of a guy, in spite of age and fatherhood. "You are still the same ol' Cubanazo that you were back in '76."

"And you are the same kidder you were back then. But we are still buds. No matter what. Us Cuban guys must stick together." Hector was buttering me up. But for what? "As I was telling Sue the other day, you are quite a guy. One of a kind. Even if you are queer," he laughed.

"How's Sue?" I asked, slightly exasperated. Though Hector gets on my nerves at times, I have nothing but love for Sue. Any woman who would get Hector to settle down, put up with him for nearly twenty years, and give him two boys and two girls, deserves an award of some kind.

"Oh, Sue's fine, taking care of the kids and the house. She wishes you well." He paused. "Are you still single?"

"Yes, I am. And I plan to stay single, if I can help it." I would have been with someone if you'd stayed, I said to myself. "I like to be by myself. Besides, running my lumber company keeps me busy, and I don't have time to get involved. I am a confirmed bachelor and I like to stay that way."

"Well, we had our good times. But that's over. Now is the time for you to settle down, get married and have kids. Just like I did." Another pause. "And speaking of kids, there is something that I want you to do for me. It's about Andy."

"What about Andy?" Andy is Hector's oldest son, a teen. The last time I saw Andy he was six years old and a spoiled brat. "Did he get in trouble?"

"Oh, no, nothing like that, Vic. Andy is a nice boy. In fact, he just graduated from high school and is now traveling the country. In fact, he is down there in Miami this very weekend." Another pause.

"Hold it! I know what you want! You want me to let Andy stay over at my place, right. Well, he can't!"

"Oh, come on, Vic! Andy will give you no trouble. He'll be nice and quiet and even help you around the house if you want. He might even learn something if he spends some time with a bud of his old man, a guy who made it in the world. Think about it."

"I am beyond thought."

"It'd only be for one night. He'll come in, hang out for a while, go to sleep, and be gone the next morning. How about it?"

"I don't know. . . ."

"Do it for me, bud. C'mon, for old times."

I groaned. "Oh, all right! Andy can spend the night! When will he get here?"

"In a couple of hours. He is over at a friend's house on South Beach. I'll give him a call and he'll be on his way."

"I'll get the spare room ready."

"Thanks, Vic.. I owe you one."

"You owe me a lot," I smiled. "Just tell Andy to come on over right away. I'll be staying in tonight."

"Good for you. Take care of yourself, Vic."

"You too, Hector." I hung up. Putting down the phone, I thought of the good times Hector and I had, two muscular young Cubanos hot for each other's cock and balls and ass. I wondered if 18-year old Andy was anything like his old man. I'd soon find out, I said to myself, as I made the bed in the spare room. When I bought the house a few years earlier, I figured I would rent the room out to a roommate, or a boarder. But since I loved my privacy too much, I let the room stay the way it was. Empty.

Having made the spare room livable, I went outside to wait for Andy. There I saw my next door neighbor, Floyd Jenkins, a Dade County firefighter. Floyd was my best straight friend, and we often met by the fence to talk about Dade County politics and the fires and rescue operations that he was involved in. Today we talked about the weather.

"It's an unusually hot day today, Victor. You are going to fry if you stay outside too long." It was, in fact, too late to fry, for the sun was well on its way down the horizon.

"I'll try not to." I smiled. "How are things going at the fire department?"

"I'll find out soon enough. My shift starts at eight. With weather like this, fires are bound to happen."

"Do you expect any rain?" It was, after all, summer in Florida, when precipitation is a way of life.

"I don't think so. There is a hurricane brewing out in the Atlantic Ocean but they don't expect it to head this way." He looked to the skies, as if for inspiration. Stars began to appear in the sky. "Weren't you working today?"

"No, I closed the lumber company at noon. There is no business today. Besides, an old college pal of mine asked me to let his kid stay overnight. I am now waiting for him."

"Is that him over there?" asked Floyd, pointing behind me. I quickly turned around, expecting to see an overgrown six-year- old. Instead, I saw a strikingly handsome 18-year old, with a suitcase in his hand, standing by my front gate. "Are you Victor Gomez?"

"I'll see you later," nodded Floyd, as he headed back to his house. "I better leave the two of you alone." Though Floyd was the straightest guy around, even he was impressed by young Andy. Of medium height like myself, Andy was lean but muscular, with a tight body that showed through his white T-shirt and blue jeans. Andy's swarthy features combined the best of his Latino father and his Asian mother: straight dark hair, almond-shaped eyes, a firm nose and chin and thick, sensuous lips. Andy was a far cry from the bratty kid I had met so long ago. Our hands joined in a firm handshake as I let him through the gate. He was a stranger to me, but we were immediately familiar, as if we were somehow related. Considering I'd fucked his father, this was a bizarre kinship to be sure.

Andy smiled shyly. "Thanks for letting me stay here."

"Never mind. I'd do anything for your dad." We entered the house, where I immediately took Andy to the spare room. "What are you doing down here in Miami?"

"I came to check out some friends and see what it's like down in South Beach." He smiled. "I kind of like it here. In fact, I might want to go to school here."

"Miami College is a great school. Me and your dad went there and we came out all right." Andy nodded as he looked around the room. "Would you like to rent out this room?"

This pissed me off. "No, I wouldn't. And I am not going to rent it to you."

"But . . ."

"And let me tell you right now. I am only letting you stay here 'cause your dad is, well, an old friend. I like being alone and I intend to stay that way. Comprende?"

"Yes, sir."

"And while you're in my house you are going to abide by my rules. I don't want any friends here. Or loud music. Or drugs. Or booze." Though I was quite a boozer and doper in my younger days, I've been in recovery for some time and intended to stay that way. "Is that clear?"

"I guess so."

"If you don't like it you can go somewhere else."

"Hey man, I'm cool! I'll do what you say."

"I am glad."

"My dad told me you two were quite a pair, back in school."

"That was then and this is now." Did Andy know about Hector and me? "Your dad's married and a father of four and I am ... a different man than I was then."

Andy was silent. "In fact, I am going to stay in tonight. I am tired," I added, pretending to stifle a yawn. "I think you should settle down too."

"I don't think you want me here!" The boy was not afraid to speak his mind. Like father, like son, I said to myself, stifling a smile, this one quite genuine.

"You're right. I guess I really don't want you here." I paused. "But it's only for one night, so let's make a party out of it, okay?"

"Okay."

"I am now going to fix us some dinner. Just get yourself ready and we'll eat in half an hour."

Andy was quiet for the rest of the evening. We barely spoke to one another as we ate my chili and watched a baseball game on television. It wasn't long before the two of us headed for our separate bedrooms. He's quite a boy, I said to myself, as Andy closed the door of the spare bedroom. He's cute. And smart. And sassy. Just like his dad in the old days. With that in mind, I drifted off to sleep.

The next thing I knew there was a sharp knock, as somebody yelled my name. It was all I could do to put on a pair of jeans as I headed for the door, still half asleep. There, fully dressed, was Floyd, with several other neighbors behind him. What's going on, I said to myself?

"Turn on the TV, Victor," Floyd said. He was quite shaken. "Hurricane Andrew is headed this way."

"What!"

"You heard me. I turned on my TV when I got back from work this morning and I saw that weather guy, Bryan Norcross, make the announcement. Andrew is heading this way and he'll be here tonight!"

"We better do something," said a voice behind me. I turned around to see Andy, in his shorts, as startled as I was.

"You better take care of your house," said Floyd, as he turned away to take care of his own home. "And you might want to open up the lumber company today. There'll be plenty of business today."

There sure was. Andy and I spent all morning at the lumber company, selling off every last plank. Then we visited several grocery and hardware stores, where desperate mobs fought to buy everything that wasn't nailed down. Fortunately for us, my house was already well-stocked with necessities, and those that I didn't have I was able to buy. Then we returned home, where Andy helped me board the windows and bring the lawn furniture into the house. Though the lumber business kept me in muscular shape, I could barely keep up with Andy as we worked around the house. There was no question of him leaving now.

"I guess you'll have to stay here again tonight."

- 122 -

"I guess so." Having done all we could do to secure the house, Andy and I settled down to a restless evening, eating leftover chili, watching Bryan Norcross on television and listening to the wind blow outside.

Around midnight, the lights went out. Somehow we found our way to our respective bedrooms, where we removed our clothes and tried to sleep. No sooner did I lose consciousness then a loud crash woke me up with a start.

"What the hell!" I said. Reaching for a flashlight, I rushed to the living room, completely naked. There I literally ran into Andy, also naked, wet and frightened.

"A tree branch broke through the window, Victor! And the roof is leaking. Water is coming through the roof and the window! And I am scared!" Andy and I rushed out to the spare room, which was already flooded. There was nothing we could do for now, so we closed the spare room, laying towels under the door to keep the water from seeping into the living room.

"You can sleep in my room." I tried to calm Andy down. "Don't worry. Everything will be all right," I said, as I admired the 18-year old beauty who stood naked before me. His lithe, swarthy, muscular body was hairless, except for his underarm and pubic hair. His balls hung low and his cock was thick and uncut, for Hector refused to clip his sons. Andy's buns, smooth and round, glistened in the dark. Sweat poured down from his body.

"Please hold me, Victor."

Without a word, I took Andy in my arms, embracing him with an ardor I had not felt for anyone since the old days with his dad. I intuitively kissed his tender lips, our mustaches touching each other as our tongues explored each other's mouth. Our hands reached for each other's cocks, pulling back the foreskins to stroke our hard, restless cock-heads.

"You're a beauty, Andy," I muttered. "I want you so bad it hurts!" So Hector has a queer kid, I said to myself. I wondered what Hector would say if he saw his old college pal, loving his son! "Let's go to bed."

Andy and I fell on my bed, where we continued to kiss and caress each other passionately. Though a hurricane blew outside it ceased to exist as far as we were concerned. I had my own storm inside my room: a wild teen!

"I want you to suck me and fuck me, Victor," said Andy. "I want to feel a man's mouth around my cock and a man's cock inside my ass." Without a word I reached for my young lover's uncut pinga, taking it into my mouth. Andy moaned with pleasure as my tongue worked its way around his young man-muscle, going down one end of his shaft and up the other. As I swallowed Andy's dick deep inside me, it felt like a rod of steel that burned in the furnace of my mouth and throat. My hands grasped at Andy's plump young balls, stroking them even as my mouth worked on his stiff prick.

"Eat me, Victor! Eat me!" moaned Andy, as my mouth and hands worked on his cock and balls. An 18-year old is at the height of his manhood, with urges that could only be satisfied by another man. When we were both 18, my mouth serviced Hector's enormous uncut pinga and low-hanging huevos. Twenty years later, I was doing the same to his handsome, half-

Chinese son, heir to two of the most beautiful races on the planet. Andy went crazy with pleasure as I worked my cocksucking skills on him, the result of twenty years of experienced man-love. Though my own cock remained hard, I willfully ignored it, opting to concentrate on Andy's pleasure. It wasn't long before my young lover arrived at the point of no return.

"I am comin', Victor! I am comin'!"

I quickly took Andy's hot rod out of my mouth, grasping it in my hand as cum began to shoot out of its cock-hole. Andy yelled in ecstasy as gallons of jism spewed out of his manhood, his lithe young body shaking with immeasurable pleasure. All spent, Andy lay still as I took him into my muscular arms. After we kissed for a while Andy took my cock in his hand and whispered in my ear.

"Take me, Victor. I want you to fuck me! Just like you fucked my dd!" Startled by this knowledge, I did nothing, but Andy took matters into his own hands. Taking my hands, he placed them upon his firm, round buns. "I've never been fucked before, but I want you to fuck me first. Will you? Please?" Andy stroked my cock, readying it for his virginal young ass.

"Okay, I'll fuck you, Andy. Because I want to. Not for your dad but for you." The rain poured and the wind roared outside as I reached for a condom that lay on my dresser. Andy took the rubber from my hand and slipped it over my hard cock, preparing it for its assault upon his tender, virginal asshole. As I threw Andy's legs over my shoulders, I slipped lubricant into his young rectum.

"I am going to fuck you, Andy. Like I never fucked anyone before!" Andy groaned as my hard, restless pinga slipped inside his virgin hole. Soon Andy's groans of pain turned into groans of pleasure, as my thick prick began to thrust inside his restless young culo. My hands held Andy's body tight as my mouth tasted his beautiful face and neck.

"Fuck me, papi! Don't stop! I love you!"

"I love you too, Andy! More than you can imagine!" I wasn't fooling. I never felt before the love that I felt for this 18-year old Adonis, whose virgin asshole opened wide to receive my experienced man's cock. As Hurricane Andrew raged outside, my prick took possession of the "eye" of Hurricane Andy, thrusting again and again into the warmth of Andy's tender bunghole. The world might come to an end but we didn't care. All that mattered to us was a thirtysomething man and a barely legal boy, together in that most basic of acts, male fucking male. My entire being centered on my cock, thrusting in and out of the boy I love. It wasn't long before the force of Andy's passion, and my own violent thrusts, drove me into an unprecedented climax.

"I'm comin'! I'm comin' for you! Shiiit!" I yelled. Loads of semen shot out of my dick, filling the rubber with my hot jism. Slowly slipping out of Andy's asshole, I fell over him, completely spent. We kissed.

"I wasn't kidding when I said that I love you," I smiled, as we continued to kiss.

- 124 -

"And I love you too, Victor," smiled Andy. "That's why I came to Miami. To see you and be with you."

"And those friends in SoBe?"

"Just friends."

We kissed passionately. But there was still a burning question in my mind. "How did you know that I fucked and sucked your dad when we were going to Miami College?"

"Because he told me about it. He knew that I was queer from the time I was ten, and he didn't want me to fall into the wrong crowd or take risks. He said to me, 'Andy, I want you to see my old pal Victor. He'll take care of you.' 'Cause you see, Dad knew that I have the hots for muscular papis like you, and he knew you'd have the hots for me once you took one look at me."

"Well, your dad was right." It was daylight, and Hurricane Andrew had come and gone. Still naked, we went around the house, looking for damage. Fortunately, the storm had spared my house, except for the spare room. Saying a silent prayer of gratitude, I held on to my young lover.

"I guess you'll be leaving now. But I wish you'd stay."

"Is that an invitation?"

"I guess it is. I've been lonely for too long. I need a young guy like you to help me around the lumber company by day. And to warm my bed at night. You can still go to school. Will you do it?"

"You know it."

"I am glad." We kissed again. "I got to call your dad and thank him for this."

"Oh, no, not my dad. Thank Hurricane Andrew. He's the one that did it."

I never thought I'd ever be thanking a hurricane for anything, but there I was embracing one.

SMALL WORLD
Tim Scully

"It's a small world."

I put the letter down on the desk. My hand was shaking so much that I couldn't read any more. It was from our rep in Abu Dhabi in the Gulf, and mostly in connection with the contract we'd recently negotiated.

It was the handwritten postscript which had me worried.

"I was in the bar of the Intercontinental Hotel here the other evening and ran into an old school friend of yours: one Adam Wheelwright. He looks after the Sheikh's defense contracts. I mentioned that our Mr. Scully would be coming out soon. He said he knew someone of that name at school and behold – it turned out to be you. It's a small world."

Adam Wheelwright! Of all people he had to meet Adam! Why couldn't he have met one of the others: the boys I'd just been friendly with, played squash with, and discussed non- existent girl friends with? More important, what had Adam told him about me?

"Anything wrong, Mr. Scully?" Jane asked.

"No. Just this bloody Abu Dhabi contract. I don't think I'll go after all. Adrian can do it."

"But you liked the place last time you were there."

"Too much work here, Jane. I'll have a word with Adrian."

I did. Adrian was booked for a maintenance trip to Iceland. It had to be me.

Fittingly, in view of his name, Adam had been my first but Yarbridge School was no Garden of Eden. We were both in our lower teens at the time. I can't remember my exact age. There were supposed to be three boys to a room but the school was going through a difficult time and the third bed in our room was unoccupied.

I can't truthfully say that I liked Adam at first. There were several other boys I would have preferred to share a room with. Adam was a show-off. He was good at sports. As an athlete he was superb. I was a squash player; quite a good squash player, but in schools like Yarbridge, it's the athletes who count. Win a squash tournament and you might get a medal. Win a race and the cup you get would keep a thirsty man happy for years. Adam's challenges irritated me. "Bet you can't do this!" as he swung from the lintel above the door. "I did a hundred press- ups today. Bet you couldn't even do twenty!"

Then, one night I lay in bed waiting for him to go to sleep so that I could attend to an urgent need in private. The urgency had been brought about by the sight of Simon Reade in the showers earlier that day. Just a glimpse of his slim body under the cascading water had been enough.

"Bet you can't do this," said Adam.

"What?" I turned over onto my side.

"This." He was lying on his back. He'd turned his head to face me.

"What? I can't see anything."

"God, Scully! You're so thick! This, you idiot."

I was still at a loss. "What am I supposed to be looking at?"

His hands were above the quilt. He pointed to a conical projection in the middle of the quilt.

"Anybody can do that," I said. Had he only known, I'd been gently manipulating mine for the last fifteen minutes, getting it ready for a two minute erotic fantasy starring Simon Reade.

"Ah, but I never touched it," he replied.

"Bet you did."

"I didn't. I do it by thinking."

"Nothing wonderful about that."

"Okay, you do it then. Show me."

I let go of my half-hard member and put my hands behind my head.

"You have to tell me what you're thinking," said Adam.

"You didn't tell me what you were thinking about." Simon's image began to clarify in my mind. Simon under a shower, his long, thick cock swaying slightly as he moved.

"Don't stand there gaping, Scully. Come in and join me."

"Do you mean that?"

"Of course I do. Come on, get those shorts off. There's room for the two of us."

Peeling off my shorts; blushing slightly as I stepped into the cubicle; the feel of Simon's hands on my back....

But then what? Would he let me touch his? Would he let me hold it and feel it throbbing into life? What would it feel like? Like mine at that moment or even harder? Simon was, after all a year older than I was....

"Is it working?" asked Adam.

"Yeah!"

"I can't see anything. You sure?"

"Course I'm sure." My voice sounded odd.

"Prove it."

"Come and see for yourself."

He climbed out of bed. He was naked. I guessed he must have shed his pajamas under the bedclothes as I had. He pulled my quilt back.

"Hmm. Not bad. Not bad at all," he said, peering down at my erection. "Do you want me to finish you off?"

He didn't wait for an answer. He reached down. I felt his fingers encircling my cock. The first fingers other than my own that had touched it for years. It was a great feeling and he was good. He seemed to know exactly where my most sensitive spots were. Within minutes I was squirming in delight and heaved upwards as it ran down over his hands.

"You can do me if you like," he said. So I did, but certainly not as expertly as he had handled mine. He gave a triumphant gasp and warm semen flowed down over my frantically working fingers.

"You ever tried sucking?" asked Adam a few nights later. (By this time I had become more proficient with my fingers.)

"No."

"It's good. Open your legs a bit. That's right. Let me know when you're going to come."

I'd never experienced anything like it. The feel of his tongue on my thighs and my balls was enough to get me going. When he actually had it in his mouth and I felt his cheeks sucking in against it I was in a private seventh heaven. I remember he took his mouth away to tell me to try and keep still. I couldn't.

"I'm coming. I'm...." I gasped. Like a shot he lifted his head and, for the first time in my life it actually jetted out, splashing his face and shoulders.

"Now your turn," he said. We changed places. I was a bit nervous. "Lick my balls a bit," he commanded. I did, feeling the soft crinkled skin against the tip of my tongue.

"A bit harder," he said. "That's right. Get your tongue right under. I like that."

I confess that I wondered where my roommate got his expertise from. By the time I was licking his stiff shaft, my own was beginning to wake up again. When I actually had his in my mouth I think I would have come again had it not been for the constant flow of instructions.

"Put your lips on the head. No. Not like that. Up a bit. That's good. Now slide your mouth up and down a bit. Watch those teeth. They hurt. That's better. You're doing quite well. Not bad at all. Now suck it. Suck hard. Oh yeah! That's good. Oh yeah! Watch it. Just a few seconds. Here I...here I... go!"

And go he did! It shot everywhere. There was even a patch on the wall which, when it dried, looked like the image of an inverted teaspoon.

Soon Adam's bed became almost as redundant as the spare one. He spent most of the night with me, going back to his own in the early hours of the morning and often returning before the waking bell.

Simon Reade was soon forgotten. Adam was much more interesting and much more available. Going to sleep with his cock in my hand is an experience I still remember clearly.

During the day, I was ignored. He hung about with his sporting and athletic friends whilst I spent most of my spare time in the library.

One evening, he suggested that we should go 'all the way'. I had a vague idea of what he meant. He'd got hold of some Vaseline from somewhere. It hurt. It hurt badly and, looking back, he was as clumsy and as inept as I was but, after a week or so, we managed it. I wanted to do it to him but he wouldn't allow that. I didn't mind that much. It was just so good, in the sterile environment of a boys' boarding school to have someone who cared.

We'd lie in bed afterwards, whispering to each other, holding each other, feeling each other and (or so I thought) loving each other.

And then came the annual Sports Day at school. An occasion for family visits, speeches and strawberry teas. My parents came. Adam's too, together with an uncle and aunt and his teenage cousin. He'd been on about this cousin for weeks. He was at university and, according to Adam, was the best student they'd ever had.

I only had one race. The two-hundred meters for boys under fifteen. I came in fourth, which wasn't too bad for me. I sat with my folks and watched the other events. Adam was as good as ever and I got a real thrill out of watching his long legs pounding along the track, leaving the others behind. I cheered as loudly as his father as he won race after race. My friend, my personal friend, was the best sportsman in the school!

When it was all over he'd collected seven cups to add to the row on the shelf in our room. I got as much pleasure about that growing collection as he did.

Mum and Dad went off to try and have a word with the French teacher. Boys were not allowed to sit on the chairs unless their parents were present so I lay on the grass and closed my eyes against the bright sun.

"Here he is." It was Adam's voice. I opened my eyes. Adam and his cousin towered over me. I sat up.

"Congratulations. You've done well," said the cousin.

"Yes, congratulations. I suppose I shall have to help polish the damn trophies," I added. They both laughed.

"Beautiful legs," said the cousin.

I was slightly mystified. It seemed an odd thing to say. What came next made me wonder if I was dreaming.

"He's keen," said Adam. "He'll do anything. He's got a nice tight ass too." The cousin laughed.

"Been in it?" he asked.

"Not recently. He'll be nice and tight. That was the arrangement," Adam replied.

"Possibly a bit too young," said the cousin. "I reckon an ass is best at about sixteen."

"Please yourself," said my one-time friend.

"Only problem is where," said the cousin. "With all these boys going in to take showers, your room is a bit dodgy."

"Not if I come too. I can stand with my back to the door so nobody comes in."

"And watch me suck your roommate? I thought you might be working up to that."

"You had a friend there when you did it to me."

"That was different. Where's a place where nobody's likely to disturb us?"

"The chapel. It's always open and you can go up into the choir loft. Nobody goes up there. It's marked PRIVATE and even if they did, you'd hear them on the stairs."

"Would somebody mind telling me what you're on about?" I asked.

"My cousin's going to suck you," said Adam.

"He bloody isn't!"

"Don't be daft. Of course he is. You let me do it. Why not him?"

"Because... Because...." I was so angry that I couldn't find the right words.

"But you'll like it," Adam protested. "He's good and he's got the most enormous cock you've ever seen. He'll let you play with it if you want."

"As much as you want," said the cousin.

"I don't want. Piss off!" I said.

"But I promised him," said Adam.

I stood up. "Well, you can bloody well unpromise! You're disgusting! Both of you!"

I went off in search of my parents. Out of the corner of my eye I saw Adam and the cousin head towards the chapel. I was so angry that even my folks detected that something was wrong. I didn't tell them of course.

The amazing thing was that my refusal to let him anywhere near me that night actually surprised him. I went to bed early, feeling more miserable than I had felt for years. He came back from the showers with a towel draped round his middle, dropped it and said, "Get a mouthful of this."

The argument lasted well into the night and continued on several succeeding nights. I don't think he was aware of my tears.

The trophies on the shelf got yellower as the weeks went by and I got more and more frustrated. There were occasions when I succumbed. I always regretted them afterwards. He never said anything about wanting to be friends again. He never said hew was sorry. It was just "I'm in a randy mood tonight. Want to suck it for me?" and I, fool that I was, obliged.

I suppose it was some sort of psychological reaction that caused me to start hunting for other partners. Not friends. Just partners. I never even thought of friendship when I had my hands round Tim McCormack's ample buttocks and his equally adequate cock was in my mouth. I can't remember the names of some of the boys I wanked and sucked over the next few years. Who was the lad whose cock I covered in sugar before devouring it? I remember the cock very well but the name of its owner escapes me. And as for the one and only boy I actually screwed, I remember what he looked like spread-eagled over the work table in the library office. I remember his yells as I went into him and the feel of his soft butt writhing against my groin but that's all.

Adam's cousin continued to visit the school on Sports Days and Founder's Days. I kept clear and watched from a safe distance as they sloped off to the chapel. It was on one such visit that Adam (who must then have been about sixteen) lost his virginity and I confess to having been rather pleased. Faint moaning sounds came from the direction of his bed that evening.

"What's up with you?" I asked.

"Nothing."

"Something to do with your cousin?"

"Yes."

"What?"

"Nothing."

"He's fucked you hasn't he?"

"Yes, if you must know."

"Nice?"

"It hurts a bit. We had to do it in a hurry. There was a choir practice. It was good though. You were a fool not to let him do it to you."

I think that was probably the last conversation we ever had.

- – -

The flight to Abu Dhabi seemed endless. It's a nice place. I like Abu Dhabi and I had liked their Intercontinental Hotel on my previous visit. Unlike some big hotels, the Intercon at Abu Dhabi seems friendly. The staff are helpful. The food is good and their swimming pool is superb.

"There is a message for you, Mr. Scully," said the desk clerk when I checked in. My heart sank.

"Welcome. Waiting for you at the pool. Adam Wheelwright," it said. I had half a mind to go out but that wouldn't have helped. He'd only have come back the next day.

It happens that the restaurant overlooks the pool and, apart from the airline breakfast I hadn't eaten for some time. I went there for lunch and selected a table next to the window.

I spotted him almost at once. There was no mistaking that strong-jawed face and dark hair. I looked away. There was no way I was going to get involved with him again. I took a few mouthfuls of food. Another sidelong glance. He was good looking. He still had the firm belly that I remembered so well, especially when it had glinted with his spunk. No. Definitely not. I turned my attention to the meal again.

"Is it to your liking?" the head waiter asked.

"Yes, thanks. Very good." He was good too. I looked again. Funny to think that those long fingers had been round my cock. Odd to think that his lips had encompassed it. His mouth seemed to be the same size as it always had been. I wondered if he'd still be able to take all my cock as he had done at school.

No! I was not going to let it happen! I think I'd have been all right if it hadn't been for Neil and Dhasan and Barry – all of whom I had met in the last year. When you've had something good, you inevitably want more.

Adam turned over. That made it worse. All my new friends had nice asses. Dhasan's sleek brown butt was an instant turn- on. Neil was a bit bonier but still nice. Barry's was soft and buttery. Adam's was the most aesthetically pleasing behind I'd seen for a long time. Age I suppose. At eighteen, Dhasan was good. Barry, seventeen, was nearly as good but now I was looking at an ass that had matured. It still had the tense look of the athlete but the dark hairs on his thighs had not been there at school, nor had it been so exquisitely suntanned.

Then he spotted me. My fault. I hadn't realized that I'd been staring. He waved. I lifted my hand. There was nothing for it. I had to go out and speak to him.

"Good trip?" he asked after we had shaken hands.

"Not bad."

I took a lounger next to his and took off my jacket and tie.

"I recognized you at once," he said. "You haven't changed that much."

"Neither have you. A bit more hairy perhaps. Still into athletics?"

"A bit. What about you?"

"Still playing squash."

I couldn't keep my eyes off him. He turned over. The five and a half inches he'd been so proud of when we shared a room was now at least seven inches and formed a soft-looking pad in his swimming trunks.

"I've got all the contract details in my room," I said. "You ought to see them really. I'll go and get them."

"Better not," said Adam. "I'll come up with you."

He slipped a toweling robe on and followed me to the elevator.

My room, on the sixth floor, was like all hotel rooms everywhere. Superbly comfortable, clean but, even with my luggage spread over the spare bed, it still seemed impersonal.

Adam sat on my bed. I opened my briefcase. "Basically, our strategy with this contract is going to be to move fast and decisively. It's a good opportunity for the company and I believe in seizing opportunities quickly." I explained.

Adam laughed. "You never moved fast or decisively in your life!" he said. "As for seizing opportunities, you threw up the chance of being blown by the best cocksucker in the world."

"Who, as I recall, brought tears to your eyes when you were sixteen," I replied. "He can't have been that good. I seem to remember your saying that it hurt."

"It wasn't as bad as all that. I got used to it."

"Did you do it a lot with him?" I asked. I shouldn't have asked. It was none of my business but the bath robe had parted slightly and I was looking at a long suntanned stretch of thigh.

"Once or twice, yes."

"And it got better?"

"Yes."

"What about since then?"

"Sod all. I dare not. Not in this job. What about you? Still leading a celibate life?"

"Reasonably," I replied. Dhasan, Neil and Barry would have been hysterical if they could have heard me.

"They were good times," he said. He lay back on the bed. The robe parted wider. His legs were beautifully suntanned. I took hold of one end of the belt and played with it.

"Mind you," he said, "you were a fool not to let my cousin do it. He was good."

"No interest whatsoever," I replied. "You weren't so bad yourself."

"I was good," he replied. "Sex is like everything else I've done. I was the best. My cousin said so, and so did his friend. It's a pity you can't get trophies or certificates for sex or I could prove it to you."

I don't know what happened to me in that moment. Something inside me snapped. So, incidentally, did the loops securing the belt to the bathrobe.

"What the...?" said Adam, staring at me. The robe had parted completely. His cock, swollen and huge, poked out from under the swimming trunks and looked more appetizing than it had ever looked.

"Better prove it now, then," I said. I put my fingers into the waistband and pulled as hard as I could. Something tore. He yelled and then pulled me down on top of him.

After that, all I have are blurred memories. I only wish I could tell you exactly what happened. My clothes seemed to be torn away. My shirt certainly ripped. Fingernails digging into my back, the feel of his lips crushed against mine, the smell of sweat and swimming pools.

Then the licking and the feel of his nipples against my tongue. His tongue finding my navel. His pubic hairs in my teeth as I bit into his flesh.

Adam groaned as I parted his legs; call out as I licked down into him. He wanted more but I want to suck him first. It's been a long time since I tasted his cockhead. He shook his head from side to side as I licked into his slit and round the tip. I felt his hands on the side of my head and listened to him groaning. I put the palm of my hand under his balls and sensed their warmth and their readiness.

A pause. Adam said, "My turn."

I was too far gone to comply. We fought. The bedside lamp crashed to the floor. He'd pinned me down. There was nothing I could do. I struggled but he had my cock in his mouth and if I struggled too much he might bite. "Not too much!" I gasped. He was all over me. I could feel his tongue lapping against my flesh. He was getting me ready. Yes, that was what he was doing. He was getting it wet and slippery so that it would go into his ass easily. far more easily than his despicable cousin's.

I told him so. "That's right," I said. "Get it slippery so that it'll go into that first class ass of yours. Get it hard too so you can feel it going in you."

That turned him on even more. I could sense it. He made little whimpering noises as he slurps on my cock.

"Just think," I said, trying to keep a clear head. "It's never been in your ass before. Feel that ridge? Boy, are you going to enjoy feeling that against your button. That's going to make you squirm." (Would it? It did to Dhasan, Neil and Barry but they were considerably younger. Perhaps reactions changed as people grew older.)

"Just about ready," I said. "This lot's not going to make stains on the wall. This is all going right up into your ass."

He stopped. There was another struggle as I heaved him up into a kneeling position. Another crash. The picture of an Arab fishing boat fell from the wall above the bed and landed on the pillow. I sling it onto the spare bed.

Adam was moaning now. He wanted it and he didn't want it. He's afraid. Adam, the athlete, the champion at everything was afraid. I parted his cheeks. They felt soft and cool. I could see it. A little brown slit with a few straggly hairs growing round it. I got into position. I was holding his waist. I watched his head rise as my cock pushed against him. I glanced in the mirror on the door of the shower cubicle and saw his tongue hanging out. I held on tight. I pushed hard. Then harder. Surely it was to be possible. I would get into Dhasan and Neil and Barry. Was there an age when an ass becomes impenetrable? Surely not. Gripping him as hard as I could and feeling my nails dig into his skin I shoved against him with all the strength I could summon and it happened. Adam cried out loud. I was in him, in the school's best athlete! Into Adam. 'Bet you can't do this.' 'God, Scully, you are so thick!" Well, now he knew how thick. Thick enough to bring tears to his eyes. I could see them in the reflection in the mirror, streaming down his cheeks as my cock pushed farther and farther into him, feeling the warmth there, the softness. Softer and silkier than Neil. But then Neil was a bit skinny. When my hands were on Neil's waist I could feel his hip bones. Adam's waist was smooth and soft. Neil's buns were nice, but Adam's were softer. A nice plush cushion feeling.

But what's his prostate going to feel like? Tiny and hard like Dhasan's? Big and spongy like Neil's or will it be like Barry's and feel like a lump of modeling clay pressing against me? I wriggle a bit and push harder.

"Aaaah!" I had found it. I didn't need to look at the mirror. His whole body stiffened. I felt it pulsing through the thin membrane. Another shove. The stiffness disappeared. He was panting now. Good. I enjoyed that. It reminded me of school races, of Adam pounding along the track panting. But then he was winning. He was the leader. No longer. Adam had become my slave. I was on top now. I was punishing him; hurting him. A few more thrusts. Sweat dropped from my forehead onto his back. I let go of his waist to rub it into his skin. There was blood there too, from the punctures my finger nails made. That's even better. I'd never seen Adam's blood before. One of his life fluids seeping out and my life fluid going into him....

Any minute now, I told myself. Could I hold on for a bit longer? No, I simply could not.

"Ah! Ah! Ah! Ah!" That's Adam. Or was it? I was panting too.

"Oh, God you're...." What was I going to say? I didn't know. It was jetting out of me, pumping into him. I could feel it building up and hear the squelching noise of my prick still heaving into him. He stiffened again. I reached under him. It was hard as hell and sticky. I gripped it as hard as I could and felt it throbbing in my hand. Then he came. Powerful spurts of semen squirting down onto the bed cover. Who cares? Hotels don't have disapproving matrons who counsel boys about their wet dreams.

We collapsed onto the bed.

I could feel his muscles squeezing it. "Don't take it out," said Adam. As if I could. As if I would.

For the next three days, Adam hardly ever left that room. I told the hotel staff that he had been taken ill and that he could stay in my room. They brought his clothes up from the changing cabin but he never wore them.

I went out in the mornings to work on the contract. By the time I got back to the hotel, he had eaten his lunch. I put the dirty plates out in the corridor and tied the DO NOT DISTURB label on the door handle. A bit of essential business. How had I got on with the Sheikh? It might be an idea to see Mr. So and So tomorrow. Make a few notes and then the really essential business. Peeling back his bedclothes, just as he had done to mine at school. Looking down at that luscious, eager cock, feeling it. Stroking the legs of the school's number one athlete. Feeling under his balls and tickling his anus. Getting him ready again. There was no need to hurry. Gradually conquering him; feeling him squirm as I bored into him. He was good.

"I'll tell you one thing," I said as we lay by the pool. It was my last evening in Abu Dhabi.

"Hmmm. What?"

"Your cousin was right. You really are good."

"So are you. Just what I need," he replied. His hand moved over and touched mine.

"What happened to your cousin? Do you still see him?" I asked.

"Sometimes. But you know him better than I do."

"Me? How?"

"Alec Parsons. He's your boss."

"What?" I nearly fell of the lounger.

"How do you think your firm got the contract?" said Adam. "Alec got me this job as adviser on armaments just so that I could put the business his way. Didn't you know?"

"Of course not."

"Hasn't he recognized you?"

"Well if he has, he hasn't shown it."

Alec Parsons – Mr. Parsons – was a distant figure in the firm. I hardly ever saw him. His office was guarded by a battery of secretaries and personal assistants.

I got through this human barrier on my return.

"Ah. Scully. Just back from Abu Dhabi. How did it go?"

"Very well. I met your cousin."

He was embarrassed. I could see that. He stubbed out his cigar.

"Keep quiet about that connection," he said. "If the papers got to hear.... Now I'm very busy. Report to your immediate superior. There was no need to come to see me."

"Actually, there was, Mr. Parsons. You said something once."

"What?"

"You said a sixteen-year-old ass was perfect. But, you know, a twenty-three-year-old one is pretty good, too."

He stared. "My God!" he said. "You're the boy. The squash player."

"Right. The one Adam tried to line up for you."

He didn't know what to do with his cigar butt. He put it down, picked it up, put it down again and continued to stare at me.

"You're not trying to blackmail me?" he asked.. There was a slight quaver in his voice.

"Of course not. We've both enjoyed the performance of a very good athlete."

He smiled, then lit the cigar again.

"Not bad is he?" he asked.

"Very good indeed," I agreed as I left his office.

A few days later, I was promoted, jumping three grades. My salary shot up accordingly, and, at last, I had an office of my own. The same week, I noticed a paragraph in the firm's magazine about the remarkable success of my trip to Abu Dhabi: "Mr. Scully penetrated a difficult market with extreme skill and sowed the seed for a possible expansion in the Gulf area."

READY FOR IT
Tim Scully

Water splashed round our bare feet in the shower basin.

I was playing my favorite game. By putting my hands on Neil's shoulders and changing the position of my fingers I could direct a stream of water down his back. As my hands moved lower I could aim it, first over one buttock, then over another, and finally between the cheeks of his ass.

He was worked up too. I'd noticed the promising bulge in his jeans when I arrived at Dhasan's apartment. Usually, by the time I got there, Dhasan had already had him.

"I hope you're feeling fit," said Dhasan when I arrived. "Neil's more than ready for it."

"That's good news," I replied. "You mean you haven't beaten me to it?"

"Not today. I've got a college assignment to finish."

"So you're feeling dirty?" I said, addressing Neil who sat, blushing slightly, in one of Dhasan's armchairs.

"Uh huh."

"How about a shower," I said. He stood up and grinned.

"I'll make you both a coffee later," said Dhasan. "You'll need a stimulant."

I said something about being sufficiently stimulated. Neil stood up and followed me into the bathroom. "Stimulant indeed!" I said, locking the door behind me. Neil did likewise to the door linking the bathroom to Dhasan's bedroom – not that there was any real need to do so. Both Dhasan and I had become accustomed to watching each other in action with Neil.

In the eight months we'd known him, both Dhasan and I had grown really fond of Neil. He was then nearly seventeen and a student at the exclusive St. Bede's College, which lay just outside the town. He had an open, friendly sort of face, a good sense of humor and a superb torso. More important to me was lower down. Out of a dense bush of bristly hair grew a cock that was at least eight inches long and over an inch thick. That made up for the flatness of his butt. At that time I had very little experience but the difference between Neil and my friend Barry was remarkable. Neither Dhasan or Neil knew about Barry. He was seventeen and lived in the midlands. Thrusting into Barry and feeling his padded cheeks slap against my groin was a delight. Screwing Neil was rather like putting my cock into a hole in a not very well upholstered wooden bench and just about as exciting. Barry groaned and waggled his butt under me. Neil yelled a bit as it went in. After that, nothing.

Dhasan once said that the great thing about Neil was that he didn't mind what he did – and that summed him up perfectly. Barry enjoyed every second. Perhaps that famous private school ethic about not showing emotion was to blame. I remember going into Dhasan's room once to find him in action. Neil knelt on the bed in front of him. Dhasan, perspiration running down his face and shoulders, was well into him. I stood there for a moment watching that massive brown cock, glistening with oil, disappear between Neil's white buttocks. Neil cried out and then caught sight of me. He smiled and then winked.

There was nothing I could do about his butt of course. It was pure chance that made me discover the remarkable effect of a shower. Neil and I had been helping Dhasan paint his living room and went into the shower together. His hair was hardly damp when he suddenly lost control. His cock sprang up. His hands were all over me. It was like being with an octopus. That day he shot more spunk than he had ever done. It went everywhere. It wasn't long before the mere mention of the word 'shower' turned him on just as effectively as the faucet turned on the water.

"No Dhasan today then?" I asked, watching him undo his shirt.

"No. Like he said, he has a college assignment to finish."

"Good news for me. I like the creamer to be full," I said, undressing.

"It is. Haven't touched the handle since Wednesday."

He pulled off his sneakers and socks and undid his belt. Being rather less tidy than he was, I was already naked and my clothes lay in a pile on the floor. I sat on the laundry basket and watched his golden-haired thighs come into view as his jeans slid down. His cock showed against his pale blue boxers. He looked down at the protuberance and grinned.

"You?" he asked.

"Of course. Come closer."

He took a couple of steps towards me. I put my thumbs between the elastic and his warm, moist flesh and slid the shorts down. Liberated at last from restraining clothes, his cock sprang up – inches from my face. I caught a whiff of excited boy – surely the most exciting odor in the world – and feasted my eyes on its swollen, purple head; the dense bush surrounding it and his massive ballsac.

"Going to lick it?" he asked. I did most weekends but then he'd already come at least once for Dhasan.

"Not today," I replied. "In you get."

"Ha Ha. It's going to be one of those sessions, is it?" he said.

"Right first time."

He went into the cubicle, closed the sliding door and turned on the water. The frosted glass became slightly more transparent as the water flowed over it. What looked at first like a ghost in the mist became more substantial. The hair on this head; under his armpits, and the dense patch of pubic hair appeared as unconnected black blobs. Then flesh came into view. The pink of his face and torso, the startling white background to his pubes and the honey color of his legs. He turned slightly to one side. His cock brushed against the glass, leaving, for an instant, a horizontal stripe of dry glass.

"Ready," he called. I opened the door as rapidly as I could and stepped in. He said nothing but handed me the soap and turned to face the faucets.

My cock slapped against the back of his thighs as I soaped his neck and his back. He raised his arms so that I could get to the bristly hairs under his armpits.

Desperately willing myself to go as slowly as possible, I plied the soap in circles on his shoulder – blades and down his spine. Then, holding my hands out of the stream of water, I lathered them liberally with foam and went to work on his buttocks. Firm, flat flesh – solid muscle but pretty sensitive. Instinctively, he parted his legs. I pushed my fingers into the cleft. He shuddered.

Dhasan would have had good reason to thank me that night. I managed to get two fingers right inside. If he'd been anybody else I'd have shoved my cock into him there and then but I wasn't fooled. I knew somehow that he was grinning at the tiled wall and congratulating himself on bringing me to the boil so quickly. I withdrew my fingers. He tensed up, obviously waiting for something more substantial to replace them. Instead, I moved down to his thighs and then back to his shoulders and played my water game. It gave me time to cool down and him to warm up. I felt his heart thumping. Then he started to make little whimpering, pleading noises. Neil was over the barrier.

"Your turn," I said.

The feel of Neil's long fingers on my skin is one of the best turn-ons I've ever experienced. He began, as he always did, by tentatively stroking my chest, tweaking at my nipples and then moving his fingers inexorably downwards, twining them in my bush and then playing with my highly aroused cock.

"I really like this," he murmured. I did too but said nothing. One look at the expression on his face told me that there would be no more conversation. His eyes sparkled. His mouth was half open. I put my hands on his shoulders and drew him towards me. Our lips touched gently. He groaned and pressed himself against me. I felt his cock against mine. He reached down and did something. I don't know what it was. I dropped my hands to his butt – forcing him even closer. My tongue brushed against his teeth. My cock slid between his thighs. He panted. His balls felt soft and moist against my cock head. His hands dug into my back. He was like an animal. His nails scratched my skin. His tongue pushed into my mouth. I felt his butt tighten as he thrust his cock between my tightly constricted thighs.

The sound and the feel of the cascading water were forgotten. He was mine – all mine. Nearly seventeen, highly intelligent, endowed with a wonderful sense of humor – the sort of person anybody would value as a friend – and he was mine. We hugged, we kissed and we clawed each other oblivious of everything else.

"Oh yeah!" he groaned. "Oh yeah – yeah – yeah!"

A wet warmth suffused my thighs – nothing to do with Dhasan's plumbing. My own load splattered (I think) on the tiles. His trickled down my legs to my feet. I was just in time to see it form strings in the swirling water before it vanished into the drain.

"Nice?" asked Dhasan when we joined him later in the lounge.

"Very," I replied – not quite certain as to whether I was commenting on the coffee he had just made or Neil's performance.

"Sorry to be such a poor host," said Dhasan, "but I have to finish this assignment."

"As a matter of fact, I've brought some work to do. I thought you and Neil would be occupied," I replied

"Just you two carry on. I can watch TV until you've finished," said Neil. So, for the first time ever, Dhasan and I sat at his dining table working. Neil flicked from channel to channel on the TV, apparently found nothing that appealed to him and wondered over to look over my shoulder.

"Oh, sorry," he said, noticing the 'SECRET' stamp on the folder.

"Don't worry. It's all old stuff and you're no spy," I replied.

"What is it?" he asked.

"It's an amour-piercing missile."

"You ought to come and give a talk to our school science club one day. They'd be interested."

"Do you reckon?"

"Sure. Rockets – explosives – stuff like that. It's interesting," he said.

"Bloody boring as far as I'm concerned," I said and carried on doing my calculations.

Dhasan finished. He put his books to one side.

"There!" he said. "Carcinoma treatment by penetration of gamma rays covered in five thousand words. Now how about a bit of penetration of another kind or is the target still a bit sore?"

"Unused," I said. "No point in using missiles before you've emptied the enemy's armament store."

"I thought we were friends," said Neil.

I reached out and stroked his butt. "We are. I spoke metaphorically," I said.

"To my satisfaction," said Dhasan with a wide grin. He stood up and put a hand on Neil's shoulders.

"You'll take a nice long time to come. Just how I like it," he said. "You can have a double load of mine in your delectable little ass before you come to the boiling point. Come on."

They vanished into the bedroom. I concentrated on the computer steering of the new 'BLISTER' which was far from being as old as I'd told Neil.

Concentration, I confess, was not a hundred percent. Neil's yell and subsequent gasps; Dhasan's frenzied panting and groaning were rather more interesting then the specifications of heat sheathing cable.

"Oh yeah! Yeah! Yeah!" Neil groaned.

"On target," I muttered to myself.

"Oh, ah! Ah!" he shouted a few minutes later.

"Missile has homed," I muttered.

"Oh God! That's so good!" said Dhasan. At that moment, as I knew so well, millions of Dhasan's sperms were hurtling around in the tight interior of Neil's ass – just as violently as the scattering of sharp-edged shrapnel that BLISTER discharged into an enemy tank, but infinitely nicer.

On the following Tuesday, Dhasan and I were at the squash club. We'd just come out of the court when Mr. Low, Neil's Headmaster who was on the club committee, came up.

"Mr. Scully," he said.

"Oh! Hi, Mr. Low. Good evening."

"Good evening. Young Webb came to see me this morning."

"Oh, yes?"

"Says you're prepared to talk to the science club. Awfully nice of you. I just wanted to say thank you."

"Well... as a matter of fact.... "

"Many of the lectures we arrange are, I am sorry to say, rather too abstract," he continued. "To have someone like you is a great privilege. I'm sure the boys will find missiles more interesting. I mentioned it at our assembly this morning and they seemed very keen indeed."

If he hadn't said that I'd have tried to get out of it. As it was, I was stuck. I could have strangled Neil (or, at least, given him the screwing of his life) for mentioning it. There was nothing I could do save agree. The lecture was fixed for a Tuesday evening two weeks hence.

"They're a bit of a wild bunch," said Neil the following weekend. We were at Dhasan's again and Dhasan had obviously had no college assignment to finish. It had taken a full ten minutes to get Neil's cock erect and although my heart was pumping hard, he just lay there on Dhasan's bed with his legs apart and his hands behind his head as I nibbled at his balls.

"In what way?" I said.

"Oh – the older ones are a bit of a handful," he said.

"So is this," I said, stroking his foreskin.

"Mm. I like that," he replied.

"A mouthful is even better," I said. After that, the Science Club wasn't mentioned.

The firm was helpful. They let me borrow models of 'BLISTER' 'RED ARROW' and 'COBRA' and a couple of dated video tapes showing them in action.

The lecture was in the school library. Not being used to that sort of thing, I felt a bit nervous. When the audience filed in I felt rather more at ease. The senior boys filled the front rows. At first I was tempted to ask them to sit at the rear so that the little lads could see more. But two of them, one blond, the other dark, both about eighteen, changed my mind. They were absolutely

- 143 -

beautiful. One of them stretched his long legs out in front of him and I found it difficult to stand my model 'BLISTER' upright, my hands were shaking so much.

Neil stood at the back by the light-switches and winked encouragingly. I smiled back and began.

Briefly, I sketched the history of missiles. "The big problem there," I said, showing a slide of a V2 trajectory, "was that you got it up but had very little idea of where it would land."

"A bit like my evening with Mark Forbes," said one of the two very good-looking boys. "I got it up all right but that's about all." His companion laughed. He said it in an undertone but I was near enough to hear.

I moved on to the 'RED ARROW'. "This," I said, "is a heat- seeking missile. Fired from an aircraft behind another, where do you think it will head for?"

Hands went up throughout the audience.

"Yes, you. You at the back. Where do you think?"

He was barely a teen. "The other plane's engine, sir?" he stammered.

"Excellent. Absolutely right. To be specific, it will seek out the source of the heat exhaust gases."

"Sensible rocket!" said one of the two boys in the front row. "The source of all those lovely little bubbling farts. Mine's the same."

I could hardly believe my ears.

"Whereas 'COBRA' is a so-called intelligent missile," I continued. "'COBRA' is computer-controlled, which is where I come in. 'COBRA' seeks its target, senses it, follows it and finally moves in for the kill."

"You've just got yourself a new nickname," said the dark- haired boy to his blond friend. "How long did it take you to seek, sense and follow Peter Mason before you moved in for the kill?"

"Six weeks. Worth every minute. I went right up his little jet-pipe."

By the time I'd got round to 'BLISTER', there was no doubt at all in my mind. They laughed at the phallic shaped war-head. I expected that. We'd laughed enough about it at the firm.

"Why is it that shape?" asked one boy.

"Good question. It isn't wonderfully aerodynamic but it's the perfect shape for what it has to do."

"Perfect size too," the blond boy whispered. "Just imagine how Simon would react with that in his ass."

His companion chuckled.

I explained that 'BLISTER' was an air-to-ground missile. I got through the very complex process by which 'BLISTER' melts steel before bursting in the interior of a tank, making mincemeat of it occupants. Most of the audience shuddered. The two in the front row smiled. I tried to ignore them but that proved impossible. Both had spread their long legs out in front of them and one of them – the blond – had quite a package under his grey worsted pants.

Lots of them asked questions. The clock moved to seven o'clock. Neil gestured to his watch.

"I think that had better be it," I said. They applauded and filed out – all except the two in the front row. Neil busied himself coiling up cables and packing away the video equipment. The two boys came up to the table to examine my models.

"Aren't you going down to dinner?" I asked.

"We have ours later," the blond one replied. "Do you mind us hanging around?"

I didn't of course. Quite the opposite. On the other hand, Neil made it very obvious that he minded very much. He threw a cable into a box, banged down the lid and then kicked a chair out of his way.

"Go and have your dinner, Neil. I can do that," I said.

He glared at me and left, slamming the door behind him.

"Daisy's having one of her tantrums," said the dark boy.

"Daisy?"

"Our name for Neil Webb – he gets jealous if he sees us talking to anyone else."

"Why should he do that?"

I thought – I may be wrong – that the blond boy blushed slightly. I know I did. Memories of delightful sessions under the shower; me thinking of Neil as 'all mine' – it was all balls. Neil obviously got laid whenever and wherever he could. I knew about him and Dhasan of course. That wasn't too bad. Dhasan was my buddy, my partner. The thought of Neil doing it with a couple of big-mouthed teenage louts was infuriating.

I said nothing of course. That would have made things worse.

"Can we give you a hand packing these?" said the dark one. His hand rested on the nose of my model 'BLISTER'.

"Sure, if you've got time."

"Always glad to provide a helping hand," he replied and, as he spoke, he moved his fingers up and down the model and grinned. There was no mistaking that gesture. He smiled. His friend smiled. I smiled – and all inhibitions fled. Two handsome eighteen-year-old gay boys – Dhasan and me? Dhasan's apartment? It might be possible. My imagination went into overdrive. As we dismantled the models and replaced them in their boxes I learned that the blond one was Richard. His friend was Thomas. I'd guessed their ages correctly. Both were due to leave school that summer.

"I guess quite a lot of the boys will miss you and what you do for them," I said with what I hoped was a mischievous grin. It probably looked like a leer.

"There'll be others to continue the tradition," Thomas replied.

"Like Neil?"

"No way. He's going through the change."

"Change?"

- 145 -

"Yes. Give that guy another six months and it'll be girls, girls, girls and if you try to remind him how much he enjoyed male company, he'll deny it completely. It happens to most of them, I'm sorry to say."

"We think he's started on the downward slope already," said Richard. "He spends weekends away. It's pretty obvious that he's got a girl somewhere in town."

It was hard to keep a straight face. A girl somewhere in town' indeed! If only they knew!

I had planned on leaving the school no later than eight o'clock. In fact it was after nine thirty when I finally drove though the ornate gateway. Mr. Low had given me a glass of sherry and thanked me – and I'd arranged to meet Thomas and Richard for lunch in the 'Lobster Pot' on the following Saturday.

I called Dhasan the moment I got home.

"Can you think of a way of putting Neil off this weekend?" I asked.

"Why should I want to do that?"

"Because, Dhasan old dear, I've found two gorgeous kids."

"Sounds interesting. How?"

I told him about the lecture and what had happened.

"You're sure?" he said.

"Hundred percent," I replied.

"Okay then. Leave it to me. When do I expect them?"

"I'm meeting them for lunch. Should be with you at about three."

The 'Lobster Pot' was busy on Saturday. Fortunately I'd reserved a table in an alcove. Richard and Thomas enjoyed their meal – and the bottle of wine I'd provided. Gradually, the conversation shifted from St. Bede's and missiles to matters more interesting.

"Do I gather correctly that you have it off with the other boys?" I asked.

"Right first time," said Thomas. "The Stallions of St. Bede's, that's us. Man, woman or dog. The men and the women are all married. Mr. Low's Dalmatian lacks sex appeal so it has to be boys. Not that we're complaining. The Greeks had the right idea."

"And how many have you had?" I asked.

"No idea."

"How many this month?"

"Twelve at the current count."

"He had Simon Saunders last night – lucky sod," said Richard.

"And how was Simon?"

"Good. Very good."

"Better than Neil Webb?"

"I wouldn't say that. Neil's good – or was. Simon is – what did you say in your lecture? – an admirable soft-skinned target."

"And your missile penetrated?"

"Penetration achieved and explosion occurred well inside target," said Thomas. "He's away this weekend but I have another test firing planned for Monday."

For over an hour they thrilled me with tales of their exploits. When it was time to settle the bill, I was so excited that it was all I could do to stand up. Excited but also annoyed. Annoyed with myself. Here were two youngsters who had so much more experience than I had – and who were able to speak about it so openly. I was nervous too. What if they refused? There's hell of a difference between screwing a hero-worshipping young teenager and being on the receiving end.

I let them walk to the car in front of me. They really were out of this world as far as looks were concerned. Both had long, powerful legs, and full, well-padded butts filled their designer jeans. Their broad shoulders and backs were set off to perfection by T-shirts that looked as if they'd been molded on to them.

"Who's this guy you're taking us to see?" Thomas asked, clicking the seat belt round him. I'd ascertained during the meal that they had nothing planned and suggested visiting Dhasan. "Oh, Dhasan. He's a student at the university. A nice guy. Youngest son of an Indonesian prince actually." That always impressed people.

"Rich then, eh?" said Richard.

"Very and interested in the same thing as you and me."

"Sounds interesting."

"He is."

I could tell from the way Dhasan's brown eyes sparkled when he opened the door that he approved of my choice. We sat in his luxurious lounge sipping drinks from engraved glasses. They admired his new flat screen TV and hi-fi equipment. He put on a CD that they liked.

Looking back on that afternoon I have to admire Dhasan's skill and his patience. I didn't at the time. Very slowly – far too slowly I thought at the time – he led the conversation along. As he described the climate of Indonesia I wondered which of the two I would have. Was it going to be Richard's long blond hair on my pillow or Thomas's dark curls? At that stage neither seemed very likely.

But inhibitions, like the ice cubes in our drinks, melted. It must have been two hours after our arrival at Dhasan's apartment when he said, "Which of you two is the biggest?"

"How do you mean?" Thomas asked.

"Who's got the biggest cock?"

"Me." They spoke in unison.

"That would be too much of a coincidence. What do you reckon, Tim?"

I glanced at their hands. "Richard," I said, "by about a quarter of an inch."

"Balls!" said Thomas.

"We'll measure them later," said Dhasan. "I'll put a fiver on Thomas."

"You're on," I said – and put a five pound note on the table. Dhasan did likewise.

"Winner gets the money," said Dhasan. "Now, if Tim can come and sit with me on the sofa...." I did so.

"And you two stand in front of us."

"You're serious about the ten pounds?" Thomas asked.

"Absolutely. Come on."

They stood up and moved towards the sofa.

"What do you want us to do then?" asked Richard.

"Nothing. Come a bit closer. That's it."

As far as I could see, there wasn't a sign of an erection on either of them. Certainly not Richard whose wide hips were less than two feet away from my face. For the first time I noticed that his belt buckle was engraved with the letter 'R'.

"Stroke them a bit first," said Dhasan – and following his lead and watching him out of the corner of my eye, I ran my index finger up and down the centre of Richard's jeans. They were fitted with a zip fastener not buttons. I could feel the serration's – and a few minutes later I felt something else. Slowly, like a long balloon being inflated, the denim filled out under my finger. First, a thumb-sized bulge, which began to swell. Then it began to lengthen. It was if a snake were moving down, pushing its way under the denim towards the top of his right leg. The thumb became a sausage. The sausage hardened. Richard was breathing harder and so, to my right, was his friend.

"I rather think I'm going to be right," said Dhasan. I looked over. Thomas's cock was straining against his jeans – as, I confess, was mine. Dhasan seemed unmoved.

"Never!" I said. "Richard's is much bigger."

"Only one way to find out for sure," said Dhasan and, moving so quickly that Thomas wouldn't have time to object, he pulled down the zip.

Thomas didn't object. He winced slightly as Dhasan's groping fingers brought his cock into view.

"Eight inches by, say, an inch. Uncut. What have you got?" asked Dhasan. I was only too happy to find out. I'm not sure that Richard was but when your friend's cock is being admired and there's ten pounds on the table, shyness has to be overcome.

With some difficulty – and a lot of excitement – I managed to extricate what looked like a bit more than eight inches of extremely hard meat from the pale green Y-fronts that seemed to have been designed to make the operation as difficult as possible.

"I hereby declare Richard to be the winner," I said, holding it (though it did not need any support) in the palm of my hand.

"I'm still not convinced," said Dhasan. "If Thomas and Richard could get completely undressed...."

"Only if you do as well," Thomas interjected.

"Yes. Let's see which of you is the biggest," said Richard with a laugh.

"No contest I'm afraid," I said, "but happy to oblige." Dhasan had the biggest cock I'd ever seen.

Soon, the scent of four naked bodies wafted round the room. That, and the sight of Richard's butt really turned me on. You know my preferences already. Richard fulfilled all my criteria. Like freshly peeled, hard-boiled eggs, his buttocks gleamed, separated by what looked like a fine pencil line. There wasn't a hair on them. Below the fold and down his thighs fine hairs glittered, becoming a veritable golden fleece on his calves.

Predictably, Thomas was much more hirsute. Thomas was a very hairy boy indeed. A nice butt – slightly more rounded and tighter looking than Richard's but he even had hair on his back.

"Oh, you're so beautiful!" said Dhasan. For a dreadful moment, I thought he was talking to Richard. He wasn't. He sat on the sofa, pulled Thomas gently towards him and stroked the boy's thighs.

"Good enough to eat," he said – and I knew exactly what he had in mind.

I led Richard to the sofa and sat down.

It's funny how some memories stick in the mind. Richard's thick, honey-colored bush; the incredible thickness of his cock and the blue veins on its surface are as clear to me now as they were then. I remember his large and wide-open piss slit and his huge, pear-shaped scrotum.

"You can suck it if you want to," he said – as if I hadn't already planned on doing so.

"Two's better than one," said Dhasan. "Come over here and stand by Thomas."

I was choked – and quite certain that Dhasan would be. He got them standing so that their cocks touched and then took both of them into his mouth. He looked like a gerbil biting two Siamese twins apart.

"Oh, yeah! That's feels good!" said Thomas.

"Yeah!" Richard gasped.

With a hand on each of their butts, Dhasan took more and more of them into his mouth until their bellies were pressing against his ears. God knows how he did it. I've tried it since then and failed as miserably as I did on that afternoon when it was my turn. I opened my mouth to get a bit more of Thomas – and lost Richard's. And when, at last, Richard's cock-head was bashing my gullet Thomas's was brushing against my cheek demanding entrance.

One cock at a time is, and was enough for me. They tasted different. Thomas's was sharp-almost acid. Richard's was sweeter. The rank taste of perspiration wasn't so strong. Luck was on my side that afternoon. A drop of pre-cum landed on my tongue. Richard was close. Very close. I wondered, as I savored the taste, what the next move in the Dhasan master plan was going to be. Fortunately, I didn't have to wait.

"Bedroom," he said.

"Why can't we stay here?" Thomas asked. "Nobody can see us"

"Because I like to fuck in comfort," Dhasan replied.

"We don't do that," said Richard.

"But you do it to other people."

"That's different."

"Do as you expect to be done by. A Christian philosophy I believe," said Dhasan firmly. "Come on."

"What about me – us?" I asked.

"All taken care of. Follow me," said Dhasan, and together we shepherded the obviously rather nervous boys into his bedroom.

I'd been in that room a good many times without realizing that the king-size bed of which Dhasan was so proud could be divided. In its place were two smaller beds, each with a separate, sheet-covered mattress and a neat stack of towels. For planning, as I have said before, Dhasan gets top marks every time.

"A new prize," he announced. One hundred pounds to the pair who make it last longest."

"How much?" said Thomas.

"One hundred pounds."

"We don't know who's won the tenner yet," said Richard.

"Oh! Sorry. I'd forgotten. Hang on. There's a ruler in my desk," and believe it or not, the next five minutes were spent measuring cocks. Five minutes of good screwing time wasted whilst it was established that an eighth of an inch entitled Thomas to a couple of five pound notes. I was furious with impatience.

"And how do we know who wins this round?" Richard asked.

"I'd have thought that was pretty obvious. The ones still humping while the others are getting their breath back!" said Dhasan, and he led Thomas over to the bed nearest the window.

Dhasan, as you know, favors what he calls the doggie position. I don't. I take his point. It makes entry easier and allows your fingers easy access to the boy's cock whilst you're fucking his ass. But, I don't know, it seems undignified and a little too animal like to me. Nonetheless, I found it exciting to watch him get Thomas into the right position. So, I noticed, did Richard. His cock kept rising until it was almost parallel to his belly.

"....Knees a bit farther apart," said Dhasan. "That's right. That's perfect."

He was. I wouldn't have minded screwing him myself. His ass cheeks were white and smooth. His balls hung down and his cock pointed forward to his chin.

However, in a race – especially with a hundred pounds at stake, it's a mistake to pay too much attention to the opposition and I had things to do!

Obediently, Richard lay face down on the bed and parted his legs for me. "It won't hurt, will it?" he asked, which made me wonder if all he and Thomas had said was true. At least some of the dozen boys they'd screwed that month must have yelled as they lost their cherries. He could hardly be scared of the size of my equipment, which was no bigger than his.

We had to wait for the oil. I should have brought my own. Dhasan used a swan-neck bottle of oil he gets from the medical school. I don't think Richard or I minded waiting. We watched. Richard lay with his head to one side. I sat on the bed as Dhasan insinuated the nozzle between Thomas's cheeks. We listened to the bubbling of the liquid and Thomas's gasp as cold oil flooded into his rectum.

Thoughtfully, Dhasan wiped the bottle carefully on a towel before throwing it over to me. I parted Richard's cheeks, thrilling to the sudden anxious tightening of the muscles as I did so. His asshole was little bigger than the orifice of his penis but as red as his lips. It was as sensitive as lips too. He flinched as the nozzle touched it.

"Try to relax," I whispered.

"I am," he replied. I pushed. The plastic pipe bent. I pushed again. I might as well have been pressing against concrete. I stroked his back and his buttocks, maintaining the pressure on the nozzle. That did it. It slid into him quite suddenly; rather too much of it actually.

"Ow!" he said. "That hurt!"

"Sorry." I squeezed the bottle. He gasped. I felt a spasm run through his body. Then he lay still.

I pulled the tube out and parted his cheeks again. His ass blew an oily raspberry.

I turned to Dhasan. At first sight it appeared if he were doing nothing but merely resting his hand against Thomas's ass. It was Thomas himself who belied that impression. His tongue was hanging out, his face was red and his prick was jerking. Dhasan's long brown finger was hard at work clearing the way for something more substantial.

Richard was much more reluctant to accept mine. Again, constant pressure, constant re-assurance and stroking worked. He yelled a bit but, by the time my finger was into the knuckle, he'd quietened down and lay there breathing heavily with his eyes closed.

I love the feel of a boy's ass. They're all different too. I'm no doctor. I suppose, anatomically, they're identical but Barry, my midland boyfriend, is a spasmodic gripper. It feels like your finger is being chewed. Dhasan is a smooth slide. Neil is uniformly tight and feels like you're pushing your finger into a tightly closed fist. Richard was different again. He was tight but soft, like a vise lined with warm, moist sponge.

All I could see was the base of my finger growing redder by the second in the grip of his sphincter. What I felt was quite different. He was opening up. I could wiggle the tip of my finger inside him and did. He liked that. He grunted and squirmed around as though trying to get more. Richard was ready. Gently, I withdrew my finger and wiped it.

"Ready?" Dhasan asked.

"Ready."

"When I say go! Three-two-one-go!"

I put my hands on Richard's shoulders. He tensed up again. I had to reach down to get my cock into position, not that it needed a lot of help. I felt the oily softness of his still-gaping asshole and pushed as hard as I could.

I don't know who screamed first; Thomas or Richard. Their frantic yells merged. It was as well that Dhasan's neighbors were not at home. The din was indescribable: a long, drawn-out, rising duet. Then silence; a silence punctuated by heavy breathing. I remained still.

"Christ! That hurt!" I heard Thomas say. Having been on the receiving end of Dhasan's monster once or twice. I knew what he meant.

"Is it all in?" Richard whispered.

In fact it wasn't but I didn't tell him that. My cock-head was nowhere near his prostate. At least I couldn't feel it.

"Just lie still and get used to it," I said.

"I'm trying to."

We lay there for some minutes. Then, as always happens, he seemed to come to life. I felt his buttocks soften against my thighs and I pushed again, more gently this time. I found it. I was on the firing button. He shuddered violently. I pushed again and he was launched. He groaned and squirmed, trying to screw as much of my cock as possible into his tight little passage. Now all I had to do was to go as slowly as possible. I was determined that we would win the prize. Unfortunately, physiological factors can over-ride will power. A boy with a cock in his ass can't be controlled and it's just as difficult for his partner.

Richard's behind gyrated wildly under me. I felt him trying to lift it off the bed.

"Oh, yeah! Yeah! Yeah!" he panted-and I thrust even harder into him.

Louder sounds came from the next bed. "Ah! Ah! Oh, yes!" Thomas gasped.

"Oh! Oh!" Dhasan cried. Their bodies slapped together.

I held on to Richard's shoulders as tightly as I could.

"Oh, God! Oh, Jesus!" Thomas called. I turned my head towards them and was just in time to see it. A stream of semen jetted from Thomas's throbbing cock. He lifted his head but still caught quite a lot on his chin. The next lot splattered against the headboard of the bed.

I think Richard came at about the same time as Dhasan. I saw Dhasan collapse over Thomas's kneeling body and Richard gave a deep groan and lay still. My own orgasm came a few seconds later but I managed to convince Dhasan that I was still in action after he'd finished. The hundred pounds was ours. In fact, of course I gave it all to Richard.

"Neil Webb doesn't know what he's missing," said Thomas later. We'd taken them both out for a meal.

Dhasan said nothing but reached down and patted Thomas's butt.

"Me too," he said. "You'll have to come again."

Thomas laughed. "A bit more slowly next time," he said.

LOVING EVERY INCH
James Hosier

When I last wrote to you, I told you about Michael, who very kindly patched up my leg after I got a thorn stuck in it and who then parted with quite a lot of money for services I rendered three times a week, school vacations included. Good services they were, too. Worth every dollar of the fifty I charged. The customer comes first. In fact he never did. It was I who did the coming. I told you that he had this idea of both of us spending a short vacation in Florida. His intention was to screw me. Mine was to screw him, for as much as I could.

Well, we both reached our objectives. I came back with a sore ass. He came back less a thousand dollars but with a happy smile. Like I say, the customer is king. If you've got a bit of real estate and some guy wants to drill in it, you let him – for a fee.

I think I managed to convince him that I enjoyed every minute (or should I say every inch?). I took his quite considerable cock with a lot of lubricant. As for his promises of lifelong affection: I took those with a very large pinch of salt.

Which was just as well. Did I tell you about Phil Clay? Phil Clay was seventeen at the time. A year older than me. He's in the swimming team. He's a good swimmer, better than I am. More important, he's got a cock that wouldn't be out of place on a donkey.

Now, Phil is a funny guy. Like me, he hated gays. When we were much younger we used to hang around outside the 'Pink Angel' and watch them come out, holding hands (ugh!) and get in their cars and drive off. Then we'd go back to Phil's place or my place and imagine what they were getting up to. ("Up" is certainly the right word!)

Well... (Sorry about the flashback but you ought to know everything) when I was about fifteen, we went on a school field trip. The details of the trip are not important. It involved laying a grid on the ground and counting what was in each square. A real bore. But coming back on the bus we were sitting on the back seat and I guess it was the bouncing of the bus that gave me a hard-on. Phil noticed. I may have told him. I can't remember. He said there was only one thing to do so he put his raincoat over both of us. He pretty soon had my jeans open and had it in his hand. I did likewise. Gee what a tool, I thought. God, it was huge! It felt like steel too. I managed to get a handkerchief out of my pocket. I am happy to say that I came first. I wanted to stop then, but he insisted so I carried on and one wet handkerchief became a soaked handkerchief. I remember the teacher saying how impressed she'd been by our quiet behavior in contrast to the singing fools up front.

End of flashback. It never happened again. Having someone else do it for you sure beats jerking off in bed in the middle of the night but I read a book (or maybe it was a magazine article) that said that fifteen was a very impressionable age and that habits picked up then might stay with you for life. Not wanting to end up like the poor sods in the Pink Angel, I went for the birds. So did Phil, officially. He made sure everyone knew about the dental receptionist, the girl from Alabama and the French girl he screwed during one of the Clay family's many European vacations. He had photographs of himself with each of them; Phil with his arm round a girl grinning with expectations based on a large cock and a wallet to match. The Clay family are not just rich, they are loaded. I have no doubt that the girls enjoyed meals out, expensive drinks and possibly the occasional dance. I doubt very much if any of them even saw the monster between his legs.

Talk to any of the guys in the swimming team and they'll tell you that Phil is a great guy and completely straight. I'm the only one (I think) who knows the real truth. By the time I met Michael I was fed up with telling Phil to fuck off or to keep his filthy hands to himself. Generally speaking, the pool was a safe area because the other guys were around. An occasional underwater fumble was all he dared try. In school he made sure he was surrounded by girls. The problem was that my dad had gotten friendly with Philip Clay senior. They had some kind of business deal going and that meant compulsory dinner parties at the Clay house or ours. The dinners were okay. It was the after-dinner times that frightened me. "Why don't you two boys leave us? Show James your new software, Philip," or "James, why don't you and Philip go up to your room?"

Being alone with him was like being shut up with an octopus. What made it more infuriating was that he keep telling me that I wanted it. There was me pushing a hand away from my front while another one rubbed my butt. "Come on, Jamie. Ease up. You want it real bad. I can tell you do."

And the awful thing was that I did. If it hadn't been for that article I would have let him. If I am to be totally honest with you, there had been several jerk-off nights when the image of the girl I had selected was replaced with Phil Clay. Odd things, the handlebars of my bike or a baseball bat reminded me of the incredible hardness of his cock that day in the school bus.

Then, as you know, I met Michael and, one afternoon as I lay on his sofa and he was on it like a desert Arab with an ice lolly, I told him about Phil. Not about the bus of course. Just that there was this guy in the swimming team with about nine inches of cock.

My dad, as you know, sells fitted kitchens. I learned one hell of a lot from helping out in his showroom. Michael's reaction was just like the punters who come in to buy a kitchen. He finished doing what he wanted. The cream fountain worked. He got his fill and sat there licking his lips. I just waited.

"That one isn't bad," they say. You know damn well that they want it. They've read the pamphlet thru and thru at home. They've discussed it night after night but there is something about people that prevents them from being too enthusiastic. Then, in a totally uninterested voice they ask an almost irrelevant question, which is answered in the pamphlet: "What sort of wood is that door made from?"

"He's a swimmer, this guy Phil?"

"Yeah. He's good."

"Mmm"

Now, "Mmm" in the showroom is the point where you move in fast and tell the customer the really relevant facts. That teak is well nigh indestructible. That the super ceramic cooking surface has an automatic cut out – and you demonstrate.

Well, I didn't have Phil with me to demonstrate but I did go into a good sales pitch.

"A really huge cock," I said. "And you know what swimming does to a guy's ass." He sure did! The original contract was for me to go round to his place three times a week for him to get his mouth over it. Those were the jeans-round- the-ankles days. That soon gave way to naked James having his ass licked out and after the Florida vacation, the Sunday afternoon appointments were in his bedroom. Naked James with his legs in the air, feeling like he was sitting on a flagstaff.

"What days does he use the pool?" (In other words, "I'd like to have a real good look at it.")

"Fridays, mostly. About five o'clock." ("I can have one here by Friday at five o'clock, sir. Would that be convenient?")

"I can't say definitely. I may be out of town Friday." See what I mean? They hate to appear too keen. If I had a dollar for each time I've heard "I can't say definitely," I'd be a rich lad. In the showroom they've always got to consult someone first. The bank manager probably, though they never say that.

So, Friday came. A sunny, warm day. Just right for demonstrating something that was a pleasure to use and needed just a wipe-down with a damp sponge afterwards. No need to recommend the occasional rub-down with teak oil. Phil had been pretty liberal with the suntan oil. That and the hot summer, made him look the same color as the "Bavaria" kitchen with its teak and mahogany finish. More attractive too.

I'd told him that I knew a guy of about thirty and that I had mentioned Phil as being a really nice guy and that Michael wanted to meet him some time. That seemed to please him.

"No idea if he will come today or next week," I said, glancing at my watch. "How's that knee?"

"Oh, it's okay now. It was just a sprain. What's this guy's name?"

"Michael."

"I can't stay around too long. Got a date for tonight."

"That's bad luck. Michael wanted to take you and me to Roberto's."

"Roberto's? The steak house?"

"Yeah."

"I guess I could call her."

Well, I can honestly say that I never saw him make any calls that evening but, as Shakespeare says, "I run before my horse...."

When Michael arrived, Phil was lying on his front trying to get his back the same color as the front of his legs. I pointed to him. The customer nodded. One aspect pleased him. To be quite honest with you, it pleased me too. I'd been struggling with a potential hard-on for some minutes. Phil had the sort of butt that seems to flow from his back and you're never quite certain where cheek ends and thigh begins. Do you know what I mean?

"Phil, meet Michael."

Phil turned over. "Hi!"

"Well, hi!" He was impressed. So he should be. A cock like Phil's doesn't exactly hide itself in swimming trunks. Michael couldn't keep his eyes off it. (Okay. I admit it. I was staring at it too.)

In Florida we spent most days in and around the hotel pool recuperating from the previous night's activities, so I knew that Michael was a reasonably good swimmer. Nothing wonderful but competent and in Florida he had no interest whatsoever in improving his style. One look at Phil and it was a different story! Did Phil have the time? Would Phil mind? He thought possibly his leg action was at fault.

Soon they were both in the water and I sat on the side watching the performance. When Michael finished a length by putting both hands on Phil's shoulders, I knew I had a sale. Just like that moment in the salesroom when the wife puts both hands on the ceramic cooking surface and stares into space imagining all the wonderful meals she's going to cook on it. It was just a question of agreeing on terms. Handsome young men and fitted kitchens have one thing in common: They are both designed to be used. But handsome young men have to be persuaded to fulfill their function. Phil had the hots for me. I knew that but I wasn't at all sure if he'd agree to what I had in mind for him.

Michael made an amateur attempt in Roberto's that evening. I doubt whether Phil had even heard of Leonardo da Vinci and Michelangelo. The information that they were gay made no impression at all. He just sat there tucking into the biggest steak I ever saw and said nothing. He's not a great one for academic conversation, especially when it's likely to interrupt his protein intake.

"Michael and I were in Florida together," I said.

"Yeah?"

"It was great. You been there?"

"Yeah."

So it went on. It was like talking to a paper shredder.

I went to the toilet. When I got back to the table they were actually talking to each other. Okay, it was only about swimming but at least they were talking. Tactfully, I left them again and went to have a chat with Roberto about Italian wines. He gave me a couple of glasses to sample so I sat up at the counter and watched progress from there. They laughed about something several times. It was looking good.

Michael made no attempt to get Phil back to his house. At least I don't think he did. When it was time to leave, Michael's credit card took another bashing and he drove us both home, dropping Phil at the Clay villa before me.

"What do you think?" I asked. You're not supposed to ask customers to make up their minds in a hurry but I was anxious to know.

"About what?"

"Phil of course."

"Oh he's a nice guy."

"How about that cock? Did you ever see swim shorts with that much meat inside them?"

"Yeah. He's certainly well developed."

I went into my full sales pitch. I described parts of Phil that I had never actually noticed or seen.

"You're pretty keen yourself," said Michael. He must have noticed the lump in my jeans. I denied it of course. The next stage is to negotiate terms. Seventy five dollars seemed a reasonable price for a mouthful of Phil. He'd spent more than that on three steak dinners. That would be, say, thirty dollars for Phil and the rest for me. I couldn't guarantee that Phil would allow anything else but if he did – well, it would be expensive but well worth the money. "Quality like this is expensive, sir."

"I'm not sure. I'd have to think about it." A normal customer reaction. I ignored it. He said he would let me know.

Days passed. No word. I was on the couch for the third time after the dinner at Roberto's. He was wiping his mouth. I cleaned up a bit and pulled my jeans on. "What about Phil?" I asked. "Did you decide anything?"

"Yeah. Why don't you bring him with you on Sunday?"

Sunday, as you know, is my big bucks day. I didn't want to lose out. I said something about Sunday being our special day and how I looked forward to Sundays. Just saying it made me feel nauseous. The truth was that I kept my eyes shut for a long as possible and tried to forget that I was being screwed by a guy nearly old enough to be my father, and rode home on what felt like a red hot bike saddle. Business is business. I said I would see what could be done.

I saw Phil in school the next day. He must have been surprised to see me make a bee-line for him. I'd been waiting for a chance to catch him alone. He was looking at the notice board.

"Mike wanted to know if you're free Sunday afternoon," I said.

"Yeah, sure."

"He's a funny guy," I warned. "Gets a bit over-affectionate at times. Probably something to do with living alone. I go round there three times a week. Sort of keep him company if you know what I mean."

"Yeah, I know. He told me."

I was a bit at a loss for the next bit. It isn't covered in the sales manual. "To be honest," I said, "If he gets a bit carried away, I let him. He pays well and who cares?"

No reaction. I expected something on the lines of "Just let him lay a hand on me!" or "Sod that!" Phil just shrugged his shoulders and carried on reading.

"I could meet you on the corner. Say about three o'clock?" I said.

"No need. He gave me his address. I'll see you there."

I don't know why but that annoyed me. It was as if the factory had been dealing with the customers direct. That's how salesmen lose their commission. But there was nothing that I could do about it, except have strong words when the occasion arose.

Sunday came. I thought it would be a good idea to get to Michael's place early. After all, once things had been set in motion, I'd have to leave. He wouldn't want me hanging around though the prospect was pleasant enough to cause a hard-on under my jeans.

When I got to the house Phil was already there. It was he who opened the door to let me in. Michael was sitting on the couch.

"Hi!" he said, without getting up.

"Hi! Phil found his way here then?"

"It's not difficult to find," said Michael. I was about to sit next to him on the couch but Phil beat me to it. "So...you two been getting acquainted?" I asked, pulling out the other chair.

"I guess we have," Michael replied. "Don't sit down."

"Why not?"

"So we can both have a good look at you." He turned to Phil. "Yeah. I see what you mean," he said.

"See what?"

"Oh, we were talking about what swimming does to a boy's butt muscles."

I was embarrassed. Being talked about behind your back is bad enough. When what is there is the subject of the conversation it's worse. I muttered something about Phil being a more regular swimmer than I was.

"Yes, I can see that," said Michael. "Yours is coming along well though."

Coming along well! A few weeks previously he'd kissed it, licked it and called it beautiful!

"What would be interesting," he said, "would be for the two of you to get undressed and stand together. Just to see what difference a year and extra swimming make."

To my surprise, Phil agreed. I wasn't too sure. Sure, I'd gotten undressed in that room a good many times but you know what they say – two's company, three's a crowd. Besides which, there's something about being in close proximity to Phil that makes my cock do strange things and it

- 160 -

was beginning to take an interest. I sure as hell didn't want him to know about it.

But we did. The chair I'd intended to sit on was soon covered with clothes. I deliberately didn't look at Phil. Michael sat on the couch beaming like one of those Chinese gods.

"Hmm." he said when the last stitch was off. "Come and stand here." We did and that's when I noticed it. My half – hard six and a half inches was nothing! Phil's stood out rigid from that dense bush of his. I'd guess it was all of eight inches; a great, stiff, purple-headed monster.

Michael told us to come nearer. We did so and I shook my head, trying to warn him not to go down on Phil suddenly. He didn't. He took mine in his hand and said something about me being slow to warm up. Phil laughed.

"Why don't you do it? You're probably better than I am," Michael said. He let go and for the second time in my life I felt Phil's fingers close round it.

"Shit, man!" I exclaimed. "Leave off!" It was too late. It sprang to attention. I felt his other hand stroking down my back and over my butt. He whispered something. I didn't catch the words. I felt him pulling me down onto the carpet. A cushion from the couch landed near us. Then I was lying on the floor and Phil was biting my nipples. I felt his cock pressing against my thigh. I reached down to touch it. He grunted and started to lick me. In an attempt to stop him going too low down I put my arms around him. I remember feeling the soft hairs on his back. I might just as well have tried to stop a locomotive at full speed. His tongue went everywhere and I really do mean everywhere. I had it in my ears, my mouth, my navel, lapping over my cock and finally ... well I don't need to tell you. By this time, of course, I was too far gone to care. I was dimly aware of Michael's presence. I don't think he said anything. He handed Phil a tube. Instinctively I raised my legs and felt the cushion being shoved under me. Then that all-too- familiar cold, damp feeling and the strange sensation that you're like a block of wood being split apart. With Phil it didn't seem to hurt as much as it did when Michael did it.

"Jeez! You feel good!" he said. I don't know what I said. I recall that it made Michael laugh.

Then it was pressing against my ass. Pressing hard. It was the moment I always dreaded with Michael. Once a cock is in you, it's not too bad. It's the entry that hurts. Michael was bad enough but the thought of Phil's pile driver made me sweat with fear. I remember the feel of his shoulders against my legs and his hands on my hips. He grinned and shifted his position slightly. "Come on, Jamie," he said. "Ease up!" Moments later, "Oh, that's it. Oh yeah!" Inch by inch it slid in. I think I must have yelled when he was all the way in. I'm not sure. All I can recall of the next few minutes is the crack in Michael's ceiling, Phil's gleaming teeth and the feel of his balls slapping against me. It was painful but it was a strange sort of pain. Like the feeling you get towards the end of a swimming race. Every muscle hurts like hell but you know it has to be like that.

He let go of my hips and started to play with my cock. That felt good. At first I tried desperately to hold back to make it last but that was impossible. His cock was rubbing on my button and I had had enough experience with Michael to know the inevitable result of that.

He gave one more, huge heave and I knew he'd come. I'd only felt it before jetting out into a handkerchief. It felt a hell of a lot nicer going into me. I sensed the spurts. You can't honestly say that you feel them, especially when the same thing is happening to you. I saw mine arc upwards and felt it splashing down on my belly.

"Jeez!" he said again. He started to drag it out of me. That hurt. He waited and then tried again. It was better that time.

I was suddenly aware of the fact that we were both panting for breath. A drop of sweat landed on my face.

"Well done!" That was Michael's voice. Consciousness returned. The dirty sod had been sitting there watching!

"Good value?" asked Michael.

"Sure was," Phil replied. "Like you said, it's worth paying the extra – for quality."

THROB
Kevin Bantan

Leigh's hungry eyes were riveted on the beautiful white boy dancing in the middle of his table. His tongue moistened his lips, lasciviously, as he watched the dancer's muscles undulate lewdly for his entertainment. The white, lightly-oiled skin glistened over the boy's rippling sinews. Only a lustrous black satin pouch swaddling his genitals kept the boy from complete nudity. That, and the large, polished piece of onyx in his navel, were the only material additions to his smooth, flawless skin.

The boy knelt now at the edge of the table, inches from his face, still stirring seductively. Then he bent backwards onto his hands and opened his thighs wide, affording the patron a full view of his generously-filled satin prison and issuing a silent invitation to it.

First, however, Leigh leaned forward and kissed the duskly-shiny navel ornament. He licked it, sending a shiver through the boy. He was fascinated by this erotic addition to the dancer's anatomy, because he had never seen a male wear one before.

Only after he had satisfied his need to know the stone did he lower his head to press his lips to the glossy pouch, which harnessed the boy's sex. He inhaled the sweaty musk exuded by the bound crotch. Then he leaned back to savor the olfactory treat. His eyes continued to scrutinize the harnessed bulge, which had grown rounder from his kisses.

The cute face, topped with short black, blond-highlighted hair, bent toward him and kissed him with lips as generous as his own. He received the tongue, gladly, and sucked on it for a few seconds before the boy withdrew the offering.

The dancer rose effortlessly to his feet and lithely stepped down from the table. In a near pirouette, he settled lightly into Leigh's lap. He continued his movements, while smiling invitingly at him. All the while, the boy's hard hemispheres ground into his needy crotch.

But instead of fondling the satin lump of his desire first, Leigh fingered the glinting ebony jewel filling the exotic dancer's navel, as the boy's arms went around his muscular neck. The firm body squirmed in delight, as he meticulously traced the edges of the black belly button.

When the boy kissed him soulfully a second time, Leigh allowed his fingers to track down the ridges of the lower abdomen to the obscene display of maleness. He fondled the pouch and squeezed it. The dancer's lips moved more feverishly on his and the young man's ass cheeks abetted the erection straining up at them.

"You're beautiful," he whispered into Leigh's ear. "I want to take care of your needs after Ryan entertains you." He kissed Leigh, tenderly, and smiled, before reluctantly relinquishing his seat on him.

Leigh watched the boy's naked round posterior muscles work like human pistons, as he walked away. He turned once, to smile and purse his lips at the customer. His body was in profile, so that Leigh could enjoy the distention of the glorious male basket he sported. The blondish sex machine's name was Casey.

Ryan was nearly a physical copy of the white boy, except that his features were as captivatingly African as Casey's were European. His black hair, too, was frosted. His skin was a rich dark brown. The juxtaposition of it with his white pouch and pearl navel jewel began to stir Leigh's sex again.

The black dancer was as sexy as his counterpart, which was dire news for Leigh's challenged hormones. Ryan's movements were as fluid and erotic as Casey's, his kisses now more arousing in Leigh's heightened state. The youth straddled him during his lap dance. He arched his back and sucked in his abdomen, so that the patron would play with the large gem embedded in his midsection. He had evidently noticed the man's fascination with Casey's.

As they kissed, Leigh fingered the smooth, iridescent stone, which was as slick as the youth's glistening, coated skin. Ryan moaned into his mouth as he fondled the boy's enhancement, as if waves of pleasure were being telegraphed from the stone into his body.

"You are so gorgeous," the dancer whispered, and nuzzled his ear. Leigh's hand rubbed the solid muscles of the youth's groin before settling on the hard, white lump and caressing it.

"You can have us both, if you want," Ryan said, pulling back to smile at him with teeth as white as his belly button. The customer definitely did.

So it was that Leigh Alan Jackson was following four perfect ass cheeks up the carpeted wooden steps to the bar's second floor. The boys turned down a hall at the top of the stairs, as his tented erection pointed at them like a sexual divining rod. They were barely legal, he was thinking. If that.

He didn't consider their ages for many more seconds, because Casey opened a heavy, paneled door and stepped back to allow Ryan and Leigh to precede him into the room. It was sparely furnished, but neat. The bed was king-sized and draped with a spotless champagne-colored satin comforter.

They undressed him slowly, alternately kissing him and teasing his interested manhood. When he was naked, each pressed against his side and slid their hairless legs slowly up and down his in a gesture so provocative, that his sex bobbed in response.

They then guided him to the bed, where he lay down in the center of it. The boys crawled on either side of him and bent to take one of his already-rigid nipples into their mouths. He caressed the short hairs on their heads as they suckled on his dark, sensitive nubs.

From there, they tongued down his tight body, Casey pausing at his navel to make love to it with his lips and then to ream it leisurely, tantalizingly, with his tongue. Ryan continued down his abs, licking the ridges as he went. When he made pubic fall, he lingered over the kinky hairs beside the erection vibrating helplessly over Leigh's belly, teasing them into goose bumps.

But it was Casey's tongue which made him squirm more. The boy looked up and grinned with teeth as blinding as Ryan's. "We have a belly button fetish, in case you didn't guess," he said, looking sheepish.

Ryan paused and gave Leigh a smile identical to the other dancer's, and said, "We're really not all that kinky, but you know, whatever makes you throb." He shrugged.

"You two make me throb, for sure."

"Thanks. That's sweet of you to say," Ryan said, as Casey joined him at Leigh's crotch.

They began to lick and kiss his engorged penis and taut scrotum. He breathed heavily as his nerves screamed in pleasure from the sensual lips and tongues, which were ravishing him. He began to gasp and thrash as the dancers slid their soft palms over his torso and legs. His cock jerked and pulsed, begging for release, but the talented boys gave it no such satisfaction. They backed off, when they sensed that he was close and shifted to the insides of his thighs in order to allow his shaft to cool off. They were unbelievably gifted teases.

When they resumed their attention to his erection, they took turns covering him with their mouths, mingling their saliva on his glans and shaft, making them glisten like their oiled skins. It excited him further to see his rod shiny with their combined lubricants on it.

Then, when he thought that he would pass out before he came, they decided to have mercy on his beleaguered organ. Together they tongued the sensitive underside of his prick insistently together, which brought him to a quick, explosive climax. When he ceased spasming, they cleaned out his slit with their oral fingers and then lapped at the white pools on his abdomen and chest.

After they had licked up all of his essence, they smiled at him.

"Man, that was great," Leigh said. "You guys are unbelievable."

"Thanks. That was just act one," Ryan said, joining the white boy to Leigh's right.

He turned on his side and watched them kiss, sharing the remnants of his come with each other. As they embraced orally, they undid the snaps on each other's neutering pouch. He looked on in anticipation as they removed the rounded satin material from their respective genitals. He sucked in his breath, when he saw their cocks spring to freedom. They were almost identical in their lengths and girths and definitely blessed in their endowments.

Ryan's nearly black cock angled up against Casey's pale member creating the impression of crossed swords at the beginning of a duel. They continued to kiss each other enthusiastically. Their erections jerked occasionally, caused by the passion searing their lips. It was obvious that they had engaged in this type of foreplay many times, so in harmony they were with each other.

Slowly they closed the gap between their bellies, forcing their shafts to slide up the other's body. Their convex gems touched just above the slits of their penises, white against black. Beautiful, he thought. Like them. When the stones were in contact, he noticed that they were like live contrastingly-colored bookends kneeling there in front of him.

The same silky palms, which had recently stoked the fire on his skin, were now roving over the sleek surfaces of their partner's body. This was a far better show than the ones downstairs had been, despite the fact that Leigh was simply an observer in this one. Well, that wasn't quite accurate, because, incredibly, his recently-spent cock was beginning to respond to their lovemaking.

Ryan lowered himself onto the bed, still attached to Casey's lips. Once they were horizontal, the white boy began to kiss down the black boy's body. His neck, his chest, his abdomen were covered with dozens of moist lip prints. He skated his tongue around the jeweled navel, causing the black boy to sigh. He maintained the skating technique, as he zig-zagged over the smooth skin, which stood in sharp relief over Ryan's toned muscles, until he encountered the mushroom head of the boy's erection. Without pausing, he engulfed it with his mouth.

Ryan stroked the streaked hair as Casey's lips lavished deserved praise on the lovely male organ. He teased the sac into retreat with his nimble fingers. Layer after layer of saliva he applied to the tensed rod, making it slippery with his moisture.

Somehow, Ryan seemed to pass a silent signal to the fellating boy, and he ceased his ministrations. He kneeled up the black boy's body until the ebony cock nestled between his classically-curved cheeks. Slowly, he lowered himself onto the phallus, making it disappear into him. When he was impaled, he leaned down and kissed the full lips pouting from Ryan's face.

Then Casey fucked himself with studied deliberation, as they began to tell each other how beautiful he was, what a great body he had and what a terrific lover he was. Their sex talk was disembodied lovemaking. Leigh found himself more and more turned on by the two studs coupled next to him. It was manifest that their relationship was far deeper than he would have guessed, which served only to heighten his enjoyment of the performance.

He resisted the urge to wrap his hand around himself, choosing instead to let it wave freely in front of him. He suspected that the longer he witnessed this hot mating, the more likely it would convulse of its own accord.

When Casey bent again, it was to suck his partner's small, dusky nipples and areolas. Then he licked them, and sucked them again, in turn. The supine youth appreciated this attention, gauging from the low moans escaping from his mouth. Ryan remained buried inside him the whole time, no doubt kept throbbing by Casey's nipple worship.

Although enjoying the intense action, Leigh picked up the discarded black pouch, fondly remembering his nose's first encounter with it. The satin felt sensuous to the touch inside and out. It was seamless and elasticized around the edges with black snaps on top, where Casey secured it onto his equipment. He considered using it to further his own pursuit of pleasure but decided that his hard on was having enough fun on its own.

He did bring the damp material to his nose and inhaled the male scent suffusing it. He liked it so well the second time, that he picked up Ryan's white stringless G-pouch, curious to smell him, too. Their boy perfumes were remarkably alike, which he didn't expect. Perhaps the satin imparted its own strong scent, which made their odors strangely similar, he thought.

He turned his complete attention back to the dancers. He had never seen a black boy and a white boy make it with each other, but he couldn't have chosen two better representatives of their races for such a tryst. They were ideal, as his hardness attested. He also found the presence of the black and white stones on their naked bodies highly erotic. It was a crowning touch, to see them bejeweled as they were.

Ryan was now returning Casey's favor, only he was pinching, pulling, twisting and flicking the firm dark brown nubs of the white boy with his fingers. Casey loved it and began to move faster on the cock sheathed in him. His tempo on the black rod continued to increase, making him look as if he were an elegant bronco rider. This made the black boy take the vulnerable erection into his hand.

The sight of the brown fingers encircling the white penis drove Leigh's sexual regulators to a higher concentration. He licked his lips as Ryan masturbated his partner as easily as if it were his own manhood which he was stroking. Casey was mewling sex noises as Ryan came closer and closer to pulling his trigger. At the same time, he began to buck into the young man, making the rodeo analogy suddenly more fitting.

Then, before Leigh could reach his version of coital nirvana again, Casey arched his back and cried out, sending his first volley onto his partner's face. The second hit his neck; the third his sternum. The last fell harmlessly onto the rises of the black boy's abs.

As the white boy shuddered in orgasm, Ryan sharply reported his own release, evidently brought over the edge by Casey's convulsions. They remained where they were for a few seconds, panting, their skin shinier than ever from their sex play. Then Casey's body relinquished his partner's cock to kiss him and rub his nose. They chuckled.

They sat next to each other facing Leigh, as if joined at the hip, with an arm around the other's waist. They grinned at him. He grinned back. Even without coming himself, his body felt as if it had participated in another three-way with them, their ardor having taken him on a wild hormonal ride to his own body's exhaustion.

"That was unbelievably hot, guys," he said. His boner corroborated the statement.

Casey said, "Yeah, dancing makes me throb. And pleasuring someone as gorgeous as you does the trick, too. But nothing makes it throb more than making it with my beautiful twin brother." He kissed Ryan, as Leigh's mouth dropped open.

The guys laughed at his shocked expression.

"What's the matter, you couldn't tell," Ryan asked and they chuckled some more.

"Ryan and Casey O'Toole, at your service," the white twin said, grinning.

"Our mom's black and our dad's white. We just happened to come out the strange way the DNA color dice got rolled," Ryan said.

That helped to explain the close resemblance of their body shapes. And the longer he looked at them, the more similarities he saw in the facial characteristics he had previously believed to be so different. The soft brown eyes under arched brows; the same cheekbone structure; their exquisite puggish, flared noses. The sultry pairs of lips.

They were beautiful, but more than that, they were, indeed, black and white versions of each other.

"We're obviously fraternal twins, although when people see us side by side, they get really weirded out, because they know it isn't possible for us to look identical. We think that the skin color gene is the only one we don't share. Otherwise, we're alike," Casey said.

"You are. It's uncanny."

"Yeah. But we were bonded from the start as if we were identical. We cried if the other wasn't near us. We were inseparable growing up. There is no one in the world that I could possibly love, except my brother," Ryan said. They looked so lovingly at each other that Leigh's heart contracted.

"Not a chance. I think we were doing it with each other as far back as the womb, somehow, because mom said that we were a bitch to carry during pregnancy, kicking her as much as she said we did. We've been playing around with each other for as long as we can remember outside of it, too," Casey said.

"Yeah, we have. So here we are. This our uncle's place, and it's perfect for us, because we love to dance and to please horny customers," Ryan said.

"And you've certainly satisfied this one, believe me," Leigh said, somehow knowing that soon the twins would again ignite his body, and before long it would throb.

THE TENNIS CLUB
Scott Anderson

Stewart ran down the stairs from his bedroom to the hallway below. He was dressed in his whites for tennis and carried a sports bag and a tennis racket to confirm his intentions. "I'm off, Mum. Shan't be late," he called out.

"Right, Stewart," came back a reply.

"Where's Mum?"

"In the kitchen."

"Oh, right," Stewart acknowledged as he made his way towards that particular room.

His mother was wiping around the sink area as he entered. "Thought you'd be finished," he said. "Where's Dad?"

"Finished now. Your dad is somewhere in the garden. Anyway, is that you off now? Hope you enjoy your game son. It is a very hot night so don't you be over-exerting yourself, and be careful driving." She smiled with a look of caring tenderness and pride that only a loving mother seems privileged to give.

"Thanks, Mum. Shan't be late." And he bent down and gave her a quick kiss on the cheek. "Bye," he said, as he turned and exited from the scene.

He deposited his tennis racket and bag on the rear seat of his coupe, with the roof already down, climbed into the driving seat of his pride and joy, and was soon reversing down the driveway into the street. Stewart set off in the direction of his friend's home. The warm breeze ruffled his golden blond hair as he sped along in the balmy summer evening air. He hoped George would be ready when he arrived, otherwise they might have to wait a while to get a court, even though they had previously reserved one. The rules of the private Tennis and Social Club were clearly simple. If the party was not available at the time allocated, the court could be given to someone else. George appeared from his house as Stewart drove up, much to Stewart's relief.

George and Stewart had been friends during and since their school days. They were both keen sportsmen, which in reality, was the only interest which bonded their friendship. George that projected a truly macho image whose main topic of conversation was disco, drinking and girls. Stewart had often wondered how he ever managed to become qualified as Surveyor. Where he had been concerned, he had studied hard for his degree with honors. George only ever said that he had obtained his qualification. Stewart had gone out on a few other occasions with him, mainly to make up a foursome to partner a chum of one of George's current girlfriends. It was never his scene though, and lately he had declined such invitations. Even their nights out for sport were becoming fewer. As the car sped along towards the Tennis Club George was relating most graphically his latest conquest with a redhead. According to him, every girl ripped off her knickers about half an hour after meeting him, begging for it. George was becoming too repetitively boring and letting his fantasies and imagination cloud reality. Stewart was relieved to turn the car through the gates of the club and park. The only good thing about George was he made an excellent adversary at tennis. Stewart never worried who won. It was always the hard-fought worthwhile contest that was important.

They both left the court following their game, their faces running with perspiration and their wet shirts clinging to their bodies.

"Let's get a shower and into some dry gear. My balls feel as if they are lying in a bucket of water." George spoke into the strings of his racket, which he stupidly carried directly in front of his face.

"As bad as that? Sign of old age coming on," Stewart joked.

"Sign that my balls and the rest of it is too well developed or my pants are too tight," George smirked leeringly.

Stewart decided to let the intended banter end there. He knew what would emerge from it. George would suggest that he invite one of the girls from the club into the shower with him and his fantasies would run wild once more.

They climbed the steps leading to the clubhouse in silence. The routine would be the same as always. They would report to Reception, which also served as the bar and shop, and confirm their court was free. George preceded Stewart across the foyer and seemed to strut aggressively rather than walk towards the counter. As they approached, the young, dark- haired attendant stood up from the chair on which he had been seated. He had been at the club about a month now, and, being part-time, was not always on duty. In fact, when they had reported in Old Charlie was acting as the receptionist.

"That's court number four free. What showers are available?" George spoke in a superior, demanding tone.

"Court number four you said, Sir?" the young man asked politely for double confirmation.

"That's what I said," George spat out his reply.

"Showers for two, Sir?" the young man asked, looking towards Stewart who had stood slightly to the rear.

"No! For three. One for me, one for my mate and one for the Invisible Man."

The young man never flinched, simply retained a quiet superior dignity. "Showers three and five are cleaned and available Sir. Here are the keys," he said, handing them over. As he did so, he gave Stewart a look that seemed so tender and yet full of question, or, was it one of sympathy?

Stewart felt confused and was sure he was blushing, although he could not understand why he felt that way. He merely gave a friendly smile in response.

George spun towards Stewart, "What do you want to drink after showering?"

"Oh! Oh, I'll have a fresh orange with ice please," Stewart replied.

"That will be a pint of lager and a fresh orange with ice," George instructed, adding, "And I suppose you won't be stupid enough to put the ice in the lager?"

George turned away abruptly from the counter. "Right, mate, let's get freshened up," he addressed Stewart in a friendlier manner.

"Why were you so aggressive and cocky towards that guy?" Stewart asked as they made their way to the changing rooms.

"Him? That guy is so polite, he irks me."

"He's paid to be polite. If he wasn't, no doubt you'd be the first to complain and report him!" Stewart snapped.

"No doubt about it. And if I say 'jump' to him, I'll bloody well make sure he jumps," George retorted.

"Get off the guy's back, George."

"And why have you suddenly become so concerned? Don't tell me you fancy the guy. Do you want to be on his back?" George asked sarcastically.

"Don't talk wet. Because you lost tonight, don't take your bad sportsmanship out on everybody. Maybe once you've had a shower you'll feel better, so in the meantime, just shut your mouth." Stewart could feel his temper rise.

George looked at Stewart as they reached the changing rooms. The angry expression on Stewart's face forced George to remain silent.

The friendship between them was still under strain while they sat silently with their drinks. When George suggested they should leave and head home, Stewart was readily willing to agree. Normally, George would have had quite a few drinks, but not tonight. It had been habitual when Stewart drove George home for a possible further meeting to be arranged. All George said was "Thanks, I'll maybe phone you sometime." Stewart knew he had no intentions of doing so. The future interests for the leisure hours of George now obviously focused elsewhere.

A short time later Stewart stripped naked and lay on top of his bed. It was so hot and stuffy. His mind was confused and seemed to race irrationally. He pulled the top sheet up to his stomach when he remembered he had forgotten to put his soiled tennis gear into the laundry basket, and his mother would no doubt appear to extract them from his sports bag. He was still annoyed with George's aggressive attitude at the club. The young man did not deserve to be subjected to such treatment from an overbearing prig like George. Forget George. What had been done, had been done. He began to think about the young man and the gentleness in his eyes. The look that had passed between them had him puzzled. Stewart conceded he had always received a rather friendly look, but that did not mean anything strange. He possibly was the same with all the members. There was something about him though. Something that deeply interested Stewart. There was something different about him, some sort of magnetism.

In a sudden moment of panic he felt afraid. Why did this young man seem to be of such importance, now? Why did he arouse feelings within him? These feelings had occurred once or twice previously, though he had cast them quickly aside. This time it seemed so overpowering. Other fellows of his youthful age were already married and fathers. Why could he not get a real interest in girls? His heart began to beat faster at the thought that he might be – might be – different. What was wrong with him? He broke out in a cold sweat and pulled the top sheet up to his chin. Again the vision of the young man pushed foremost into his mind, which strangely made his inner panic begin to subside.

At last Stewart fell asleep, dreaming. He saw himself running naked beneath a long avenue of trees. The touching overhead branches changed and became the high ceiling of a vast cathedral, and the stout tree trunks formed the strong pillars supporting the arches. It was so beautiful and very peaceful. He knew that there was an elusive figure running on the other side of the pillars. Sometimes the figure seemed to be behind and then in front of him, but he did not stop running. Suddenly, a naked young man appeared a little way off in front of him with his arms outstretched, but he did not stop running. As he approached the figure, he felt such elation when he recognized the young man at the club. They clasped hands and kept running, but suddenly the scene changed. They were now running, still naked, hands clasped, and laughing freely and happily as they made their way through a field of long grass, as if it were being filmed in slow motion. At last the young man stopped running and pulled Stewart round, so gently, to face him. The soft, tender look in his eyes expressed adoration which was matched with a smile so warm, so beautiful, so sensual. The young man released Stewart's hand and slowly placed his own on Stewart's cheeks. His head came forward very slowly and, as he was about to kiss him, Stewart wakened with a start.

The following evening Stewart knew that he had to return to the club. He had to see him again, face to face, as he believed it was the only way to erase that thoughts which had given him such a dream. Perhaps someone might be looking for a partner for a game. Whether he played or not was of little importance. What was important was to straighten himself out and rid his mind of utter stupidity and nonsense. He hoped the young man would be on duty, but when he arrived, Old Charlie was behind the counter. Stewart's spirits dropped, but he went through the formalities of saying he was available as a partner. In the meanwhile he would have an orange juice and a seat in the foyer. He lifted a motor magazine and thumbed through it, flicking over the pages with none of his usual interest in cars. Raising his head, he directed his eyes towards Reception. His heart missed a beat when he saw the young man standing behind the counter looking over in his direction. As their eyes met, the young man smiled and gave a quick wave in recognition.

Stewart's mind started racing again. This was not the way his plans were supposed to go. He began wishing that he had not come to the club, but that thought passed. At the very least he could apologize for George's behavior the previous evening. Yes, it was a good idea. It is what he would do. He would apologize for George. What he must not do was make a complete idiot of himself. He finished off his drink slowly and deliberately, lifted his empty glass, and walked over to the counter.

"Good evening, Sir. I believe you are hoping to be partnered for a game. Nothing so far, I'm afraid. Is your friend not with you tonight?" the young man smiled.

It was the same smile in the dream. For a moment Stewart's mind again became befuddled. Regaining his senses quickly, he told himself that he must continue with his quest to stop the ridiculous situation. He must not allow himself to be sidetracked.

"No. No, he is not with me tonight and I don't know when he will be back. Can I have another orange please?" Stewart imagined that his voice was trembling.

"Certainly, Sir," as the young man turned to fill a glass of orange. "And your usual ice?" he asked as he turned to face Stewart.

"Yes, please."

The young man placed the glass on the counter and Stewart handed over the cash. As their hands touched, Stewart felt his heart give a thump and a tingling sensation around his stomach. It was not going the way he had planned.

"Thank you, Sir," the young man said softly as he accepted the money.

"Look," Stewart began hastily. "Look, I want to apologies for the rudeness of my friend last evening. It was quite uncalled for and in extremely poor taste. Forgive me, please."

"Oh, that's all right. You don't have to apologize for him. After all, you weren't rude." The young man still spoke softly as if he were reading Stewart's mind, and trying to soothe his mental stress.

"No. That's true, but I was embarrassed. It was just so unnecessary."

"Thank you. I do appreciate your concern."

"Can I ask your name?" Stewart requested, gaining more confidence and inner composure.

"My name is Paul," the young man replied.

"And my name is Stewart. Have you another job besides this one in the Club?"

"Not really. I'm at University and I take any odd job going to eke out my pennies. I hope to get my degree next year and after that, a permanent job."

"Do you belong to these parts?" Stewart asked.

"I belong to London but had to come here, for a place. I sometimes manage to visit home at the odd weekend. My only sister is there on her own now. My parents are both dead."

"Oh! I'm truly sorry," Stewart said with sincere sympathy, as he thought of his own supportive, loving parents.

"Thanks, Stewart. It was quite traumatic at the time. They were both killed in an horrific car accident. I missed out on a year's study because of it all. That was two years ago now, but we both manage okay. My sister's working and we manage, as I've said. My sister and I have always been close and that helps a lot. What about you?"

"I live with my parents and work locally. Nothing very exciting I'm afraid. Just a school teacher who has high hopes of becoming a lecturer. I'm also studying for even more qualifications."

The conversation ended abruptly at that point. They both stood engrossed with their own private thoughts. Stewart's mind was quickly evaluating what Paul had said. The guy had gone through a bad time losing his parents and being separated from his sister, who maybe needed his physical and moral support. He seemed a really decent guy, a gentleman in fact, who was perhaps lonely. One can be so lonely in a city, in a crowd, and even among the fraternity. Stewart told himself that perhaps this was the empathy between them. A simple basic friendship. He had mentally accused George of not facing reality, and he had allowed his own mind to play tricks on himself. Perhaps Paul felt that he needed a friend and that he could be the friend he needed. Paul was not really able to suggest it as he was an employee at the club and unable to overstep his place in case he lost his job. Stewart made his decision and broke the silence.

"Do you have many friends here, Paul?"

"Not really. I study a lot whenever I can. No Stewart, I am afraid I do not have any real friends."

"Would it be forward of me to suggest we could perhaps meet sometime soon and go for a coffee, a drink, or play sport or something? Please say if you'd rather not." Stewart gave an encouraging smile.

"On the contrary, it sounds really good. I'd like to meet you very much and look forward to it." Paul's reaction expressed a deep sense of gratitude. He obviously wanted to say something more, but was unsure of himself. He hung his head for a moment.

Raising it again, he looked directly into Stewart's eyes as if searching for an answer to a question not yet asked. The tender look and the warm, beautiful smile on his lips were again the same as in the dream that had so confused Stewart.

Paul swallowed hard, then said, "I think we may have a lot more in common than we each want to believe."

Stewart nodded, although he had no idea what Paul meant.

GOING DOWN
Rick Jackson, USMC

Life is funny. Sometimes you get more tail shoved into your face than even a Marine can handle; other times, because of biorhythms or the Fates or the intervention of alien visitors or whatever, you can't score tail with a hundred-dollar-bill hanging out of your fly. When you're an anatomically dick-advantaged, six-two Marine with a boy-next-door face, muscles out the ass, and foxy green eyes to woo the romantic, the dry spells may not last long; but after a steady diet of Marine Corps workouts underway, four days of handling yourself on leave away from the Corps can seem for-fucking-ever. The pressure can even build up enough for a guy to use lines he wouldn't believe in fuckflick, and we know how true to life those things are, don't we?

I'd taken a room for a couple weeks at the Hale Koa – a great hotel designed and built at public expense so grunts on R&R from Vietnam would have a nice place to fuck. It's still run by and for the military, but most of the guests are now retired Gray Panther types or their dependents. The $24 rooms are as good as any in the state and are smack on Waikiki Beach so I can't really kick. I'd expected to run across more firm government-owned flesh but had only seen one prime candidate – and he'd been in the lobby the day before so I wasn't even sure he was registered at the hotel. The single glance I got of him was enough to tell me he had what I was looking for. The guy was just under six feet, with curly brown hair and enough tanned flesh stretched tight over perfect muscles to make my dick dance like a dervish. The brief look I had at his strong chin and brow, sparkling blue eyes, and prime-quality dicksuckable lips made me stroll out the door behind him. By the time I was on the beach, though, he wasn't. I spent most of that afternoon sniffing around for his ass until I got disgusted with myself. I'd been moping about like an adolescent with a bad case of hero worship so I did the sensible thing: I went back upstairs and took care of business myself.

Early the next afternoon, dressed only in shorts and zori, I took the elevator down with the idea of finding sunlit solace on the beach – and maybe more, besides. As the elevator doors open, who should be standing there but young Spunky, naked but for neon orange swim trunks that only served to highlight his obvious advantages. Stunned by his classic beauty as much as by the suddenness of his appearance, I said the first idiotic thing that came to mind: "Going down?"

Since we were already on the ground floor, a normal person would have shaken his head or said, "No, dickweed, get the fuck out of the elevator." Brad gave me a long, slow look up and an even slower look down before he parted those suckable lips to brag "Anywhere, anywhen."

I managed to hold off until the click of my door guaranteed privacy, but my discretion had been a near thing. On the ride up 17 floors in the elevator, Brad's beachy smell of man-sweat and salt was more aphrodisiac than I needed. Granted, that's not saying much. After four days of palm-driven pleasure, I'd have gotten hard for a tax audit or root canal. Brad's compact, muscular frame and curly hair, his radiant smile and sparkling eyes, the stench of tropical man and glow of his noble-savage tan were more than any mortal should be asked to take at one time. Taking, though, was just what I had in mind – and Brad was more than ready to give.

Driven by instinct and need, my hand reached out and pulled him to me, slipping from the small of his back, across a few stray grains of sand, and down to separate his ass from those orange shorts. A morning spent lying in the sun had heated his solid ass until it was tinder for the lust that had long burnt out of control inside me. His soft, supple skin stretched tight across sweaty, Corps-quality cheeks. As my fingers slipped from his spine, across his tail-bone, and down into the narrow, sweaty crevice between those beautiful buns, his whole body shuddered a welcome like an earthquake in an aspen grove. Our eyes locked together first, then our lips.

My left hand joined my right inside his shorts, each digging deeper than the other until his butt was pried apart and my fingertips were slipping across his pulsing asshole, ripping sensation from the secret recesses of his soul while my lips sucked at his, limbering them for the pleasure that lay inevitably ahead. His hands were all over me, too, sliding along my flanks, cupping my ass, tweaking my tits, pulling in great handfuls at the hair covering my chest, caressing my neck, and generally worshipping my hard marine body the way I agreed it deserved. Even through the rough, rust-colored thatch on my chest, I felt his stiff tits digging into my pecs as he ground up against me, a squid-bitch in heat.

Brad's lips escaped mine and slid down my neck, sucking and licking their way to my shoulder. I tore into his salacious scent like a satiric vampire, slurping my way from his Adam's apple around to his scruff, scraping away his sweat and special sea-bred man-musk with my bumpy tongue. His body shivered under my touch as my tongue and fuckfingers played with him like a cat before the kill. By now, our cloth-clad dicks were grinding together, begging to be free so they could breed one tight pleasure-hole after another.

His lips and tongue found my ear and sent shrapnel ripping through my universe as he burrowed his way into my brain and left me hopelessly, helplessly heaving in his arms. When the slut tired of tongue-fucking my ear and let me come back to consciousness, I found we'd somehow lost our clothes and were writhing about on my bed, our dicks darting along between our hard bellies, gushing enough slick pre-cum to lube a mastodon orgy. The glorious scent of man-sex saturated the air, transforming the artificial, air-conditioned atmosphere with the most ancient and urgent of man's natural needs. I had great handfuls of his soft, brown hair, using them to smear his face into mine while our dicks dueled. The cocky bitch slipped the hands he'd had all over my back down to my ass and felt me up. I suppose since most jarheads love nothing so much as a stiff squid dick up their butts, he figured

I'd be easy. Before he could adjust to the idea I was that uncommon Marine who did instead of got done, my rod was rubbered and his faggot, fairy-assed legs were pointing towards the ceiling.

I took the time to watch his face as my dick followed the path my fuckfingers had blazed through his asshole. Something about hanging suspended over a guy's face, watching every muscle react as my warrior's weapon slams up his ass has always rung my chime almost as much as busting the nut itself. Young Brad was a special rush – because he was so fucking cute, because being on the bottom seemed such a surprise, and because the guy reacted as though having my thick nine inches of Marine meat rammed home were the event of his young life. Most guys don't take what I have without flinching, but old Brad damned near passed out. His eyes were like a stellar catastrophe, bugging out and flashing nova-bright in shock and the first throes of agony one instant, and then cascading in upon themselves like the birth of a neutron star. His jaw clenched tight, great knots of muscles stood out at his temples, and even his cute little ears snapped back against his head like a pussy cornered by a wolf. His lips parted to beg for a moment's mercy, but I had kept the final, thickest inch of dick for last and gave it to him with a brutal thrust of my hips that stunned him stone-still and rock-solid. Then, once everything I had hard was rammed up his tight, tenderized little butt, I gave him a minute to catch his breath and entertain me with his twitches and soul-shattering moans of awful, abject acceptance.

When he was almost ready to be ridden, I slipped his legs over my shoulders, gave his ass a nasty grind, and yanked my dick up until the head slammed hard into his sphincter. His guts went from massive gut-stretching overflow to dick-starved vacuum before he could even yelp, but my piston pounded back down into his cylinder to ream out an even larger bore on the next stroke. The pussy-assed slut was still grunting and growling in between grimaces, but his hole had spread wide enough I could pick up my ramming speed without doing much permanent damage. My ass answered the call, arching upward to gain maneuvering room for my meat and then curling inward and down with a brutal rolling stroke that shoved my thick marine bone rapier-fast and sledge-hammer subtle hard into the tight hole wrapped around my throbbing crank.

By my third real stroke, though, I knew I'd switched into overdrive too soon and blown it. Four-day virgins ignore style and technique. Four-day virgins only know about busting a nut in the quickest, tightest hole going. If shooting too soon was a disappointment, shooting too fast was a serious trauma. My dick always does me right, slipping by easy degrees from one stage to another. It becomes a hard-headed, ramrod used to crash through tight muscle and stretch a hole to fit. Then as the guy's slick guts flutter and ripple across the super-sensitive head of my dick, I forget the thrills of conquest and domination and relish the tight, tender depths of the wonderful country streaking past just outside my rubber tour bus. Finally, after ages of fun and games, of poking and prodding, of having my balls bounce off the tight butt below me and frenzied nails clawing my back, my balls do their duty and, my milk bone filled to capacity, I focus on pumping the last legal ounce of pleasure up the butt before our brief, fleeting fuck flares into history.

That afternoon, though, my trusty tool fucked me, too. I'd only managed to slam Brad about twenty feet of dick total when I skidded straight through all my Zen technique and lost my load like a beardless boot. One moment I was male vigor triumphant; the next I was sprawled helpless across the altar of sensuality. In the few hectic seconds between annunciation and advent, I had every sensation I would expect in the longest, wildest, sloppiest, call-home-the-cows fuck I could imagine – compressed into twenty seconds soul-shattering savagery that would make any sane man give up sex forever. Instead of gently filling with froth, my dick exploded in one orgy of heaving, spurting, thrusting, slashing spume after another – at exactly the same time every nerve in my dick lased to life. My whole fucking body convulsed in a whirlwind of violent sensation too gloriously painful to describe. Cells exploded, time stopped, the heavens spun, and I blew enough USMC prime spooge to all but rupture my left nut.

When I came to and found that I was somehow still in the same space-time continuum, I didn't worry about catching my breath or giving Brad a supportive, caring pat on the head. The sole force driving me just then was to do it again. Before Brad could begin to recover, I'd swapped rubbers and had pulled him up onto his knees. If looking at that boy-next-door face was going to make me a two-minute marvel, then I'd fucking well do him like the bitch he was. This time around, I didn't worry about his firm ass or the rippling texture of his flat belly. I ignored his soft curls and the hard texture of his swollen tits. I was almost even able to forget the tangy scent escaping from his pits as he struggled to stay on his knees with me slamming away up his ass. My arms held him tight – first by the shoulders and, later, when I wanted to get more acrobatic with his ass, tight across his thighs at the crotch. My sole surrender to romance came after five or six minutes of rough-riding when I noticed my first, very full and exceedingly sloppy rubber lying on the bed. A single flick of my hands dumped most of that monster load onto Brad's bronzed, sweat-streaked shoulder blades. My thick, white strands of marine jism jolted into new patterns with every butt-busting, bone-crunching thrust of my hips into Brad's beautiful bubble-butt. Brad's hot skin and our locomotion quickly separated out some of the goo into milky streams that rippled down across his flesh, leaving untouched cloud-like strands of foam behind. My tongue slipped low with every fuckthrust to skim off one wave after another of the retreating tide. When only the sperm-spume remained, I burrowed my bone deep up my boy-bitch's butt and ground it out to give myself leisure to lap of the sweetest of the cream.

By the time my balls got the breeding instinct again, I was ready to enjoy and remember every slick, satisfying stroke – and Brad had settled in for the duration. We had, after all, sealed our bond of warrior brotherhood with our own jarhead jism and that's a glue that lasts a lifetime.

A BOTTOM FOR RICO
Thomas Wagner

When I was in college, I got more than an education: I got Rico up my ass and in my veins. Now that I've graduated, I can look back and say – with a definite twinge in my cock and balls – that the night our involvement began was the most memorable and twisted of my life.

Up to that time, I was so closeted, even to myself, that I was by far the biggest homophobe on campus. In fact, I was always ready to pick a fight with some well-built stud when deep down, I guess, I just wanted to fuck him. At the time, I wasn't really into self-awareness, but that isn't to say I wasn't very aware of myself. On a whim, I pierced my nipples and threaded wide silver hoops through the nubs. Since I spent a lot of time working out, I got hit on constantly. It was like every guy knew but me. Some dude was always staring at my rock-hard ass, and whenever I went swimming, I couldn't take a lap without feeling someone groping at me.

Anyway, I thought I was the sexiest thing with a pair of balls on campus until I saw Rico, who was by far the most charismatic guy I ever laid eyes on. He had a body that seemed made of the same steel as the studs on his leather jacket. He was at least six-two, and he always seemed to look right through me.

Rico had a swarthy mystique to match his body; his attitude was as huge as his motorcycle. I didn't even know he was gay until I ended up watching him walk into an all-male bar near the college. At that point, I knew I had to take him on – in any way I could.

For at least an hour, I waited for him in the alley outside the bar. While I stood there in the warm, close air, the sweat was dripping down me and my blond hair took on a greasy sheen. My torso became liquid fire down to my crotch. My curly bush became drenched. Reaching into my inside pockets, I gripped the rudimentary tools of bondage I'd brought with me in intense anticipation.

After a while, Rico appeared and stood in front of the entrance, talking with some guy. The minutes seemed endless as I watched his every move like a jaguar about to spring on his prey. My eyes roved over his lanky body, noticing that his damned jeans always seemed a size too small.

When he and his friend finally parted ways, I immediately sneaked up behind Rico. Taking advantage of the element of surprise, I overpowered him so quickly he didn't have a chance. I used the two pairs of handcuffs I'd bought just that day at a novelty shop to get his hands and legs locked up. Then I maneuvered him face-first onto the ground. I gagged him with my old bandanna.

When he was totally at my mercy, I growled into his ear, "Hey, Rico, I hear you like guys – so let's see how you like this."

His only response was to thrash around on the ground, which did him no good at that point. My face was a lusty mask as I undid his belt and pulled his pants and underwear down.

My hands were damp from nervousness and exertion as I rolled him onto his side. His swelling hard-on glistened in the steamy moonlight. The uncut tip stretched halfway up his long torso. His smooth, heavy balls rubbed against the coarse hairs on his upper thighs.

I stood there for a moment, mesmerized by his arousal. Then I lost control, reached around his body, and wedged my hands deep into his hairy ass-crack. It was the first time I'd ever really touched another man's naked ass. His skin felt silky and firm at the same time. Though I struggled not to reveal it, I loved the friction between his skin and mine.

It was then that I caught the expression in his dark eyes. Though he was still putting up a half-hearted struggle against my probing hands, Rico was clearly enjoying this. And I had to admit that I sure as hell was, too. For the first time, I understood the smoldering forces that had propelled me to follow him, and so many others like him.

My gaze moved lower, to his vibrating erection. The purple veins pulsated with every push of my fingers near his asshole. His conspicuous pleasure made me go at him harder until I'd bruised his butt considerably. I saw him grind his teeth into the bandanna with barely repressed lust.

After that, I used my other hand to pull apart his cheeks so I could get a look at his tan hollow. His pucker hole appeared tense, twitching with anxiety. I couldn't resist nudging roughly at his dark, hair-fringed rim, finally entering his ass with my forefinger. It constricted in reaction to my explorations. But each fold felt warmer and more inviting than the next as I slithered in deeper.

Without reservation, I pushed three of my fingers into him. As I felt my way around inside of him, he loosened slightly. Then, working steadily at stretching him out and curling my fingers against my palm, I took the initiative and sneaked my whole fist up his ass. He moaned so deeply that I could feel his innards pulse against my knuckles as I turned it around inside of him, inching toward his prostate.

His ass felt like a suede cocoon, and pretty soon I was moaning with excitement, too. His butt involuntarily thrust back with each of my motions, and I could see his cock twitch with excitement. I let my balled hand wander like I was on a feverish expedition, fighting his constricting flesh for more room to plunge myself inside him.

Before I got my fill of this venture, the contractions in his ass grew stronger. Finally his cock twitched and blew a thick jet of creamy cum, which spurted all over my sneakers. Wad after wad sputtered onto my ankles and socks. My own stomach was pulsing hungrily as I felt my boner go stiff.

As the last trickles slithered down my legs, I slowly pulled my hand out with a loud suction noise. With only a grunt in his direction, I threw the keys to the cuffs at him. Then I left him there on his side in that stinking alley.

In record time, I ran the mile back to my tiny apartment. Locking the door behind me, I pulled off my shorts but left the cum-stained socks and sneakers on my feet. I loved the feel of the stickiness oozing through my toes.

I wiped some of the excess from my shins and got hold of my balls, wiping Rico's cum all over my groin. The ooze crept into my sensitive skin. I lubed my hands with it and got a tight hold of my cock.

Working fast, I squeezed its rock-hard dimensions and raced down the length of it from base to tip and back again. Up and down, down and up. In no time, I came to the vision of Rico spouting all over my shoes.

The whole scene kept playing in my mind as my prick exploded all over my gooey legs and belly, mixing his cum with my fresh batch. I massaged all the cum together with my fingers, dipping my fingers into the glop. Then I licked it off of them, savoring the tangy flavor of the cum. I fell asleep, exhausted and truly satiated for the first time in my life. That night, I dreamed of Rico's orgasmic manmeat, as I did on many other nights that followed.

Since I was still afraid of my own predilections, my only sex life for the next month was beating off with the cum-saturated socks I never laundered. Nor did I ever tell any of my friends what had happened. I even thought that Rico would never find me. I was never more wrong.

Like I said, beating off kept me going for a while. And after going at myself for hours I'd finally nod off. But then the magic wore off.

And, night after night, I couldn't sleep at all because of how badly I wanted Rico again, even though I was avoiding him for fear he'd kill me or just find out how enslaved I was to his desire.

One humid evening, I thought I was having another dream when I heard my window creak, the curtains billowing from a reluctant breeze. I thought I saw a shadowed figure moving across the room toward me. The figure turned a little, revealing the silhouette of a boner at full mast. A moment later, I stared at the flood of cum dripping down the foot of my brass bed, unmoving and unbelieving.

Suddenly, I heard a familiar snarl. "I think I owe you something, Ethan," the voice whispered. "It's payback time, asshole." He moved into a circle of moonlight, and I could both see and smell that he was wearing a pair of thick leather pants. The snap fly hung halfway open, exposing the swell of his fat cock, and when he moved his arms, I noticed two large rings of sweat under the armpits of his white t-shirt.

I'm not sure whether Rico knew how much I wanted his attentions, but in any case he gave me the full treatment, jumping me and cuffing each of my limbs to the four metal bedposts. Just hearing the metal clang made my erection more painful than ever.

As he bound me hand and foot, Rico's body radiated with sheer fury. And he seemed somewhat baffled that I barely put up a fight. "And here I thought you were a tough guy," he whispered. "Well, you're a wuss and I'm going to make you into a man."

I remained silent, still half-believing I was dreaming. He took complete mental control of me as well. I knew I'd do anything he asked me to as long as I could taste his hot cum again. He had mastered me completely.

I heard the swift popping sounds as he undid his pants all the way. Moving with lusty, jerky motions, he tore the clothes from his shadowed body and hung them on the bedpost. I salivated just from looking at his taut pectoral muscles. And for the first time, Rico got a good long look at my exposed, blond-haired physique.

By the looks of his giant boner and famished stare, I understood that he especially approved of my silver-pierced, erect nipples. Every hair, every fiber of my body stood on end. When he was naked, Rico straddled my torso with his powerful legs and gave each of those shiny rings a strong pull.

Torrid vibrations sped through my bullet-like nubs and tore through my system. But when I groaned with pleasure, Rico gave me a forceful slap across the chin. My jaw trembled. I felt a sort of relief when I tasted the blood in my mouth. It wasn't as good as cum, but in the heat of the moment, it was close, and I felt my groin give another powerful lurch.

"Suck my cock – and make sure you do a good job, or I'll kick the shit out of you." Rico suddenly grabbed hold of my neck and held my head up in mid-air, aiming it at his engorged boner, still streaked with the cum he splattered on my bed.

His hot balls wiped the trickle of blood down along my neck. I felt the harsh touch of his jet-black bush burn the stubble on my chin. Then he shifted his body, putting his weight on his knees. His groin was in my face as one of his hands slipped higher to grip my ear. With the other, he held onto the bed to balance himself on my face. I held my neck up as stiffly as I could, reveling in the smell of his musky sweat and drying cum as it wafted right under my nose.

My mouth had a will of its own as I began by licking his spongy balls. I pulled on the kinky hairs around them with my teeth. He really got into that, grabbing my ear and twisting the lobe with excitement.

"That's it, Ethan. You're a fucking natural," he wheezed. With that remark, he slammed his meat into my half-open mouth. I gagged severely, feeling the swollen head bruise my tonsils, but he wouldn't let up. In a panic, I struggled to open my jaws around his tool and gasp for breath. My reward was a sudden, harsh twist to my right nipple ring. Fire shot down my body.

"If you gag again, you'll be sorry."

It took a few seconds of intense concentration, but I finally discovered a way to breathe at the same time as I was inhaling him as deeply as I could. I even managed to get my tongue back in motion up and down that huge salami stretching out my face.

As soon as I could, I sucked him halfway down my throat, licking his base at the same time. He thrust into me with all his might, fucking me hard. I became like a rag doll in his grasp, his big tool slamming my head back against the brass bars of the bed.

Then he rasped, "I'm there, you fucker. Swallow it! Swallow every drop!"

Bursts of his luscious cum flew down my throat while he continued to thrust faster. I licked and swallowed until he started to finish off. He groaned huskily, "Oh, yes, you dirty little cocksucker! Suck it all in! Suck it!"

I sucked him with intense ferocity, milking every ounce. Once he was empty, he pulled out and wiped the saliva and cum all over my face, using his cock like a paint brush. The gooeyness got me even hornier, but I knew my only function tonight was to satisfy his insatiable lust. I lay there waiting to fulfill his next demand.

"I'm going to reward you for your good behavior," he mumbled, when he'd recovered his powers of speech. "Open wide." I opened my mouth, feeling my jaws begin to ache after that other workout. "Wider, shithead."

I opened as wide as I could and just got a glimpse of the yellow waterfall going in my direction. Then I felt the warm spray of piss and leftover cum spray my face and slide down my throat.

My eyes teared up with the strong smell and the heat suffusing my head, and I instinctively closed them. For this I received another vicious twist on my nipple ring. For one wild moment, I thought he would tear it right out of my tit. In that same moment, I thought it seemed like an incredibly sexy idea!

As the hot stream sizzled against my face, Rico immediately ordered me to swallow. I made up for my former misdemeanor by gobbling his piss-and-cum cocktail as it slithered into me.

"Now that you're cleaned up, I have one more lesson in manners for you."

He freed me, turned me on my back, and then swiftly re-cuffed me. I felt even more delicious trepidation since I could no longer see his angry face. I heard the belt swish out of the loops in his pants, then felt the stinging crack on my ass.

Pain shot through me, driving me wild with desire. Then, once again, the leather came down on my cheeks. He went at me until there wasn't an inch of me that wasn't welted. But my cock just got harder and harder. I could only anticipate what other kinds of punishment awaited me!

I felt that any second, I wouldn't be able to stop myself from coming. But I knew if I called out in pain or excitement, my punishment would increase. When he'd stopped whacking me, I slowly turned my head. I saw him position himself to fuck my virgin ass.

I tried not to tense up, because I knew he wouldn't lube me. I broke into a cold sweat. My ass-crack became a mini-river, my sweat rushing down to my inner thighs like a flash flood into a canyon.

As I'd expected, Rico parted my ass with both hands and plunged inside me with one quick thrust. I was sure my body would split in two. He thrust as harshly as he could, and each time he hit my prostate, I knew I was a lost man. I practically fainted with lust when I felt him copiously unload in my vacuum-like asshole.

My own cock went berserk and spewed wad after wad onto my sheets.

My body bucked and trembled as he kept up the action even after he'd emptied his milk into my ass.

I felt beaten and exhausted and really high. My skin tingled and burned with a harsh desire I'd never experienced before.

From then on, I was hooked on bottoming for Rico.

Night after night, for more than a year, he'd return to beat the living daylights out of me.

So, I ended up an accomplice in his revenge plot against me – but I also had the ultimate satisfaction of giving myself to the sexiest man I had ever seen.

A RICAN POUNDING
Jack Risk

"Hot fuckin' Puerto Rican man: Five-ten, one-seventy-five. Eight-and-a-half inches, five inches 'round, uncut. Lookin' for a nice, smooth bottom to slide this horny Puerto Rican dick into... Peace."

All right, I'm so sick of hearing these Hispanic guys leaving outgoing messages like: "Black brothers and banjy boys only" or "homeboys need only apply." Okay, I'll admit it: I'm a white boy who loves dark dick. I love the way my cream-colored skin looks next to caramel or chocolate-colored complexion. I love playing with the skin on an uncut cock. I love being with someone who was raised in a culture so completely different from mine. I love that their culture leaves the special skin on their little baby boys so now that those little boys are grown up, some of that skin can end up in my mouth.

I respond right away: "Hey, man, five eleven, one-sixty-five. Dirty blond hair, crew cut, greenish-grayish eyes, pretty smooth, very cute...really nice butt."

I press #2 twice, not needing the computer voice to prompt me on how to send my message (not that I'm on the line all the time or anything like that, you understand).

The peppy but droning recorded voice informs me, "Your message has been sent."

I scroll through other outgoing messages, wondering if hot fuckin' Puerto Rican'll like my weight and my coloring, and my height, wondering what he wants in his bottom boys. I hope the way I said "really nice butt," pausing right before I said it (in the same way he paused right before he said "uncut") will make him as hot for me as I am for him and that he at least will send me a message back. My dick starts to drool, and I pull my underwear right up under my balls, getting lost in hearing the sound of him describing himself, also loving the way he said "peace." I'd like to be his hot fuckin' Puerto Rican peace.

A cartoonish kind of sound effect from the phone line suddenly alerts me:

BU-WONG KWONGKI
The peppy but droning recorded voice makes it known that:
"You have a message from..."
A tough voice with a familiar accent:
"Rico."

Now I don't know that much Spanish, but I've been injected by enough Colombians, Ecuadorians, Mexicans, Dominicans, and Puerto Ricans to know that "Rico" means "rich."

"Yeah, Papi, que rico.... yeah, man, that feels good!... Yeah, man... rico, man, rico."

Yes, I've heard that word more than a few times before. It's usually been directed towards me from behind by some Spanish guy getting off on getting into my ass.

Rico responds: "Hey, Papi man, this is Rico, man, drop me those digits so we can get this thing goin'. You got me so fuckin' hard thinkin' 'bout that nice tight butt of yours, man."

Damn! He's ready right now. Didn't even ask me any questions about how I'm hung or anything! Really, he just wants my butt really bad. I didn't even tell him it was tight!

I'm shaking, suddenly a little bit nervous, holding on tight to my dick with the hand that's not holding the phone.

"Here's my number, um, Rico... 553-6511." Then I repeated it, for good measure. "Just leave me one more message letting me know you got the number, and I'll hang up and wait for you to call..."

I press #2 twice with my right thumb, having learned how to do all the button-pressing with my right so my left is always free to touch whatever part of my body gets turned on. That way, the phone never gets sticky or spitty.

"Your message has been sent."

What if he's full of shit, just asking for my number, knowing he's never gonna call me? That's happened to me so many times before – I get off the line, and wait for the guy to call, and he doesn't, and I end up lying here with a hard-on, wondering what I said wrong, wanting to get back on the line, but afraid if I do, that he'll call right then and end up getting my voice mail through the telephone company.

The cartoonish sound effect comes on again.

"You have a message from...."

"Rico."

"Yeah, Papi, hang up. I'm gonna call your ass right now."

I hang up and feel more drool from my dick dripping down as I press the talk key to hang up and set the cordless phone on the pillow next to my head. C'mon, Rico, call me. C'mon, Rico, c'mon. I wipe some of the pre-cum on my stomach, slip a finger down to feel my ass. Squeeze the bottom-side of one cheek to feel what his hands'll hopefully be feeling soon. I like my ass. Wish I could see it myself while he pounds that Puerto Rican prick into it, that is if he actually calls and ends up wanting more than to just get off on the phone. I slide my finger down my crack, wondering if he'll eat my ass. Stick my middle finger in the hole to test the tightness, hoping it's tight enough to squeeze on that huge, uncut cock, but not so tight that he'll have trouble shoving the thing in. Of course, it could be hot if he got a little frustrated and started to get a little bit rough like that time the hot Dominican kid from the subway followed me home...all the way home!

The phone rings and brings me back to the current cock. I let the thing ring twice.

"Hello?"

"Hey Papi, man, what's up with that butt?"

"Not much...until you get that big dick over here. All eight inches!"

"Eight and a half, man....sometimes nine, man." He laughs just a little, turning me on a lot because he can laugh and still sound so sexy. Good gets better as Rico goes on: "...Think you can take it all?"

"Fuck yeah, man. Get your balls over here."

I let myself laugh a little, feeling vulnerable, even though he laughed a little first.

I tell Rico where I live in uptown Manhattan. He says he's gonna come pick me up and take me back to his "crib" (with as many guys as I've gone home with, I've never been to anyone's "crib" before) because he doesn't want to leave his car out on the street in my neighborhood. He's coming from The Bronx. I love the way The Bronx sounds, like every street has hundreds of homeboys just hanging out in front of their "cribs," ready to pacify their "babies" with something to suck on. But even though it's only about twenty blocks from my house and I've lived uptown for two years, I've never even been to the Bronx. I like that my first trip to the Bronx is gonna be with a homeboy who wants my ass.

Rico speaks: "Hey, man, before I come all the way up there, you let me know now, am I gonna be disappointed?"

I'm not sure what to say. Anyone can say that they're cute, but what I say is cute about me may not sound cute to him. And although I feel like I have a nice body from being a dancer for fifteen years, in this age of the body-builder fantasy, I'm still a bit unsure how I measure up to other dudes – except for my butt. Fifteen years of ballet built this butt solid, and I can always confidently say that I have a "nice" butt.

"Well, I'm a cute white boy, and you like white boys, right?"

"Yeah."

"You like to fuck white boys, right?"

"Oh, yeah, man."

"And I definitely have a nice ass."

"Oh, man, I'm coming over." He blurts it out the last three words all strung into one, and hangs up without even saying PEACE.

Better get this "nice ass" in the shower now.

I lather up, washing my hair and scrubbing my armpits kind of quickly. I suds up my back, running my hands down over the curve of the ass that's gonna get at least eight uncut inches in it within about a half an hour. I stick my middle finger in again. As my sphincter muscle squeezes around the relative thickness of the finger, I'm relieved that it still feels tight even while I stand up in the shower. Rico said something about it making him hard thinking about that tight butt of mine. I hope I can squeeze my butt this tight once his thick, "five inches 'round" is deep inside me.

The phone rings. I think it's him, but it's only been ten minutes. It's not. It's Jorge, this other guy I met on the line, who I hooked up with without ever having sex. I've gone out with him three times, and he's really nice, but he just doesn't do it for me.

Jorge sounds peppy but droning: "Hey, what are you doing?"

I can't help but sound like a slut: "I'm all wet. I just washed my culo, and, ..."

"Eeugh!" Jorge cuts me off.

Too bad Jorge can't get down and dirty when I talk about making my culo clean. Culo is the word for butt in his own language, and I can even say culo with a really good accent, but it not only doesn't turn him on, it turns him off. No wonder he doesn't do it for me. I want someone who wants my butt in any and every language, and who likes to talk about it.

I tell Jorge that I really have to go because I'm on my way to the grocery store.

"Well, okay, I guess I'll talk to you later...movies again this weekend?"

I try to sound like Rico just sounded like: "Yeah, I'll see your ass on Saturday...."

"Would you stop with the talk about that?"

"Okay, I gotta go anyway. Bye."

"Fuck, man!" I say out loud to myself, feeling a little bit bad that I had to lie, but glad that I got him off the line a lot easier than I usually can even though I had to talk like a slut (I mean puta) to do it. When I hit the talk button on the cordless phone to hang up, the dial tone's changed to alert me that I have a message. Fuck! Now this is one of the times I wish I had call waiting, not just automatic voice mail through the telephone company.

I can tell the message was sent from a cellular phone:

"Chris, it's Rico. I'm outside your house! Chris, man, pick up! Chris, man, get your ass on the phone."

"Fuck, man!" I throw my shirt on, pissed off at Jorge for choosing to call me at such a stupid time, wishing I'd explained to Rico about my voice mail, wondering if he'll wait for me. Maybe he thinks I was in the shower. Should I wait for him to call back?

I try to sixty-nine the call. "The number you are trying...." I hang up on the droning, recorded bitch who I know is gonna tell me that the number I want can't be reached by this method. I wonder if I take the phone with me down the four flights of stairs if the reception will work while I am outside to see if there's a cream-colored Audi waiting. Fuck it! I run out the door and down the stairs, feeling the firmness of my ass leading the movement of my legs as I pound down the steps.

I jump from one landing to the next as I get outside the building, more conscious of my butt than ever before, and as I come around the corner, there it is! The Audi! I can only see the short-shaved, black-haired back of his head as I slow down my stride to look cool. Then the side of his face comes into focus, and as I bend over to look into the passenger side window, I feel a little stretch in the part of my backside where I just washed so well.

"Rico." He rolls the "r" and tilts his head back.

He smiles at me with unevenly-spaced, bright-white teeth and full lips, protectively surrounded by a rough mustache and goatee. He's got a gold chain on with a gold cross hanging right at the hollow of his throat. I lift my eyebrows and grin to signify I want to get in. He makes a "come on" motion with his chin. I make sure he gets a little glimpse of my ass as I turn to the side to slide into the seat with what little room there is between the car he's double-parked next to. I can't see the look on his face as my ass is going in, and I have to look around for a moment to find the space in the side panel to stick my fingers into in order to shut the door. As my gaze turns to meet his, I catch him looking at my crotch, but then he quickly looks up.

"So, okay, man?" I say, knowing already by the smile on his face that my ass is exactly what he expected.

"Yeah man. How 'bout me?"

"Yeah, great."

There's a little bit of silence while we check each other out for a second, and I almost ask him if Rico is a nickname or if someone gave him that name because they knew he was gonna be good. I stall a second thinking about how I'm gonna say it, and then he raises his eyebrows and suddenly says it himself, "Yeah man, I think you're gonna have a really good time."

He's got on one of those nylon tank tops with little holes all through the fabric, and as he switches the gear into drive, I see some of his chest hair poking through those little holes. Nice. He's got on nylon pants too, and I can't see whether he's hard or not because of the ballooning of the fabric over his crotch. The right leg of the pants is pulled up into that homeboy thing I've seen so often on the subway. I used to think that they pulled up one pant leg to keep it from getting caught in the spoke of their bike chain. But then I met this black guy on the phone line who came over a few times to pound my butt before he went back to his military base in Georgia. He told me, as he was putting his own nylon pants back on over his nice, big, thick dick, that pulling the pant leg up was just a fashion statement. Rico's making a statement of his own right now as the thick, black hair-covered calves of that exposed leg are pumping up and down, firmly and self-assuredly, going from the gas pedal to the brake, and then back to the gas again. There's something about the way that his calf muscle releases and flexes as he pumps on the pedals that tells me he's gonna be really good at pumping in and out of my ass.

"So, what's up?" he asks, taking his gaze from my crotch up into my eyes, maybe meaning to be suggestive, maybe just being naturally homeboy hot.

"I like how you look. I like your lips a lot. And I like your teeth."

"Thanks." Rico smiles unevenly as he grips the wheel a little tighter.

"Are you gonna kiss me?" I smile at him, remembering that I forgot to say that my favorite thing to do is make out. I always feel like I'm taking a chance suggesting something these top guys might not be into.

He glances over at me with a look in his eyes like he could pull me over with one thick black hair-covered arm (while still steering with the other) and cover my whole mouth with that mustache and goatee right then.

"I don't know, man. I usually don't kiss. I usually save that for my girl."

Girl? Oh well, even though kissing is the thing that most turns me on, I'm sure I could be satisfied just by sucking on his cock and once I got it good and hard, having him slide all those incredible uncut inches up my ass. Besides, if I had wanted to make sure he would make out with me, I should've said something about it on the line, but then maybe I would've never ended up hooking up with him.

When we get to The Bronx, he sees that his homeboys are hanging out right in front of his home as we slowly drive close to the corner of the street that his house (I mean his crib) is on. Rico apologizes like a gentleman but still sounds like a homeboy.

"Fuckin' shit! I'm sorry, man. I'm gonna have to drive around a little bit. I don't want these boys knowing my business."

He asks if I want anything at the store, and I realize that he's not just hot, and not just a gentleman, he's fucking adorable. I tell him I want some gum. Even though he says he usually doesn't kiss, and I already paid as much attention to brushing my teeth as I did to washing my ass, I figure I'll keep drawing attention to my mouth, whether it's for him to keep contemplating kissing me or for him to visualize my lips wrapping around his dick.

He leaves me in the Audi all alone as he hops out to go into a corner store bodega. I like that he feels that comfortable with me. I take a deep breath to smell the scent that he's wearing still lingering in the leather upholstery, excited that he thought enough of me to take the time to put on cologne.

He gets back in and gives me the gum.

"Too bad your butt's on the seat where I can't see it."

I give him a little grin as I slide a stick into my mouth, at the same time rolling all my weight onto my right cheek. Then I slide my ass all the way over to the edge of the seat, pushing the right side of my body right up onto the edge of the door panel. I nestle my head between the window and the head rest, looking out onto the street as he slams his door shut and pulls away from the store. I can see his face in the reflection of my window as he tries to keep one eye on the road and still take in all of my ass.

"Damn, man! Fuck!" He sounds both nervous and excited about driving around his own neighborhood with a white boy pressed up against his passenger window.

He reaches over with his right hand and pushes into the back of my jeans, sliding his middle finger into the crack of my ass, pressing his palm into the flesh around it. My dick presses up against the door panel and activates the door lock – it makes a deep thud rather than a light click like I would've expected.

"That's sounds like the way my dick is gonna fit in your ass, man."

He keeps on driving, pumping that pedal, and having to readjust himself in his seat. I can tell he's getting hard even though I can't see it sticking up. I readjust myself too over the new seat he's made for me – his big hand makes a nice solid surface for me to shove up against, and his big middle finger keeps me steady. I push my right cheek out to the side so his finger slides right against my pucker.

"Goddamn!" he says, turning the corner with one hand.

As the car lurches, the metal of my button fly scrapes against the door panel.

"Don't fuck up my interior, man! I'm the one who's gonna fuck up yours."

Even though that sounds kind of stupid, like bad porno dialogue, I've said plenty of stupid things myself in sexual situations, and I twist my head around to look at him like I really liked what he said. I actually really did like the way he said it.

He pulls his right hand out from underneath me and uses both hands to start to parallel park. I think maybe I pissed him off, and he's stopped to check out a possible scratch in the leather, but then he stares right through me and says, "I'm takin' you in the back way."

We go through an alley and he tells me we have to hop the fence to get into the backyard space behind his house. He tells me, "Your ass is goin' over first," and as I get a foothold in the fence, and start to hike myself up, he grabs hold of my waist and pulls me back down a little, biting my butt through the denim. He holds me there for a minute, pulling down, sinking his teeth in a little, making an "mmmmmh" kind of growl, and I feel the wetness from his mouth easily soaking through to my skin, since I don't have any underwear on. He shoves my ass over the fence, and then pulls himself up onto it, and I finally get an idea of how big his cock is as he straddles the top of the fence for a moment before throwing his other leg over. He hits the ground and I see the fucker bounce heavily in the dark blue nylon. He looks right in my eyes as he puts his hand in his pants to reposition himself. He grins without showing me those hot unevenly spaced teeth, letting just the head of that Puerto Rican cock ride above the waistband of his pants as he strides past me towards the door.

He's got one hand still on his cock as he looks around suspiciously sticking his key in and shoving the back door open. He grabs the front of my pants and pulls me in quickly. He kicks the door shut and locks it, never releasing his hand from my pants, even letting the top button fly open as I hear him latch the door locked from the inside. He keeps one hand working on my fly while he's handling his own cock through his pants with the other. I still can see only the head of it, the foreskin sliding around on the skin of his hairy belly.

I pull him up against me, and in the jerk that we make coming close to each other, our faces almost meet, and I swear he almost puts his mouth on mine, but then seems to remember what he told me before about his girl. I slide my hands around his ass and push the as hairy as the exposed calf of his right leg, and as I get down on my knees to pull those pants all the way down, I see his legs are also thick and hairy all over. The gray fabric of his midway brief is a bit darker right around the fly. Looks like he's been leaking too.

I look up at him from below, and he tells me exactly what I want to hear: "I want you to get me real hard."

I love when a guy has such a big cock that it takes a little time to get it all the way hard. With Rico, I don't mind working on it with my mouth for half an hour, watching how he gets more and more turned on seeing how I'm savoring the different states of firmness that his cock goes through, from being half-hard to rock-solid to just about ready to blow a load. He's got lots of skin too, and he pulls it back for me every once in a while, so I see the delicately sensitive pinkness of the head slipping through the protective hood of brown outer skin. It is simply perfect: perfect size, perfect shape, perfectly-colored Puerto Rican prick in the 'hood.

"Te gusta?" I say in between sucks, letting his cock slide out of my mouth just long enough to slobber the words, loving making love to that cock.

"Oh, yeah, papi. Me gusta mucho ... How 'bout you, man? You like that big Puerto Rican dick?"

"Rico," I gurgle, giving him the best little grin I can give while I'm giving him the best head I think I've ever given anyone, even guys I was in love with.

I keep showing off my lips to him – both the set on my face and the set between my bottom cheeks. I pull him down on the floor and get in a sideways position so he can play with the thing I'm getting his cock ready for. He's fully hard now and it is every bit of eight inches.

"You ready, man?" says Rico.

I don't say anything. I just roll up over his torso, with my knees straddling his hips, sticking my butt in his face. I look back between my legs so I can see the look in those big brown eyes as I reach back and hold one cheek in each one of my hands, feeling the hair of my crack underneath my fingers, never letting the uncut skin of his cock come away from the soft skin of the back of my throat.

"Aw, fuck man." Rico sounds real good saying that.

With my mouth still full, I show him my hole, and I can see through the space between my thighs that he doesn't know how he's gonna keep from pulling my ass right down onto his mouth. But he said he wasn't even gonna kiss me. He slaps my ass and pushes me off his dick so I end up face-down on the bed. He holds my face down so I can't see, or maybe because he's so turned on that he can't look at me. I'm wondering which it is as I hear the familiar sound of condom packaging being ripped open with teeth. He needs two hands to slide the latex sheath onto that big cock, so he releases my head, and I turn around to watch him.

He struggles with the packaging, looking like he's gonna shoot his load without his dick even going in my ass. He focuses fiercely on his dick, concentrating on the condom and on not coming too soon, throwing his head back while smoothly sliding latex over foreskin and unraveling the rest of it over the five-inch thickness. He falls down on top of me, pushing his palms first onto my forearms and then sliding his thick fingers over the backs of my hands to intertwine his own fingers with mine. Although it's a forceful pinning, I feel like there's more to it than to hold me down. If this was just a fuck, he'd hold onto my wrists. He sticks his dick right up against my pucker and pushes firmly over and over like a piston, trying to get that monster even a little bit in there.

I like the pressure and pulse of the pistoning, and I really like the balance of determination and sensitivity that I can feel in the way his stomach is spread across my lower back without all of his weight just slammed into me. I raise my ass a little off the sheets both to let him know how bad I want his cock up inside me and to be able to release my own dick off the bed. The head of his cock finally goes in just a little, and then he holds it there, going, "Ohhhh...," for just a moment before he starts sliding the shaft in. I usually make a guy hold it there for a minute until my muscle has a chance to relax a little bit, but with Rico, I push past the pain and just shove right back onto that cock, showing him that I can be a forceful mother-fucker, even if I'm the one being fucked.

"Now pound me, man. Fuckin' pound me."

He's surprised at my aggression, but it gets him going. I didn't say I wanted him to kiss me in my outgoing message, and he didn't say he wanted a submissive bottom. He starts digging down into me, and I can see his ass going up and down in the mirror he has leaned up against the wall next to the bed. I push my own ass up and back onto that cock – that uncut cock that had been described to me just an hour ago, that cock that I'd imagined, that made my dick drool just thinking about it, and now that exact dick, better than I'd even painted a picture of in my mind, that cock was not only all the way up my nice white boy butt, but it was pounding away at me from the orders I was giving.

"Yeah man, Rico, pound it, man! You like that ass?"

"Oh, yeah, man. You like this Puerto Rican dick up in you?"

"Yeah, man! Fuckin' pound me, pound my butt. This ass is yours, man,

"Oh, yeah, this ass is mine, man...mine!"

"Yeah, you like that? You want this ass to be all yours? You want it all for yourself?"

I twist my head around and give him that same little grin I gave him before, and that's it, I see him trying to hold back, see him trying to slow down, but there's this thing going on between our eyes, and I slip my arm out from underneath me and throw it around his neck, and pull his face down onto my mouth at the same time I push my ass further onto his cock. Both of us thrust as Rico starts to come at the same moment his tongue slides past my teeth.

My left hand reaches for his ass as my neck twists around some more to suck that Puerto Rican tongue just as hard as I sucked that Puerto Rican cock. Our teeth knock against each other as our mouths push more firmly together, and I love the smoothness of his lips pressing through the soaked-with spit brush of his goatee along with the sudden unintentional slight scrape of his teeth.

I can see in his widely-opened brown eyes that Rico's trying not to think too hard, just saying to himself, "Oh, fuck it, man, fuck it." His moaning turns into almost a whine as I force his hand around my cock as I start to shoot my own load. His cock is in my ass, my tongue is wrapped around his, and his hand is wrapped around my dick, spurting out stuff in the same rhythms as our moaning, like neither one of us is ever gonna stop. Each time I feel him thrust farther in, I thrust back, and his hand slides farther down on my cock, and his mouth spreads more widely onto mine, and there's one more spurt coming out of each of us for what seems like a full fifteen minutes.

Both of us are breathing hard and his dick's still inside me, staying hard even half an hour after the last of our loads shoot.

I twist my head around once more to look at him, my backside sliding easily over the sweat of his hairy stomach, hoping he feels okay about kissing me, his saliva all over my cheeks, lips and chin, my saliva in the same places on his face, the mustache, goatee hairs, all stuck to the skin.

"You're fuckin' good, Rico. So fuckin' good!"

I roll my "R" the same way that he did when he first said his name.

He smiles at me with those unevenly-spaced bright white teeth, pushing my head back around so I'm facing the sheets, then kissing me firmly and wetly on the back of my neck.

"Yeah, you too, man. You, too... Hey, man, I like the way you say my name. Do you know what Rico means?"

MY YOUNG COMPADRE
William Cozad

One spring some time back, I was driving to the Sierra Mountains, the most beautiful place in the world as far as I was concerned. It was there that I went when things became too much for me. I was escaping the concrete and steel city where I worked. Beyond the Sierras was the Reno valley, with its green felt jungle of casinos, another world without windows and clocks. They say that if you're unlucky at love, you're lucky at cards. I'd had my share of disappointments, lovers and tricks who'd slipped through my fingers like quicksilver. I had to be lucky at gambling. Besides, just getting there was uplifting; when I looked at the forest and the snowcapped mountains, I knew this had to be the face of God.

I pulled off the freeway and bought gas. I wasn't prepared for what happened when I left the 76 station. At the entrance to the freeway, I spotted a youth hitchhiking. He was dark with a thatch of black hair and flashing coffee-colored eyes. A Mexican with a dark mustache. A young Aztec god if I ever saw one. I never picked up hitchhikers, aware of the dangers. Like I never went to the baths anymore. Fear ruled my life instead of trust and love. I felt that was confirmed when they closed paradise, the 21st Street baths, the last bathhouse in San Francisco.

But then I thought, if I was willing to risk my money in Reno, why wasn't I willing to take a chance on a hot man? Surrounding the bathhouse in the Mission district was the Latino barrio. I never looked on these macho studs as Latin lovers; they were fucking Mexicans, not a putdown because I thought they were the most beautiful hombres in the world. For a moment I forgot about the Latino youth gangs in the violent Mission district that bordered the Castro gay village, the teenagers who bashed queers.

What made me stop my car? Like the Church Lady on television says, perhaps Satan? Oh, but I love Mexican men; they're so hot. My very first lover was a mojado, a wetback. Isn't that special? I heard Church Lady's voice.

"You gimme a ride for Sacramento?" the Mexican said.

To me, Spanish sounded like music. I was gone. I'd have taken him to Tijuana. Just looking into those sad dark eyes blew me away. He was of barely legal age and wore a black tank top that contrasted with his bronze skin and blue sweatpants. Rolling along the interstate, I thought about his tool and glanced at his toolbox. He smiled at me with his even white teeth and luscious thick lips. I thought that was the way Pancho Villa probably looked at the gringos before he cut their balls off. He had a wolfish grin, this young man.

"What do you do in Sacramento?" I asked.

He probably watches out for immigration officers and chases pussy. Mexican men are incurable flirts. Even my first amor was that way but when he fucked me like one of his bitches, he changed my life forever. I looked for

Mexican men everywhere, like Lancelot looking for the Holy Grail, which they said turned out to be a gay bar in Jerusalem. Is that what I'd find with my hitchhiker, a cruel joke or my doom?

"I work, save up money, go back to Mexico."

With more than a thousand pesos to the dollar he could live good in Mexico where they worked for five dollars a day. Besides, they said that Reagan had this country so screwed up that Mexicans were sneaking back across the border.

"What are you doing in Vallejo?"

"Visiting. My uncle lives down here."

I didn't know what to believe. I don't care what they say about the Mexican image. Mexicans are like the Frito Bandito character. My first boyfriend was not only an asshole bandit, he ripped off cars and went to jail or back to Mexico, I don't know which.

"Me cansado. I didn't sleep while visiting my uncle. We drank all the time."

"You can sleep in the car but it's not comfortable."

"All the time I sleep in a car. My compadre and I live in his car. I haven't slept in a bed for months."

I spotted the billboard that said Big 6 motel at the next exit. I was thinking of my passenger, wondering if he had a big six. Or eight. Even better.

"I was thinking about getting a motel room tonight," I lied. I was only fifty miles away from home and rested. I could easily make it. "Maybe you'd like a nice soft bed?"

"I no got much money."

"Hey, that's okay. I'll pay for it."

He nodded.

I don't know if the Mexican got my drift or not. I was thinking more like he had a hot tamale and was looking for a free-holie.

The freeway exit loomed up and I headed for the motel. I had to be crazy to take a chance like this. They'd find my dead body and stolen car.

On trips I always carried a cooler full of beer. I'd stop at the highway rest stops and check out the shithouses and guzzle some suds, then continue.

I checked into the Big 6. There were several rigs parked around. This would be a good place to cruise for horny truckers, I decided when I looked into rooms with open drapes and saw men sprawled out on single beds. For now I was occupied with thoughts about getting south of my hitchhiker's border, down into his crotch.

Inside the motel room, my hitchhiker sprawled out on the bed. I hoped he wouldn't just go to sleep. I'd make a move on him and if he didn't go for it, I'd split and leave him to sleep alone, I opened us each a tall, cold can of Bud.

"I love cerveza."

"Salud," I said.

I introduced myself and he told me his name was Jorge, which he pronounced "hor-hey," I flipped on the TV and there was a Rob Lowe movie. I absolutely loved Rob Lowe; he was always prettier than the girls he played opposite. They spent a lot of time screwing in this flick.

"Mamacita," Jorge moaned and rubbed his crotch.

After the movie he flipped the channel to a cable station that played shows in Spanish for the Sacramento-Stockton-Modesto area which had a lot of Mexicans. I understood bits and pieces of the story about the hombre who captured a woman and had a chain around her boot. They were pursued by her father and soldiers on horseback. He sang to her and she fell in love with her abductor at the end.

I'd about drunk myself to sleep. Jorge seemed to get a second wind with all the beer. He was the one who was supposed to be tired. "I wanna take a shower," he said.

"Sure. Go ahead."

I listened to the shower running. I thought about what he looked like naked. He was Aztec Indian, which meant a smooth chest and thighs and a dense pubic bush. I used to love to watch my first boyfriend bathe. He'd soap up his bronze skin and want me to wash his back and blow him afterwards. I had to restrain myself from going into the bathroom and looking at my hitchhiker in the nude. I didn't want any violence, like a reverse of the shower scene from Psycho in the Bates motel. Maybe he had a knife on him.

There was a Bruce Lee martial arts flick playing on the TV when Jorge came out of the shower with a towel wrapped around his waist. I was right about the smooth chest. A couple of wild strands of hair sprouted around his nipples.

Jorge pulled off his towel and revealed his soft brown cock with the pink cockhead. He was cut, unlike my first Mexican boyfriend. He had a crotch of wiry, black hair like on his head and bulging, strong thighs. His work in the fields reflected in his rippled torso and muscular arms.

He lay down naked on the single bed next to mine and fondled his cock and balls. I watched. I couldn't speak; I'd only stammer hama-hama-hama like Ralph Kramden. I guess Jorge assumed I was interested in his body. I knew I was drooling at the mouth. I crawled over to his bed, like a dog begging for a home. I could tell by his glazed eyes that he wanted me to help him take care of his hard-on.

Kneeling between his legs, I grabbed his cock and jacked it into a proud, thick seven-plus inches. Pre-cum oozed out of his pee hole. I swabbed my tongue over the bulbous pink cockhead and held it while I licked the veiny, brown shaft. I tongued his balls which were darker than his rod and sucked on them one at a time.

"Ayeee," Jorge moaned.

In a rapid movement that caught me off guard, he shoved me down on my belly on the bed and mounted me. For a brief moment I thought maybe he would tie me up with the sheets, gag me and rob me. But I was wrong.

Jorge had a gun to my back but it was bony and full of spicy cum. He pulled off my white cotton briefs and mounted me.

My ass was happy, no denying. It twitched, anticipating this Mexican avenger. California had once belonged to Mexico and we'd taken Nevada, Utah, Colorado, Arizona and Texas from them.

This was going to be a rough fuck, because he didn't use any grease. Just a little spit and pre-cum lubed my Americano asshole.

Jorge plunged into me, hard. I screamed into the pillow and thought he was going to ram me through the headboard, through the wall into the next room.

I listened to his heavy breathing and felt his sweat drip onto my body while he fucked me with ass-stretching cock-strokes.

"Chinga su madre. Chinga su culo, puto. Ayeee."

He swore in Spanish and groaned while he rammed his cock up my ass. I responded by wiggling around and fucking back at the Mexican cock that stuffed my asshole.

"More! Faster! Harder!" I begged like a slut.

"I gonna shoot! Shoot my leche up your culo. Ay, motherfucker!"

I felt the jets of cum squirt up my asshole and fill my guts. I wrapped my ankles around his and squeezed his cock with my ass muscles until I got every drop of cum I could out of those dark balls in their wrinkled sac.

Jorge's cock plopped out of my butt hole. I rolled over onto my back and my cock just exploded. Gobs of smooth white cum like heavy cream spurted all over my belly and chest. While he watched me, I rubbed the gooey stuff into my skin.

I tossed and turned that night with my ass full of the stud's cum.

I must have fallen asleep, scared as I was that my hitchhiker might turn violent and do a number on me. I was really paranoid and nervous, although I listened to his even breathing from the bed next to mine.

At dawn I was awakened, not knowing where I was or who I was with for a moment.

"Is cold," the Mexican said.

He crawled under the covers and snuggled up against my back and I felt his hard cock against my naked butt. I thought he wanted to fuck me again, and I wasn't about to stop him, although my butt was sore from the fucking last night.

Jorge had other ideas for me and his hard-on. He rolled me over onto my back and straddled my chest.

His cock was stiff and he pushed it between my lips and fed it to me for breakfast! At one point, I looked up at the bronze god with his dark eyes, and I thought how much he looked him like an artist's conception of Lucifer I'd seen once.

He fucked his cock down my throat, massaging my tonsils. His cock got steely hard and I knew it was going to shoot off right away.

I wasn't prepared for the hottest cum I'd ever tasted gushing into my mouth as quickly as it did, but I managed to swallow every delicious drop of the cum.

He wiped his cock on my cheeks and lips, smearing them with the last of his goo.

While I stared at magnificence of his genitals, I reached between my legs and tugged on my own prick.

I looked up into the stud's flashing dark eyes and I shot my wad.

I quickly showered and, when I finished, he was watching cartoons on television.

At the coffee shop near the motel we ate a big breakfast together.

Back in the car, Jorge listened to music on the Spanish station on the radio, and I dropped him off outside of Sacramento, near the American River.

As I continued my trip across the Sierras to Reno, I thought about Jorge and felt sad that I'd never see him again. But I was grateful for the night I had with him. He'd work in the fields, save his money and go back to Mexico and probably have a family.

The beauty of the drive across the Sierras filled me with wonder. In Reno, I'd try my luck in the casinos and escape for a few days. Then, I'd return to the real world and work. But I'd always have the fantasy of my young compadre.

- This story was adapted for this collection from material originally appearing in Torso magazine.

JOHNNY HAYSEED
James Hosier

More often than not, you don't really know about a guy until you've been with him for at least an hour. I guess you know what I mean. Some of them take as long as three weeks before they make the first move. "Come round for coffee some time." You go round. You have coffee. You leave.

Next time there's a casual reference to gays, usually in connection with some film or pop star. "People say he's gay. Not that it matters to me," – said with a glance in my direction to see how I react.

It takes weeks before I make a sale and go home with an aching ass and a wad of greenbacks.

Sure, there are direct guys. Usually encountered in public toilets: "A dollar if you let me suck it." I guess you could say that, in the two years I've been pursuing my secret spare time occupation, I've come across everything. Nevertheless, Tom Holt came as a shock.

On Saturday mornings in the summer months the swimming club has exclusive use of the pool in town for just one hour; seven-thirty to eight-thirty when most people are still in bed. After that, they let the general public in. Inevitably, most of us hang around after eight thirty.

I'd been cruising up and down the pool, practicing my backstroke and trying to eliminate some of the splashes I'd been making lately. I noticed this guy standing on the side looking at me. That was the other difference. I've gotten used to guys who wear sunglasses on the dullest days so that I can't tell where they're looking. Then there are the sideways glancers, apparently talking to someone but with their minds on something other than the conversation. Tom just stared. I did a few more lengths. He was still there. A few more. He hadn't moved. He was beginning to put me off my stroke.

One of Dad's business rules that I have adopted is never to turn a potential customer away. (I don't count single dollar offers as customers.) I waved. He waved back. It was time to make the deal. I clambered out of the water and went back to the changing rooms. Like I thought, he followed me. I wondered what the approach would be this time.

"You're a very good swimmer." That was the usual one. Or, "You remind me of somebody." Or, "Haven't I seen you before some place?"

After "Thanks," or "I don't think so," they bring up the imaginary friend. He is either a talent scout with the Olympic Games in mind, a doctor with an interest in athletic bodies who'd like a photograph of me for the textbook he's writing, or some guy he knows who's frightened of the water and would like to learn to swim. Whatever, it ends with a business card and "Call round some time when you're free and we can talk about it." Sometimes I do. Sometimes I don't. It depends on my fiscal position at the time and the age of the guy. Needless to say, I never get to meet the friend.

Tom shattered me. "I'm Tom Holt," he said. "Looks like you've got quite a weapon between your legs."

It's not a disappointment. I grant that much but it isn't enormous and it doesn't match up (in my opinion anyway) with some of the things that have been said about it over the two years I've been doing this." Beautiful," "magnificent" and "mouth-watering" are not terms that I would personally use but, like Dad says, if a customer praises a product, go along with him. So.. I just said "Thanks," and waited for the next move.

"You could earn a lot of money with that. Looks a nice straight one," he said. I switched on my "innocent country lad"- look which I'm told I do well. I'm not sure that I didn't even tousle my wet hair.

"How?" asked Johnny Hayseed a.k.a. James Hosier, wide eyed and interested.

He went into one of the cubicles and emerged with a business card. "Call me sometime," he said. "Two hundred dollars," and then he went back into the cubicle and bolted the door.

I looked at the card. I knew the street well. It's one of the new streets on the south side. Bungalows mostly, each with a garage on either side and occupied by up-and-coming young executives. Coincidentally, it's one of Dad's best sales areas. They can't wait to strip out the brand new kitchen and replace it with a Kookalux unit.

Rather expecting to hear the bolt being drawn back again and the door to open invitingly, I hung around for a few minutes. Nothing happened. I could hear him getting dressed. I went to the communal changing room the swimming club uses, put the card in my pocket and thought no more about it for at least three weeks.

Then circumstances intervened, as they sometimes do. Michael went away to a conference for two weeks. That meant a loss of income. My computer crashed out and needed a new I – board. If there is one thing I hate, it's spending more than is coming in. I thought it over – and called Tom.

You're going to ask why I didn't call one of my regular customers. Any one of them would have welcomed an extra nibble of the cherry. (Some cherry!) I don't know. It was curiosity I guess and he wasn't bad looking. I draw the line at the over-fifties with bald heads and beer bellies.

On Friday evening at 7 p.m. exactly, I pulled up outside his house. It was a neat enough place, freshly painted and with the usual flower border. I rang the doorbell.

"Ah! Spot on time," he said.

He closed the door behind us. "I do it in the attic," he said. That worried me a bit – even more when he lowered a step ladder leading to a small square hatch in the ceiling. If a guy comes on weird in the main part of the house there's a chance to get dressed and run. Attics are not designed to allow a quick getaway. When we were up there, I got even more worried. A solitary, bare light bulb hanging from the rafters cast sinister shadows. I could just make out a table in the center and a long bench down one side. On a shelf over the bench were what looked like gallon paint cans. It was very different from the couch or bed I'm used to. No elaborate booze cabinet either. ("You ever tried whisky in your Coke? Here. Try it.")

The smell of the place was eerie too. I've gotten used to josssticks and strange cigarettes. ("They're a real turn on. You'll see.") Not for this lad. This was a sickly, sweet smell. Some sort of instinct told me that it was inflammable and that a single match would take the roof off. At least I wouldn't be offered anything to smoke. That was a slight relief.

"I should put your clothes over there," he said, and pointed to some hooks screwed into one of the roof beams. I don't mind admitting that I was getting more and more nervous. I glanced out of the window. Down below was a concrete patio. No chance of doing a dramatic dive through the glass. I didn't want to end up looking like a heap of strawberry jam.

"I'm meeting somebody at eight," I said.

"Oh yeah? Where?"

"Outside. I told them I'd be here."

Normally that would have had an immediate effect. I'd have been shown out of the house so fast that my feet wouldn't touch the doormat.

"Buddies of yours?" he asked.

"Yeah. One of them's in the Marine Corps. He's home on short leave."

"A Marine eh? I could be interested. Anyway, the quicker you get undressed, the sooner you'll be free to join them."

Amazed, and, to be honest with you, a bit frightened, I started to undress. He busied himself at the bench. I couldn't see what he was doing. He had his back to me. It was unbelievable. There are some guys who like to watch me strip. There are some who like to do it themselves. In either case, their eyes are practically popping out of their heads.

"Lie on the table when you're ready," he said.

I have to admit that my heart was thumping a bit. It wasn't the enjoyable pounding I get at the prospect of shooting into some guy's mouth or over his sheets. There was something distinctly weird and worrying about Tom. I should have known of course. He'd have to have something really kinky in mind to offer two hundred. Hell, my regulars pay a hundred for unlimited access.

I climbed on the table. It had been covered with a sheet. He stayed at the bench. "Ready when you are," I said. It came out sort of croaky. He turned round.

"Get it hard for me," he said.

Two hundred bucks and he hadn't even looked at the goods, let alone touch them! Most of my customers get tetchy if it's even half hard before they start on it.

There was nothing for it but to do what he asked – or try. It wasn't easy. It was probably the smell of the place. None of my usual fantasies worked. Susan and me in a forest was a dead loss. Susan and another girl licking each other out whilst I looked on had to be dismissed on the grounds of total impossibility. Me and Phil Clay? No. Me and Steve Marshall? It stirred very slightly. Steve Marshall was a minister's son at school and well on the way, at sixteen, to becoming a saint. When he said he was only with us temporarily nobody knew whether he was referring to the school or the world. He was a keen member of the swimming club but he always went into a cubicle to change and made it very plain that the usual banter about cock sizes and where they had been recently did not amuse him. I wasn't the only one who tried to get him to change in the communal room. Steve was one of those real good lookers. He looked "big" in every possible way if you know what I mean.

The sound of pouring water came from the bench. That, together with the smell, began to do the trick.

"Will it hurt, doctor?"

Turn off the tap with my elbow.

"Not too much. It has to be done."

"I'm meeting somebody at eight."

"You were. Now let's have a look at it. That's a nice cock you got there son. You ought to look after it. Give it a bit of open air exercise. Like this...."

Steve wriggling and protesting. "This is nothing. When you're ready, I'm going to screw that tight little ass of yours. You're not ready for it yet though. I want to feel this get hard as steel...."

"That's it," said Tom. "Great! Just like I imagined it would be. Soon to be the most famous cock in the United States."

How so?" Desperate to keep it up I continued to play with it as I spoke.

"You'll see. I'm nearly ready for you. Just make sure the saw is sharp enough..."

I think I passed out momentarily. Two things happened at once. He picked up a little gadget from the bench and ran it up and down his arm. I could hear it buzzing. As he turned round to face me I caught sight of something on the bench. It was a human penis; a long, black penis. It lay next to a stainless steel hospital-type bowl.

I don't know what I did. I must have yelled. I know I would have gotten off the table pretty fast if I could. You read of people being paralyzed by terror. It isn't an exaggeration.

I was suddenly aware of Tom standing over me with the bowl in his hand. "It's gone down a bit," he said. I remember shouting at him. I don't think I actually hit him though I tried to. He put the bowl on the floor.

"Hey! What's gotten into you?" he asked.

I think I gasped out something about him not getting away with it and he laughed. He actually laughed.

"What do you take me for? A queer?" he asked.

"I know bloody well you are. A fucking pervert as well!"

- 204 -

"I wouldn't say that," he said.

"What's that over there on the bench then? Which poor bastard was that?"

"Hardly poor. He's two hundred bucks richer. Here, have a look." He went over to the bench, picked it up and handed it to me.

"I'm not touching the fucking thing. Fuck off!" By this time I was standing on the floor and mine had shriveled to nothing.

"Go on. Hold it. It's set now."

Set? I put out a finger and touched it. It was rubber!

"It's a dildo!" I exclaimed.

"Of course it is. I thought you realized. Didn't the other guys in the team tell you?"

"Which other guys?"

"Phil or Karl or Mike."

"No."

He laughed again. "I begin to understand your concern," he said. "I've modeled them all. It was Phil who suggested you might make a good one."

By that time I'd begun to see the funny side of things. It was typical of Phil not to tell me. Phil led his life in watertight compartments. I guess I do the same.

"I've got them in here somewhere," said Tom. He opened a drawer in the bench. "Yes. Here they are. This is Phil for sure. And this is Karl. I think Mike is this one but I can't be sure."

He gave them to me and I held the cocks of my three best buddies. It was odd but the thought turned me on again fast. There was no doubt about Phil's. It was enormous and I'd recognize the banana bend anywhere. Karl was interesting. Much bigger than I'd guessed. Mike was a bit of a shock. I'd seen it often enough after swimming. It was difficult to equate the dangling, rubbery object I'd seen in the changing room with this six-inch-by-one-inch rod. I knew his balls were big. Seeing them close up like that was quite an experience. I could have counted the wrinkles.

The only one I had experience of was Phil's. An ass full of Phil leaves no room for anything else. I ached for days afterwards. Karl is so slim and slightly built that his monster was quite a surprise. I could understand why the guy he met in Germany was crazy about it. As for Mike... well, if he didn't object to having it modeled, maybe he occasionally went a bit further but who with?

Not with Phil, I thought. They never seemed to get along that well. You sort of know when two guys have a thing going. It often isn't sexual at all. There are no fulltime gays on the swimming team.

The only guy who really seemed to like Mike was young Tom Ansell. I know he often went round to Mike's place. Could it be? Well, it was possible.

"That's it. That's really good," said Tom. He slipped a piece of plastic with a sort of key-hole shape cut in it round my cock, put a rubber over it and started slapping bits of warm, wet cloth round it. "Try to hold on to whatever you're thinking," he said. "I hope she's nice!"

"She sure is," I replied. I had Mike's cock in my hand and the softness and warmth enveloping mine felt good.

"It's good of you to show me," said Mike. "I wouldn't know what to do."

"Think nothing of it. See, how I've got my cock in his ass? Not too far at first."

"What does it feel like?"

"You'll feel for yourself when I've got this hard enough. He's great. A nice soft feeling."

"Just going to brush some oil on your balls to stop the plaster from sticking," said Tom. I opened my legs a bit. That felt good.

Soon, my entire groin area was covered by plaster cloths, which began to cool and stiffen.

"Hold on to those thoughts for as long as you can," said Tom. He stood back and wiped bits of plaster from the table and his hands.

The soft tissues of Tom Ansell's sweet virgin asshole metamorphosed into a cool, hard hand. Phil's hand.

"I hear you've had this in Tom Ansell."

"Only a little way. I was getting him ready for Mike."

"I don't like the idea of you doing it with kids of that age. Much better to let me give you a wank like we used to when we were kids. Remember?"

I sure did. On the back seat of the school bus once. We were only kids then but the memory stayed with me.

"Guess it must be the bouncing. My cock's gone hard. What about yours?"

"Same."

"Want to give me a wank?"

"What here? On a bus?"

"Sure. Why not. Here, I'll put my coat over us. Miss Treadwell will think we're cold.

Then that hand, burying itself into my jeans. "Hey! It feels bigger than it did last time."

"I'm fourteen now. Makes a difference...."

"It should be ready," said Tom. "Keep absolutely still. Don't move a muscle." The buzzing noise started. The motor must have had a built-in fan. I could feel the draught on the insides of my thighs. Having a saw blade quite so near your balls is not an experience I would want to repeat. It must have had some sort of guard though. I could feel metal on my skin as it sliced through the plaster, up and over my balls and along my cock. Suddenly, the tightness vanished and I felt cool air. Tom held two chunks of plaster in his hands.

"Perfect!" he exclaimed. "If you want to wash and dry, use this bucket. I haven't got running water up here yet."

He gave me a cloth and I wiped myself. "What happens now?" I asked.

"Your bit's finished. I put the two shells together and make a mould. Then it's filled with liquid latex. That's just the prototype. The factory does any final cleaning up necessary. This should be in production within a month. When you're dressed we'll go downstairs and pay you."

There's an amusing sequel to this story. I think it's amusing anyway. About six months later I was in a hotel room with a certain gentleman. That's all I'm going to say. If I were to tell you the name you'd either not believe me or you'd spread it around. Let's just say that you know him pretty well.

We met after one of his concerts. I was keen on the supporting group. I was never one of the thousands who almost worship him. I was standing outside the concert hall waiting for my dad to pick me up. Going to concerts on a motor bike is really not on. You sit there or stand there in leathers and with a crash helmet in your hands feeling completely out of place amongst all those people in tee shirts and jeans.

Behind me were two enormous double doors marked SCENERY. The stage door was round the corner and you couldn't see it because of the thousands of people clustered round it. Suddenly, a small door inside one of the big ones opened.

"Night George," said a voice. I turned round and it was him!

The doorkeeper said, "Good night," and the little door closed.

"Hello. Who are you?" said the person.

"James Hosier."

"Pleased to meet you. John said you'd be here. The car should be coming round about now."

Before I could ask who John was or how John knew I'd be at the concert, an enormous stretch limousine appeared. Quick as a flash we climbed in.

"There he is!" somebody shouted and a stampede started behind us. The driver put his foot down and we soon left them.

It didn't take me too long to get the message that time or to put two and two together. My dad was going to find a hustler standing in the appointed place. I wasn't too worried about that. In fact it was an amusing thought. If the hustler had been told what was expected of him, my dad was going to have an embarrassing few minutes.

"You look quite well built," said the person. "John did a good job." He pulled on a glove and stroked the front of my jeans. "Nice," he commented. "Long legs too. Should mean you've got a good ass."

In the hotel room I had to undress in front of him and parade in front of a mirror.

"Let's see that arrogant look!" he said. Feeling like a not- very-good actor portraying a (naked) Nazi general, I strode up and down the floor.

"Good! Come here. Let me get it really hard."

I stood, with my feet apart, in front of him, wondering what his fans would think if they could see him or hear him.

"That's right," he said. "Look at it! Swelling with pride. I guess you're real proud of this, eh?"

I didn't answer. I was wondering what his next move would be. If he didn't make it soon, he was going to get a face full.

He made no attempt to get down on it; just kept rubbing it and gloating over it.

He made me kneel on the floor. The oil he'd squirted in from a bottle was running down my legs into the carpet. I guess when you've got that kind of money, you don't have to worry about hotel furnishings. He reached into a bag, brought out a box and there it was. James Hosier II!

I have a tiny little spot on the left hand side of my cock down near the base. It's always been there. I recognized it at once.

"Let's see you squirm like I had to," he said, and the first inch was pushed into me. I gave an artificial groan.

"Hurts doesn't it? Good. Have some more."

The groans became genuine. I could feel my insides twisting up as he screwed it into me. Suddenly he stopped. I hadn't shot my load; neither had he. I felt it being pulled out.

Fifteen minutes later I was lying on his bed with his head between my legs and he was sucking on it like a baby on a comforter. The pain in my ass subsided. I just lay there with my hands behind my head thinking how weird people are. It took me much longer than usual that night. He wiped his mouth and got dressed again.

Then he told me all about it. The story the fans haven't heard. Everybody knows that his parents died when he was young. I guess some know that he went to live with his widowed uncle and his eighteen-year-old cousin. What nobody knows is that the cousin screwed him every night; sometimes twice a night from the age of ten onwards. Ten! There are some real nasty bastards in this world.

"I screw a teenage boy after every concert," he said. "I guess I'm trying somehow to get even."

We ended up drinking well after midnight. "That's quite a weapon," I said, pointing to the glistening piece of pink plastic on the floor.

"Sure is," he grinned. "I bought a dozen. I only use them once."

"In that case," I said, "Would you autograph this one for me?"

He produced a pen from behind the ornate French clock on the shelf. "Sure. What shall I write?" he asked.

"Well, that's a real sad story of yours. How about 'getting my own back,'" I said.

DIPLOMATIC PRESSURE
Peter Gilbert

"Sheer fantasy, of course," said the man in the State Department as he reached across his huge desk to hand the box back to Richard. "Strictly between you and me, we've known he was unbalanced for a long time. As for the note; I'd forget it." The Stars and Stripes fluttered behind him as a breeze blew through the open window.

"Why don't you at least send it for analysis?" asked Richard. "Then we'll know who's right."

The man shook his head wisely. "We wouldn't wish to get involved," he said. "Anyway, it's just laughable. Forget it. You're being hoaxed. Go back and run that hotel of yours and leave us to deal with the Mandanguans."

Frustrated and angry, Richard picked up the box, put it into his briefcase and got up to go. He'd spent two days in the capital, seeing the Italian Embassy, the German Embassy and now the State Department. None of them wanted to know – and he knew he was right.

On the flight home, he opened his briefcase. He fingered the box and shuddered. "Viva Italia," he murmured.

"Beg pardon?" said the man in the next seat.

"Oh, nothing," said Richard. He shuddered slightly and snapped the lock shut.

- – -

Richard hadn't been in business very long. He had twenty- four resident boys; runaways and illegal immigrants he'd picked up in his travels. They were helped out at weekends by boys who came in from the nearby town to earn a few bucks.

Things were looking good. A number of rich clients found the Garden of Eden just the place to enjoy a very "un-relaxing" weekend and an opportunity to savor forbidden fruit without worrying about the news getting out at home. The Garden of Eden was fifty miles away from the nearest human habitation, which was the reason Richard had been able to snap it up so cheaply.

The fax arrived on a Sunday. For that reason, Richard didn't pay it much attention. Sundays were a busy time. The boys and their partners generally gathered around the pool and Richard enjoyed sitting by his open office window enjoying their antics. Hairy buttocks clenched and unclenched. Boys gasped as cocks bored into their asses for the umpteenth time that weekend. They wriggled ecstatically as moustache-fringed mouths sucked on their erect cocks. It amused Richard. The same men who were enjoying themselves so openly had arrived on Friday evening looking like they'd broken out of jail, peering left and right as they climbed out of their cars and almost running across the parking lot to get into the reception area. They all asked the same question. Was there anybody registered that weekend from their neck of the woods? It quite often happened that there was. It didn't matter. By Sunday morning all inhibitions had gone. It was "Hey Joe. You had Peter yet? You want to book him for next time? What an ass! Knows how to use it too."

The fax was from the Embassy of the Republic of Mandangua. A Mr. Opaminondas, a senior official of their government, wished to visit the Garden of Eden on the following Thursday.

"Although Mr. Opaminondas is entitled to police protection, it is especially requested that the police should not, repeat, not, be informed of this visit," it continued, causing Richard some amusement.

The car was one of the longest he'd ever seen. Its occupant ranked as one of the biggest men. He was well over six feet tall and, although not exactly fat, he was certainly well built. The immaculate black suit, sparkling white shirt and tie he wore looked wrong. Some sort of flowing robe would have done his build more justice and the hole in the lobe of his left ear should, Richard thought, support some sort of dangling ear ornament.

They shook hands. Richard led him into the reception area. "How long will you be staying?" he asked.

"Oh, only this afternoon and evening. I have to fly back tomorrow."

That was a disappointment. "If you would like to give me some idea of your preferences, I'll find a suitable host for you," said Richard.

"Later. Later. First I must have something to eat. I am starving."

Aghast, Richard looked at his watch. Three o' clock. The two chefs had gone home and the boys on kitchen duty would have gone back to rest and he was reluctant to call them back. They'd be back for duty of a different kind that evening.

He apologized and explained the position. "I could rustle up something in my place if you don't mind that," he said.

"Something cold. No time to wait for cooking."

Thus it was that Mr. Opaminondas, senior official of the Government of Mandangua sat down to eat a hastily thrown-together salad with canned tongue.

"This is absolutely delicious," said Mr. Opaminondas, putting an entire slice of the meat into his mouth.

"I feel guilty about serving it to you," said Richard. "The fax didn't say when you'd be arriving."

"I'm sorry about that. The embassy should have known. Do you mind if I look at the can?"

He was obviously thinking of doing an export deal with the makers, Richard thought, as he rummaged through the garbage and produced the can. He handed it to his guest.

"Nice picture," said Mr. Opaminondas. Richard, who hadn't given the label much attention in his panic to find something, looked at it for the first time. It showed a smiling, very young farmer's boy, clad in dungarees with a pitchfork over his shoulder.

"A similar product was imported into my country once," said Mr. Opaminondas with a chuckle. "The label showed a boy. Most of our people are illiterate and it is the custom to illustrate the contents on the label. Of course, everybody thought it was canned boy."

"Must have caused riots," said Richard.

"On the contrary. They sold the entire consignment in a day. Cannibalism was once traditional in my country. The missionaries banned it. Boys were preferred because they are more tinder."

"Tender," said Richard, laughing. "Tinder is something a scout lights fires with."

"Ah, yes. The Boy Scouts. This movement is very popular in my country at the moment. The missionaries introduced it when they stopped our traditional practices. Teaching boys to be pure in thought, word and deed. Teaching them to tie knots in ropes. It is ridiculous. In the old days they'd have wanted to learn how to untie them!" He laughed.

"How interesting," said Richard. It was always useful to know a client's little foibles.

"My grandfather always used to say that a boy isn't any use if he's not tied up," said Mr. Opaminondas. "All that youthful energy restrained. Like a clock. The tension in the spring restrained by the escapement. An interesting concept, don't you think?"

Richard was running a list of names through his mind. Both Stephen or Chuck would be suitable. He wondered which one to recommend. He was dying to get away from the table to make sure that they were still on the premises. Weekday afternoons were so slack that quite a lot of boys drove into town.

Unlike most clients, Mr. Opaminondas seemed in no hurry at all to get down to the business for which he had come to the Garden of Eden.

"A well-rounded rump, wriggling in the ropes," said Mr. Opaminondas. "The first line of a poem I wrote when I was at University."

"I think it's time I introduced you to the boys." Poetry was all very well but he wasn't getting paid to listen to a recital.

"Perhaps." Mr. Opaminondas stood up, and in doing so hit his head on the light fitting. If his equipment was in proportion to the rest of him, thought Richard, one unlucky lad was likely to have a very sore backside.

He led his guest out to the poolside. Fortunately, most of the boys were there. Word of the visitor had obviously gotten round pretty quickly. Some had dispensed with swim wear altogether. Others wore theirs so low that if the boy got off his lounger they would certainly have fallen round his ankles. Buttocks of every degree of rotundity and every possible color absorbed the sunshine. Pubic hair, still wet from a recent swim, glittered as though it was sewn with diamonds.

"Now this is Trevor," said Richard, recognizing the boy's soft round butt and long legs.

Trevor turned over and, shading his eyes with his hand, said "Hi."

"A good one," said Mr. Opaminondas. Richard agreed, though he didn't know whether the remark had been made about Trevor as a whole or the huge lump in the front of his trunks.

"I'll have him," said Mr. Opaminondas.

"Wouldn't you prefer to take your time?" Richard asked. First-time clients usually spent hours talking to boys, eyeing them up and down and occasionally putting out a tentative hand before making a choice. It was if some elaborate game of musical chairs was being played on the poolside.

"No. This one will do. I don't have much time."

Relieved, Richard smiled broadly. "Take room seventeen, Trev," he said and, turning to his guest, he suggested that Mr. Opaminondas call in to his office when he was finished. "We prefer cash to credit cards, for the protection of our clients' privacy," he said. "I hope you have a good time. I'm sure you will. Trevor is very good."

He turned to go back to his office. "Where are you going? I shall need others," said Mr. Opaminondas.

"Oh! Sorry. I hadn't realized," said Richard, smiling even more broadly. There were a few other clients who enjoyed orgies. He should have realized. Four boys on a Thursday afternoon! Things were certainly looking up. He'd charged the last orgy client ten thousand bucks but that was for six boys over a weekend. He was trying to work out a reasonable sum when Mr. Opaminondas spotted Paul Sinclair.

It would have been difficult to overlook Paul. He was the tallest and the most muscular of all the boys.

Paul lay on a lounger. His swimming shorts were a lump of wet cloth on the ground beside him. His enormous tool flopped over his thigh. Richard introduced them.

"Big," said Mr. Opaminondas, staring down at it.

"He certainly is. Quite delicious, so I've been told," said Richard. Several of his regular customers had almost choked on Paul's eleven inches. A Paul orgasm was considerably more than a mouthful.

"Delicious? At his age?" said Mr. Opaminondas. "To be truly delicious a boy should be much younger. Soft, silky pubic hair and still with a bit of little boy fat in the buttocks. A boy like that, my friend, is mouth-watering."

Richard regretted that it wasn't the weekend. Young, very young, Alan Scoble came in at weekends to mow the lawns. There were one or two clients who forsook the professional hosts in favor of the little boy with brief shorts who drove the mower up and down. Officially, Richard knew nothing about it but often smiled to himself when the roar of the mower stopped. First Alan would go into the guest wing, followed a few seconds later by one of the guests, usually with hands in pockets and looking far too casual for a man about to experience Alan's long, drawn-out, shuddering and almost dry orgasm.

"I'll take him as well," said Mr. Opaminondas. "Now. Two more."

Richard shaded his eyes with his hand and looked round the pool. Stephen and Chuck would be ideal but, at first, he couldn't see them. Then he spotted them, lying together in a shady corner well out of the sun.

Chuck nudged Stephen as they approached. Stephen put a hand to his trunks and pulled them down slightly and, apparently, fell into a deep sleep immediately.

"Now these two would be very suitable for what you were talking about," said Richard. Stephen let out a light snore. Chuck opened one eye and smiled.

"Do you think so?" said Mr. Opaminondas looking down at them with exactly the same quizzical look with which Richard's head chef appraised salmon.

"Oh, certainly. Tied up and all that."

Chuck opened both eyes and grinned. Stephen stirred. Richard had often wondered what had caused them to be as they were. The discipline at the reformatory they'd run away from was apparently pretty draconian but you don't run away from a regime of beatings and solitary confinement to suffer the same again – even for money. They'd been with him for a year and caused no trouble at all. There'd been no complaints about theft, which was the cause of them being sent to the reformatory. Their clients spent happy weekends tying them up, beating hell out of them and left with their billfolds and Rolex watches still in their possession.

"And how old are they?" asked Mr. Opaminondas.

"Sixteen," said Richard.

"Hmmm. Ask them to turn over."

Chuck did so. As though waking from a deep sleep, Stephen followed suit.

"What's happened to that one?" Mr. Opaminondas pointed to the pattern of weals on Chuck's thighs.

"A client," said Richard. "But you need not worry. They won't affect his performance. You might like to add a few. Chuck collects them like other boys collect stamps."

"Certainly not!" said Mr. Opaminondas. "To spoil a bottom like that is a terrible thing. In my country the man who did that would be flogged to death. However, they'll do."

Chuck and Stephen got up. Richard waved to Trevor and Paul and watched as the most varied procession he'd ever seen walked over to the guest block. Eighteen year old Trevor led the way. Then Mr. Opaminondas, the connoisseur of pre-pubertal fat bottoms, followed by a very hairy twenty-year-old and two sixteen-year-olds.

"We've had some odd customers but you're the oddest," Richard murmured to himself. "It just doesn't make sense – still... The customer is king."

He walked back in the direction of his office to do some calculating.

"Who was that?" asked one of the boys.

"Never you mind," said Richard.

"I'll bet he's got the most enormous cock," said the boy. "I wouldn't be in the shoes of any of those four. Not for all the money in the world."

"They aren't wearing shoes," said Richard with a laugh.

"Going to fuck them, is he?" the boy asked.

"I don't know. I'm not so nosy as you," Richard replied. It was a good question he thought. It was unlikely that anyone could fuck four boys in one afternoon. Richard had grown quite skilled in assessing his clients' predilections. Even the shy ones; the men who were stealing a weekend away from the wife and kids were pretty easy. Just watching where their eyes were looking whilst they talked about baseball or the difficulty they'd had in finding the place was enough.

Mr. Opaminondas was a mystery.

It happened that rooms sixteen and seventeen were connected. A relic of the place's heyday as a resort hotel when there was a demand for children's rooms. Richard did his calculations, took the master key from his drawer and padded along the corridor. From room seventeen itself came the sound of voices. He took off his shoes and slipped into room sixteen. He put his ear against one of the panels in the communicating door. Mr. Opaminondas was holding forth on the beauties of Mandangua. So much for the man in a hurry!

"The mountains in the north are mostly not explored," he said. "There is dense jungle there."

Richard sat down on the bed and waited. What he was doing was quite wrong. Clients were promised absolute privacy and here was he – the originator of the rule, listening in. He stood up again, determined to leave but something drew him back to the door for one last bit of eavesdropping.

"All Mandanguan men drink it. It keeps us healthy," Mr. Opaminondas was saying. "It is a tradition of our country."

Richard was about to sit down again when it became apparent that his strange guest was not talking about pineapple juice. Paul gave a loud sigh and there came a sound like someone trying to mop up a puddle with a vacuum cleaner. Stephen and Chuck giggled.

Silence. Then Paul breathing heavily. Slurping noises. Paul's breaths turned to gasps. A strange slapping noise that Richard couldn't identify. "Oh yeah! Yeah! Ye...ah!" The slapping and the slurping stopped.

"Very good," said Mr. Opaminondas, sounding a bit like a Disney goldfish. "Now you. Trevor isn't it?"

"That's right."

"Stand a bit closer so I can feel you. That's it. Hmmm. A lot of muscle."

"I work out a lot," said Trevor.

"In Mandangua, you wouldn't have the chance. A boy like you would be tethered so that all your energy could go to the parts which matter. See, it's still a bit limp. In my country it would leap up as soon as someone came into the hut. A bit closer now...."

The slurping noises started again. Stephen and Chuck were whispering. Trevor sighed – probably, thought Richard, because his greatest asset wasn't being used. Trevor's weekend earnings were phenomenal. There had been one weekend when he'd serviced sixteen clients and Richard (and Trevor when he was told) laughed at what number fifteen had said. "Pretty new to the scene, eh? I can always tell. It was like putting a key into a new lock. Reserve him for me next time and don't let him get too much of a liking for it."

Trevor sighed again.

There followed a short silence and then Mr. Opaminondas spoke again.

"And you with the scars. Chuck. Let's have you next."

It soon became obvious that Chuck was a disappointment. Mr. Opaminondas cajoled him. The others encouraged him but it was all too obvious that Chuck's prick was failing to respond.

"Oh, go away," said Mr. Opaminondas irritably. "You waste my time. In the very old times in my country they would bring out the mpiku for you. Let's see if your friend is any better."

"What's a whatever it is?" asked Stephen. "Is that close enough?"

"Mmm. You are also soft."

"Just play with it a bit and tell me what a whatsit is."

"It is the special spear they killed the boys with. Ah! Good. You are hardening. I think you will be especially nourishing."

"Did they kill lots of boys in those days?" asked Stephen. His voice sounded husky.

"Usually only one. He was the special boy. They cut up the body and roasted his legs – and this bit. The chief ate the boy's cock and his balls. By doing that the boy's spirit passed into him. The elders banqueted on the legs and the rump. The rest of the body went to the women to make ornaments from the bones and the skin. But enough of history. You are ready."

Stephen grunted. Richard took his ear away from the wood. and smiled. Without knowing it, Mr. Opaminondas had found Stephen's secret trigger. Telling Stephen a gory, horror story got him going like nothing else. A film producer had discovered it first. Richard hadn't thought to tell Mr. Opaminondas. If he'd thought about it he could also have told the man that Chuck reacted to pain. The more he was hurt, the more excited he got. Privately, he suspected that the two of them had quite a thing going together. Not that he minded. They both performed well for the clients.

It was time, thought Richard, to get back to the office. He slunk out of the room, put on his shoes and returned. He need not have rushed. An hour went by and then another. He kept himself busy working on the duty roster for the next week. It was no easy task. You couldn't put a boy on kitchen duty in the morning if he'd been with an active client all night. The weekends were worse. New clients liked all the boys to be round the pool and yet the work had to be done.

Then the phone rang. It was someone from the Mandanguan Embassy, demanding, not asking, to be put in touch with Mr. Opaminondas immediately.

"I'm afraid he's busy at the moment," said Richard.

"Interrupt him. Get him!" cried the man. "I have to speak to him."

Nobody had ever telephoned a guest before and Richard was quite sure that Mr. Opaminondas would be as angry as any other guest. But the man was insistent. There was nothing for it but to take the phone down to the guest room. He stood for a few minutes by the door. Something was happening in there but he couldn't make out what it was. He tapped lightly.

"Someone at the door," said Paul. Richard tapped again.

"You go, Paul. I don't want to miss anything," said Stephen.

The door opened. Paul and his cock peered out. "Oh, it's you," he said.

"Guy from the Mandanguan Embassy, says he has to speak to Mr. Opaminondas urgently," said Richard and he went to pass the phone to Paul.

"Bring it in," Mr. Opaminondas called. Paul opened the door wider. Richard slipped in.

"Be careful as you close it, Paul," he said, looking down at the boy's amazing cock. "Don't damage it. It's worth a lot of money."

Once inside, he did a quick double take. Mr. Opaminondas' huge bulk seemed to fill the room. Naked, he looked even bigger and more powerful, a power being appreciated at that moment by Chuck, who knelt on the bed, supported by his hands and by Stephen and Paul who sat on either side of him. Mr. Opaminondas' cock was deep inside the boy and Chuck's hard organ pointed downwards and forwards and jerked with every contraction of Mr. Opaminondas' vast behind.

He stopped for moment, took one hand from Chuck's back and snatched the phone.

"Opaminondas." He gave a slow thrust forwards. Chuck shook his head from side to side.

"Nge?" said Mr. Opaminondas. Chuck shook his head again. "Soon be over," said Steve, brushing his friend's glistening forehead with his hand.

"Nge?" He gave another thrust. Chuck yelled.

"Nge. Nge."

"Ow! Ow!"

Mr. Opaminondas laughed and said something in Mandanguan. He held the telephone in an outstretched hand so that it was nearer Chuck's gaping mouth.

"Let my friend hear you," said Mr. Opaminondas. His giant, brown buttocks clenched together and Chuck screamed.

"Good, good! Again." Chuck screamed even louder and shook his head so vigorously that drops of sweat landed on Stephen and Trevor's naked shoulders.

"I think he's about to come," said Stephen. Mr. Opaminondas put his other hand under the boy and felt for his cock. He gave three more thrusts. Chuck yelled out three more times and then gave a loud sigh. If Stephen and Trevor hadn't been holding him up, he would certainly have collapsed. Mr. Opaminondas brought the hand up to his mouth and licked it hungrily. He spoke to his Embassy friend again and passed the phone to Trevor. Then he put both hands on Chuck's waist and concentrated on the job in hand. The man certainly had stamina, thought Richard. He was aware that he should make himself scarce. He wasn't wanted but couldn't tear himself away. He'd never seen Chuck in action like this.

Running the Garden of Eden was a bit like running a candy store. The first few months had been pretty hectic but he rarely had a boy these days. A client who had had rather too much to drink told him about Chuck's preferences in the bar one evening.

"That boy takes some beating," the man said. "Used my Daddy's old riding crop on his butt. Gave him the thrashing of his life. Just like my Daddy used to give me. You should have heard him scream! There he was, wriggling around like a worm on a hook." He laughed. "Couldn't rightly tell which cheek I was hittin' and boy oh boy, didn't he come good. Like a high pressure hose," he said.

"Very good!" said Mr. Opaminondas. He waited for a moment or two, then started to withdraw. The boys, who had obviously seen it before smiled. Richard stared in amazement. It was like watching a black snake being pulled out of its burrow. Four inches – five inches – seven inches – nine inches and still it came. Finally, with an audible squelch, the great plum-like head appeared. Mr. Opaminondas stripped off the rubber and threw it into the wash basin in the corner.

"Now I must return at once," he said. "There is some trouble in our country. How much do I owe you?"

Richard told him when they were in the office. He produced a wad of hundred-dollar bills that looked as thick, when he returned it to his pocket, as it had when he took it out. Richard saw him off the premises and went in search of the four boys. He found them talking by the poolside. Understandably, Chuck lay on his front.

"Easiest money I've ever earned," said Trevor when Richard gave him his share.

"More than you can say for Chuck," said Stephen.

"You okay, Chuck?" Richard asked.

"I guess so. Feels like I've been sitting on a fence post. When's he coming back?"

"No idea. But I guess he will."

- — -

But Mr. Opaminondas didn't. The television news that night announced that the President of Mandangua had died and went on to list his achievements. Then came the civil war. It was odd, Richard thought, as the months went by, how often Mandangua was in the news. He'd never heard of the place before. First of all, there was the great uranium find in the north of the country. There was more uranium there than all the other sources in the world. Then came yet another civil war. Almost every night, the television showed horrifying pictures of street fighting. Then, to his surprise, Mr. Opaminondas became His Excellency Eustace Opaminondas, President of the Independent Republic of Mandangua.

Richard invited the four boys to watch the inauguration of the new president on television. "If only they knew what we know," said Paul as they watched the motorcade glide by the thousands of dancing, clapping spectators.

It was announced some days later that the new President had ruled that the country should return to its old traditional way of life. Missionaries were expelled. The western world, presumably more interested in a good supply of uranium, protested mildly.

The Boy Scouts Association of Mandangua was abolished. There were strange rumors about missing scouts. The television showed a group of mothers protesting outside the presidential palace. The Mandanguan Government firmly denied that any Boy Scouts had been arrested. The American Ambassador was instructed not to get involved.

Then came the extraordinary affair of the disappearance of the Italian schoolboys' soccer team. Invited to Mandangua to play a few friendly matches in celebration of the country's first National Day, they were apparently captured by bandits during a bus tour of the mountainous northern region and never heard of again.

Richard began to see a pattern which, apparently, the State Department hadn't spotted but then Richard knew the President's secret. They obviously didn't, or did they? Boys visiting Mandangua who were actually seen by the president, vanished. Generally speaking, the growing number of tourists were safe. There were a few isolated reports of boys vanishing from beaches but, strangely, only from beaches near the capital.

"He'll be the next," Richard murmured to himself one evening as he watched the television report about a Russian mining expert's visit to Mandangua. Mr. Opaminondas was shown ruffling the hair of the man's fifteen-year-old son and smiling at the boy. Richard was right; just seventeen days later the distraught expert and his wife left Mandangua without young Petrov.

Six members of a German boys' choir vanished. ANOTHER KIDNAPPING OUTRAGE IN MANDANGUA! the headline said. "Kidnapping's the right word," said Richard. The oldest boy was fifteen. The article went on to say that Mandangua was the world's biggest supplier of uranium ore.

He threw the paper down in disgust, went to his desk and unlocked the drawer. The package had arrived that day. It contained a long, leather-covered box with the Mandanguan flag embossed on the top. The Order of the Golden Elephant, presented to him by the President. If only the note had been omitted he'd have been none the wiser.

The four boys had received presents too. Wallets.

"Beautiful aren't they?" said Stephen. "Look, that's their national flag."

"Hm. That was kind of him," said Richard.

"It's German leather," said Stephen. "There was a note in it to say so."

"Mine's Russian," said Paul. "Trev's is much darker. The guy's got a great sense of humor. I'll bet it's a joke about his sunbathing."

"Almost certainly," said Richard, trying to stifle a shudder. What did you get, Chuck?"

With a grin, Chuck produced two items from behind his back. One was a wallet. The other, a beautiful leather riding crop."

"The handle's made of bone," he said.

"And did you get a note too?"

"Yeah. I can't really make it out. Here, have a look."

"He wasn't as good as you were. Sincerely, E.O."

When they left, he opened the box again and read the note.

"In gratitude for a pleasant afternoon. He was Italian and quite delicious. Fitting, don't you think, for a boy who has spent years kicking leather to end up covering a box? Sincerely, E.O."

COFFEE BREAK
John Patrick

A guy named Bob picked me up at the park late one night and said he would buy me a cup of coffee. But we drove to his place. Bob lived in a condo uptown, tastefully decorated, Monet prints on the wall, nice furniture, lots of glass. It was eclectic, cosmopolitan and very neat.

"Nice," I said, looking around. I stopped myself from asking if he lived alone. It was hard to tell, what with no photographs, no notes on the fridge, nothing to tell of how his life was lived, only well-organized sterility, like a layout in a design magazine that spoke of taste but not of the people who lived there.

He brewed some coffee, his special blend, and put some cookies on a plate.

He served us in the dimly lit living room. "Hmm...." He slipped off his shoes and snuggled up on the couch, sipping his coffee. I sat in a chair across the room. I drank my coffee down, nibbled a cookie.

The cookie didn't help. Neither did the special blend of coffee. It just made me more nervous. There was something strange about this whole set-up. I felt like I did back when I was fucking Seth Elder's boyfriend, Arlo, while Seth was off at a police officers' training seminar. That was a dumb-ass thing to do. If Seth'd caught me he would have killed me. I was lucky. He pulled a gun on Arlo and told him he'd shoot him unless he told him who he'd been out with, but he kept his mouth shut.

Bob studied me for a few moments, then walked toward me, measuring my response. He knelt down and took my shoes and socks off in slow, deliberate movements. He ran his hands up my calves and thighs, spreading them apart, kissing them, reaching his hands inside my shorts, running them around back, gently squeezing my hamstrings, examining, coaxing. I felt myself grow hot, my mouth dry. I wet my lips.

He smiled. "You have great legs."

"Thanks," I said, still nibbling on the cookie. It was a big cookie, chocolate chip, my favorite. I was going to finish it.

"I wonder what the rest of you looks like."

I remembered thinking how I liked studs who knew what they wanted and how to get it, but I'd never known anyone like this guy. Anyone who could pick me up, take me home, feed me cookies and coffee, and seduce me in less than an hour was quite a fellow. Part of me was in rapture; part was scared shitless.

"Do you want to find out?"

"I do," he said, taking my hand and pulling.

"Where are we going?" I was still chewing my cookie, and crumbs had dropped all over his carpet.

He chuckled. "Where do you think we're going?"

He put soft music on the radio in his bedroom, then approached me. "May I?" he asked.

Finding no resistance whatsoever, he lifted up my shirt, eased it over my head. He twisted a nipple. Then he kissed my stomach, letting his tongue dive beneath the waistband of my shorts, letting them fall from my hips to the floor. He cupped his hand on my balls. He slid the shorts down, then kissed his way up until he took my erection in his mouth.

I lifted his shirt off. He was smooth, nicely built. He stopped sucking me so that he could take off his pants, briefs. He had a lovely cock, bigger than mine, thick. I longed for him to make me suck it. But he went right back down on his knees again, kissing, licking my cock. I ran my fingers through his dark hair, murmuring that he was a truly talented cocksucker, which he was. He maneuvered me toward the bed, never removing his fingers. He sat on the edge of the bed and began sucking in earnest. I cried out.

"Hmm. Come here," I said, pulling him near, wanting to run my hands down his back, his buttocks, his strong legs.

He released me to get on the bed, on my back. He straddled me and I lifted his cock to my mouth, taking him in, my tongue gliding around it. While I sucked him, I stuck a finger in his anus, looking up at him for protest. He didn't. I loved doing this, filling every orifice, giving sensation and pleasure to all the places that seek touch, that quiver with delight. He glided back and forth, crying out for more. He lowered himself over my cock, and I felt him press against me. I put my hand on his, covering his fingers as he jacked himself. Tanned, long fingers curling around the thick prick. He gasped and collapsed, taking me down with him.

"Oh, I'm sorry. But don't stop. Fuck me."

"I will." I remained deep inside him. I ground into him furiously. Then he started to fuck my dick again. He was untiring, his long, firm strokes even and precise.

Then, somewhere in the distance, the phone rang. It rang until the answering machine picked up and still those long even strokes, growing harder, my moving against him and wanting more. All I heard between the beep and the click was something like "I love you," and "I can't wait to get home." It was a woman's voice. He stopped.

"Don't stop," I begged. "Please don't stop."

But he did; he got on his stomach, wanted me to finish that way. I began to feed my cock into his ass. I heard him suck in his breath as the head poked inside, then he cried out as I inched the shaft in. When my balls hit his ass, he let out a deep sigh. I began to thrust my hips back and forth, starting out slowly. Then I picked up speed, fucking him with vigor. He soon picked up on my rhythm and pushed his ass back on my cock. "Harder!" he demanded.

As I fucked him, I leaned over and reached around, grabbing his stiff cock in my hands. I jacked him off as I plunged into him. His body began jerking and I knew he was close.

"Oh, yeah, I'm gonna shoot," he cried.

Every muscle in his body seemed to convulse as I pulled on that big dick of his. Then he let out a howl as jets of cum spurted onto the bed. I never let up on his ass, even as he was coming. I began to feel that overwhelming surge of being so close I cannot stop, no matter what. I came with such intensity that it completely drained me of whatever energy the strong java had given me.

I kissed his naked shoulder, then fell back on the bed next to him, panting.

He leaned up on his elbow and stared at me. The phone call drifted back. I could see it in his face.

I ran my hand across his face before he began. I said, "I knew even before I heard her voice."

"How?"

"I guess I can always tell."

"It doesn't bother you?"

"No. In fact, I prefer it."

We slept together that night. In the morning we fucked again, then had coffee. And he heated up a big coffee cake. We had spent a single night swept up in carnal passion. Beginning with coffee, ending with coffee.

When I left, the phone was ringing.

I don't drink coffee much anymore. The smell, the taste of it, reminds me of Bob, making me crave his touch, a craving worse than caffeine or those nicotine kisses. Now when some guy asks me to go for coffee, I wouldn't dare.

FARM-FRESH
Jason Carpenter

My trip from Texas to Iowa to visit relatives should have been uneventful – seven-hundred miles of good road all the way – an easy drive for someone accustomed to the distances I traveled within Texas making sales presentations for a Dallas software company.

The first indication of trouble began as I crossed the border from Oklahoma into Kansas. The sky suddenly became black, as though a dark veil had been drawn across the horizon. A strong gust of wind from the west shoved my car half-way into the center lane and fat, arrogant rain drops "spatted" against my windshield.

I popped out the CD I'd been listening to and roved the channels on the radio until I picked up a local station. The D.J. was in the middle of a weather report.

" . . . and heavy thunderstorms with golf ball-sized hail. The National Weather Service says that this storm front has the potential to produce dangerous straight-line winds or even tornadoes. So, be alert and stay indoors.

"Now, the first of ten in a row on KOKY, here's Garth Brooks singin'"

I switched off the radio, shivering as a chill crept over me. The outside temperature was dropping dramatically as the storm pushed through. The map on the seat beside me indicated no town ahead for fifty miles or more. I stomped the accelerator, feeling terribly alone on the highway.

My speedometer read sixty-five when marble-sized hail blasted out of the lightning-split sky and disintegrated against the windshield. The hammering racket on the roof was enough to tighten my sphincter and make me clutch the steering wheel in fear.

Before I could slow down, a hail stone the size of a man's fist shattered the window beside me, covering me in a frightening spray of sticky safety-glass. A thin line of warmth on my cheek told me I was bleeding.

Up ahead I saw an exit off of the highway. Wrenching the wheel, I took the exit just as my rear window imploded from the hail. Nearly blinded by the wind-driven rain, I could barely make out a large shape to my right – a house or a barn, I decided – about fifty yards from the road, down a partially washed out graveled driveway. Rear wheels skewing, I plunged up the narrow path, wanting nothing more than a shelter from the storm.

The wind growled through the broken windows, gaining in intensity.

When I got closer I could see that the building was a two-story house with a wide country-style verandah all along the front. Pale light spilled from an open door. A figure jumped from the porch and ran to my window. A youth, wearing only mud-caked boots and tight, water-soaked jeans, he shouted to be heard above the whistling wind.

"Around back – there's a barn – put your car in there!"

He ran ahead of me, leading the way. I followed, driving in after he opened the wide, swinging, double doors. He closed them behind us, his muscles bulging with effort as the wind threatened to tear them from his grasp.

The hail, which had stopped for a few minutes, began anew, pounding the barn like thousands of insane carpenters with heavy hammers. To go out into the fusillade would invite a concussion.

· I crawled shakily from the car and leaned against it. "Thanks," I told my rescuer. "It was getting scary out there."

He shook his shock of corn-colored hair, slinging droplets of water. "TV said a twister touched down 'bout five miles from here," he said, coming closer.

I marveled at his chest and arm development. Hard work was no stranger to this kid.

A frown crossed his serious face. "Hey, you're bleedin'."

I put my fingers to my left cheek and drew them away smeared red.

"Hang on, there's a first-aid kit on the wall," he said. Moments later, after tenderly cleaning and bandaging the cut on my face and another on the nape of my neck, the boy stuck out his big paw. "Brian – "

"Joseph Caster – Joe," I said, shaking his hand.

Was it my imagination that he held my hand a couple of beats longer than was necessary? I sincerely hoped not. "You here alone, Brian?"

"Yeah. Folks went into town earlier. I thought it was them comin' home when I saw you drive up. They'll probably stay 'til this blows over."

I shivered, dressed as I was in shorts, polo shirt and sneakers. It had been in the upper eighties when I left Dallas.

"We need to get out of these wet clothes. I'll get us a couple of horse blankets from the tack room," Brian told me. Seconds later he returned with clean-smelling blankets, tossed one to me, tugged off his muddy boots and wet socks and unselfconsciously unzipped his jeans and let them drop to his ankles. He wasn't wearing underwear.

His pale dick hung down from his thatch of curly, blond pubic hair. He looked up and caught me staring at his meat. A knowing look passed between us. Then he stroked himself and smiled.

I hurried out of my clothes thinking, "Oh Lord, for what I am about to receive, I thank you!"

Brian and I moved together in a clumsy embrace, our cocks springing to hardness. I took him in my hand and stroked the silky smoothness of his circumcised rod. He cupped my pulsing balls in his big hand and fondled them gently. Our lips met as thunder shook the building.

"Over here," Brian whispered, taking my hand.

"Wait, I need my wallet. I've got rubbers – "

I fetched several condoms and went back to Brain's side. He led me to a horse stall with fresh, fragrant hay covering the floor and an entire bale leaning against one wall. We lay down, facing each other just long enough to don the rubbers, then assumed a sixty-nine position. I filled my mouth with Brian's hot meat and shivered as he twirled his tongue around the crown of my own bulging tube.

The smell of his vibrant youth and earthy, farm-fresh maleness nearly made me come. I massaged the ripples in his muscle-ribboned stomach and drew him deeper into my throat. He worked a couple of thick fingers up my ass and stroked my sensitive insides, making me buck with lust.

I let his thrusting shaft slip from my lips and crooned to him in the soft light. "Fuck me, Brian. Fuck me hard up the ass, sweetmeat."

He rolled away from me and stood up long enough to pick up the bale of hay and set it before me. "Lie over that, Joe." And, with dry straw tickling my chest and belly erotically, I draped myself over the hay bale, offering my puckered rosebud.

Brian got to his knees behind me and screwed his nine-inch, pulsing dickmeat between the cheeks of my ass and, with a gentle thrust, into my silky, hot, love passage. "I ain't real good at holdin' back," he grunted, fucking me with long, slow strokes that teased my prostate and made my own cock jump with excitement.

His hands cupped my hipbones, dragging me with excruciating slowness onto his rigid pole. The straw made my balls tingle. Brian's humping became faster, more rhythmic as he pounded my butt cheeks. Suddenly he reached around me, gripped my engorged tool in his callused hand, and began fisting me in concert with his fucking. When he leaned over my back and gently bit my neck I squirted what seemed like a pint of jizz into the rubber while wriggling my ass against Brian's pelvis. I tightened my sphincter muscle and heard Brian howl.

"Lord A' mighty, I'm comin'! In ya, in ya, spurtin' my hot cum up in ya! Ahhhh, unngh, unngh!" He groaned and I felt the heat of his seed bathe my guts. He stayed buried up my bunghole until he slipped out, soft and, momentarily, sated. We curled together, kissing, covered by the blankets, unconcerned with the whistling wind and pounding hail outside.

It was only a matter of minutes until our pricks rose and became turgid spears of man-meat. Brian fondled me.

"Ain't never had it up the ass – would you, you know, pop my cherry?" he asked innocently.

I nodded, rolled him over onto his stomach, and put a rolled up blanket beneath his muscled abdomen to raise his pretty, round globes up for me. I pulled his asscheeks apart and viewed the tiniest little ass-blossom I'd ever seen. I wet my condom-covered prick with saliva and eased my swollen dickhead into Brian's tight, puckered butt hole, stopping when I had a couple of hard inches in him. "Okay?" I asked.

"Hurts a little, but I want you to assfuck me, Joe. Do me any way you want," he said, shivering beneath me.

I gripped his strong shoulders and pulled myself up and in, filling him with my nearly nine inches. He gasped and his breathing became heavy. Never had I been in a guy so tight and hot. Slowly I withdrew, then plunged back up his youthful chute, over and over. His firm buttocks clenched and unclenched, driving me on harder.

I felt my sizzling jizz sluice from my balls and, like an uncapped oil well, spew up the derrick of my cock and explode in a geyser of creamy fuckjuice up Brian's recently virgin assmeat, flooding his slick insides with my load.

I pounded into him, both of us bucking and humping for maximum penetration. When I fell away from him, emptied, I heard his soft crying. "Thanks, Joe – thanks for makin' me a man." He fingered his own fucked-red ass-ring and smiled happily.

Now to pleasure him. I rolled him over onto his back and slipped a rubber down over his pink meat. I began at his inner thighs, licking and nibbling his skin, then took his solid ball-sac in my mouth and sucked and rolled his cods together with my tongue, slowly. When I took his dick crown between my lips he laid his hand at the back of my neck and urged me on.

I held his engorged staff in one hand and, reaching up his body, pinched and rolled his nipples until he cried out. "Eat me, Joe. Let me fuck your face, fuck your throat, suck the fuckin' cum outta me, Joe!"

I engulfed his hammer until my lips touched his blond pubic hair then tightened my lips and sucked his throbbing dick hard against the roof of my mouth, up and down until he was a mass of uncontrolled, wriggling farm boy ready to shoot his pure white load. "Now – I'm gonna shoot now," he breathed.

But not yet. I circled the base of his cock with my thumb and forefinger and held back the flood. "Wha?" He moaned.

"It gets better," I said, before relaxing my throat and going down on him again, taking his dick down my gullet up to his hairy balls. Suddenly he rolled both of us over so that he was above me. He throat-fucked me hard and deep while I drew my fingernails over his rock-tight asscheeks, his smell and taste making me dizzy. I closed my eyes tight and gave myself up to his hunger.

"Shit, shit, shhhiit!" He screamed, ramming his dick to the hilt down my compliant throat and spurting his copious dick-honey with tornado force into my hungry mouth. I could feel the heat of it even through the rubber, smell the pungent scent of his farm-fresh spunk; taste his saltiness in my mind.

Brian scooted down beside me and we hugged and kissed, him fondling my dick while I screwed two fingers up his sweet ass and toyed with him.

When the raindrop fell on my cheek, cold and wet, it dawned upon me that the hail and rain noises had stopped. Thinking that the roof must be leaking I looked above me.

There was no roof – only gray-smudged sky, beginning to clear to blue! Brian and I had been so engrossed in fucking each other we never noticed when the storm lifted the barn's roof and took it away without touching anything inside!

Brian and I got dressed just as his parents pulled into the driveway. They were appalled at losing the barn roof, but ecstatically happy that their son was safe. After they made me stay for a great country-cooked meal I told them good-bye and Brian and I returned to the barn, which was still fragrant with our sex.

My car was beaten all to hell, but driveable. After cleaning the glass out of the seat, I kissed Brian good-bye out of his parent's sight and promised to drop in on my way back through in three days.

"Maybe my asshole will be healed by then," Brian kidded.

I cupped the bulge in his jeans. "If it isn't, I'll kiss it and make it better. I'll fuck you so hard the walls will fall down next time."

I drove away down the mud-washed driveway, watching Brian through my rearview mirror. He waved until I reached the road. I had a feeling the next three days were going to go by slowly but be filled with fantasies of the next time I met my farm-fresh fuck-buddy.

STRANGER ON THE MOUNTAIN
Sonny Torvig

I glanced up to the high ground ahead, the road clambering like a camouflaged snake to the high pass beyond. On the flat I could have covered those miles to the border in no more than a couple of hours, but flat was the last thing this part of the country had on its mind. Only an hour from the lodge and I was into the foothills, the first hint of the sun's warm breath on my back.

I had stormed away from the lodge early, and in a mood that matched the cold and damp air of dawn, John's blatant ogling of room service beginning my morning on completely the wrong footing. I was angry; and then I was cold. Without much thought, I had seen myself heroically struggling up the last hairpin to the peak, blazing out my suppressed fury in a sprint to match any of our tour's best climbers. In reality I was chilled to the bone as I struggled those first few miles over the foothills. But I had burned off the worst of my anger, and certainly warmed my blood. The day did not look so black as time wore on.

I tried to keep a rhythm as I rose and fell over the gentle slopes, liked to think it was the same rhythm timber wolves kept as they trailed their fleeing prey, ceaseless and chillingly inevitable. The hard tires sang over the coarse surface of the narrow road, the metallic symphony as chain met gear teeth occasionally cracking into a short burst of automatic fire as I dropped or raised a gear. I had dropped more than raised so far, but there was another chain-ring still to go – fortunately.

Your mind takes to wandering as you approach such a long climb, while you are still fresh and the effort needed is not too painful. (And the toxins haven't had time to accumulate in your muscles!) My thoughts turned to John, and I wondered what he would be doing now, or who. I knew it was my own reaction to room service that was at the root of my hurt; that had I been alone and, without John, I too would have asked the young Adonis to my bed. That tightly wrapped package I had almost drooled over as he bent to put the tray down! I had to admit my anger with John stemmed purely from the fact that he put into words the things I only furtively imagined. We were really struggling to remain as a couple lately, and after being together for these four years it made me sad, and angry, to think that I might lose him. He was dangerous, he was exciting, and he wanted more out of life than I seemed able to offer him.

I went over that morning's disastrous beginning in my head, running through all my possible responses in an attempt to understand how I might have avoided those outright hostilities. I could have called his bluff, and invited the house boy to our bed. I shivered, John would have loved it! But I knew I couldn't have done that. He was my lover, and there was no way I was going to voluntarily share him, despite the youth's beauty. What was done was done, and picking up the pieces would have to wait until later, it would give him time to think if I stayed out of the way for the day, he might even miss me.

I reached down and raised a gear, getting out of the saddle to build up the speed again, make it hurt a little more for a while. The sun was doing more than breathing on my back now, and bathed the wooded surroundings in clear warmth. The scents of the forests were light and clean as they teased my passing senses, with only the heavier sweetness of dry wood smoke to bring them to earth. My spirits began to rise from their cool depths, like dolphins rushing to the glittering surface.

I wasn't ready for him when he came by me, so wrapped up was I in the freshness of the day. I had never heard any warning from behind me that there was another rider close, and the suddenness of his passing drained my mind of daydreams instantly. It was him – and he was flying! I had a quick glimpse of a tangerine-colored frame and the frosted sheen of all Italian alloy, set alight by the glittering of chromed spokes. And then all I had to watch was his backside. But it was that which had me out of the saddle and trying hard. It was the unmistakable sweet rear of the room service lad. Those same tight buns I had tried to imagine naked under me. My eyes fixed on the accentuating sheen of his ultramarine lycra pants, I raised another gear and went for it, the rhythmic swooshing of my tires as I threw my weight into each push sounding like a flat. He must have heard me putting the effort in, but I saw no hints that he had any intention of letting me bridge the steady distance between us. He was managing to maintain it without any visible increase in his efforts, which only added frustration to mine. I very quickly began to feel myself out of my depth as he unhurriedly drew away. I sat back down in the saddle, and snarled.

Up ahead, he never missed a beat as he began to edge away, his lean body so steady as he rode. I admired his fluid style as he wore me down, but mostly I admired his physique. He was not big, with a deep tan that shone with health and oil, his skin tight shorts and top showing every muscles as he powered away. I momentarily imagined myself catching him, leaning over to give him a track rider's sling, but not gripping the saddle to catapult him into the fray, oh no. To feel that smooth lycra moving beneath my open palm was a much better idea. Such a tight and perfect arse, and I had absolutely no chance of getting to know it better! My thighs burning, I eased off and dropped back down to a more comfortable speed, trying to ignore a new sensation. Attempting to ride with a hard and frustrated cock is not comfortable at any speed.

An unpleasant aura of unrequited lust settled like a cloud around me as I watched the focus of my daydreaming crest a rise way ahead, and slowly sink from sight. Hell I was eager, all of me was eager. I thought of turning around and heading back to John, but it was still too soon. If I went back now I would have given him the victory, and the very thought stuck in my throat.

I gradually dragged back to the reality of the morning, the heat now making the road's tar soft. One by one I pounded around the inside line of the hairpins, slowly but surely looking down over the wooded valley below. The scents were now of hot tar, and the occasional drift of a coconut-like scent from the rich yellow gorse lining the higher ground. And then he was there again! I looked up as I sat back from the struggle of another hairpin, to see the bobbing ultramarine as he sprinted away. Had he been waiting for me, watching over the barrier as I struggled around the hairpin? There was certainly nothing else on this short stretch to warrant a stop, and I was suddenly aware of the sharp tingle of exciting possibilities beginning in my stomach.

I launched myself at the straight and raised a gear, chain cracking into place as I threw my full weight into the attack. With my legs burning deep and my breath becoming ragged I bore down on the retreating figure, the scent of victory lending me greater strength. I was two bike lengths from him when he leapt out of the saddle and sprinted. I cursed, but still threw all I had into those last few feet between us. One bike length, but my pace was suffering now, my legs on fire and my chest fit to burst. The son of a bitch was stretching it out again, his head down and back to his previous style, hardly moving on the bike as he notched up another gear. I was furious, getting my head down and throwing all I had left into one last attempt. The distance gradually diminished, the sounds of the woodland we rode through unheard as I stared fixedly at his glorious arse. I could almost feel the warm silkiness under my hands as I tore down his lead.

For the first time he looked back, and, his shoulder length hair blowing over his mysterious dark eyes, he smiled – a welcome, almost an invitation. I read all manner of things into that easy greeting, and something uncomfortable began to drag at my attention again.

He straightened up in the saddle, and put his hands on his narrow waist to wait, reaching out to pat my shoulder as I came alongside.

"You are your own worst enemy on the mountain...?"

I felt an edge of irritation that his first words had been so damning. "No, I was pacing myself to make it to the pass."

He smiled over at me and put one hand on his flat stomach. I remained doubled over with my grip low on the handlebars, acutely aware of possible embarrassment. "Besides, you sound as if you live here, and that gives you an unfair advantage."

He looked across at me and raised an eyebrow, a smile dancing at the corner of his full lips. "John said you were very quick to defend yourself."

That hit me like a boulder. "Where the hell do you know John from?" I felt myself coloring up as I imagined John's touching him, stroking those tanned legs with their sheen of oil, kissing those luscious lips. "Shit, can't I get away from his flirting anywhere I go?" I forgot myself and sat bolt upright in the saddle, zipping up my jersey. "I'm going back down, no offence meant by that, I just want to be left to myself." I slowed to turn around, and glanced across. He was looking directly at the jutting eagerness within lycra. Then he looked up, and our eyes met.

"If you want to go down, feel free. But I was only asking him about you. It is, after all, you who rides, he does no more than play games with his admirers."

That stung, despite my recognizing its truth. I was about to turn, but something in his look cooled my burst of anger. I breathed out the breath I'd forgotten to take, and reached over to rest a hand on his shoulder. "OK, let's start again from the beginning. What am I doing wrong when it comes to the mountains?"

The next bend was close as he led me out, my eyes torn between the road ahead and his bronzed thighs. He half-turned in the saddle and pointed ahead. "OK, I watched you, and on every corner you cut close to the inside line. Why?"

What did he mean? It was obviously the shortest way round. I said so.

"Well, maybe, but it is the steepest too. And on the hills the important thing is to establish a rhythm, and struggling round a steep curve scrubs away at that. Just try this bend the way you would normally take it and see how it goes."

Determined to impress I threw myself at the task and all my weight into keeping up a rhythm. It was a tough one, and I ended up having to drop a gear just to keep any speed. He came alongside, and braked. "Come on, James, go back down and try it again. This time go around the outside." Loathe to give up conquered ground, I swung about and descended, mentally preparing for the assault to come. This time however I kept to his line, and, surprise, it was easier going.

He was stood at the crash barrier watching me as I came round the last of the curve, and in the high sunshine his upper thighs seemed in shadow. I swallowed hard, he was straining the elasticity of his shorts with that beauty! I pulled up beside him and climbed off, the sight of his urgent erection spurring me on. I threw caution to the wind and placed my open hand over the tight heat of him. "Thanks for the advice, but let's forget the hill?!" I squeezed. His hand closed over mine, pressing me hard against his engorged cock. His voice was husky and matched the feverish glow in his eyes.

"Back down James, there is woodland I know well. We can be alone there." His hands slipped down around my butt as he pressed close into me, our bodies sleek with sweat and oil. "Follow me." His lips were soft and warm against mine, his tongue hot and wet across my teeth.

The descent and the pathways to the woodlands were no more than a blur, so eager and flushed with lust had I grown. Forget John, here was a god for the taking! This divine creature had actually sought me out for his pleasures. I watched the way the rough ground bumped his saddle upward, his buttocks quivering and shaking as if being fucked. I practically dribbled. As we burst into the clearing the air became electric, bikes thrown aside into the soft grass and the pair of us fierce in each other's arms.

We tore and struggled with tight fabrics, his hands impatiently yanking at my shorts when they caught over rampant cock. It burst eagerly into the warm air, jutting upward and twitching with primal desires.

Wet heat engulfed me, all of me, and as I looked down I saw that his face was buried in my curls. Fingers sought out my balls, the hot spot behind them, and the even hotter spot behind that. I jerked onto my toes as a wet finger slipped up inside me, at the same time his panting breath squashed against my groin. I found myself gripping his head as I began to lose control, pounding his succulence against me. I had never reached such heights so fast, dreaded coming for that would mean an end to this ecstasy. Nearer and nearer I panted as the finger in me wriggled and pushed harder.

I couldn't hold back any longer, and burst into him with a force that had a recoil, as one finger hit my prostate and another the spot behind my balls. I thought I would never stop, creamy ooze trickling from around his loudly sucking mouth. Again and again he pumped his face against my belly, wetter and wetter the noises that added to the intensity of my orgasm. It was almost a pain, so deep and urgent the feelings of explosive release. I felt my knees begin to shake as the last of my offering was sucked down his slippery throat, his grunting and moaning as he lapped at my glistening cock, which was gradually diminishing.

I slipped wet and temporarily sated from his last kisses, and sagged to the floor to join him. Only for a moment did I look at his splashed face, my creamy ooze slowly running down over his chin, before I swept my arms around him and kissed those creamy, salted lips.

He allowed my tongue to immerse its length in his cum-filled mouth, our teeth crashing together in my frenzy to taste myself from inside him. I was desperate, and reached down to run my wet fingers through his lush curls, down further to the hot rigid cock beneath, my hand closing around its silky warmth.

He groaned as I pressed at his chest, forcing him back to the sun-bathed grass, his stiff cock pointing to the sky and waving its ample head in excitement. I bent low and sucked him as deep into me as I could manage, my mouth filling with a live heat, my nostrils filling with the scents of man-sex, sweat and sun oil. I drew deep breaths of ecstatic pleasures and began to move around on him. My hands swept over his tense belly, feeling his heavy breathing there and on his chest. His nipples were rigid and begging for the marks of teeth and suction, wanting the same treatment his cock was wallowing in. My forehead slapped loudly against the line of hair that swooped down from his navel to those curls, my nose rubbing into his crotch.

His nails were digging into my shoulders as I felt him growing more tense beneath my weight. "Don't swallow, James. I want to share with you. Bring my cum to my lips and let me lick it from your face." I bobbed my head as I added my hands to the game. His balls heavy and warm, his ring tight and hot. I raised my head from his length and squeezed him, fingers slippery on his wet skin. He groan and dug his nails deep into my flesh, the muscles I nestled against rigid in anticipation. I gathered up all of my patience, and stopped.

"You..." He seemed to take several seconds to register my having stopped. "You fucker!" He tried to press my head down, but I twisted aside, keeping a tight grip around the base of his throbbing cock. I was struggling myself now, eager to taste him, swallow him, possess his every fiber for our brief sliver of time. I could hold out no longer and went down again. Down to the wet and pumping length of his sex, down to the very base with my hungry lips. I knew that he would be mere seconds, and I knew what I wanted now.

I drew back from my rhythmic sucking and pumped his slippery length by hand, keeping my face as close as possible. I desperately wanted those first jets of cum to hit me in the face. To feel the wet heat dribbling down over my cheeks and lips, to rub him into my skin with the pumping length of him. His arse arched off the grass in his attempts to impale my hungry mouth again, even as the first splashes of his cum hit the side of my nose. I pumped once more, another jet of creamy heat splashing against my lips, then I had him in my mouth again, sucking his cum from deep within his arching loins, filling myself with him, his heat, his solidity, his generous helping of cum. I slathered, I gobbled, I filled my cheeks with him. I ground my wet face into his wiry curls.

He groaned, he writhed, he pumped into me. The pain of his nails raking my shoulders began to subside, and the urgency of our want began to melt. I slipped from his softening cock and into his arms. Our slippery mouths met to share their riches. We were soft in each other's embrace, our kisses, our licking, our nipping. Our faces grew wet and slippery as we anointed each other with the rich mixture of our cum.

With the sun's dappled light warming our bodies, we lay together, stroking, caressing, sharing. I began to feel a firmness growing against my thigh, prompting my own cock to gain new enthusiasm. Almost imperceptibly the touching grew more firm, the embraces more ardent. My mind began to notch up a gear, from loving to lusting once again.

Led by my throbbing erection, I arched into indecision. I wanted to feel him inside me, sending ribbons of hot cum into my eager arse, but I wanted to possess him too. I wanted all of him, every pore of his skin. I ached to melt through him, become one in passion with him. To be as one, inside each other, enmeshed, to explode like some awesome firework. He arched up from the grass and firmly rolled me onto my chest, an open hand slapping my arse so hard I jumped. The stinging felt good, and I wanted it all. I heard myself moan, words I never intended, things I had never heard myself utter before.

"Take it! I want so much of you it burns." I raised my arse a way from the cool grass, the tickling as the blades stroked my skin only inflaming my cock the more. His weight crashed down onto me, pounding me into the ground. His arms encircled my waist and his grip became almost painful. His breath was fierce against my cheek, teeth catching my earlobe. "I've never felt so powerful before, never wanted so much so soon." I felt the warm and solid tip of him find my eager hole, tried to push back over him, tried to magnetize his full size deep into me. "Fuck it!"

His teeth bit down hard and I whimpered. "Now, fuck me!"

And he did. I cried out as he rushed deep into me at the first onslaught, the slap as his belly hit my arse sounding wet. I bit my lip as I pounded back as best I could, feeling his glorious cock push deep up inside me. I wanted to feel him so intensely I reached back to try and grip his buttocks, force him deeper. All I managed was to feel the rigid muscles there as he powered away into my wet hole. He tensed against my back and nails bit deep into my belly as at last he erupted into me, his loud gasp as the heat of his cum seemed to fill my belly a joy to my ear. I clamped onto him, wanting to wring him dry. His intake of breath was long and shuddering, as with small jerks into the furthest point he filled me with his ardent offering. It felt good. I felt sore, but full. I felt complete.

I held him inside me until I could grip him no longer, his wet and softening length sliding into the warm air. He left me empty, he left me incomplete. We slid into an embrace under that summer tree, dozed awhile and tried to gaze into each other's souls when we woke, dark eyes darting from one to the other blue. And then we made love. It was that I am sure, for never again have I felt that complete. It was slow and tender. It was warm and slippery. It took care and time, and we sank into the splashed grass in each other's arms when we had spent all we had to spend.

I have a piece of him even now; I have never washed out the stains of our passion. I take them out occasionally and stroke the bright fabric, feel the sheen beneath my fingers and think back. I wonder how frequently he touches mine for that same purpose. Or if he ever does. I have been deluded so many times it is hard to believe in words of love. I left the lodge on my own, and never saw the room service lad again. In fact, as I tried to catch him on that fast, twisting decent from the pass, my last sight of him was what I would have wanted it to be.

STRANGERS ON THE DUNES
Daniel Miller

A few years back, I lived near a certain stretch of grey sea and ivory sand where horny men were known to congregate. I had my share of carnal encounters in the hazy shadows behind the dunes, but I remember one afternoon in particular.

I'd been at the beach for hours, watching the dark waves swell and bob under a deceptively tranquil sun. The hazardous look of the water intrigued me, even though I was disappointed in the current crop of guys who had gathered to enjoy the weather. Tourists, mostly, they were lying around on blankets or hiding underneath silly striped umbrellas. Horny but apprehensive, they eyed each other over the tops of trendy summer magazines and salivated over every pair of tight male buns that sauntered past.

A few surfer dudes, college-aged, like me, were playing Frisbee by the water, their bathing thongs looking more like g-strings than swim gear. A few times, the handsomest one in the group turned and looked in my direction. His attentions seemed playful rather than determined not quite what I was in the mood for. Instead of responding, I leaned back on my towel, my fingers straying down over the front of my own scanty Speedo. My imagination was already making up for the lack of real-life prospects, and I could feel my cock harden, the warm head thickening against my hot ballsac.

I half-closed my eyes, raising my hand to my nipples and pinching them roughly between my fingernails. The blade-like edges sent a satisfying tingle through my chest and down to my crotch. It wasn't much compared to the effect I could get at home with my private collection of wooden clothespins and black metal binder clips, but I didn't think my fellow beach-goers were quite ready for that sort of display. In spite of the area's reputation as a notorious cruising spot, it had been a long time since I'd even seen a guy sunning himself naked. Quickly, I began to get bored with the whole scene.

My sensitive nipples eventually grew numb under my continual prodding and squeezing. Resentfully I sat up, intending to scan the baking sands one last time for some dangerous-looking character who struck my fancy. If nothing did, I figured, I'd head for home and get creative with the contents of a certain locked trunk I kept under my bed.

It was then that I spotted the three men sitting a few feet away from me.

They must have just shown up, I figured; otherwise, I sure as hell would have noticed them before. They were lounging on a frayed white grey blanket and staring directly at me like a school of hungry tiger sharks. They were a study in contrasts: one was blond, one kept his head shaved almost totally bald, and the third wore his dark hair long enough to touch his shoulders. All three appeared to be in their early to mid-twenties, and had the kind of incredible bodies I wanted: steely abs and butts, chiseled quads, healthy tans, and an appealingly malevolent attitude. The bald guy had an unusually pointed scar running along the length of his cheek like a single, perverse sideburn.

When I met his flinty eyes, he flashed me a narrow, predatory grin that bent his scar to a jaunty angle. Then he opened his legs and brushed aside the leg of his bathing suit. My pulse quickened when I caught a glimpse of his bulging red cockhead, speared through with a tiny silver barbell. He flicked the rubbery dome with his fingers, then tucked it away again.

His friends were smiling, too, as they got up and rolled the blanket into a sand-flecked ball. Walking single file, they sauntered a few hundred yards down the beach, heading away from the midday crowd. Finally they passed through a weather-beaten lattice-work fence, apparently erected to block off a long, privately owned stretch of grass-speckled dunes.

I waited a while, not wanting to look too eager. I never look twice at desperate men myself, and I wouldn't expect anyone worth my time to, either. Just as they were about to disappear from sight, I gathered up my stuff and started walking after them.

The sand was scorching hot under my feet, but I didn't want to stop long enough to put my sandals back on. I followed them to an isolated spot, shielded by a row of huge, slumping dunes, where a sign proclaimed that I was trespassing on private property. At that point, the three of them stopped walking and turned to look at me again. My heart began to beat rapidly, their chilly leers arousing me and making me nervous at the same time.

At that point, I noticed that the tall dark guy was carrying a black leather knapsack, which I figured contained some toys. My erection grew in proportion to my curiosity. I felt all the blood in my veins rush into my cock. The thrill made me dizzy with a greedy horniness.

The light blond guy turned to the dark guy with an upturned lip. "Looks like the little fucker followed us over here, Stew."

The dark guy snickered, not too pleasantly. "Sure does look that way. You see that sign, asshole? Private property. Colt, here, likes to hunt down trespassers. Shoots them on sight, don't you, Colt?" He flashed Colt a knowing smile and ran his fingers up his friend's muscle-kneaded neck. The two of them were lovers, I assumed where, then, did the guy with the shaved head fit into this nasty little triad? My eyes sought his, but he was staring somewhat lower right at my crotch, in fact.

In response, Colt's long, tanned fingers groped his own crotch, fondling the growing outline of his eight-inch prick. "Maybe we could let him stay and watch for a while," he decided. "But how do we know he's for real?" At that point, Colt swung his head around and addressed me directly. I could see how he'd gotten his nickname, because he moved with the short, jerky movements of an impatient pony. "See, we don't do just anyone around here, though we're never short of volunteers. We got bored with the typical fuck 'n' suck a long time ago."

I didn't know what to say. I didn't even know if they really wanted me to respond. Things seemed too far gone for me to bow out now, but I wasn't at all sure that I wanted to. My fingers tightened around the towel I still held bunched up in my fist. The bald guy smirked and finally spoke. "Maybe he got bored with it, too."

"Well, one thing's for sure: this is the perfect spot to find out," Stew said. He took the beach blanket I'd seen before out of the backpack and spread it on the weed-stubbled sand in front of us. For a moment no one advanced towards me, their hot stares burning into my skin like the sun on the ocean. Then Colt took a step closer. His eyes glinted like a bull shark closing in on a wounded seal pup.

"Yeah, you like it rough, all right." His eyes flicked to baldie. "Jeff, you get his suit down. How's this for a start, tough guy?" Colt took a firm hold of my right lat with his left hand, while with his right hand he tweaked my already erect nipples. The blades of his nails bit into my sensitive flesh. Their pink hue turned crimson, and an oddly sensual pain rippled through my torso.

Colt glanced back at his friend, who was busy pulling my bathing suit down over my thighs. When he was finished, he kicked off his own, the silvery ampellang glinting in the brutal sunlight. My violently erect woody jerked up from its matted patch of brown hair to salute their leering gazes. "Hmm. Not bad, for a fucking little wuss like you," Colt commented. I wasn't sure if he meant my nipples or my hard-on. He squeezed my tits again, twisting slightly. I sucked in my breath with a hiss of pain.

Without letting go, he moved in a step closer, until the head of my dick just touched the swollen pouch at the front of his swim trunks. I felt the heat of his breath on my lips, and could almost feel the steady pulse of his balls through the Spandex barrier between us. At that point, a strange mixture of excitement and panic settled over me and gripped my guts with a clammy fist. My vision dimmed with the sudden image of myself being caught in the gnashing, razor-lined jaws of a shark on the prowl. I imagined my body twisting helplessly as the beast's sinewy body thrashed, dragging me to the tomb-like shadows beyond the surf. Now, rebelling against that hopeless sensation in my limbs, I felt an overpowering urge to challenge Colt, to break the hold he had over my body and over my lust.

My fingers went straight for his buns. I dug my short sharp nails into his taut muscles, sinking ugly scratches into his flesh. Colt let out a wail as I mashed his groin into mine. The stiff end of my cock jabbed up into the high-cut leg hole of his swim trunks. There our blood-engorged shafts jousted like malicious harpoons.

"You cheeky son of a bitch." With an angry look, Colt gave me a rough push. Naked, I staggered back a few steps and bumped into Stew, who stood behind me with the backpack at his feet. My ankle brushed against it at an awkward angle, and I would have gone down on the ground if his long arms hadn't slid out and clenched around my waist. He pulled me up tight against him, still chortling under his breath, the coarse hairs on his forearms scratching my tenderized nipples.

Jeff and Colt had closed in again, Colt's face scarlet with rage. Stew opened his mouth and bit the lobe of my ear painfully as he shoved me back onto my feet.

"Don't get impatient, now," he smirked, hooking his foot around the back of my knee and toppling me forward. I went down into doggy position with a grunt, my earlobe stinging with the marks from his teeth and my rigid cock trembling between my splayed thighs. "There's enough of me to go around, and then some."

They crowded around me, and I heard the backpack being slowly unzipped. I felt Stew's fingers prying open my butt-cheeks, and then something blunt and full was prodding at my exposed sphincter. I sucked in a breath as he rubbed the broad tip of what was obviously a huge dildo up and down on my clutching pucker.

"They always say two are better than one," Colt remarked, settling his hand over the back of my neck. His fingers suddenly clamped down hard, pushing my face into the tightening bulge in his swimsuit. "Lick me," he snarled, digging his fingers into my scalp. "Lick my cock out of this fuckin' swimsuit."

With that, he gave some kind of signal to Stew, who thrust the dildo forward and plowed it deep into my ass. I could tell right away that there was a lot of it, but I didn't realize just how much until it drilled well past the point of comfort. It began to invade my guts, grinding roughly against the tender walls of my ass-canal, stretching my ass-rim until I could almost hear the flesh there creaking. Still the thick rubber plug kept moving forward, cleaving my ass-cheeks wide and forcing my insides wide open. Tears spurted from my eyes as I felt it tunneling deeper, harder, twisting down into my bowels. And still the solid column of its bulging shaft kept burrowing.

One of Colt's hands was under my chin now, tipping my head up to his crotch. The fingers of the other were grabbing my hair. Spreading his legs apart and tilting his hips, he wedged my nose against the hard, cylindrical outline of his shaft, crushing the rubbery mound of his balls against my lips. The warmth of his body, and the pressure on my bowels, made my face and neck flush with a dark, smoldering heat. Stew was still screwing the dildo into my ass. My hips would buck and shudder involuntarily with every rough push. My horny groin moved back and forth, humping the air.

Colt shoved his crotch hard against my face, jarring my tongue against my teeth.

"I said to lick it," he growled, a powerful whiff of sweat and musk escaping from his tight swimsuit. I inhaled his sharp aroma desperately, then opened my jaws and flattened my parched tongue against the moist fabric.

Moaning, he leaned back and humped the flat of his cock against my open mouth. Though I could feel the pulse of his ripe, round head against the flesh of my cheek, it lay just beyond the reach of my tongue, pointing toward the elastic waistband of his Speedo. Though I maneuvered my head in every direction I could think of, fighting to concentrate despite the cramps in my abdomen, it remained just out of reach. In spite of my frustration, I don't think my cock had ever felt so hard and so long.

It occurred to me that I had lost track of Jeff, and I began rolling my eyes to the side in search of his lanky form. I finally caught a quick glimpse of him standing beside me, half-smiling as he enjoyed his voyeuristic thrill. When he saw me looking, he hastily stepped to one side.

Stew was pumping the dildo in and out of me now, alternately suctioning up the pain and then filling my body with it again full force. I could hear him grunting with the effort, and felt rivers of acrid sweat dripping down the crack of my bruised ass to baptize my loose-swinging balls. My long-held breath escaped in a hiss when I paused in my attentions to Colt's still-growing cock, and he rewarded me by roughly smacking the side of my head.

Suddenly disoriented, I reeled from the blow, dimly aware of the dildo crashing back down inside me even deeper than before. I also became gradually aware of a new sensation on my left tit, almost like fingernails, but sharper and tighter. In fact, it was more like a tiny set of jaws, clamping down hungrily on my throbbing, swollen bud. Blistering pain spread rapidly outward, bathing my pecs in a fierce inner heat. I gasped and twisted, trying to shake loose whatever was imbedded in my flesh, but every shake of my torso only tightened its grip. I realized that the paltry tweaks and tugs I'd given my tits, even during my wildest masturbation sessions, had been nothing compared to this.

Again I lifted my head from Colt's groin, bracing myself for a blow that never came. "What, what is it?" I rasped.

I heard Jeff's bitter laughter as the agony intensified in my chest. His hand came up between my nose and Colt's swimsuit, turning over a glinting silver object in front of my eyes. Through a searing red haze, I struggled to focus on the second nipple clamp. In the harsh white glare of the sun, the tiny metal jaws almost resembled a shark's angry, ragged teeth.

"Can't wait to feel the other one, I'll bet," Jeff whispered. "Trust me the first one will feel a hell of a lot better once it's on." He reached under me, and then Colt and Stew were laughing, too. I held my breath while the metal cut as viciously into my flesh as the first one had. Jeff gave each a strong tug, then ran his hand along my stomach to grasp my balls. He squeezed me three times, hard, then turned to yanking my cock instead. The combination of the pleasure and pain whipped my senses into a kaleidoscope of flame.

I drove my head into Colt's crotch, hard, loosening his hard-on from his swimsuit in one swift lunge. I slurped it out over the top elastic and sucked it down in one fierce pull. His plump cockhead reeled into my mouth, the fiery bulb sinking down past my tonsils. Meanwhile, Stew kept grinding himself into me from behind, forcing my butt-cheeks farther apart. The three of them swarmed over me like a school of predators over vulnerable prey.

Never had I been fucked so hard or so long. Both ends of my body were being invaded by thick, horny cock, my throat muscles convulsing around Colt's relentless boner, Stew screwing me with the thick rubber dong until tears of pain and excitement spurted down my cheeks. No sooner had my sphincter stretched out to accommodate its thick circumference than Stew licked two fingers and shoved them into me alongside the latex plug. Moaning and rocking on my knees, I tried to will my guts to open as he plunged down into my bowels, reaming me out until my entire lower body was cramped and convulsing.

Meanwhile, Jeff had gotten down on his back underneath me, sucking my cock hard while he yanked furiously on my clamped nipples. The stubble on his shaved head raked my abs and scoured the insides of my thighs as he bobbed up and down on my shank. His long tongue curved around it, sucking and pressing on it, while I opened my jaws wide to receive the steaming load that had finally spurted from Colt's depths. As thick surges of pain and fear that alternately razed and refreshed my whole body, I felt my own nuts untwist with an equally powerful blast. I shot into Jeff's furiously sucking mouth, splashing his tonsils until he stopped me, by biting down on the base of my cock, hard.

I was about to cry out, but the forceful feeling of Stew yanking the dildo, and his three fingers, out of my ass stopped me cold. At my other end, Colt pulled away, too. He yanked his dripping tool from my jaws, then wiped his cockhead on the side of my face. A sticky glob of leftover cum stuck there, drying slowly in the humid air.

My ass and throat burning with emptiness, my wilting shaft imprinted with Jeff's molars, I knelt and groveled in the hot sand. Only the fierce clench of the nipple clamps, still searing the roots of my nipples, reminded me of the sublime agony I'd felt moments before.

Giving his cock a final shake against my down turned lower lip, Colt stepped back. At the same time, Jeff slid out from under me, and Stew gradually wandered around to join them. The three hovered over me, exchanging smirks and tilting their hips so that their damp, flushed rods dangled only inches from my chin. Only Stew was still in his swimsuit, the tight amber pouch straining with the weight of his boner behind it. He held up the fat black dildo he'd been plowing my ass with, pushing it under my nose and turning it around slowly around. I began to salivate when I both saw and smelled my aroused ass-juices on it.

"You think he's ready?" Colt asked, stroking himself again, quickly. His cock began to swell up to full size again in only minutes. Seeing it made my bowels clench with desire.

"I'd say he's nice and stretched out," Stew announced. His fingers strayed to the front of his swim trunks, pinching at a mound that seemed to be growing much bigger under his casual touch. "And he was sucking on this thing like he was trying to get the whole thing inside that puny asshole. So, yeah, I think he can take all of me. And if he can't...." He closed his fingers around his Spandex-covered cock then, and a slow, icy leer spread across his narrow lips. "...Well, if he can't, the three of us will just have to help him along."

Before I had time to react, they were on me. Colt gripped me by the scruff of my neck and dragged me, on my knees, over to an anvil-shaped rock. Its jagged surface bit angrily at my naked stomach and bruised cock as he heaved me onto it. At the same time, Jeff reached into the black knapsack and pulled out a pair of handcuffs. They jingled as he swiftly clipped my wrists behind my back.

Securely trussed, I lay on the rock. Unable to use my arms for balance, I had to keep my entire body still and tense. My legs were splayed open, my toes stretched wide to dig into the bone-colored sand.

Stew moved up to loom in front of me. His hands were still at his crotch, performing some action just out of my visual range. The muscles in my neck ached, and my face felt flushed as I craned my head to gaze up at him.

He had been untying the drawstring inside the front of his trunks, I realized, loosening the waistband so he could push the suit down over his taut, meaty thighs. At that moment, it became clear why they had all been so interested in the elasticity of my butt hole. Stew's hard-on had now flared to its full, magnificent, ball-boggling length. Even I, who'd tricked with some of the best-hung men who'd ever strutted their stuff on these competitive sands, had never seen anything remotely as large. At least eleven and a half inches long, it was mapped over with a web of bluish veins that rose from a maroon bed of cockflesh in sharp, pulsating relief.

He punched his hips forward, balancing the ponderous weight of his tool in the palm of his hand. For one wild moment, I panicked as I realized he was preparing to shove the whole thing down my throat, or up my ass. It seemed that I would hardly be able to take all of him in either orifice, however willing I might have been to attempt it. That swollen, rigid club would surely split me in two, or choke me to unconsciousness.

His two friends were standing off to the side now, waiting and watching to see what might happen next. I could hear their shallow, nervous breathing. I felt a cold tendril of sweat trickle down between the trembling globes of my ass.

Time seemed to stand still for a while, marked only by the hiss of the sweat between my legs and the rasping heaves of my lungs. Then, as if he were moving in slow motion, Stew moved forward and crushed the pulpy tip of his cockhead against my lips. It felt as big and hot and as impossible to swallow down as a hard-boiled egg. All the same, I opened my mouth and allowed him to flatten my tongue with its mass.

"Get me wet first," he growled. "It'll go easier for you that way."

Densely thick and as unyielding as marble, his enormous truncheon flailed its was down my gullet. I barely had time to moan before its immense breadth clogged my windpipe, choking off my breath. Colt's cock had blazed the trail, but Stew's wrenched it nakedly open. While he thrust himself into me, he twisted his fingers into my scalp and snapped my head as far back as he could without doing me permanent injury. Hot stabs of pain spiraled from my hair's roots to the inflamed base of my spine. A single, drawn-out gag bubbled up from my lungs as Stew's cock pushed the breath from my body and clogged my esophagus.

He held himself motionless, churning his hips back and forth and burrowing into me. Down, down, he plunged toward my lungs, which felt like they were swiftly collapsing. Twin streams of oxygen-starved saliva spurted from the sides of my mouth just as corresponding tears erupted down my cheeks. Still he pushed forward, and before long it seemed like an ominous black veil, dazzlingly specked with silvery stars, began to drop down over my eyes.

Then, suddenly, he was pulling himself out. My overpowered membranes seemed to turn inside out at his retreat, simultaneously pulling at him and begging for more.

"You did better than I expected with that part," he said gruffly. His hand was absently burnishing the underside of his shaft as he stepped back from my mouth. His fingers traced slow, angry patterns in the glaze of spit and sweat. "But now let's do the real test." And he began to walk away from me, finally settling himself between my open legs. I felt his sweaty thigh brush against the curve of my left buttock..

I tensed on the rock, bracing myself for the pain I knew would consume me any moment. Stew reared back, laughing, and it did.

It would be difficult to describe the complex interplay of agony and transcendent pleasure that consumed me at that moment. And it would be even harder to explain what, exactly, it was like as he stuffed his unrelenting pole up my backside. It was probably closest to having a smoldering log from a campfire, or a fat champagne bottle, bottom-end first, that had been heated over an open grill for half an hour, crammed up my chute with one severe, merciless shove. In and out, in and out he plugged me, until my entire body was limp and his smoldering cum, mixed with the blood from my tattered ass-rim, streamed down the backs of my legs. My own cock was bloated and stiff against the rock and my stomach. The sea-roughened surface bit into it like shark's teeth.

"Good, Stew?" I heard Jeff asking, his voice awed and obsequious, as I lay moaning. In response, Stew laughed again. His voice was a bit breathless. He must have come harder than he usually did. The quantity of spunk swilling around in my ass-crack was proof.

"Not bad at all, though I seem to be a little dirty. Hold his head while I clean myself off."

"Sure, Stew, you got it."

With that, Jeff scrambled into place by my head. I didn't bother to open my eyes as he yanked my head back with one hand. His other forced my jaw as wide open as it would go without popping. Then that gigantic prick was in my throat again, humping back and forth against the bump of my tonsils as he polished away my pungent ass-juices.

Still laughing, they started to walk away from me then, all three of them. I was left naked and ravaged, my cock so desperate to get off that I could have rubbed it wide open against that craggy slab of sea rock.

In the distance, I heard Stew's voice rise above the surf's whispered pulse. "Don't forget your hand-cuffs, asshole," he said, and Jeff came loping up the sand to unshackle me. I sat up, my cock red, swollen, and bruised-looking, while Jeff's eyes raked my body with a peculiar mix of scorn and pity.

"Please, man," I whispered, pointing down at my raw crotch. The fact that he got down and sucked me off was, I suppose, less an admission of his desire for me as an attempt to draw off the sticky vestiges of Stew's cooling fluids. When he was finished, and I was still lying slumped against the rock, he hauled his own cock back out and pissed on my chest.

When he was gone, I groped around for my discarded possessions. My bathing suit was gone, but luckily I still had my towel. I wrapped it around me, and with my ravished ass hanging out the back, I walked back to the beach. Eventually, I waded back into the surf to rinse off the blood, cum, and piss, but the sting of the salt in my wounds was more than even I could bear.

I sat naked a while, ignoring the stares and a few lame come-ons from men I wasn't interested in. And I did the same thing the next day, and the next, but I never saw Stew and his buddies again. I haven't been back to that particular niche of rough coast again. Still, every now and then, even when I'm walking in the city, I hear that nasty, mocking laugh of his again. When I turn to look, he isn't there, but the dull throb that's never really left my cock and scarred asshole reminds me that, one day, all three of them will be.

THE PICK-UP
John Patrick

"John Barrington caught up with Noel Coward in the Gents toilets at the Cafe Royal. Coward gave him a big wink and said, 'Hello, dear boy, how's trade?' John responded, 'It's been rough, but it's picking up.' Coward laughed and replied, 'Naturally old boy! Picking up's the thing!'

Another wink, and he walked out." – Rupert Smith in "Physique"

Joey is getting ready to leave Shorty's bar, take a rest. It has been a long day. He's taken three out-calls today and just stopped in to pay his pot supplier. Then, when he turns around, he sees Roy, about forty, trim, dark hair, across the bar, watching him. Joey gets up, walks over.

"Hi," he says.

"Hi," Roy says, lifting one eyebrow.

Over the space of fifteen minutes of keen observation, Roy has become infatuated with the young hustler, with his high, delicate cheekbones and his aristocratic nose combined with a strong jaw line and cleft chin. Roy is also attracted to the shiny blond hair that tumbles down nearly to his shoulders. Best of all, Joey's tight jeans leave little to the imagination.

Two beers are ordered, and Roy tells Joey he always comes to Fort Lauderdale in March, when it's sunny and 77 degrees. This is the last night of his week in the sun, Roy tells the boy, and he has spent the whole time looking for someone like Joey. "Now here you are," Roy says. Joey smiles; he says he is also from Ohio. Joey says he left the Buckeye State in October and he's been here ever since. He has a job, he says, at the Marriott, but, he admits, he's behind on his rent. Roy would like to help him out. Joey nods, lets Roy buy him another beer.

Joey's ascent up the stairs to the door of Roy's room at the Royal Palms bed 'n' breakfast is blessed, his ass inciting Roy to open the door urgently. Roy leads the youth through the door, and, street-smart as he is, Joey is checking for intruders lurking in the shadows.

Roy clicks on the lamp on the desk and Joey collapses, sinking back into the welcoming mattress, legs loosely apart, exhausted.

While Roy starts undressing, Joey closes his eyes and reclines seductively on the double bed, waiting. Roy goes to the bathroom, pees. When he returns, Joey has taken off all his clothes, except for his red nylon briefs, and has rolled over on his belly.

Roy stands over the bed, clad only in his trousers. He smiles down at the lascivious display, and his bittersweet blackberry eyes savor the sight of the youth's ass. Throbs of intense lust power through him. Impishly, he pushes the nylon deep into the hidden valley and watches the cheeks clench instinctively.

Now he lays a flattened hand across Joey's bottom, relishing the silky smoothness of those taut mounds and, spanning his asscheeks with his splayed fingers, he clasps them together, squeezing while Joey turns and twists in heated passion.

The incredible sight and feel of the excited youth squirming hotly on the bed while he plays with his ass brings Roy to an immediate state of full arousal. He is barely able to restrain himself as he snatches at the waistband of the boy's briefs, eager now for the final unveiling and the act they both now know that will inevitably follow.

And so he draws the briefs down, Joey lifting his hips to help. Roy yanks the briefs away and for the longest time he lets himself contemplate the lovely sight of Joey's upturned bottom: two smooth hemispheres, perfectly rounded. Joey closes his eyes and waits expectantly.

Gazing at that trim, appealing bottom, Roy finds himself enchanted anew by the hustler. He can't help caressing him. Slowly, almost reverently, he cups the pleasing curvature of the buttocks. He strokes them, and murmurs, "Such a perfect little ass."

Roy brings a hand up along the back of Joey's leg, idly stroking his extended form, lightly moving his hand up and down, feeling the curve of the back of a thigh, the contoured rise of the splendid ass. Joey rolls over and reaches up to get at Roy's belt buckle, which Roy left hanging open when he peed. Joey manages to pull the belt completely free, then undoes the front of the pants and pulls down the zipper. Through the fabric, Joey grips Roy with surprising urgency considering how tired he was before, fondling him with a determined hand. He squeezes tentatively, as if testing his hardness. Roy opens his mouth but no words come out; Roy is putty in the hustler's hands. As Joey struggles to work the loosened pants down over Roy's hips, the increasingly impatient man reaches back to help, twisting out of his pants and pushing them farther down in a fevered rush of excitement. Once the pants have been removed and Roy is standing completely naked before Joey, the hustler is stunned to see the size of Roy's equipment.

"Ummmm...I want this," he says, his voice soft and husky, as he squeezes Roy's penis.

Roy looks down on the kneeling boy and nods, dropping his hands to Joey's naked shoulders so he can hold on as he surrenders to the waves of pleasure and the tender ministrations of this determined youth. He groans as the knowing fingers explore his incredibly large cock. Through half-closed eyes he watches as one hand lightly cradles his balls, while the other wraps around the thick shaft. He feels those hands pass lightly over his cock, examining every inch, playing in his pubic curls, easing along his inner thighs, clasping his hips and then sliding around so that he can hold him by his butt. Joey extends his tongue and draws it wetly all the way up the entire nine-inch length of the underside of Roy's erection, sending wild tingles pulsing through the older man. Roy tightens his butt as Joey leans forward and covers the throbbing crown with his lips, letting Roy push so that Joey has the full knob in his mouth and then taking it all deep down his throat.

"Oh, god!" Roy groans, squirming uncontrollably, helplessly tossing his head from side to side, arching his back and struggling to hold on.

The boy continues to demonstrate an incomparable talent for fellatio, hollowing his cheeks rhythmically. Roy tightens his grip on Joey's shoulders while the taut ring of lips slide up and down on Roy's shaft, up and down, up and down in a smooth, piston-like motion. After a few minutes of this, Roy is feebly trying to stop the boy before he comes. He steps back, causing his lust-swollen prick to pop from Joey's mouth. Roy's cock stands proud, glistening with Joey's saliva.

But Joey won't stop; he reaches out for the cock, demands more of it, and Roy is soon moaning again. Joey is not bothered by the moaning so much but because the moans are so regular, and they come so predictably. Normally, Joey likes it when they're quick about it. He is patient, waiting for them to get off. Sometimes he wants to count, to count down. "Okay, now," he says. Then there are the guys who never come at all. Those are the hardest. It takes so much time; if only he could charge by the minute. If they are nice, he'll work at getting them off. They say they just can't, but they've never had Joey.

"It doesn't matter," they say. Sometimes they act irritated, disappointed.

"We can always try," Joey tells them. He likes nothing more than a big, thick, hard, cut prick.

Roy sighs, trying to overcome the overwhelming urge to shoot. Joey realizes Roy is close and he pulls the prick from his mouth. Joey looks up at him. Roy clamps the boy's head rigidly in place and bucks his hips furiously, fucking his face in a frenzy that soon has him teetering on the brink of orgasm. At the last possible moment, he wrenches himself free, extracting his cock.

"Okay, that's enough. I'll give you what you want."

"Thank you," Joey moans.

Roy slides on a rubber and caresses the lube all over it.

Joey remains on his back, which surprises Roy. Roy is unsure if he might change his mind. Relinquishing sexual power must be hard for a boy like Joey; boys like him are such schemers. Yet here he is, on his back, legs wide.

Roy decides he will be the boy's benefactor and give Joey the fuck he craves – on his terms. He climbs on top of him like he has watched people do a thousand times before in porn videos. Joey, seeing how huge the cock looks now, shows fear for the first time. Roy can tell in the tension of his mouth, the way he bites his lip, holding back the demand as Roy guides it between Joey's splayed legs. Rubbing the head against Joey's sweet asslips, he slowly taunts Joey. Then, in one movement, Roy pushes his way in until he is buried deep inside Joey. Grasping Joey's hips, he begins to stroke in and out, building tempo until he is pounding, slamming into Joey, and Joey's body is rising and pushing into each stroke.

"Oh, good boy," Roy says. Roy shows no mercy; he immediately starts driving into him. He stares at Joey, watching him sink into another place, perhaps another man in Roy's place. Sweat from Roy's face drops on Joey's face as he lunges heavily into the boy. It is a voracious hole, Roy thinks, as Joey's legs wrap around him, clasping for deeper penetration. Gasps and grunts greet Roy's astonished ears. He leans on one arm, biceps pumped up with the strain, and grabs at Joey's luscious prick. Now with his body quivering in orgasm, with barely suppressed sobs, Joey is done. Roy is concentrating on keeping his cock inside Joey. He lowers himself onto Joey and holds him tightly. "Oh fuck it," Joey whispers in Roy's ear.

Roy's excitement builds. He gives him another stroke, his cock burning into Joey's ass, and then another and another, until he can't hold back anymore. Finally, he is moaning and crying out, delirious with orgasm. Joey is rocking his tight little ass into Roy and spreading his own fresh cum all over Roy's face and into his mouth.

As Roy lets his post-orgasmic body slide down Joey's sweat-drenched torso, Joey looks at Roy with a bit of real embarrassment, perhaps for enjoying it so much.

Roy disappears into the bathroom again. When he emerges, freshly scrubbed, Joey is on his belly, undulating his hips.

"You want me to fuck it again?" Roy asks, bewildered.

"Oh, please. Be good to me, and I'll be good to you," he says, almost pleading. He begins grinding his hips, his buttocks pushing into the air, his fingerings preparing the way for Roy.

Pressing on, Roy reaches around and touches Joey's cock to find, reassuringly, that it is rock-hard once more, slick with pre-cum. Roy plucks at Joey's still-sopping asshole, prying the buttocks back. Joey waits tensely. Roy's wet tongue begins to lap at the splayed lips, sending Joey into a spasm of delight. He tightens his buttocks and wags his hips as though to shake off the flood of lewd sensations, but Roy offers him no respite. Roy's tongue is flicking deep within the boy, and Joey is bucking his hips furiously. Next, Roy's finger slickly penetrates Joey, to be immediately joined by a second, then a third. Roy begins fingerfucking the hustler, who is flinging his head from side to side moaning, begging for Roy to stick his cock in him once more.

After a few minutes, Joey is being driven crazy with passion. Roy pulls back and the mattress sways as he gets into position behind Joey, applying a new rubber to his hard prick

"Yes, yes," Joey says as Roy holds his hips in his hands and teases the opening with the head of his cock. Roy gazes down at the magnificent ass as his now fully-erect cock slides slowly into it. Roy is methodical, the cock moving in a smoothly mechanical stroke that keeps Joey begging for more. Roy raises Joey's excitement to fever pitch, holding him there teetering on the edge, then withdrawing the glistening shaft till only the tip remains buried in the boy's ass. In and out he goes, with a fucking that is slower, deeper, and more satisfying than Joey has ever known.

But by now Roy's own restraint is breaking down. He pulls back, withdrawing the glistening shaft, forcing himself to hold off a little longer. He eases back on his heels, only to have Joey fall back and in one powerful thrust, bury Roy's cock to the hilt. Roy falls back on the mattress, Joey over him, slamming his ass onto Roy's prick. Joey at first doesn't move, he just holds the big cock in him.

At first Joey's fucking is wildly erratic, but somehow he manages to slow down and it becomes more rhythmic, even smooth. Soon Roy is meeting each plunge with his own pelvic thrust. In this way they ride to new heights, and quickly Roy can feel the tension rising in Joey's sweating body. Soon Joey is jerking furiously, at last coming, with a violent tremor, crushing Roy's groin against his ass, burying Roy's penis to the hilt. Roy reaches around to feel the cum spurting from Joey's cock. He lets it ooze all over his fingers.

Joey lifts himself away and drops to the mattress, exhausted.

Roy knows he should get up and shower but Joey's smell is too good to wash away. As he drifts into a deep sleep, he thinks about the times when his friends have accused him of never living life for the moment, like it was gonna run out and leave him stranded, suspended between visions of possibilities. But, boy, if those friends could see him now!

In the morning, Roy dresses and packs quietly, not wanting to awaken the sleeping hustler. As he leaves the room to catch his flight, Roy plants a final parting kiss on the back of Joey's head.

Later, when Joey wakes up, he finds he is alone in the bed. He realizes immediately Roy has vacated the room. He also realizes he didn't get his fee upfront and there has been nothing left for him. Joey hadn't been kidding, his rent is due, and an overnighter would have cinched it for him. This is not the first time he's been fucked over, but this one doesn't hurt as much as the other ones. What hurts more than anything is Joey's asshole. He decides to partake of the amenities of the Royal Palms. He grabs a towel, wraps it around his waist and heads downstairs to the hot tub.

Jerry, a thirtysomething vacationer from California, is sprawled out languidly on a chaise, working on his already formidable tan. Joey lowers himself into the steaming, whirling waters, then looks over at Jerry, smiles. They are alone in the courtyard, so Jerry decides to play with Joey. He spreads his hairy thighs and is soon displaying a proud erection that rivets Joey's attention. Almost reverently, those long elegant hands explore the swollen shaft, caressing the prick. Joey sighs in silent admiration. With loving care Jerry works his cock, one hand easing down to cradle the wrinkled sack of his balls while the other clutches his erection in a loose fist. Jerry's grip tightens and he begins to pump his fist up and down in slow, steady strokes. He arches and mutters something, and smiles up at Joey with a lewd, sexy grin. Joey slides out of the hot tub and kneels down over Jerry, bringing his mouth close, to plant a single kiss on the sensitive flesh just below the ridge of the tumescent crown. Wrapping his fingers around the base of the shaft, Jerry tilts it toward Joey. Joey excites the throbbing sex with delicate, fluttery kisses.

Quickly changing tactics, Jerry asks Joey to show him his asscheeks. Like most men, Jerry delights in the sensual feeling of Joey's hairless leg as Joey stands up, and in the boy's low moans as Jerry's eager fingertips travel a few inches higher, and explore the asslips. He presses his finger in, testing him, and getting a soft shuddering moan of pleasure from the blond.

Jerry spends a few leisurely moments delighting in the warm, satiny feel of Joey's splendid ass, affectionately fondling those heavenly mounds, then moves his hand in a slow caress up the boy's back. Joey says he would love to stay here, playing, but, with a reluctant sigh, he says he is eager to get to the main event. He wraps his towel around him as he leans down and brings his lips close to Jerry's ear. "Come up to my room," he mutters.

Jerry nods, slips on his swim trunks, and they make their way quickly upstairs. Jerry stops at the door to his room, just two doors down from Roy's. Joey agrees to enter, and, tossing off his towel, flings himself immediately on the bed. Jerry dumbly nods acquiescence. Joey begs Jerry to begin, his body tense with anticipation, breathing audible in the quiet room. Without being told, Joey parts his legs in invitation.

Joey watches with widening eyes as Jerry tugs off his swim trunks and he climbs between Joey's legs. Joey blinks, reaches out to stroke Jerry's renewed cock. Joey is pleased with the cock, it is not too small yet no way near as large as Roy's monster. Jerry takes a lubed condom from the nightstand and applies it to his cock, then he reaches down to insert it into Joey's well-fucked ass.

Joey throws back his head and groans at the breathtaking swiftness of the penetration. Jerry soon has Joey writhing in frantic urgency as he drives the shaft up into the boy. Joey is flinging his head about, mumbling incoherently as Jerry presses all the way home. Now Jerry starts fucking, using short, choppy strokes, while Joey utters a series of tiny grunts through clenched teeth, his pretty features distorted with the throbbing hurt. Lines of distress etch his brow as he steels himself to endure the fuck.

Wildly excited by Joey's sensual squirming and the soft moans of pleasure he is making, Jerry pumps even more furiously, driving the frenzied hustler to even greater heights of ecstasy.

Soon Joey is whimpering as he senses the imminent approach of Jerry's orgasm. Joey begins gyrating wildly, totally out of control, thrashing about on the bed, snapping his head from side to side while his legs flail in the air. Joey raises his hips high off the bed, bucking up to meet Jerry's pounding strokes, and he moans long and desperately. Soon Joey's eyes are clenched tight, his breathing heavy through his parted lips, as Jerry labors over him until his body stiffens and he is caught in the throes of an all-consuming orgasm.

On his way back to his room after a late breakfast, Lance, a thin, 24-year-old vacationer from Virginia, stops when he hears the hiss of a desperate whisper coming from one of the rooms just down the way from his own. He can't quite make out what is being said. He moves down the hall, listening alertly, his head cocked to one side. Then comes an unmistakable groan, an animal growl of helpless passion, and he knows without a doubt – two guys are fucking and the door has been left open!

Instinctively, Lance turns in the direction of the sounds. As he peers into the shadowy interior, he distinctly hears a second groan, longer and deeper. For a brief second he struggles with inner doubts; then, on impulse, he reaches down to stroke his crotch. Fired with an intense curiosity he simply cannot contain, he moves stealthily towards the sex-sounds. This is sick, he thinks, yet he can't help himself as he is drawn inexorably to the hidden possibilities behind that partially opened door. Hardly daring to breathe, he creeps closer to the doorway, being careful to keep well back from the opening, leaning in just enough to peer around the door frame.

Just then, Jerry explodes inside Joey, letting out a long satisfied sigh. A little sigh also escapes Joey's lips.

So stunned at the sight of Jerry coming deep inside Joey, Lance falls against the door and it swings open. He stands there, just inside the room, taking in the riveting action.

Joey turns toward the doorway, his body motionless, submissively accepting the last thrusts of Jerry's cock.

Seeing Joey's eyes on him, Lance is petrified, caught in his voyeurism, his hand frozen in place over his hard-on. After what seems like an eternity, Joey smiles at Lance. His heart racing, Lance takes the smile as an invitation to step deeper into the room.

Lance approaches the bed and Joey extends his arm toward the man. Lance stands with his legs pressed against the mattress. Joey squeezes the bulge in Lance's swim trunks. Lance looks over at Jerry, who is still slowly sliding his cock in and out of Joey, unwilling to give the ass up even though he has come. Jerry smiles at Lance, and Joey tugs at Lance's trunks. Lance backs up and slips out of his suit, freeing a cute, cut erection. Joey grabs the cock and stuffs it in his mouth. Joey's cheeks become hollowed as he sucks Lance, looking up at him from beneath his long lashes, watching his face for each subtle reaction, playing him like the pro cocksucker he is. He soon has Lance groaning weakly and tossing his head from side to side.

Jerry finally pulls out of Joey. He accepts this intruder grudgingly, gradually reviving his spent prick watching Lance's succulent member enveloped by Joey's mouth.

Lance's hands fumble to hold Joey by the head, his fingers digging in the thick mass of blond hair. Sensing his need, Joey freezes, letting Lance hold his head steady while he fucks his face, his hips bucking up and down in frantic rhythm.

Jerry studies the hairy-chested stud standing before him having his cock serviced by Joey. He climbs off the bed and steps behind Lance so he can catch a whiff of the manly smell of the stud. He feels Lance's body surging with lustful urgency. Jerry runs his fingers up the inner walls of Lance's thighs, and bends over. His lips force open the asscheeks and he buries his tongue inside Lance.

Jerry is aware Lance is so desperately hard that it was painful for him, and to continue would send him off like a shot. Joey is totally immersed in the task at hand, licking and lapping at the glistening cock. Jerry rises and holds Lance, peering over him to watch as Lance returns to stabbing Joey's mouth repeatedly until he lets out a long, shivering moan and reaches down to clutch a fistful of Joey's hair as he comes.

Joey lies exhausted on the bed, his labored breathing gradually subsiding. Lance grabs his swim trunks, bends down and kisses Joey on the forehead, then turns to Jerry. "Thanks," he says.

"See you later," Jerry says, slapping Lance's ass as he passes him.

Jerry goes into the bathroom and turns on the shower. Joey is still for a few minutes, catching his breath. Then he rushes from the room. He hears Jerry call out as the door slams shut behind him, but he doesn't look back.

In Roy's empty room, Joey hurriedly showers, dresses. Suddenly, a key is being turned in the lock. Joey stands still.

"Oh," Gino, the youthful janitor, says. "I thought you'd checked out."

"I did," Joey says, "I just had to pee."

Gino sets the vacuum cleaner he has in his hand on the floor and says, "I'll come back."

"No, that's okay. I'm done."

Gino smiles at Joey. "You sure?" His eyes are riveted at the bulge in Joey's jeans.

Joey shakes his head. "God, I don't fuckin' believe this."

"What?"

"Is there something in the water here or what?"

Gino's smile becomes broader. "I don't understand."

"Everybody is on the make here."

Gino closes the door to the room. "Well, we are pretty free here."

"Well, I'm not. Free, that is. I have my rent to pay today."

"Didn't make enough last night?"

"No. He ran out on me while I was sleeping."

Gino steps closer to Joey. "How much do you need?"

Joey brightens. He steps up to Gino, grabs his crotch. "How much you got?"

"Eight inches."

"That's enough."

Joey drops to his knees before the well-built janitor, bringing his hands to Gino's crotch. Joey's hand slowly unzips the shorts, and his hand is moving fast, snaking up between Gino's legs to capture his balls, softly cradling them, then caressing, squeezing the hairy sack while the other reaches up to grab the turgid, uncut prick. He lets the dark shaft rest in his cupped palm, while he bends forward to nip at the foreskin.

Gino's eyes close and he sighs blissfully as Joey makes love to his tasty foreskin. Gino, aching for sex, runs his fingers through the silkiness of Joey's hair and, grasping him by his hair, he pulls Joey's head against his straining erection. Thus, Gino can now control Joey's movements, guiding his head, restraining him just out of range, forcing him to extend his tongue out as far as possible to reach the now fully erect, swaying cock. Gino wiggles his hips, teasing Joey with it. He watches delightedly as Joey's talented tongue slithers lavishly over the whole crown, circling it before concentrating on the sensitive flesh along the underside, pleasuring Gino with quick, fluttery strokes.

Gino closes his eyes, and clenches his fists as Joey thrills him. Joey then switches to long wet strokes along the underside of the shaft. Gino grunts as he struggles to hold on, driven to new heights by the insatiable hustler. Joey works with the determination that is his trademark, working his tongue up and down along the sides, over the top ridge and then sliding down underneath once more, until he comes to the balls. Here he licks the ample, cum-filled sack thoroughly, soaking the dark hairs, and then opening his mouth wider to suck Gino's balls ever so gently. Groaning helplessly, Gino tightens his fists on the handfuls of Joey's hair. His prick is incredibly hard now, gleaming with the wet sheen of Joey's saliva. He looks down at the blond, a smile on his thin lips. Joey grabs the throbbing shaft, and, bending his head, he slips the crown between his parted lips, lightly scraping the shaft with his teeth, and drawing Gino's prick into his mouth. Joey works his jaw, bringing into play his mouth, tongue, and lips, using everything he has to work Gino over, while Gino groans and twists in ecstasy.

Gino holds on to Joey's locks, twining his fingers in it, his eyes closed, rolling his head from side to side. The eager hustler bobs his head up and down in a slow, even rhythm. Joey knows instinctively when Gino is near climax, and he abruptly slows down, even stops for a moment, while Gino hangs clinging to the edge. And Joey waits, perfectly still, letting Gino catch is breath. Then Joey gradually starts again, slowly building Gino up once again. Gino can stand it no more; besides, he has to get about his work. In a heated rush he holds Joey's head rigidly in place and bucks his hips, pumping the shaft in and out of Joey's mouth, fucking his mouth with incredible urgency. At last, Gino lets himself go completely, arching back, plunging his thick shaft deep into Joey's mouth as his hands clamp the sides of his face. Spasms of pleasure shot through Gino's body as his exploding cock sends his cum into Joey's now relaxed mouth. Gino's orgasm seems to go on and on, and Joey pulls it out of his mouth and squeezes it, watching the cum drop to the floor.

Finally, Joey falls back weakly, collapsing onto the floor, Gino's softening cock sliding from Joey's fingers. Joey looks up at Gino.

"Was that enough?" Gino asks.

"Oh, yeah," Joey sighs, lowering his head and leaning forward to snuggle against Gino's leg, his head resting against Gino's thigh. Gino takes three twenties from his wallet and drops them on Joey. Joey grabs them, smiles back at Gino, then gives the cum-coated cock a tender parting squeeze.

As he starts to leave the Royal Palms, the three twenties wadded in his hand, Joey reaches into his back pocket for his wallet. He withdraws it and opens it. He stops dead. He cannot believe it. Roy hadn't fucked him over after all. He pulls out two crisp hundred dollar bills. He laughs out loud and, putting the twenties with the hundreds, slides them into his wallet, and returns his wallet to his back pocket. He'll be able to pay his rent after all, and, in celebration, he's going to sleep the rest of the day.

As he enters his little apartment near the beach, the phone is ringing. At first he thinks he'll ignore it, just crash. But he relents and picks up the phone. It is a john; he saw Joey's ad in the gay bar guide and wants to meet him.

"Where are you stayin'?" Joey asks.

"The Royal Palms," the john says." I just checked in."

Joey puts his hand over the mouthpiece and howls.

A STRANGER IN THE HOUSE
Carter Wilson

Barry got off the freeway and followed the familiar, second-nature winding of his hill almost to the top, turned the corner and popped up into his own driveway in the space next to the Toyota. Lewis, the young man he'd just met, got out and stretched. Ventura below them was misted over, but beyond it was clear, the sea flat, distinct and silvery in full moonlight.

"Who else lives here?"

"No one."

"You could get a sticker that said, 'My other car's a Toyota.'"

Barry laughed, hoping his visitor wouldn't notice all four of the Toyota's tires were sunk to their rims.

Inside, Lewis surveyed the fireplace side of the room, then turned his attention to the view out through the slider. He asked for a vodka tonic and, while Barry was getting it, Lewis went and found the switch and put out the overhead lights and stood there smoking and gazing out at the shiny plate of the Pacific. Barry set the vodka down on the table and asked Lewis if he could kiss him. Lewis said, "You go right ahead."

When Barry put his arms around him, Lewis sighed and came to him and turned his mouth up. He kissed gently but in earnest, letting it go on, taking Barry's tongue into his mouth briefly, his bony, smaller body full against Barry's bigger, softer one.

Barry led Lewis by the hand into the guest bedroom. Lewis took off his boots and put his socks in them, then stood by the bed waiting for Barry to undress him. A thick band of moonlight crossed the bed. Barry thought of closing the curtains, but no one would see in and he did not want to stop what he was doing. Naked, Lewis turned out to be smooth, nicely constructed, not built up in the shoulders or chest but strong-enough looking, meaty, full butt and cream-colored skin. (He drove agricultural equipment from location to location for one of the big companies, he had told Barry at the bar.) His cock hung down, still soft. Barry sat on the edge of the bed, leaned over and took the head of it in his mouth. Once it hardened up it was probably eight inches, and even thicker along the shaft than at the plump head. "Get it down your throat, try and get it on down your throat, man," Lewis begged softly.

After a while Barry stood and pushed down his own pants. "You want to suck me some?"

"I'm not much of a sucker," Lewis said. He got under Barry's shirt and rubbed his belly while he ran his face back and forth over Barry's beard. "I like that, though," he said, his voice down to a whisper, "want you to get naked with me now."

"Nekkid" it sounded the way Lewis said it.

- 259 -

Barry finished taking off his own clothes and they lay out together, Lewis on top humping gently, their tongues back and forth in each other's mouth, Barry holding Lewis's ass. Under them the guest bed made a merry, squeaky, sawing noise. When they stopped, there was no sound anywhere around. Well after three, into the night's silent watch.

"Think I could have a refill?"

"Sure."

Barry got up and flicked on a lamp.

He had the drink made and was out of the kitchen on his way back when Lewis called to him, "And my cigarettes? They're there on the table." Barry located the box in the dark, the black butane lighter sitting on top. As he was picking them up, he thought, Have one. And then, Why not? The question made his heart beat hard. Going back to smoking came up for him nowadays only in dreams and was usually enough to wake him, a danger sign.

It's all so fine. A new life here too. Have one.

He turned toward the mantel, making a kind of wordless supplication to protect him against that voice, even though it was a thing of his own. He couldn't see anything of the figure in the photograph up there, only the dull, ghostly glint of the frame. But his appeal worked anyway, the dreamy, insinuating other voice ceased, desisted, old loyal life reasserting itself.

Getting back in, Barry pressed his body up against Lewis's and so they stayed, propped up on their elbows, comforter pulled up on their legs, while Lewis smoked and drank his drink. Then Lewis put out his cigarette and went in the bathroom and when he came back there was mint toothpaste on his breath.

"Can I put out this light for a little while?"

"Sure," Barry said.

Lewis found the lamp switch, turned it, snuggled down against Barry. Barry put both arms around Lewis and held him.

"What color would you say your eyes were?"

"I don't know."

"They're hazel, aren't they?"

"Well, yes, sir, I suppose they are. I'm part Cherokee," Lewis added, as though that somehow explained where the color of his eyes came from. "My grandmother was a full-blood, so that makes me a quarter, right?"

Barry nodded. "Um."

His grandparents had had a farm, Lewis said, and they had been the ones to raise him. So he had been brought up around pigs and rabbits and always had chores to do, feeding the animals, keeping the wood supplied for Gram's stove.

Barry wondered where Lewis got his energy. He was nineteen, he had said, which maybe counted for some of it. Barry was only eight years older, but he was half asleep by now, content with the soft skin of Lewis's nipple and the thump of Lewis's heart under his hand. No longer attending to every word, he began to half dream, seeing what Lewis was saying in pictures – an old gabled house, in the middle of the yard a trunkless palm tree (in his mind's eye it was a green explosion in the sere plane of browned summer lawn), a high-ceilinged hallway with red-carpeted stairs, a dusty silent room with drawn yellow shades, bags of feed sitting prim as church visitors on the sprung chairs....

"I was the one found my grandmother when she died."

Barry stirred and came back fully awake.

"How old were you?"

"Oh, this was just two weeks ago. I been back living with her in Camarillo, and I was asleep in my room and I got up in the morning and went in and there she was."

"How old was she?"

"Gram? Oh she was an old-enough lady. Eighty-one. It was her time, I guess."

"Still. That must have been hard."

"It was. But I'm getting over it now."

As though that were what was expected of him.

Barry said, "Turn around here." Lewis moved promptly. Barry helped him roll over and pulled him back to his own body. He milked Lewis's penis and cupped his balls and said, "I'll just hold you like this for a while."

At first Lewis didn't seem comfortable with Barry's still-hard dick pressed up to his ass, but after Barry had been rubbing his beard on the back of his neck and kissing him there a while, Lewis sighed and let go and settled in against it. His breathing began to come steady. His own cock was starting to get hard again. Barry slowly humped against him and Lewis moved his butt back, falling in with the motion. Then he sighed, stopped. "Hell, I've only been fucked once in my life," he said.

"And you didn't like it?"

"Not really. I think I'm too small back there."

"Would you like me to suck you some more?"

"I sure would, man."

Barry pulled back the covers. He got down and kissed the head of Lewis's cock and sucked it a while, then sat up and lifted Lewis's legs. In the moonlight, he could see the little pucker in the cleft of Lewis's ass.

"What you going to do?" Lewis said.

"Nothing. Just looking."

They lay together again, Lewis up under Barry's arm pressing the whole length of his body up against Barry's. Barry said, "I was never much of an ass licker, but in another time I think I would have licked yours."

Silence. Then Lewis saying, "Uh oh."

"'Uh oh' what?"

"Nothing. Except I think I could go a little for a guy like you."

"What's wrong with that, Lewis?"

"I don't know. Something, though. Isn't there always bound to be something?"

"Well, what if it really was just only a little – on both our parts?"

Lewis seemed to be thinking that one over. He snuggled in even closer. "I guess that could work," he said finally.

Lewis had warned Barry he might talk in his sleep, and before the light began to come up, he did. His body tensed suddenly, bringing Barry immediately awake. "Didn't close the car doors," Lewis said. "Have to go do that." His voice was loud, staunch, reasonable.

"No, Lewis," Barry said, "I remember closing them myself."

"Nope. Got to get up now!"

Then silence. Lewis's body relaxed and the easy shushing of his breath began again.

Barry's heart was thumping. Gene, the man in the photograph on the mantel, had always told Barry he was no judge of people. "Some day, when I'm not here anymore, you are going to bring home some nut case and it is going to be all over for you," Gene would say. Was Lewis that man? Barry felt surely not, though the evidence was only the trusting way Lewis spoke and the way he let Barry hold him. Not a nut, he thought, moving back toward sleep, not this time.

A while later – the guest room window had already turned to a block of gray – Lewis spoke again, this time in Spanish and without the tensing of his body. "Whatever happens," he said, again completely reasonably, "you don't ever want to get your mayordomos angry with you."

In the morning when Barry asked what mayordomo meant to him, Lewis said, "That's what the Mexicans call their crew leaders." He didn't remember what he had said in the night about either mayordomos or car doors, and he didn't want any coffee or breakfast, just a cigarette and some more talk, then a shower and to get on the road. He didn't appear hung over or even tired after only four or five hours' sleep, but he did ask Barry would he drive again.

They had come in Lewis's red Buick, leaving Barry's old wagon in the lot behind Pati's. It was going to be another hot day. The lanes of 101 coming toward them were already slowed almost to a standstill by Angelnos fighting their way out to the beaches. Lewis slouched in the passenger seat controlling the tape deck, idly running his hand along the inside of his thigh.

"Were you always attracted to other boys?"

"Were you?"

"From the beginning," Barry said.

Lewis nodded.

"One time – I don't know how old we could have been, six maybe? – me and this other kid got caught messing around by his mom."

"Doing what?"

"Playing with each other's dick. The other kid's mom took us into the bedroom and told us, 'OK you boys, take your pants down now and have yourselves a good look because this is the last you're going to see of it.'" Lewis laughed. "But she was wrong about that one, least in my case."

Five miles later, Lewis said, "There was a couple of my half brothers and one of my cousins I'd get it on with too when we were little. They're all married now. The one of them – he's with a Mexican lady – he won't do anything anymore. Least not with me. One of my brothers, though, he lives in the Imperial Valley and whenever I get down there if I give him a call he'll still come on over to the motel and fuck me."

Barry's was the only car left in the bar's gravel parking area. He pulled Lewis's up beside his, left it in neutral and they got out and strolled over toward the shade. Here in Oxnard the morning smelled of peppery eucalyptus resin. Way off in the bright sun beyond the trees and a railroad track a little scattering of men and women moved hunkered down along the rows picking second-crop strawberries.

Lewis scuffed the dirt with the toe of his boot and then said, "If there wasn't people around, I'd kiss you."

"That's OK, Lewis. My mouth's all out of shape from the kisses you've been giving it anyway."

Lewis stuck out his hand. "I'm glad," he said. "I'll call you."

Home again by early afternoon, exhausted now, Barry thought maybe he should prepare for a crash, a bad day or two. Instead he found himself buoyed by even the little recollections of what had just happened: the way Lewis had picked Barry's hairbrush off the bathroom counter and used it without asking was it all right (and the way Barry, usually fastidious about combs and brushes, hadn't minded at all); Lewis's palaver about being the singer in a rock band back in high school and how the girls had just "lined right up" for him and how sorry it'd made him not to be able to tell them why he wasn't interested ("Well, not that I wasn't interested, really. I've slept with a woman, and that was all right, but I just lay there the whole time thinking, 'What'n the hell am I doing here? I'm gay, aren't I?'"); the country, or at least country-music accent that clung to certain of his words – not only nekkid, but also wuh-min for "woman" and the way he said look-it sometimes instead of "look"; how this morning when Melanie and Ashley had come barking up from the dog house, Lewis had without much ado reached over the fence and grabbed one muzzle, then the other, and said to them, "Hiya, pooches"; his excitement when he was flipping through Barry's old LPs and he came across the Simon and Garfunkel album "Bookends" – "I've been looking and looking for this one. Could you put it on?" and then without waiting Lewis singing "They've all gone to look for America" all on-key in a throaty sweet baritone; even, in a funny way, the charm of the fact that he hadn't asked Barry anything about what he did for a living or even how old he was.

What Barry felt sure Lewis had liked best, more than the sex, was the part where Barry held him while he slept, even though that hadn't gone on very many hours, and some of the chance to talk. Barry had sucked on Lewis again after they woke up in the morning, and this time Lewis got good and hard. When Barry asked him to, he willingly lay up almost on top of Barry and traded long hot kisses while Barry ran one hand all over Lewis's backside and a finger up and down the smooth crack of his ass and jacked himself off. Twenty minutes later in the shower, Lewis reached down and said in his most country voice, "You got another boner there, mister? Well, you are a horny toad, aren't you?" and without being asked, he started beating Barry's dick. He continued, going back and forth between sticking his tongue in Barry's mouth and sucking hard on his nipples until Barry shot off again.

But in the whole time he was at the house, Lewis himself hadn't come. The realization surprised Barry, made him wish he could go back, change the script. In the moment suggesting to Lewis they could try caring for each other "just a little" had seemed about right. Now Barry wished he had been a lot less careful.

Out to Xuma, then up Fresno and Salinas way, down to Santa Maria on the way back and maybe down into Mexico – Sonora, Baja –

Though Barry told himself to expect nothing, the itinerary Lewis had mentioned began to run over and over through his head. No way of knowing how long it might take to complete. A couple of months at least, Barry figured, though for all he knew it could be six months or the whole cycle of the growing year.

ABOUT THE EDITOR

JOHN PATRICK was a prolific, prize-winning author of fiction and non-fiction. One of his short stories, "The Well," was honored by PEN American Center as one of the best of 1987. His novels and anthologies, as well as his non-fiction works, including Legends and The Best of the Superstars series, continue to gain him new fans every day. One of his most famous short stories appears in the Badboy collection Southern Comfort and another appears in the collection The Mammoth Book of Gay Short Stories.

A divorced father of two, the author was a longtime member of the American Booksellers Association, the Publishing Triangle, the Florida Publishers' Association, American Civil Liberties Union, and the Adult Video Association. He lived in Florida, where he passed away on October 31, 2001.

n the park. He was wearing these really tight jeans, so tight you co

ng any underwear. "Excuse me," I said, having a hard time lookíng

led by that bulge in his crotch. "but don't I know you?" "Maybe," I

of te   bout a m

Ray   God, you

ser?   in?" he as

"Lik   s stronges

ody   e on Gree

he l   I ever sa

to t   ny ideas?

king   e same

coul   ery long t

raci   ne swell.

with   e in store

go   behind so

see   in public

" he   vent to the

acy.   grabbed

d. I

raci   t, so firm

t, ha

h m   bing dick

g, I   n cock, be

ound of unzipping filled the small space. I don't know who's hand

t before I knew it, I had his rod in my hand, and mine was in his. "

do?" he asked, his tone challenging. I knew exactly, and sank to n

answer. By the way he carried on, I could tell I was giving him th